THE WITCHES' BREW

Spatterlight
Amstelveen 2020

THE WITCHES' BREW

Dan Temianka

Cover art and illustrations
by Tom Kidd

Published by Spatterlight, Amstelveen 2020

Cover art and illustrations by Tom Kidd

ISBN 978-1-61947-385-0

SPATTERLIGHT

www.spatterlight.nl

Foreword

My huge stylistic debt to the magnificent late Jack Vance will be immediately apparent to many readers. I will never be able to pay it off, although I made a diligent effort in that direction by compiling his coined words in *The Jack Vance Lexicon: From Abiloid to Zygage*, also published by Spatterlight Press.

It will be equally obvious that this little novel, which I wrote back in the 1980's, is 'overwritten'. I love archaic words, and have stubbornly resisted the urging of my wonderful wife to rewrite it in a simpler manner. "No one will understand it," she insists. I foolishly respond that quantum physicists are also not widely understood, as is the poetry of Ezra Pound, the music of Béla Bartók and so on.

The psychiatrically inclined reader may surmise that the exercise of writing this book was a substitute for years of psychoanalysis, to come to grips with my relationship with my late mother. But she was not a witch. The symbolism of Grandmage Mentharch could also be dissected, but my father, unlike the quixotic wizard, had an exceptionally stable and courageous character. Both of my parents were gifted artists.

Writing a novel was the most difficult and challenging experience of my life, not excluding divorce and running a hundred miles in less than twenty-four hours, respectively. I shudder at the all-but-irresistible prospect of writing a sequel. But as Noel Coward observed, "Work is much more fun than fun."

In these parlous times it is a comfort to reflect on the warm, affectionate relationship between Milord and his faithful mascot Flick. I hope my readers enjoy meeting them as much as I did.

Dan Temianka
Pasadena, California
March 2020

Contents

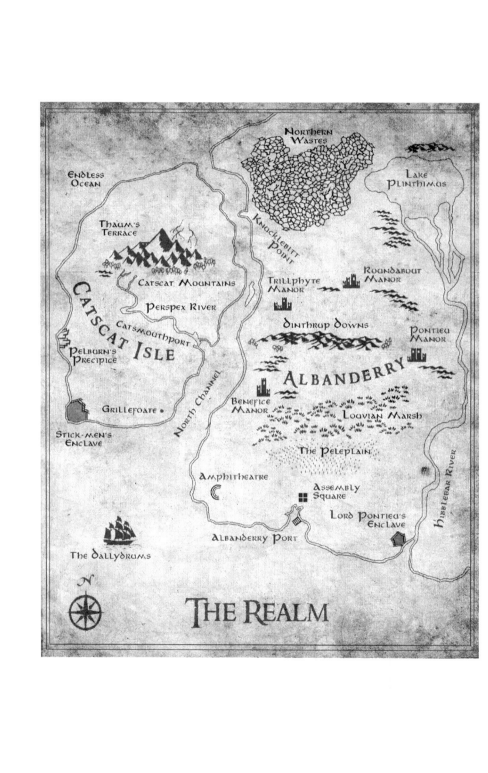

THE REALM

I

A CURSE

t was a deliciously sunny morning when we first learned of the curse. Milord arose as usual at the crack of ten o'clock. He padded to his toilette, sat down before his gold-veined mirror and placed his knitted nightcap on its stand. I hopped to my perch on the back of his chair and watched quietly over his shoulder; he does not like to be disturbed while he dresses.

He folded his hands in his lap and lowered his eyes. "Manservant Mumphreed, if you please," he said quietly.

Mumphreed popped instantly out of his closet. "Yes, Milord."

"Grade IX attire, Manservant, with heraldic markings and *coiffure bouffant*."

"At once, Sire." Mumphreed glanced quickly through two of the room's twelve armoires. "Perhaps the empyrean tunic, Milord," he murmured, fanning its dazzling gold embroidery over his wrist. "With the green serge trousers, Your Grace," he added.

"An excellent choice," said Milord. Mumphreed set about preening him as Milord cocked his head this way and that. From time to time Mumphreed peered discreetly at my master from the side and delivered a judiciously inflected "Ah," or said, "Mm-hmm, yes, just so," with a note of pleased surprise.

Mumphreed assisted Milord with his *complet*, carefully powdered his wig, implanted a purple silk boutonniere in each lapel and helped him to draw on a pair of white lambskin gloves. "Sire, you have attained a pinnacle of cosmetic and sartorial perfection," he said at last.

"Thank you, Manservant." Milord now turned to me and pointed invitingly to his vest. "Are we prepared for the day, Flick?"

I squeaked my agreement and hopped into his pocket. My full name is Flickamerry Hansombear, but Milord calls me Flick for short unless he is put out with me, which is seldom. My small size — less than that of a ripe orange, but larger than the average field mouse — allows me more easily than most of Albanderry's mascots to accompany my master, Lord Gracewright Cantilouve Benefice, on his errands and social outings.

He stood up and moved with a sublime and stately air to the landing. His magnificence was worthy of an envoy from the stars — a celestial diplomat! — and as always I was thrilled to be at his side. Waiting below were the household staff, formally arrayed and bowing. Milord smiled with genuine pleasure. "To all the loyal denizens of Benefice Manor," his voice rang out — he looked around, silently counting heads, alertly noting whether any were less than entirely bowed — "to all a pleasant day." The entourage murmured in response.

Milord proceeded to his morning room, where Masterfootling Farberwile hurriedly adjusted his cummerbund and bowed.

"Masterfootling, I regret that I shall require a somewhat swifter service than usual, as the morning's schedule presses."

"Very good, Your Grace."

Two liveried dwarves delicately lifted Milord's coattails to right and left while two others presented a brocaded couch to his backside. He settled himself before a sumptuous, thirty-foot knurlwood table heaped with exquisite delicacies and condiments. "What remarkable colors and textures the Kitchenmaster has prepared!" he said. From a hollow emerald concealed within the ruffles at his wrist he extracted a tiny pinch of snuff, dispatched it and sneezed briskly.

The Manor's priest-in-residence, a coal-black shaman dressed in ritual African robes, entered ceremoniously and stood at the foot of the table. Today's subject was *apeiron* — "the indefinite primal principle of all matter," according to Anaximander. Milord lowered his gaze reverently as the priest discussed the concept in substance, intoned a brief dedication and withdrew.

Milord nibbled at a crumb or two, hardly enough to fill a hummingbird's cheek. He cleared his throat, by which everyone understood that the repast was at an end, and moved to the lavish mahogany desk in his adjacent receiving chambers. He had scarcely arranged the day's parchments when there was an urgent knock at the door.

"Yes?"

It was Masterfootling Farberwile. "Milord, an emissary arrives. He represents Grandmage Mentharch himself, to judge by the extraordinary appearance of his vehicle." There was an undercurrent of excitement in Farberwile's voice, for the Grandmage is a hoary and powerful old wizard, the recounting of whose sorcerous accomplishments fills an entire wing of the Paradiplomatic Archives. I could not recall an instance in which he had taken the initiative to communicate with a Lord.

Milord stroked his chin thoughtfully. "What business could possibly bring him here?"

"This I cannot say, Your Lordship." He hesitated. "The Gasmaster advises a formal reception in the courtyard."

Milord pursed his lips, frowned and stood up. "Very well. Re-schedule this morning's appointments for the morrow."

To either side of the front steps a hushed breeze played on curved hedges and terraces. A score of retainers in bright red uniforms, with long-pikes and halberds bristling at their sides, had hastily assembled around the turn-circle below.

An outlandish coach approached on the entry road. Its lumpy body was splashed with lavender and strawberry and corn-yellow, so bright that my head swam. Its chassis was equally lopsided, so that the entire contraption shuddered from one side of the road to the other, much to the regret of the exhausted horses in its traces. Surely the carriage was an impudent joke contrived by some drunken glass-blower!

But as it turned slowly in the circle in front of us and presented its broad sides, I saw famous scenes from the history of sorcery illustrated in living motion: the invention of Telestic Asportation; Furibund's ingenious deployment of hagstones against a Cosmic Mistress; and the dramatic rescue of Lord Munchfirth — by Grandmage Mentharch himself — from a witch's Snare of Gummosity.

The driver wore a slender frock coat and green top hat, and around his neck a heavy collar of coarse leather, which he fingered frequently and with conspicuous discomfort. "Where is it now?" he asked in exasperation, fumbling through the numerous pockets of his jacket. "A simple riding crop, the tool and symbol of my trade, and I've misplaced it again. Damnation!" He turned and rummaged irritably in a chest behind him, also with no result; then ransacked a satchel under his bench; and began rifling his pockets all over again, all the while pulling at his odd choker. Belatedly noticing the Manor, he pulled sharply on the reins and the brougham herky-jerked to a stop.

Trumpmaster Rampbleu stood at the curb. He blew a stirring fanfare on his cornet and replaced his white gloves with ones of ceremonial scarlet. Taking his tricorne hat under one arm, he stepped to the carriage door with a flourish of his coattails and bowed deeply. "Hail and welcome to Benefice Manor," he announced.

The door remained closed. Towards a pursuivant with the high rank of Trumpmaster, this was a shocking snub! The driver glanced down disinterestedly from his bench. Rampbleu took several disgruntled steps back, replaced his hat, blew another animated charge on his cornet, stepped forward once more and repeated his salutation.

Again there was no response. The driver muttered something to himself, crouched behind his seat and disappeared into the cab. There was protracted rustling within, and the door flew open. A forbidding individual sat shrouded in a voluminous black cloak elaborately embroidered with mystical designs. Protruding from under its hem were large slippers of purple velvet with long, coiled toes. A deep hood concealed his face, but the same leather collar was visible. I poked

Milord's shirt front; he whispered that he too had noted the odd necklace and its coincidental presence on both driver and passenger.

The Trumpmaster bowed. "Hail and welcome to Benefice —"

"All right, very well," the envoy said testily, assembling the folds of his cloak. He rudely shunned the Trumpmaster's proferred hand and descended. Behind him followed a one-armed dwarf in a baggy suit of pink brocade.

"The Grandmage wishes to present a token of his favor," the tall one said curtly. He shot a stern glance at his diminutive assistant, who turned and struggled unsuccessfully with his one hand to extricate a large round object from a rack on the carriage's fender.

"Before evening, Gwarph," his master hissed, delivering several cloak-hampered kicks to the wretched fellow's back. This served only to inhibit his small efforts, but presently Gwarph staggered backwards from the coach, grappling with a spherical cage of plaited fishbones and blue toadflax. With enormous relief he dropped it onto the red welcoming carpet.

Within the globe were a vicious desert skink and an equally deadly black scorpion. They darted and snapped at each other, or froze suddenly in threatening stances like wrestlers looking for an advantage. At some undetectable signal they interrupted their hostilities and grazed as blandly as cows on their imprisoning bracts of toadflax, oblivious to each other.

"Present the thing properly, Gwarph," said the envoy, administering another kick.

"Yes, Master," he whimpered. With a heave he set the cage rolling like a tumbleweed toward the Manor. Milord's guards instantly impaled it with crossed halberds.

The Masterfootling stepped hastily forward. "My Lord would have an explanation of this strange embolus!" he demanded in alarm.

"Beadles and bumfuzzle!" said the envoy, as nearly as I could make it out. He abruptly re-entered his carriage and slammed the door, while his dwarf scrambled to a perch on the fender. A moment later the driver climbed again to his station, snapped his reins and moved off.

"What significance can there be to this?" asked Milord.

The Masterfootling spread his palms in a gesture of bewilderment. "The Grandmage is notorious for his conundrums and perversities.

Perhaps the quarreling of the caged animals implies that discussions with Your Grace will take place under constrained or even adversarial circumstances."

Milord scowled and slashed the air with his arm. A squad of retainers immediately double-timed from their positions and blocked the road. The colorful barouche careened to a halt, its horses bowling over one another and neighing in protest.

The driver dove back inside; the envoy bounced from his seat, waving his balloon sleeves; Gwarph again trailed behind him like a duckling. "What is the meaning of this?" he demanded, charging up to Milord. In the shadows of his oversized hood his yellow eyes blazed with anger. Gwarph imitated his master's gestures and glared at Milord with his beady red eyes.

"You may take back your rolling vivarium," said Milord. "Inform the Grandmage that I am unable to interpret its significance, but will consent to a personal interview if that is his desire."

"Well, you should have said so!" With a snap of his fingers the envoy plucked off his cape, condensed it in one hand and stood revealed as the Grandmage himself. He now wore tight green stockings and a sleeveless tunic of orange duffle, edged in white; and the odd leather collar. A great shock of white hair, decorated with glittering bangles, radiated from his narrow head like a corolla.

Milord chuckled. "Perhaps Grandmage Mentharch would care to refresh himself after his long journey…"

"Who said it was long?" he asked irritably.

"I withdraw the question." Milord began strolling back to the Manor. "To what do I owe the honor of this call?"

The Grandmage plucked a crabapple from his sleeve and nibbled it. "An impairment," he said curtly. Milord tilted his head in sympathy, as though this laconic comment were ample explanation.

Mentharch reclined casually in midair and discarded the crabapple. He sighed and scratched his head. Milord ensconced himself in a comfortable armchair brought by the Floorsteward. I cannot recall a stranger sight than that conversation in the courtyard: the Grandmage suspended in air, with Gwarph and his odd vehicle behind him, while Milord and I looked on amidst our retainers!

Mentharch stared blankly at Milord. "It's a terrible bit of housekeeping, isn't it?"

My master was taken aback. "I —"

"But it was housekeeping we were discussing, wasn't it?" he persisted.

"You referred to an impairment," Milord said uncertainly.

The Grandmage knitted his white brows in an intense effort at recollection. "An unpleasant matter, yes. And this collar, for instance — a bit of impudence from a scrawny mountainwitch, slipped over my head in an unguarded moment.

> 'Be bedighted with a collar —
> Wear this necklace with an itch!
> Til it's plucked off by a hybrid
> Of a savage and a witch.'

"Such was her insipid verse, just before she vanished. The blasted thing chafes me raw! And what in Thaum's name did that guttersnipe mean by 'hybrid'?"

Milord made a sympathetic clucking noise. "Surely she intended no more than an unpleasant pleasantry, so to speak … Of limited duration, one hopes."

Mentharch stared hard at Milord. "I fear not." He attacked the nape of his neck with a small back-scratcher from his belt. "Were it not for Gwarph's vigilance, she would doubtless have sabotaged my energy vats as well." Gwarph permitted himself a small but proud smile.

The magician's face darkened. "But her second quatrain was far more disturbing:

> 'As night's sun waxes and declines
> From slice to globe to blackest black,
> Your mind will parch like grapes on a vine
> And wither to an empty sack!'"

The roadside cypresses were cuffed by a sudden gust of wind, and thrashed back and forth. Milord twisted uncomfortably in his chair. Gwarph's tiny red eyes pleaded with me.

The Grandmage himself, cursed! He cleared his throat twice; his eyes wandered absently among the huge eucalypti flanking the Manor. I realized with dismay that he was trying unsuccessfully to marshal his thoughts.

Milord scarcely breathed. In a whisper he asked, "How...how may I be of service?"

With a crooked finger Mentharch probed the fold in his left cheek. At last he said, "There is only one possible solution." Again he paused.

"The Protectioners' Guild, perhaps?"

He drew a deep breath, and seemed to regain himself. "No. I must have their brew."

"The witches' own brew?" Milord asked in amazement.

"The very same. Many times in the past I have attempted without success to bargain it from them out of professional interest. But now I must have it before the new moon — less than a month from this day — or the volume between my ears will become an empty space, scoured by cosmic winds!" Mentharch closed his eyes and pressed his slender palms against his white-haired temples, as though to prevent the escape of the fine, magical intelligence burning therein. With an effort he resumed. "Consequently you must obtain it for me."

"I?" Milord blurted. He sat bolt upright, giving my holster a jolt. "By what means could I possibly obtain that vicious sewage?"

Mentharch shrugged and picked a thread from his sleeve. "This much you must determine."

Now I must explain that Milord shares one attribute with the witches: he is a most competent concoctor of essences and vapors. Often I have watched as he fiddles with the tubes and retorts in his upstairs workroom, pouring a greenish liquid into one, distilling a bright mauve fluid or hazy exhalation in another. In each category he has evolved a nearly perfect form. For example, one selection produces a bland euphoria, a sense of well-being unsupported by any specific rationale; he is wont to sample this variety prior to leaving for the opera. Another vapor imparts exceptional vigor, even under conditions of extreme exhaustion or hunger; this 'Vimplicate XII' has been in great demand by soldiers and fishwives.

Thus it was somehow logical that the Grandmage should approach

Lord Benefice for help in this situation. But a witches' brew — that was another matter altogether! I shuddered with fright.

"Perhaps a double dose of my Clarissimus Magnus would be of some benefit," Milord suggested weakly. This preparation exacts an extraordinary attensity, or mental clarity; I can easily determine when Milord has been breathing it, for his glance becomes as sharp as a robin's and sagacity wreathes his face.

The Grandmage shook his head firmly. "No, Lord Benefice, the problem is far beyond human skills. Only their foul milk will do, for reasons I have neither time nor terms to explain." He extracted several small, oddly shaped trinkets from his tunic and placed them in Milord's tremulous hands. "I present you with these magical implements as an aid; think of them in appropriate circumstances." He waved his hand at Gwarph, who trotted to the carriage, retrieved a caged bird and handed it to Masterfootling Farberwile. "When you are ready to contact me again, dispatch this diving petrel; I will appear within three hours."

Without further discussion Mentharch slipped down from his invisible perch and re-entered his gaudy brougham, while Gwarph jumped into a compartment on its skirts. A moment later, wearing his frock coat again, the wizard scrambled onto the driver's bench and resumed the nervous search for his riding crop. With a last glance at us he shouted, "Another aggravation: she has undoubtedly stolen my whip as well!"

The vehicle lurched into the road, and in a few moments disappeared beyond a copse of shimmering aspens. In twenty-eight days the moon would be as black as earth's bowels — and Grandmage Mentharch's potent sorcery would no longer be a bulwark against the vitriolic Mountainwitches. Who could imagine what unbridled tricks they would play then? What curses, out of jealousy for his skills, would they visit on Milord? I pulled the flaps of my pouch tighter around me in fear.

Milord looked pensively at the magical implements in his hands. He secured them in his wallet, took a deep breath and rose from his chair. "Masterfootling, you may dismiss your retainers." He looked skeptically at Mentharch's bizarre gift. "And donate the wizard's zoological appliance to the Assembly Museum."

"Yes, Milord." With their pikes, three footmen gingerly prodded the cage toward the armory.

Milord walked soberly back to the Manor. "A pretty dilemma," the Masterfootling suggested.

"Pretty indeed," said Milord, distracted. He ordered his faithful servant to summon the Gasmaster, and the three of them conferred for most of the day in Milord's study, while I toyed listlessly with a box of puzzles. It was within the Gasmaster's means to communicate at any time with the Mountainwitch Consortium, but he could devise no credible strategy by which they might be induced to part with their most sacred and treacherous substance.

Here I must say something more of the Mountainwitch Coven on Catscat Isle, and of their relationship with my Lords. The hags produce none of their own food, owing to laziness and poor soil, and are consequently dependent upon our serfs and fishermen for sustenance. In addition they are infatuated with certain lap-toys produced by our cottage workers.* The Lords therefore supply these commodities, and in return the witches dole out minor charms and incantations, to the great amusement of Albanderry's Ladies, and refrain from the application of their more destructive spells.

But the equilibrium is tenuous, pressured constantly by the harridans' penchant for evil and avarice. To maintain the balance, the Lords depend heavily on their august Guild of Protectioners. The Guild's responsibilities include the negotiation of commodity contracts (which they saturate with spell-nullifying fluid), and the maintenance of strategic vapor barriers around each Manor; their other, more arcane methods are not openly discussed. Each Manor salaries a Protectioner in Residence — in our case Gasmaster Bickle — and the Master Guildsman naturally holds a position of great prestige in Albanderry's Assembly.

But the witches sometimes give in to their tendency to excess, and then even the Guild is taxed beyond its limits. At such critical junctures the intervention of a greater magical competence is required, in the person of Grandmage Mentharch. The most famous such instance

---

* That supernatural beings should have such base needs once puzzled me; but Milord explained philosophically, "That is no more baffling than that we, who are physical beings, should have dreams and fantasies. All living creatures are a blend of element and wish."

occurred some forty years ago, when the coven acquired an ancient cache of mighty spells, and plotted to join Albanderry Peninsula itself to their own Catscat Isle. The Grandmage responded by populating our coasts with tiny iridescent butterflies, whose gentle magic effectively dispelled the threat. Even today those lovely innocent creatures may be seen fluttering along our coasts.

But now Grandmage Mentharch's powers were threatened, and the lunar clock was ticking.

II

A BARGAIN

The next two days were crowded with urgent discussions between Milord and his advisers, but passed without result. Late in the morning there was a knock at the den door.

"Yes?" said Milord. I wiggled free of my afghan and sat up.

Masterfootling Farberwile entered the study and bowed. "A gentleman to see you, Sire." Milord looked questioningly at the Masterfootling, for he is usually more precise in his announcement of visitors. "A bookless fellow, actually," he continued apologetically, "and his soiled leggings suggest a substantial journey. He presents a card, Sire." He bowed again and held out a filigreed silver tray, on which was quarantined a chip of dog-eared parchment. The name HAGGLEMAN WIMLEY was boldly engraved on the dusty card in cobalt-blue letters, and thereafter, in italics, *Supplier of Magic to the Realm.* Below this was scrawled an addendum: 'Gewgaws and Impedimenta to Suit All Circumstances.'

Milord sighed. "Show him in."

"Very good, Sire." Farberwile turned to re-open the door and was nearly knocked down as Haggleman Wimley threw it open.

"Good of you to see me, Lord Benefice," he said. In the close, firelit den his voice boomed like a cannon. His boot struck a couch leg, dislodging dried mud on the rug. "Sorry," he said carelessly and kicked the sod under the couch. He thrust his huge, raw hands into the pockets of his pea jacket and squinted around the room. I realized with a shock that the lout wasn't even going to bow!

Milord waved him to a chair. He made a show of settling himself and licked his lips deliberately.

"Masterfootling, a beverage for the Haggleman," Milord said. "A simple one," he added, with a significant look at his senior servant. The Masterfootling closed his eyes and withdrew.

"Thank you, Sire," said Haggleman. "And a sip for your pet fox, too, eh?" He thought this a fine joke, but to me it was merely another variant on a tiresome theme which we Filxxxs* have heard repeated ad nauseam since our arrival in Albanderry a century ago. I suspected that this vagrant charm-monger made an unpleasant habit of wading to the precarious edge of wit and peering shamelessly beyond into the realm of vulgarity.

But this caller was intriguingly different from the staid Lords and donzellas whom Milord usually entertains. His hard jaw and ruddied cheekbones had but recently squared the pudgy face of an impudent youth; large ears sprouted like cabbage leaves from his head. The glowing hearth soon induced him to throw off his coarse wool coat, revealing that travel and the frequent lack of a roof had effectively trimmed the fat from his tall frame.

"And now, Haggleman Wimley, you may illuminate us as to the reason for your call," said Milord. A look of sober caution settled onto his round features.

Wimley peered slyly at my master. "It's a supernatural matter, you might say, particularly well suited, in my humble opinion, to the

---

* I have used x's for the transliteration of unpronounceable second-level consonants, according to the convention established by Archlinguist Honeyquill.

interests of Benefice Manor." He waited, tapping his chapped fingers on the arm of his chair, but Milord only gazed coolly back. The Masterfootling re-entered and presented a simple glass, which Wimley drained at once.

"Well," he continued, seeing that Milord had no intention of rising to the bait, "I've been traveling for some time, which is plain to see, and I've encountered a few items which I thought might pique Your Lordship's curiosity." He patted his vest, then leaned back and smugly folded his thick arms.

"My curiosity would undoubtedly aggrandize you and impoverish me," Milord said pointedly.

Wimley chuckled. "A pleasant thought, Sire." He produced a ragged strip of cloth, blew his nose vigorously and stuffed the cloth into his sleeve. "Now then. My itinerary included the vicinity of the Catscat Mountains. Does that mean anything to you?"

Milord looked sharply at him. "Do you take me for a beef-wit? Of course I know of the Catscats. Come to the point."

The Haggleman was taken aback. "Very well," he said with an air of injured pride. "No need to be rude."

He pinched his nose in an exaggerated effort at recollection. "It was twilight. I was walking through a copse of snipsnapsnorum plants by the Perspex River — I won't burden Your Lordship with the precise reasons for my presence in such a bleak locale — when I happened to witness a frightening spectacle amongst the clouds: a clowder of witches, cackling raucously and turning cartwheels in the sky!" Waving his arms in imitation, Wimley dislodged a rare porcelain statuette from the table at his side. The Masterfootling swooped down from across the room and just rescued the fragile lady in his white-gloved hands. Milord heaved a heavy sigh of relief.

"Well, no harm," the Haggleman said airily, and continued. "They were quite drunk, and two of them strayed off toward a nearby camp of stick-men." He looked inquiringly at Milord, who only buried his chin more deeply in his collar.

"Well, as Your Lordship is aware, the stick-men use magic webs, strung between long poles, to ensnare their prey. They usually limit their depredations to large owls and clambergeists, but sometimes attack a witch, given the opportunity. They snagged these two derelict hags in their net and stunned them with clink-clubs.

"I watched from a clump of bushes as they dragged the trussed witches to a brimstone fire. What a sight! The flames were magenta and red and gold, and a dozen other colors. The heat prickled my skin where I stood, half a furlong away. The witches' rags were quickly incinerated, leaving them naked but for the crisscrossed magic webbing around them. They were trapped over the fire like scrawny pink pigs, spitted for a Freeday roast!"

The vivid description made me a bit queasy, and I considered returning to my lair behind the kitchen stove. Milord sensed my discomfort and stroked my neck.

Wimley looked condescendingly at me. "You don't think mountain-witches would be hurt by such treatment? No indeed, not a scald or a blister! In fact the flames only woke them from their drunken daze and they began cawing like crows, and laughed til the tears rolled down their leathery cheeks and went 'phisss' in the fire pit. 'Oh Petolzia,' the first one giggled, 'what a fancy!' And the other one replied, 'Fiddle-diddle, Vulgia, my heart's on fire!'" Wimley stopped and frowned into his empty glass, which the Masterfootling silently refilled.

"But what happened next turned their giggles to screams of fury: the stick-men doused the bonfire with wet sand and began sifting through its dregs, plucking out the witches' precious amulets — for that had been their goal from the start. It soon transpired that only Vulgia's trinkets had survived the flames; Petolzia's were destroyed, a fact which puzzled the stick-men considerably, and myself as well. They hubbubbed for some time, poking at the brimstone and scratching their heads in the manner of monkeys, while their two smoldering prisoners shrieked and struggled with their magic bonds.

"Presently the stick-men forgot the problem and their mood grew wilder. They dumped the witches on the ground and set about, uh…" Here Haggleman Wimley smirked and made a series of crude but very explicit gestures involving both hands. "Vulgia and Petolzia struggled and fought, but the devil-ropes held and they —" Milord coughed loudly through tightened jowls, at which the Haggleman said, "Yes, of course," in a deprecating tone which I thought very offensive.

"These violations were of course repugnant to me," he said carelessly. But if he was at all put off by the stick-men's behavior, I suspect it was only because of their lack of taste, for the witches could have had no more fleshly allure than weathered logs.

Milord looked down apologetically and fondled my ears. "Those stick-men are a savage lot!" he said with feeling. I pressed against his side in agreement.

Wimley waved his empty snifter at Farberwile and again took up his narrative. "Finally they bundled the old shrews to Pelburn's Precipice and spun them like tops out into the sea. Quite a splash they made, too."

He leaned forward earnestly. "I must tell you I took my life in these very hands, tailing vicious wights of that sort." He displayed his hammy hands, which seemed incapable of holding much more than trinkets or a glass.

Milord yawned lavishly. "Your adventures are marvelous, to be sure, Haggleman. And no doubt your brave services command a fine fee." Wimley sat up and looked at him with new appreciation. "Pray complete your account."

"Well, Petolzia and Vulgia managed to swim to shore like two half-drowned cats. Having lost all their magic paraphernalia, they were reduced to walking the forty leagues back to their hive. Imagine, witches hiking like commoners up the side of Catscat Mountain!" Milord pursed his lips and consulted his timepiece.

"But a visit to the home of the mountainwitches is too much even for me," continued Haggleman, "and in any case my instincts counseled me that a more fateful event was about to occur at the stick-men's camp, so I bivouacked there as darkness fell. They stoked their huge bonfire and pranced and brawled around it, celebrating their triumph.

"Meanwhile on Catscat Mountain their sister witches must have received the two victims with cruel scorn. They thought it no end of a joke that they had been…compromised by the stick-men." He selected this word with an effort; the imposition of such descriptive reticence was a painful task. But the tipples he had tossed down, undoubtedly on an empty stomach, amplified his interest in the lurid subject. He leaned forward confidingly, swaying a bit. "In fact, I suspect the senior witches also took advantage of their vulnerability, to, ah, take advantage of *them* as well." He snickered like a schoolboy and wiped his nose. The Masterfootling blushed and retired further into his station by the drapery. Milord studied the latticework he had made with his chubby fingers.

Wimley regained himself. "Well, I imagine the two of them pleaded and groveled, and were finally given substitute amulets and dismissed. But they continued their whining and at length persuaded the witch Council that the whole tribe had been insulted, and demanded vengeance on the stick-men; and so at last the Council invoked a frighteningly powerful curse.

"This I surmise from the events of the following morning. I was spying on the stick-men from a suitable distance. They lay about, rubbing each other with a balm of river mud and billywix dung in an attempt to recover from their excesses of the previous night. They are truly a bizarre sight, Lord Benefice; have you ever seen them?"

"Is it important?" asked Milord.

Haggleman cocked his head in hesitation, then plunged on. "They resemble enormous praying mantises, just like those in your garden, Sire, but much larger of course, and they have only rudimentary wings, which in general are of little use. And although their expressions are astonishingly animated, their 'minds', to use this term in its loosest sense, are quite blank, or so I'm told. And of course they are quite naked, so that —" Milord waved his hand in a mixture of indifference and impatience.

"Yes, well, as I looked on, they suddenly vanished." The Haggleman paused dramatically. "Into thin air. I was naturally amazed to have witnessed such an awesome display of supernatural —"

Milord interrupted him again. "May I be so rude as to catapult to what I sincerely hope is the crux of this endless tale, by posing an inference?" This caught the Haggleman by surprise. "To wit," said Milord, "may we suppose that you were able to acquire Vulgia's amulets from the remains of their rude potlatch? And that you then hastened here, knowing of my interest in such matters?"

The Haggleman rubbed his upper lip thoughtfully. "In a manner of speaking, yes. Yes, provisionally, to both questions." He paused.

Milord sat up on one elbow. "And would it be possible to clarify this 'manner of speaking' at any time, say, prior to this evening's repast?" he asked, his voice taking on an edge.

The Haggleman looked a bit uncomfortable. He seemed to recall, for the first time since his arrival, the prominent stature enjoyed by his host in Albanderry. It was easy to imagine that Milord was by no means the first client to whom he had attempted to hawk his bizarre goods, and that the vulgar incident he described had occurred considerably longer ago than he implied.

"Your Lordship, the amulets were there," he said hastily. "But there were, ah, minor difficulties associated with their disposition, Sire. Kindly allow me to explain.

"After a cautious waiting period, I advanced and inspected their grounds. It developed that the stick-men had not actually vanished, but had been instantly compressed or encysted together with their witch-plunder, within these tiny pellets scattered on the ground."

He withdrew an ornate ivory-and-gold box from his wallet, opened it and held out a few grains. They resembled ordinary wheat, except that they pulsed and changed shape incessantly, and glinted like beacons in the soft firelight.

His voice fell to a whisper. "Perhaps they hear us discussing their sad fate even now," he said, flourishing his hand in a clumsy attempt at eloquence. One of the pellets twitched — perhaps the stick-men were desperately testing their miniature walls under our eyes. I couldn't help but feel a certain sympathy for them, crude and ruthless though Wimley's tale made them out to be.

Milord studied the grains in keen fascination. "Let this be a lesson to you, Flick," he said to me excitedly. "That nature's grandeur may be concealed in the slightest button! Whole races of creatures, eons of time, even star-spatters may be reduced to a pellet for storage or other manipulation! Although in the present instance we are speaking only of a small tribe of misguided troglodytes…"

"Well put, Your Lordship," interrupted Haggleman, relieved to have kindled Milord's interest at last.

"…which reflects the relatively limited power of the witches in our Realm. Thank heaven we've none of the Cosmic Mistresses hereabouts."

"Indeed," said Haggleman with a giddy laugh.

Milord's hand idly stroked my fur. "And have you detected any evidence that the other witches pursued you?" he asked carefully.

"Not to my knowledge, Sire," Wimley said quickly. He pointed to the faint luminescence flickering like will-o'-the-wisp around the edges of the ivory-and-gold box. "I took the precaution of applying an essence which is protective against Distant Depredations of all six varieties."

"Well advised," said Milord. "And for what reason do you suppose I might wish to acquire these bits of devilry?" he asked. "Surely you don't imagine me capable of extricating Vulgia's amulets from them, while at the same time maintaining the stick-men in an enchanted state?"

Haggleman grinned. "No, Lord Benefice. But clearly, a man of your connections could exact a pretty cumshaw for them from the old ladies' Consortium," he said.

Milord studied his nails, took a deep breath and stood up. "No, I think not. Thank you for your troubles. Good day, Haggleman Wimley."

Haggleman's mouth dropped open. His hand jerked, spilling several of the pellets onto the rug. "Your Grace jests," he stammered.

Milord motioned to Masterfootling Farberwile to attend to the door. "Certainly not," he said and walked crisply out, carrying me in his vest pocket. On hands and knees Wimley fumbled with his box and the dropped pellets, muttering to himself. He jogged clumsily after us to the foyer, his jackboots echoing sharply on the marble floor.

Milord stood on the outside steps and took the fresh, balmy air. The sun shone yellow and warm, and our pinglenut vines shivered gently on their white trellises. In the high distance the snowy peaks of the Catscats reigned under a massive blue sky, in which a few brightly colored balloon-and-cabs floated on a Freeday outing.

Haggleman Wimley caught up with us, wincing in the sunlight. "But surely Your Grace would be honored to own such extraordinary items," he pleaded in disbelief, still adjusting the box in his inside coat pocket.

"Oh, perhaps ten or fifteen bezants could be found, for the sake of curiosity," Milord said casually.

Haggleman stopped and regained himself. A suspicious smile spread slowly across his pink features. He looked knowingly at Milord, then at his chipped nails; cogitated, and sighed. "No, Sire, I fear these little orphans would only mope and languish in your uncaring hands." He shook his head resolutely. "No, and no; I shall have to seek cozier lodgings for their tiny souls."

Milord flinched, but I think the gesture was noticeable only to me, resting close against his side. He affected a look of resignation. "Yes, perhaps that would be best," he said.

Wimley's worn gray buggy stood untended at the curb, its one horse nickering impatiently. Wimley hesitated and twice stated his intention to depart. "Well then, perhaps a figure of, shall we say, thirty bezants, Sire?" he asked finally.

"You feel that this sum would sufficiently improve the mood of our sad little captives?" returned Milord, raising his eyebrows.

"Oh yes, very much so," said Haggleman Wimley with a rush.

"Excellent," said Milord and plucked the box from his hands. He signaled to the Masterfootling, who had been standing discreetly behind us. "Good day, Haggleman," Milord announced with finality. Clutching me to his side, he bounded back into the Manor. Behind us Masterfootling Farberwile deftly dispensed thirty bezants from a purse. Milord bolted into his study and slammed the door.

"A first-class coup!" he exclaimed. He paced about, occasionally jabbing his finger in the air or clapping his hands, then stopping to examine the box again. The unearthly arabesque adorning its lid flickered with a lambent light. I was grateful for this aura, which was a vital protection; yet the thing aroused an ominous dread in my stomach, not only on account of the witches' involvement in it, but also because the remaining bands of stick-men might well go in search of their captured kin. Stick-men at Benefice Manor! It was unthinkable.

"It's the key, Flick! The key is in our hands!" Milord giggled with excitement. "At first they'll give up only minor potions and doodly-charms in trade, and those grudgingly," he said in an instructive tone, "but time will inflame their greed for revenge on the stick-men, and they'll bring me their notorious brew in exchange for their tiny enemies. Hah! A ransom, Flick, that's what we'll get! A handsome ransom!"

He reached to an upper shelf and drew down a thick leather notebook. The title, Summary of Essences, was embossed in gold leaf on its cover, with the insignia of Benefice Manor. Milord turned to the second section, in which his concoctions are listed in order of prestige and potency, and pointed to a blank space above the first entry, 'Clarissimus XIX'. "It would be listed here, Flick," he said softly.

The Masterfootling entered. Milord closed the volume and said, "Summon the Gasmaster at once."

"As you direct, Sire." The Masterfootling tugged an embroidered velvet rope hanging by the wall.

Milord continued his feverish pacing, occasionally muttering something to himself or bending over his desk to scribble a few notes. Gasmaster Bickle soon padded in, puffing and wiping his large pink face with a kerchief. "Your Grace?" he inquired.

"A contact with the Consortium at once!" said Milord. "Through the usual channels, but accelerated as per Article XVI, Provision 21 of the Bylaws."

"Yes, Milord. May I ask the purpose of the encounter?"

"Major items in hand, Gasmaster. Quibbling! Disbursement! Transfer of concoction!"

Gasmaster Bickle's eyes widened. "At once, Sire." He turned, momentarily wedging his ample waist against the doorjamb, and scurried off.

Milord scooped me from my pouch into his palm. "They'll prepare it in a huge, battered cauldron hidden amongst the boulders on Catseye Peak," he said, making an intense face, "stirring their vile brew with long, thick broom-straws…" He set me on his knee, wiggled his fingers and stirred his wrists in an imaginary pot of jolly evil. "Presently the straws dissolve in the bubbling muck, and the old shrews shriek and accuse one another of mismanagement and dereliction. What a contumacious coterie of crotchety fat crones they are. Ha! And ha!"

Milord loves this sort of alliterative sally. He frowned doubtfully for a moment and scratched his ear, vaguely realizing that 'fat' was out of place in the sequence.

"They love to dance around the flames, Flick, grinning and brawling as you please. Their legs clack and fly akimbo like marionettes in a fit." I feared he would attempt an imitation, not a good idea for one in Milord's enlarged condition, and he wore his elevated heels as well. But he only looked down at me with a tender smile, gave my flank a little squeeze and settled back into his wing chair. He was in a rare mood.

I wondered aloud what it would be like to visit the witches' coven. Milord looked puzzled. (He sometimes has difficulty grasping my Filxxx dialect, while I have none in understanding the simple tongue of Albanderrians, though I cannot speak it.) I repeated my question, enunciating the squeaky syllables more carefully.

"Ah. Well, perhaps someday we'll go to see them," he said, "but that's quite a risky business, you know. The witches are usually hidden in the oily black smoke of their cooking fires, so that their positions can be guessed only by the clouds of airborne parasites whizzing nearby like fireflies. They don't let on that they see you until it's too late; and then they erupt from the smoke, snatch you up and drown you in their rotten potluck."

My fur stood on end. Milord widened his eyes and made as if to clutch me with clawed hands. I yelped and burrowed deeper into my blanket. He laughed, heaved to his feet again and locked the wondrous box of demon-stones in a depositorium hidden behind a row of books.

"That's enough for now, Flickamerry Hansombear. It's time for our nap," he said, and we repaired to his private withdrawing room. The sun soon swept away, leaving only a few tatters of her glorious skirt behind. A misty gloom gathered outside, punctured by a few distant, winkling hearth lights. Milord settled into his most capacious settee, and we were soon fast asleep.

The following day Gasmaster Bickle arranged preliminary contacts with the Mountainwitch Consortium — a difficult process. Initially an *agréation* is secured, by which low-ranking representatives are selected from Guild and Consortium, respectively. They designate neutral intermediaries, who in turn select a time and place for a session of principal delegates.

This plenary meeting took place two days later. Sixteen heavily armed retainers accompanied Gasmaster Bickle and his assistant, Salvemaster Worrant; normally Grandmage Mentharch might also have been included in such an expedition, but he had given out the statement that his presence was required in his castle for the annual overhaul of his energy vats. The entourage traveled to an isolated amphitheatre in the extreme southwest corner of Albanderry, where they were met by a senior administrative witch, who, as stipulated, was alone and temporarily bereft of her deadly amulets.

In his study Milord paced impatiently, awaiting the return of his emissaries. Winter had arrived unseasonably early; flurries of snow eddied outside in a gray light. We heard the sounds of horses and carriage drawing up and shortly the Gasmaster entered, gasping even more than usual. He plopped into a chair, a familiarity which Milord permitted him because of his frail condition. It was sad to see him so afflicted, for he is one of those rare people who are quite without real malice; but such persons, I have observed, also seem somehow to lack a certain toughness, and are often easily hurt by intrigues, or smitten with neoplastic maladies. Thus it was paradoxical that he should hold such a difficult position as Protectioner, which requires great wiliness and strength of will; but by some quirk of character and good fortune he had always succeeded in dispatching his duties with masterful skill and good result.

Milord pounced on him. "What news?" he demanded eagerly, at the same time brushing a few persistent snowflakes from the Gasmaster's coat. I perched on Milord's shoulder, as anxious as he to hear the news.

The Gasmaster rubbed the numbness from his blenched hands. "The skies were disturbingly leaden, Milord," he began, "which I regarded as a portent. And the witch delegate was quite irritable, being plagued by an exceptional number of parasites, which alighted constantly to inject fulminant galls on her neck and shoulders. Indeed, she frequently interrupted the discussions to flagellate her gibbous back with a stook of thornwattle, in a futile attempt to gain relief from their pruritic effect."

He sipped at a cup of scalding tea. Milord sat down, nodding and listening patiently. "The negotiations were stormy and intense, Sire. Indeed, on several occasions we nearly broke off entirely. As you predicted, she was in one respect quite intransigent: she would give up no more than trifles for the first few grains. I acquiesced to this demand, as you instructed; and subsequently her manner softened." The Gasmaster removed his spectacles and wearily rubbed his eyes. "To shorten the account, Milord, I may say that, in sum, a satisfactory arrangement was at last consummated."

"Excellent!" cried Milord. But the battle had indeed taken its toll on the Gasmaster, for a profuse sweat broke out on his ashen face.

Milord looked at him in alarm. "Summon the physicians," he said urgently to Masterfootling Farberwile.

"Merely a chill on my liver, nothing more," Gasmaster Bickle said feebly, waving his hand in protest. He looked alarmingly peaked, and a sickly diaphoresis had quite dampened his clothing. Milord helped him to recline on a couch and spread a comforter over his legs.

Soon the three physicians arrived amidst great flurriment, bowed to Milord and removed their cloaks. But after a cursory glance at the patient, they took forever, it seemed to me, to establish which of them would examine him first; and then they spent another age in cleansing their hands, all the while discussing an obscure method of applying leeches to the earlobe of a woman in labor. Finally in exasperation Milord interrupted their conference and pointedly reminded them of the origin of their fees — "If any," he added, grating his teeth.

For a moment they looked askance at Milord. Then, clucking and shaking their heads, they bent to examine the Gasmaster. One measured the girth of his arm at various points, while the second compared the color of the patient's tongue to a series of thin wooden cards whose hue varied from an impossible shade of pink to a ghastly chlor-green. The third physician fingered the Gasmaster's frock coat and commented approvingly on the quality of its tailoring. Throughout the ordeal Salvemaster Worrant looked on solicitously, but in his eye I detected a hard gleam of understanding that he was the Gasmaster's successor apparent.

The three physicians withdrew to a corner and conferred, hands clasped behind them. Finally the first one turned with a decisive air and announced, "A compound wheezing of the spleen, without doubt. Requiring —"

The second physician looked at the first in shocked surprise. "But that is not at all what we agreed," he said. "A prolapsing kidney is to blame, possibly complicated by an excess of inflammatory bile."

"Never," snapped the third, pushing in front of his colleagues. "The diagnosis is clear: grubbulous dyspepsia, with a propensity to sallow flatulence." The argument quickly degenerated into acrimonious wrangling. Milord sat rubbing his forehead, and I feared for the Gasmaster.

At length they reached a tenuous compromise: each of them would institute a specified portion of the treatment he recommended. The first administered a draught of sour black liquid, at which the Gasmaster shuddered and clutched his bed; the second applied an electuary to his teeth and a medicinal lard to his left knee; and the third prescribed six days' absolute bedrest, to be taken in the eighth of the twenty-four Curative Postures. I was relieved that no radical surgery had been deemed necessary.

The physicians departed, loudly resuming their dispute as they left. Milord made further arrangements for Gasmaster Bickle's care, and from Salvemaster Worrant heard the details of the bargain with the mountainwitches.

The next day, in exchange for the first grain, Milord received a rather ordinary clay jar. A crippled phantom emerged in a puff of noxious lavender smoke, shielded his sunken eyes from the light and promptly retreated into his container. Milord irritably consulted the accompanying manual and recited a few advisory syllables. The phantom reappeared with the utmost reluctance, braced himself on a rickety crutch and offered, in a weak but sullen voice, to perform any six tasks.

Milord first instructed it to rearrange his garden topiary in accordance with the pattern illustrated in a rare volume he had once obtained at great expense from Grandmage Mentharch; the phantom succeeded only in dispersing a lethal fungus among the plants. Milord then directed it to several progressively simple chores, at which it also failed miserably. Finally he ordered it to remove a soiled napkin from his desk. The phantom doubled over, complained of a severe gripe and vanished.

The second item arrived unexpectedly the next night. I had been unable to sleep and sat gazing from a window of Milord's chambers. The moon was a waxing crescent, shedding an anemic light into a shadowy rear courtyard. Suddenly a dwarf witch scudded overhead, cast an object to the ground and flew off.

It was an enormous stone necklace, warranted (according to the runes clumsily scratched into its clasp) to prevent the arrival of unwanted guests at the home of its wearer. Despite its burdensome weight and pungent smell — a repulsive odor reminiscent of rotting bladderwort — Milord diligently kept the necklace around his neck for an entire day. Haggleman Wimley then came to the manor in a surly mood, arguing that he should have received an additional seven bezants for traveling expenses. Milord instructed Floorsteward Smithkline to throw him out and reckoned the necklace a failure.

But though I detected a certain impatience in his manner, Milord was not at all disappointed in these developments. That evening we sat warming ourselves by the hearth. A lovely cascade of cinnamon and orange sparks ascended from the chandler's famous cheesewood logs, which are cleverly seeded with particles of compressed wax. "Never fear, Flick," Milord reassured me. "Events are proceeding as planned." Outside, a near-half-moon hung in the sky like a broken pearl. Milord drummed his fingers thoughtfully on the clawed end of his chair's arm and summoned his newly hired clavichordist.

An asthenic man in frayed black tails slipped through the door, bowed to Milord with the speed of a fly and passionately embraced the keyboard as though it were a lost lover. He launched at once into a complex baroque improvisation, sculpting elaborate towers of music, level by complicated level. Each silvery cascade of notes was embellished with countless grace notes, mordents and trills. His fingers scooped icy balls of sound from an invisible buffet and flung them into the room's stuffy air. The music grew wild, almost fey; it became a meandering stream of indolent passion, twisting and branching into countless meanings, ever more minute, more distant and yet more intense. The musician hesitated, questioned, and a poignant shyness came into his hands.

The notes seemed on the verge of fading hopelessly away, when suddenly his mood lightened and he dispatched a bright gigue. I closed my eyes and baby reindeer pranced on the keyboard on felt-swaddled hooves, pastel scarves fluttering gaily from their necks in an imaginary wind. They took to skiis and shushed down a glittering snowy slope in bright morning sunshine. At its bottom they bowled over one another and tumbled in the snow in triple time, laughing throatily in the language of young reindeer and nuzzling each other under their furry necks. As they frolicked, Milord and I entered a reverie, from which only Milord emerged.

For it was at that moment, no doubt stimulated by the enrapturing music, that I entered *raadhxxx*. This is a developmental period, or diapause, through which all young Filxxxs must pass to allow the maturation of our *gnozzt*, an organ whose function I shall explain by and by. The process usually lasts about five days, during which we remain in a rather confused state of mind.

I remember little of that time beyond my keenest pleasures: I would secretly scamper about the household, cadging a crumb or spying on visitors. My favorite adventure was to sneak about after one of Milord's late-night feasts, sampling delicacies that portly, masterful personages had left on their plates. Such scraps you can hardly imagine! — skullnut soup, chewy twists of antwerp paste, lean fruits grown by a sect of brutal pagans beyond the Endless Ocean. One wonderful night I even tasted antennas of arctic locust, breaded in a batter of sea-cow's milk. If Mistress Breadwright had caught me, I would have been cat's meat for sure!

Those were pleasant, if only half-conscious, days, a heady recess before real life banged on my door. When I emerged from *raadhxxx*, Underfootling Thindle Spinkite was stroking my neck late one evening. "Ah, there you are again, Flick!" he said. "We've missed you."

I squeaked sluggishly in response and Thindle brought me up to date. Fellscribe Thinklefine had accidentally punctured his finger with a quill-tip; Handman Berryplain had again been reprimanded for tardiness and risked dismissal at the next such offense. Gasmaster Bickle had made a good recovery from his exhaustion. And I was saddened, though not surprised, to learn that two of my five siblings had been sent to the farms as mouse-herds because of delay in mastery of household etiquette.

Thindle said that in exchange for the third and fourth grains the witches had traded weak brews, which Milord had discarded in a remote location specially designated by the Protectioners. The fifth grain fetched what was probably a decent elixir, but the delivering witch, in a capricious fit of pique, destroyed it on arrival. The next delivery was scheduled for the morrow, and Milord felt certain that it would be a much worthier product.

A gibbous moon gleamed through the window.

III

THE DELIVERY

"I hear it. I hear it, sure." Underfootling Thindle Spinkite hopped up and down, rubbing his feet. The cart was yet ten leagues away, but its distant creaking caused a burning sensation in his soles. He looked gravely at me. "We'll feel her baneful influence for days, Flick, I can tell you. Milord's thanes will complain of itch, and Mistress Breadwright swears her dough wrestles with her hands. And my blasted feet have the ears of a rabbit."

In the kitchen there was a flurry of dropped spoons, clattering plates, hurrying legs. Urgent instructions passed back and forth amongst Milord's blackguards, maids and servants. Kitchenmaster Traysmith stood in the midst of the maelstrom, rubbing his hands, turning this way and that, shouting orders and then changing his mind. "Handman Berryplain, put this bowl…" he would begin, then reconsider; and when finally he decided what should be done with the bowl, someone had already disposed of it.

Scowling and clucking, Mistress Breadwright bore down on me. "Shoo! Get away!" she said, jabbing her broom. "I won't have *animals* in my kitchen." She treats me as though I were the first Filxxx in Milord's household (an honor actually held by my mother's father), and an unwelcome one at that. Ordinarily Mistress Breadwright and I keep an uneasy peace, but let any excitement or disturbance arise and she takes up arms again.

Thindle swept me up in the nick of time and popped me into his pocket. "Mind you don't get straws in your fur, Flick," he said, giving the Mistress a sharp look. She glared back at him for a moment, then turned and scolded one of the handmen.

Thindle ran about making his preparations, describing the delivery procedure to me as he went. "They trundle the jeroboam onto a wicker cart, Flick. The heavy urn looks as though it will break the cart into twigs, but it's made from the fired bones of dead umbs, you know, quite strong. In fact I hear they use the same cart for delivering meteors and sacred steles to their Cosmic Mistresses, so it must be stout indeed.

"Then one of the witches pulls the wagon's traces over her spiked shoulders, like this —" Thindle pulled two apron strings over his sinewy arms to illustrate "— gives out a fearful screech —" he rubbed his feet painfully again at the thought "— and hauls it down the mountain trail. And then they've a long voyage from Catsmouthport to Albanderry."

The Gasmaster scuttled past, flailing his short arms into his black frock coat as he ran to his station. A great ring of keys jangled at his waist. "Activate, activate," he reminded himself urgently, and stopped to consult his watch. He produced a large checkered cloth from his rear pocket and mopped under his chin.

"Gasmaster Bickle hastens to activate the vapor barrier at the edge of our grounds," Thindle said. "But he must first vary its location by a few inches, to take her by surprise, else she'll detect it instantly and deploy a vicious counter-spell, which would be disaster for us all. I couldn't say why the simple act of moving it slightly should deceive one as wily as a mountainwitch, but there you have it."

Bickle whirled through the back door and disappeared. "Godspeed, Gasmaster," Thindle called. He slipped a flask from his vest pocket and took a generous sip, then thoughtfully rubbed my back. "Once the biddy passes unknowing through a freshly placed barrier, she is bound by ancient assize to deliver her goods in fair state, without noxious enterprise." He stooped and pushed a few boxes under a shelf.

"Now we'd much rather meet her out by the barrier, you can be sure, instead of here in our very nest, but she won't agree to it, damn her old bones. We have to wait inside til she comes to the door, that's the ritual, and it won't do to show so much as a hint of impatience by poking our noses out any sooner. Ranktwo Sparseman committed such a *faux pas* last week: the witch singed all his hair off, hurled her cargo into the skies and blew away like a leaf in a storm. The poor fellow's hair won't grow back, and if he gets within ten yards of a fire, his scalp heats up almost to the point of flame. He'll spend many a cold winter, shrinking from our cozy hearth."

Thindle cinched up his collar, which he had the habit of wearing folded up to conceal the mark of his father's early lash. His white linen shirt, worn almost through in many places from countless wearings and washings, was heavily starched to keep its shape. I peered up at his lean face, dotted here and there with pale moles and scarred along the right cheek. Seventeen years of experience were reflected there, but not, much to his regret, in his menial title as Underfootling.

He gulped again at his flask, found it empty, and seized the opportunity, in the general confusion, to refill it from a large, smudged decanter of cooking sherry by the stove. He drew a curtain aside and peeped out a mullioned window. "Oh, Milord's laces, it's that damned whiny one with the bowlegs and the blue-black shift! God save us, she's the worst." He stamped his feet and shared a look of cordial contempt with Masterfootling Farberwile, who had taken up his position by the door.

"The pip of the lot, eh, Spinkite? And she seems to be the regular now," he said, winking and stifling a cough, for already her acrid odor pervaded the kitchen. The Masterfootling is a good man who governs his twenty-odd workers with the ease of a kindly father, and has the gift of being able to show familiarity to those beneath him without losing respect or station.

"Aye, Petolzia's charms would sour a dead man's stomach," agreed

Thindle. The Masterfootling frowned and anxiously prodded his belly with his plump hands. Petolzia! With dread I recalled that she was one of the two witches in Haggleman Wimley's tale.

It was late afternoon. In the pumpkin field an aged virago glanced spitefully right and left, picking her way quick as a sparrow. She was as shriveled as a loaf of forcemeat left too long in a stone oven, yet she radiated a menacing power. Behind her a rickety cart followed, creaking and groaning under its stony load; it seemed to move more by its own crotchety will than by her effort. Woman and wagon moved unbearably slowly, but when I blinked, they stood forty paces further along. I rubbed my eye and she was standing just outside the door, the wagon wobbling to rest. The path she had taken now had the sickly color and smell of wet grave-ashes.

"Who'll give a grimace for my glob?" she rasped, "or tasty bug, or shrunken bell, for grumous ware from Catscat Peak?"

Masterfootling Farberwile threw open the door and bowed deeply. "Good Lady Petolzia," he said, "prithee let us assist with these dainty flasks of sweet liqueur from Your Grace's kitchen."

She thrust her beady eye in his face (for the other eye was sunken and atrophied) and shrieked, "Yes yes, do assist," and cackled like a banshee, slapping her thigh til I thought it would shatter.

"Curse me if I can see the humor in it," Thindle said under his breath.

Salvemaster Worrant edged past them and inspected the shipment. To his wrist was strapped a monitoring device, which he held close by the urns; it shook briskly. "Cask in good order," he pronounced, and bowed. "Lord Benefice extends his compliments," he said with a graceful lilt.

Petolzia abruptly stopped her cachinnating and jerked her head. "Payment, payment on the instant!" she screamed, and howled til my stomach threatened to jump into my mouth. Oblivious to her screams, weighmen poured from the kitchen and grappled with the marble carboy. Sweating and staggering under the weight, they wheeled it to the larder; it grated on the stone floor, making strange musical sounds amidst the witch's noisome yells. I felt a sudden chill and snuggled deeper into Thindle's warm pocket.

The witch hopped back and forth impatiently as Salvemaster

Worrant stood by the door and cleared his throat. "Payment true and final, by avowal and consent of —" he began in formal tones.

"I'll pour scalding oil in your throat, you slimy worm," she cursed.

"— present sorceress in contract and Lord Gracewright Cantilouve Benefice," he finished, ignoring her, with hardly a flinch. Failure to complete the official phrase would have given the witch license to renege, and Sophists know what other baleful mischief besides; but Salvemaster Worrant was a tempered man who knew his job well, though I sometimes doubted him in a way I could not quite define.

Under her greedy scrutiny he then delivered a pouch from his breast pocket and plucked out a flea-sized kernel, upon which the old woman pounced in a rage. She spat in disgust and threw the pellet to the floor. Then she lifted a skinny leg from her filthy skirts and crushed it under one naked, rock-hard heel. Even before Floorsteward Smithkline could sweep up the residual bit of chaff, she and her rattan cart had vanished.

The servants heaved loud sighs of relief and slowly resumed their duties, smiling nervously at one another. Salvemaster Worrant locked up the closet and put a hand on Thindle's shoulder.

"Well, by the clouds! Another delivery secured," he said. "Milord's commerce goes well, but it's a trial for us." He helped himself to a handful of untended crullcake, spilling crumbs liberally around him in the process.

Thindle wiped his neck with a moist rag. "It's a demon's sour fart in those accursed bottles. But I trust you would know more of that than I, Salvemaster."

Salvemaster Worrant narrowed his eyes at Thindle for an instant. He shrugged and wiped his hands on the sides of his shirt, then adjusted his coat to conceal the butter stains. "In short order Milord wishes to examine the delivered tun, which I have left unsecured, Underfootling Spinkite," he said, glancing at the larder. He raised an eyebrow at Thindle, wiped his mouth on his sleeve and sauntered out.

Thindle watched the Salvemaster's slouched form as he left. "His familiarity becomes a weed choking the very air," he muttered. "And yet he imagines himself a man of substance. Hmmph!" He folded his kerchief and thrust it into his back pocket.

"Handmen Berryplain and Armright," he called. Two callow youths presented themselves. "To the larder." They wrestled the urn to a large dumbwaiter and tugged mightily at its sash-ropes til the platform had ascended the three flights to Milord's chambers.

"Come, we'll relax a bit, Flick," Thindle said and stepped into his tiny quarters behind the mop closet. Here he keeps a narrow bunk bed, a table and pitcher, a small shelf of linens. Near the ceiling a diamond-shaped window admitted a shaft of weak sunlight, whose shadows, propelled by wind-blown branches outside, turned in the dusty air like a merry-go-round. With relief Thindle dropped himself on his bunk, which creaked in protest.

He gazed up at his tiny skylight. Resentment and regret tussled on his face; both at length gave way to resignation. He sighed and looked at me. "The future's a gray spot, Flick. There was once a time when I was privileged to enjoy Milord's good graces, but now it's only 'Thindle Spinkite, dishclout'." He plumped his pillow several times, yawned and immediately fell asleep. He rolled over, pressing me uncomfortably against his hard bench.

Good Thindle Spinkite, I thought, extricating myself from his pocket — a steady man, but a thistle: blown by stiff winds, he lies down obediently, but prickles if squeezed. And this prickliness had kept him from much of the grace which Milord generally shows all who serve him, the more so as the service endures; for Milord is anything but stingy. I recall, for example, how he rewarded Fellscribe Thinklefine with an ample estate and stipend after only twenty-two years of service; and Masterfootling Farberwile certainly looks forward to the light of a comfortable candle in his waning years, even though his responsibilities could hardly be described as arduous.

Some time ago I pieced together the fragments of gossip heard daily round the hearth and came to understand the reason for Thindle's weak position at Benefice Manor. Early in his service — long before I suckled at the third of my mother's six teats — he was given the chore of receiving the daily deliveries of kitchen goods. He was but a lanky reed then, sprouting towards manhood with the speed of bamboo and considerably bewildered by it.

At that time Ranktwo Sparseman, whose position in the servants' complex hierarchy was just above Thindle's, persuaded the Floorsteward to give one of his cousins a starting position. The Floorsteward did so against his better judgment, as Sparseman's cousin was an obsequious oaf whose crude pretense of respect for authority was but a veil, thinly concealing murkier goals. I think Thindle saw that Ranktwo Sparseman would try to elevate his cousin past him without delay and was thus immediately at odds with the new arrival.

Well, not to make too long a yarn of it, Sparseman's cousin contrived to embezzle a shipment of pressed meats and condiments and made it look as though Thindle were the culprit. Thindle was confronted. Under-estimating the seriousness of the situation, and no doubt feeling that he was above replying to such deviousness in a new recruit, he resorted to flippancy and impudence instead of a frank and simple denial.

Despite much testimony on his behalf (a testimony whose ardor was tempered by the ambivalence one usually feels towards adolescents), his name was thus stained by innuendo and doubt. Sparseman's cousin died of the pox not long after, without confessing his crimes; and Sparseman and Thindle have not spoken to each other since. With each passing year Thindle's hope of proper advancement has faded, and he has become more taciturn and withdrawn. His bitterness appears only when he is truly provoked, just as a frosted window must be rubbed briskly to glimpse the fireplace embers glowing beyond it.

Thindle's chest rose and fell deeply on his sheets. His breath was laden with the odor of cooking sherry and mutton. He began to snore. I jumped to the floor and crawled through a baseboard vent into the labyrinth of fragrance-ducts which lace the castle. By their means Milord enjoys the freshness of thyme or lavender, the delicacy of saffron or paprilivole, or any of a thousand other floral scents devised by himself or his artisans, at a moment's notice. The ducts are just large enough to accommodate me, although I once forgot to contract my *gnozzt* before entering and spent a few painful moments adjusting its bulbous shape to conform to the duct.

I scurried through the sweet-smelling darkness to Milord's chambers. We usually enjoy a nap together at tea time, but today would be different. He would be most exhilarated over the mountainwitches' delivery; and in addition he was due to address the Assembly on the morrow, a speech for which he had been preparing his comments during much of the time I was lost in *raadhxxx*. I too was excited, but more by the prospect of attending an Assembly meeting than by the arrival of the brew, which aroused my intense anxieties.

Milord was seated by a window in his Terrace Room. He motioned invitingly to me and I hopped into the velvet holster at his side.

Salvemaster Worrant busied himself with preparation of the urn. "This should be the best of them, and I am pleased, well pleased," said Milord, grandly waving his hand. "A splendid mélange of Cantankerous Theories and Presumptions, such as the world has rarely if ever experienced. Distilled to a quintessence," he added, chuckling with satisfaction, and patted my sheath. I squeaked in agreement, though I didn't understand the reference to Theories and such.

Salvemaster Worrant now stood to the side, an unctuous smile on his lips. "I expect Lord Pontieu will be hopelessly jealous, Milord. His Perlimpious Fragrantia will be an excrescence, a vacuous inanity in comparison with this exceptional vintage." The Salvemaster had taken to flattering Milord in an overtly self-seeking manner, but Milord seemed oblivious to it.

"That should bring a marvelous shade of dark pink to his cheeks," Milord said enthusiastically. "And I adore jealousy."

I squirmed. Milord's velvetsmith had cut the holster a bit tight at the corners, and in any case it made me nervous to see him too self-satisfied. When that happens he sometimes swaggers about and loses his balance; on the last such occasion he stumbled into his closet and nearly squashed me against a rack of white patent Wellingtons.

He paused reflectively and gazed out the high louvred windows at the setting sun. A jury of dull gray clouds had been deliberating all day, but now they no longer seemed inclined to deliver their wet verdict. Instead they congregated on the horizon, plump burghers muttering conspiratorially amongst themselves. Their rumps were clothed in rich suits of polished pink and tangerine velvet, shining richly in the waning light. Rows of tree shadows stretched lithely across the acres of shallow rolling hills in Milord's fiefdom, jumping across gullies and swaying their arms like dark ghosts in a damp breeze. In the west a pale, nearly full moon rose like a giant silver balloon.

The edges of the fields and orchards were dotted by clusters of peasants slowly returning home from their day's work. They glanced occasionally towards us, as though aware of Milord's presence even at this distance and no doubt grateful for his beneficent oversight. Milord tilted his teacup, found only cold dregs and touched a softly glowing button on his taboret. From the recesses of the chamber a servant instantly appeared, metered boiling pale tea into the cup and withdrew.

"Now, what do you think is in it, Flick, hmm?" he asked me, turning his eyes to the urn. He pinched my ear and chuckled. "Why, fitful frights and wishful wollygoggles!" He laughed until he shook. I must have looked perplexed, for he said, "It's mindstuff, don't you see, not your witches' customary toads and newt's eyes, no! They've been traveling about, here and there, robbing minds. No wonder the Grandmage needs it!"

I recoiled and pressed my paws on my crown, fearing entry of some witch's tool through my very skullbone. Milord put his palms gently over me. "Ah, I fear I've scared you, Flick. I'm sorry. Let's to bed then, and no more of these dismal matters tonight."

My curiosity overcame me, though, as he knew perfectly well it would. I squeaked and scritched at his thigh, and easily persuaded him to continue. "You'll have nightmares, Flickamerry Hansombear," he warned gravely. In truth I think he was considering not only my welfare, but the pungent odor that nightmares bring to my fur; for I have awakened more than once from a frightening dream to hear a chorus of loud sneezes from Milord's bed.

"Well, here it is then, just as the Master Guildsman described it to me. The witches roam incognito above and below the earth's surface. Outside Albanderry, of course. They mingle amongst some thirty-two species of vertebrates: gruntibules, undines, ambassadors and other strange creatures. Really, it's astounding to think of their managing somehow to disguise their awful bulbous noses and noxious rags as they go.

"They infiltrate their victims' homes, from rude Cirilvanian hovels to the palaces of Scrimshee, prodding and poking the minds of their prey as though they were ripe tomatoes. Then they perform a sort of trephine, selectively extracting wishes, dreams, syllogisms, delusions and other mental entities.

"They pluck only the choicest morsels of thought, or what passes for it, from the species' brain-equivalents, leaving each subject more or less intact. Perhaps more 'less' than 'more', I fear. And all, as it eventuates, for the sake of trading with me!" Milord enjoyed this notion very much; but then a shadow passed across his face. He grunted and sipped his tea, and a heavy silence intervened.

"I suppose it's not right to trade with robbers," he said at length. "One shouldn't support the bandits that pillage one's fellow creatures, it's true. But they molest only non-Albanderrians; and most commerce of any consequence in Albanderry would quickly wither and perish were it not for the Mountainwitch Consortium. And in any case," he added with fresh resolve, "I must have their wretched soup to save the wizard."

His mood quickened as suddenly as it had wilted. "What an imbroglio!" he said excitedly. "Why, it's a regular mishmash, a potpourri as it were; one could even say a stew, to be plain, or perhaps a burgoo, or…"

Milord was inclined to flights of synonymy, and could spend hours lost in perseveration if not gently turned back. He once launched into such a verbal odyssey in the midst of a speech to the Subcommittee on Quaternary Alternatives, in a vain effort to recall seven synonyms for the word 'constabulary'. Such eccentricities are not well received in the Assembly, and he was treated with considerable reserve for weeks thereafter.

I coughed politely and looked meaningfully at the carboy. "Quite right, Flick, thank you," he said sheepishly, bracing himself against the arms of his wing chair. "The witches. So. And then they shake their mind-plunder into the vat — some of the more willful bits of thought-floss attempt to float away and have to be retrieved by trained bats — add a smattering of uncertainty and *voilá*!

"By the coming of dawn they've boiled it down to a gooey syrup, which they decant into this bloodstone albarello." He heaved to his feet. "…which is then stoppered tightly with an Andean cloud-core." Milord caressed a light gray stopper with his little finger. It quivered, recoiled like a snail's antenna and resumed its shape.

"And here," he said, pointing out a drop of viscid red substance applied sloppily to the stopper's edge, "this red dollop is wax made from bagwyn tallow, and as you see they've used a tiny branding iron to imprint their emblem in it." In the splash of carmine was embedded an ideographic design of marvelous intricacy. As I looked, the lines blurred and burned, brighter and brighter, until my eyes smarted, yet it became more difficult to tear myself away. Milord hastily pulled me back.

"You mustn't look too long at their insignia, Flick." He dabbed at the corners of my eyes with a silk hanky. "They're a treacherous lot — they wouldn't bother warning us about such dangerous details. And that Petolzia, she's a particularly snippy one, as I imagine you noticed this afternoon. No doubt she's still upset over her little contretemps at the hands of the stick-men." I felt a surge of admiration for Milord's wiliness in dealing successfully with the witches, even under the aegis of the Protectioners; it was tantamount to plucking a jack of hearts from a barrel of angry crabs. And I resented the witches for their ugly tricks.

Now Milord took on a serious manner. The jowls of his round face flattened, liked obedient dogs who realize their master is no longer in a mood to frisk about. He straightened the tails of his black coat, brushed an imaginary ash from his waist and signaled with a crook of his finger. Salvemaster Worrant in turn glanced curtly at his assistant, Footling Stonebrew, an obese dwarf in a suit of blue grosgrain and thick white hair combed à la pageboy. The Footling drew back a maroon velvet curtain, revealing Milord's workbench.

This was a marvel, being compressed in layers from a variety of smoky quartz, or cairngorm, and spangled throughout with motes of mica and gold. It was a goodly thirty paces wide and seemed to swim without visible supports in its large recess. Various retorts, condensers, aludels and other compound vessels bubbled and simmered there like birds chattering in a stone bath. Above the bench was a negatively vented hood to draw off the gaseous irritants being constantly produced.

Footling Stonebrew now carefully cartwheeled the tun to a small jack and raised the vessel's mouth to a level just higher than the benchtop. Milord placed a yellow silk doily over his nose, drew on heavy gloves and recited an incantation intended to muffle his thoughts against ransoms, dysphorias and other pernicious effects.

He crooked his finger again and Salvemaster Worrant applied a curved piece of sandalwood to the margin of the cloud-stopper. With a slight pop it lifted free of the carboy's thick walls. An iridescent vapor ascended several inches and hesitated like a gopher testing the air. Over the urn's top Milord quickly applied a blown-glass bell jar, to which was attached a large rectangular maze of tortuous conduits framed in thin brass plate. Like a reluctant mouse the vapor inched through one of the labyrinth's countless pathways.

"Now observe most carefully, Flick," Milord said. "We shall see which of the tubes it selects, and thereby determine its nature and quality." He adjusted several tiny fittings at the bottom of the glass maze.

The vapor moved into the uppermost channel, an exceedingly narrow, squiggly tube. It pulsed with a dark reddish glow. Salvemaster Worrant made a pleased little sound, "Grumph," and exchanged glances with Milord.

"Just as I suspected!" cried Milord. "A Vibrant Decoction — Class XX!"

The Salvemaster could not conceal a lurid smile. "A rare azeotrope, Sire. Even a dram should prove most fetching."

Milord scrutinized him closely. "You may individuate this spectacular elixir, Salvemaster."

"Very well, Milord." Worrant now placed on the bench a number of bottlettes of dark green glass. Each was no larger than a stubby, baby carrot, and was encased in a lacy tin babbitt. With the greatest care he transmitted a portion of the sinuous, smoky fluid into each bottlette. So thick were the walls of the carboy that it contained only enough brew to fill six bottlettes — no more than a few ounces. Finally he sealed the bottlettes with bungs of lignum vitae, embossed with the coat of arms of Benefice Manor: a cross patonce gules on a fess or (that is, a cross with three-pointed, concave ends, tinted a lovely dark red, on a golden horizontal bar). He turned and awaited further instructions.

Milord studied the bottlettes from his seat. Apprehension filled my stomach; I sensed that he was about to do something dangerous.

"Bring the decanters," he said quietly.

The Salvemaster's eyes widened in astonishment. "Your Gr-Grace?" he stuttered. Footling Stonebrew looked shrewdly at Milord, caught his confirmatory glance and disappeared into an alcove to fetch the decanters.

With infinite care Milord siphoned the last remaining aliquot of reddish vapor from the apparatus into a reinforced pear-shaped pot. This he placed into a detoxifying appliance, adjusted its levers and rubbed his hands with pleasure. "Soon we'll have a taste, Flick," he said.

'We!' This gave me a jolt. Lately Milord had taken to sharing his essences with me, a bit of generosity which sometimes puts our metabolic differences to a sharp test. Certain of the vapors which he finds intensely euphoric have suffused me with languor, while his Flim-vapid VIII, which left him puzzled and distracted for days, served only to induce joint pains and thirst in me; luckily I recovered in a few hours.

But a witch's brew, this was another matter! Never before had he asked me to imbibe anything other than his own carefully prepared decoctions. After his frightful description of the origins of the maroon vapor now under his excited hands, I was trembling. But I would not dare to refuse Lord Benefice.

Presently he removed the pot from the oven and decanted a tiny portion of its contents into one of the special two-holed receptacles brought by Footling Stonebrew. He lifted the silk cover from his nose, applied the container, sniffed and immediately passed it to me.

The odor made my whiskers limp and tingled my entire body. It was an extraordinary mixture of sweet plantain and sulfide, laced with burgundy. Its bouquet exploded into a pale blue light of evening planets and refracted sentiment. I shivered freely.

The laboratory whirled around us. The furniture sprouted legs and danced a lively saltarello, shuffling and smirking, then slowed to a waltz and melted into a rolling sea of rainbows. The retorts and aludels squawked and flapped about the room like threatened chickens.

Nostalgia filled me and I cried six tears, counting them in a language I did not know; the tears' salty taste invested everything I ate for the following week, even citrus and shellfish. I viewed the world from behind the faces of a thousand different creatures, then ten thousand. I saw the colors as they see them, heard sounds which they themselves cannot describe, framed their theories of the universe in the tangles of their minds. Their whiskers and feelers, beaks and dewlaps sprouted from my muzzle. I fumbled at my face, squeezed it into a ball and rolled it between my two spines, and as it bumped against each pair of vertebrae

I looked deeper into the center of time. My face-ball bounced to the floor and exploded in a puff of light yellow smoke, yet I felt no sense of loss or harm, but only a fine, soft tranquillity.

When stillness and normality finally returned, we had sunk deep into Milord's large stuffed chair. To my amazement the corner clock indicated the passage of four hours. Milord smiled like a woman who has just finished a good cry. He wiped his eyes with a pledget, which he then placed on a china plate presented by Footling Stonebrew. "Most… extraordinary," he stammered.

"Your instructions, Sire?" asked the Salvemaster.

Milord coughed and collected himself. "Maintain all six bottlettes in my superior marquetry, Salvemaster."

"Yes, Milord."

"See that the urn is thoroughly neutralized. And mind you inciner-ate the dregs with care," he added. Even the leavings from a tincture of this extraordinary character and magnitude would bring a bright penny to an unscrupulous hand. The Salvemaster bowed and attended to his duties.

"After my speech in the Assembly tomorrow, we shall notify Grandmage Mentharch that we have acquired his witches' brew. He will be greatly relieved, as am I." Milord dabbed my nose conspiratori-ally. "And when his difficulties have been resolved, we'll announce our accomplishment publicly; Lord Pontieu will chew his cuffs with jeal-ousy, and our political star will rise!

"But until then, we'll keep the matter to ourselves. It wouldn't do to boast before the sheep have been safely led back into the byre."

IV

A FATEFUL SPEECH

Thankfully when Milord arose the following morning he appeared none the worse for our extraordinary experience. I too felt reasonably well, though my thoughts remained in a rather higgledy-piggledy state for most of the day.

Milord informed me that Lords Roundabout and Pontieu were both due to join us at Benefice Manor before noon; we would then travel together to the Assembly through the Louvian Marsh, whose dangers render an unaccompanied trip very unwise. Though I am always happy to see Milord's closest confidant, Lord Roundabout, the prospect of being in close company with the treacherous Lord Pontieu for any length of time set my stomach churning.

The Manor's shaman briefly discussed the day's topic, *ananke* — "the personification of fate, affecting even the gods" — and we breakfasted. From the entry came a driver's horse-shouts and the crunching of gilded wheels on white gravel. I jumped from Milord's pocket and raced to the vestibule sash to reconnoiter. To either side of the court-yard the magnificent upper ramparts of Benefice Manor sparkled with spanking-fresh whitewash. Colorful banderoles and streamers fluttered above them in a sunny breeze. I felt wonderfully pleased to be a part, however small, of Milord's fabulous enterprise!

On the doors of the arriving carriage was Lord Roundabout's distinctive heraldry: six roundels vert and garb slipped proper on a bend argent (six round green figures and a sheaf of wheat on a silver diagonal). First to descend from the coach was his pet named Goighty, an example of the rare Glombumbulus species. Distantly related to the bulldog toads, he resembles more a hunchbacked crab with six legs; and though he is only twice my size, his ungainly anatomy forces him to waddle sideways. This clumsy locomotion, plus his rather ferocious mien, allow him to cut through any gathering a swath which is quite disproportionate to his small stature.

Moreover, despite years of assiduous training, Goighty's behavior is quite unpredictable — a source of continuing dismay for Lord Roundabout's retainers. He is quite likely, for example, to clamber without notice onto a garden statue, there to wave any combination of his seven members at an impromptu audience; or he might without warning squeeze his tube of paté with excessive force, thus decorating the gowns of nearby guests.

Today Goighty wore a bright red turtleneck sweater, woven of stout balbriggan with tweed trim and scrupulously tailored to match his unique physiognomy. This bold attempt at style in so unusual a creature produced a garish and startling effect, which set our servants and footlings atitter. I could not help but feel a certain superiority: Lord Roundabout's unruly mascot would never occupy as cozy a station in his Realm as I do in Milord's.

Lord Roundabout's entourage now assumed their hierarchical positions, matched by Milord's retinue, who had assembled in the antechamber. Ritual signals were exchanged in the prescribed sequence between coinciding members of each group, beginning with the least consequential and proceeding to Masterfootling Farberwile and Salvemaster Worrant, and finally Gasmaster Bickle, and their visiting counterparts.

This practice of bringing nearly all of one's household even on short journeys is a throwback to the days when the Lords lived a nomadic and bellicose existence. The matching of each household member is a vestige of a ritual designed to insure that neither party gained an advantage by concealing an extra warrior or spy. To vary the number of accompanying attendants and pursuivants would be regarded as a serious breach of good conduct, if not an outright threat.

Goighty scuttled eagerly in my direction with the intent of executing an esoteric nose-touching formality, but after a brief pleasantry became preoccupied with the management of his saliva and retired. I cannot deny that I was much relieved.

Trumpmaster Rampbleu raised his coronet, blew a short fanfare and announced, "Ladies and gentlemen and creatures of the Realm, His Grace, Lord Graham Fontleroy Roundabout." His Grace, the Assembly's Regional Ablegate, descended, allowing a footling to assist with each of his generous extremities. He wore his customary velvet smoker, a tired garment whose irregular cut suggested that his tailor suffered from some form of progressive palsy. He clutched at his heavily powdered wig, which nonetheless fell promptly to the ground. For a moment bright sunlight glinted from his broad pate.

"Scurfy impediment," he swore under his breath, his face reddening. Three of his retainers rushed to pick up the offending device, nearly knocking him down in the process, and repositioned it. "Thank you, Underfootlings, I'm sure," he said, regaining his balance and his breath. To the sound of the Trumpmaster's longhorn and a snare, he stepped to a scarlet rug flanked by standard-bearers and entered the manor, where Milord stood waiting.

"Closelord Fontleroy," he said, "Benefice Manor receives you with the embrace of a maternal uncle and offers our most gracious comfort." Now, the use of Lord Roundabout's middle name is a form of address permitted only to mutual members of the Assembly; but the further use of the term 'Closelord' reflects the especially cordial terms enjoyed by the two Lords.*

---

* There are seven degrees of formality amongst the Lords, from least to most familiar: 1. Lord; 2. Lordreserve; 3. Favorlord; 4. Friendlord; 5. Closelord. I have never heard the sixth or seventh degrees used.

"Your pleasure is exceeded only by mine in having done with those confounded roads, Closelord Cantilouve. They deteriorate each year, and no funds for repair!"

"A moment of refreshment would suit you then, Closelord?" asked Milord brightly.

"Indeed. This throat is parched, and a drop of Lord Benefice's justly famous liqueurs would be delightful," agreed Lord Roundabout.

Inside, a small consort of viols and lutes played discreetly, accompanied by a balladmonger. Milord's rarest fragrance, Orchid Pearl III, suffused the air. Lord Roundabout threw himself into the first chair, an embroidered wingback which groaned under his weight. Milord took a banquette next to him, and I jumped into his holster.

Floorsteward Smithkline presented an engraved silver tray with two goblets, cleverly shaped in such a way as to allow both mouth and nose to sample their contents simultaneously. Lord Roundabout raised his appreciatively to the light. "An exquisite pink hue… A variant of your prized 'Vimplicate XII,' Closelord Cantilouve?"

"Correct! A homeopathic cousin of the heroic beverage to which you refer, actually. Just the thing after a strenuous journey."

"Excellent! To potency, then."

"To gentility, Closelord. That our fates may resonate like twin stars," said Milord.

"Quite so," replied Lord Roundabout. They sniffed delicately at their thimbles and listened for a moment to the gentle strains of music.

I studied Milord's face in the windowlight. What a contrast — such sharply carved features, set above such magnificent portliness! Lord Pontieu never tires of reminding him that he has become quite *enbonpoint*, and has the cheek to do so publicly, in wittily rhymed couplets. At a banquet not long ago he even added, "Yet his nose and lips are so aquiline that his physicians fear for the adequacy of their blood supply." A churl, Lord Pontieu, you would say; and yet he is the acme of elegance, and dangerously close to complete power in the Assembly. But that Milord takes such pleasure in his own repasts, I would see him reduce his weight just to spite Lord Pontieu; and in any case the man would only find some other weakness to probe with his trenchant wit.

Milord leaned toward Lord Roundabout and confided, "Actually

I have further modified this 'Vimplicate' by the addition of a tithe-dram of Nightingale's Essence, to relax our tongues. When Lord Pontieu arrives, we shall have matters of some gravity to discuss, and stiffness would be counterproductive."

"An excellent concept," Lord Roundabout replied heartily. "I believe that the discussion of serious matters of state, like fine silver, should be swaddled in warm cameraderie and polished with the silk of badinage. Do you not agree?"

"No question. Yes, Closelord, the filigree of friendship is a perfect adornment —" He caught Lord Roundabout's look and laughed at himself. "Closelord Fontleroy, once again you have ensnared me in redundancy and excess — a trap of my own making. Touché."

Lord Roundabout chuckled good naturedly. "To repetitiousness, Closelord Cantilouve. Long may it flutter from the flagpole of metaphor." The two friends visited their snifters again.

Presently Milord sighed and said, "Now we must discuss the issue of revenues. I understand that Lord Trillphyte is considering a radical plan to restructure the collection of excise, and that its target has not yet been decided."

"A pox on it!" said Lord Roundabout vehemently. His apoplectic temperament was well known in the Assembly, where he was wont to launch into extended diatribes at the drop of a hat. "Though I confess, strictly between ourselves, that the complexity of his proposal is more than I can fathom, still my instincts inform me that it can only redound to the benefit of our wily treasurer himself, and no doubt Lord Pontieu's as well."

"Quite. We must therefore consider a counter-proposal, Closelord Fontleroy. In fact I have outlined two such alternate plans, which I shall present today." Milord displayed a small scroll in his inside pocket.

Lord Roundabout nodded. "You may count on my support, Closelord."

"For which I am grateful," said Milord. He leaned closer to Lord Roundabout and lowered his voice. "But before we proceed further, I must caution you regarding a most unfortunate circumstance. I regret to say that I have come to suspect the presence of a spy in my household."

"No!" Lord Roundabout gasped.

"Yes, I fear it were true. In recent months there have been several occasions on which curious circumstances have forced me to absent myself from meetings of the Assembly. I have reviewed the minutes of the Assembly Proceedings for those dates, and in each case certain sensitive matters were discussed by Lord Pontieu which revealed a surprising knowledge of my affairs. That knowledge could only have been obtained from a member of my staff." Lord Roundabout protested, but Milord held up his hand.

"Therefore I must take the offensive. Today I shall disclose to the Assembly certain facts which will cause Lord Pontieu considerable embarrassment, perhaps more than that."

Lord Roundabout pounded his fist on the arm of his chair. "Here here! A bit of dirt on the man's coat will be a welcome adornment."

Milord laughed grimly. "Well said. But —" He was interrupted by the braying of longhorns and stood up to look out on the courtyard. "Lord Pontieu arrives." Six jet-black chargers drew his carriage, whose windows, unlike the panes of sheer crystal in Milord's barouche, were a nearly opaque ultramarine. His coat of arms, emblazoned on the quarter-panels, was a bend sinister or charged with lioncels rampant armed gules — a diagonal band of gold bearing small red lions with claws extended.

Lord Pontieu threw open his coach door and stepped briskly from its purple cushions. Even from the manse I could see a sardonic smile set in his lean features, the smile of a man accustomed to wealth and leisure. And power, for Lord Pontieu makes bold to be the pre-eminent force in the Assembly. His political machinations have become the substance of continuous rumor, if not legend. Shrewd and irrational by turns, he is unfailingly ruthless in his consummation of the intrigues that hatch constantly in his fertile mind. This ruthlessness he applies equally to the most trivial velleity — having his way in the sequence of dishes served at a Freeday outing, for example — as to his grandest and most Machiavellian schemes, which often involve great sums of money and numerous Lords. I doubted that any called him by a more familiar degree of address than the second.

"Have you ever wondered at Lord Pontieu's use of only two lions in his blazon, rather than the customary three, Closelord Cantilouve?" asked Lord Roundabout.

"I have always supposed it to be a symbol of his willingness to say one thing and do another," said Milord.

"Indeed. And no subtlety in their blood-red claws, is there?"

Milord "hmmm'd" reflectively in response and went to the main entrance to meet his guest. "Lordreserve Ventblanc, we wish you fair-coming and health," he said.

"Lordreserve Cantilouve," replied Lord Pontieu, "my dearest wish has been realized: to step upon your hearth." He smiled wryly and extended his arm. "In friendship," he added after an uncomfortable pause.

Milord's smile weakened, but he placed his arm through his visitor's and they proceeded slowly to the receiving room. Lord Pontieu is considerably taller than Milord; thus, standing together they almost formed the figure 10, an effect amplified by Lord Pontieu's scythe-like nose.

At his feet walked Lizzault, Lord Pontieu's mascot, who resembles a small alligator. He wore a hobnailed yellow collar securely around his snout, and another over his hammerhead tail. His hide is a thick and colorless affair, thrown into thick folds and crevices which would be impossible to clothe. Even a glimpse of him sends a shudder of warning down both my spines. His rancid smell speaks repellingly of the rank muck in which he keeps his den, and persists despite his attendants' vigorous efforts to clean him prior to social outings.

At some risk, I flaunt social convention by shunning him at these encounters, and thus far Milord has overlooked my gaffe. Lizzault glanced through me with his beady eyes, curled stiffly by the door and began to 'luff', a sort of trance-panting which is peculiar to his species.

Lord Roundabout heaved to his feet and extended his hand in the Assembly's greeting gesture. "Good day, Lordreserve Ventblanc," he said curtly.

"A very good one," Lord Pontieu replied. Something in his manner must have caused me to forget myself — or perhaps it was the wary way in which Lord Roundabout used the term "Lordreserve" — for I bared my teeth at Lord Pontieu and hissed. It was an instinctive response. Milord immediately reprimanded me and apologized on my behalf.

"Perhaps we would do well to consider the use of leashes and muzzles in civilized circles," Lord Pontieu said archly.

"Such implements have their place in the Realm, to be sure," said Milord, giving me a reassuring pat on the head. "But discretion in their employment is a rarity, and I have heard that some also advocate the use of such constraints on other men."

"Men are better restrained by politics and laws," said Lord Pontieu smoothly, with an unpleasant smile. Damn the man, he could be elegant even when he was dangerous!

"Undoubtedly," said Milord, a bit lamely. "But let us put this fencing aside, Favorlord Ventblanc. Lord Roundabout and I were just now speaking of the need to don the summery garments of light repartee before taking up political matters."

"Let us hope that those raiments are not excessively embroidered," said Lord Pontieu. "Men of taste must not be offended."

"Certainly not," said Milord in an acerbic tone. "Excess is to be avoided. But I am sure you will agree that too-scanty dress, on the other hand, is a characteristic of primitives."

"Or of intimacy, which seems to be in short supply," put in Lord Roundabout gruffly. For a moment the three observed each other in wary silence, as Salvemaster Worrant presented snifters of Milord's Vimplicate-Nightingale.

"Speaking of intimacy, Favorlord Cantilouve," said Lord Pontieu, "I wish to thank you again for your extraordinary Corporeal Magnifier VI. Its effect, when taken in the company of my, ah, consorts, was quite beyond description." There was a hint of jealousy in his voice.

"You are too kind. Your own skills in this area are not to be minimized." Milord delivered this compliment perfunctorily, knowing full well that his own essences were much superior to those of Lord Pontieu.

"Thank you. From one of your rare skills, any compliment is high praise." He poised his aquiline nose over his snifter. "But I have heard of certain parties whose distillation overshadows even your best, and by a large margin..." Seeing Milord's puzzled expression, he pushed on: "In fact, one might say that its qualities are supernatural."

The color drained from Milord's face; the pocket of his vest dampened with cold sweat. "Whatever can you mean?" he said in a husky voice. Lord Roundabout looked on, bewildered.

Lord Pontieu studied Milord's face as an entomologist examines a specimen he is about to trap in a jar. "Tell me, what would a Lord have to trade for such a unique essence?"

Milord struggled to collect himself. "It could not be acquired," he stammered. "In fact, I am almost sure it could not be obtained, considering—"

Lord Roundabout looked on in growing consternation. Though he had not grasped the substance of their conversation, he awakened to the fact that his friend and ally had been cornered. "Availability is a nebulous concept," he interjected loudly, "with many aspects worthy of interpretation." He intruded himself between Milord and Lord Pontieu (an intrusion effectively spearheaded by his ample waist), inserted a little finger into Lord Pontieu's buttonhole and enlarged in increasingly vague terms on his topic.

Milord backed away and wiped his brow with a kerchief. His face was taut. He beckoned to the Salvemaster and whispered, "Fetch one of the witches' bottlettes from the marquetry. Dilute it to a factor of twenty with spring water and essence of clove, and serve it to us at once." The Salvemaster looked at Milord as though he had lost his wits, but Milord added, "Go!" in a desperate tone that sent him jumping to the pantry.

My mind raced. Why would Milord reveal his phenomenal prize — desperately needed by the Grandmage — to an enemy? It would have been much safer, and potentially informative, to serve instead a measure of his Nightingale's Essence, which might loosen Lord Pontieu's tongue; or even a simple Tranquilitas, which would dull his incessant probing. If Milord's intention were to confuse Lord Pontieu for any length of time, he defeated this purpose by diluting the brew; and in any case it appeared that he intended to serve it to himself and Lord Roundabout as well.

"...such an effort might have the most complex ramifications and repercussions," Lord Roundabout continued, "and certainly—"

Milord rejoined the two men and squeezed his friend's elbow. "Your analysis touches the subject's marrow, Closelord," he said gratefully. "But permit me to interrupt. As luck would have it, I am in a position to share the exceptional vintage to which Lord Pontieu referred just now."

He nodded at Salvemaster Worrant, who presented a tray with three tiny crystal decanters surrounding a green bottlette.

Lord Pontieu's face paled. "Perhaps the occasion is less than optimal," he said, quailing.

"What occasion could be more suitable?" Milord said pleasantly. This light riposte was actually a strong trump card, for the force of etiquette among Lords is such that to refuse an offer of another Lord's essence is quite unthinkable. But I suspect that Lord Pontieu's pride and curiosity would ultimately have led him to the trough in any case.

Lord Roundabout eagerly plucked a glass from the tray. He held it to the light, rotating it in his chubby fingers and squinting keenly through its smoky amber contents. Though himself a vintner of only ordinary skills, he is widely regarded as the most knowledgeable and enthusiastic of connoisseurs in Albanderry; his opinion is generally accepted as final when disputes of taste or classification arise. He turned to Milord with an expression of candid wonder and declared passionately, "Phenomenal!"

With a pleased smile Milord replied, "I would that I could take credit for it."

Lord Pontieu looked sourly from Lord Roundabout to Milord and, rudely neglecting to await a toast, sniffed gingerly at his glass. Lord Roundabout followed, rather less cautiously, and then Milord. Silence filled the warm room. From outside came the faint voices of the carriage drivers sharing a crude joke.

Presently Milord waggled his finger like a stern uncle and stated, "It is but a small step from the plainweave of indifference to the roughcloth of impudence." Lord Roundabout giggled and mumbled something in agreement. Lord Pontieu said nothing. The three men moved slowly to separate chairs as though in a dream. Their eyes turned to glass and they seemed hardly to breathe, til I grew alarmed and tugged at the inside of Milord's waistcoat, without effect.

Lord Roundabout's gaze lost itself in the sunlight streaming through the room's high, arched windows. Countless motes swam through the mullions' sun-striped shadows, and he exclaimed, "They vanish and reappear!" Lord Pontieu remarked in a low, gargling voice on the fact that snuff could be taken through either nostril, but that it could not be retrieved afterward. Milord's lips wrestled with themselves, and he swayed from side to side in his chair as though to control their jostling. Salvemaster Worrant slipped silently among us, collected the empty vessels and returned to his chambers.

Lord Pontieu was the first to recover himself. He walked to the window, where he stood quietly with hands clasped behind his back. Lord Roundabout roused himself and said, "A most extraordinary mixture, Closelord Cantilouve. Utterly unique. Do I detect the presence of nipplewort, or galbanum?"

"Perhaps. I myself have not witnessed its production," said Milord. Lord Roundabout began enthusiastically to pursue the question, but was interrupted by Lord Pontieu.

"Extraordinary, indeed," he said. "And worthy of an extraordinary tax. Or even impoundment, under certain circumstances."

Lord Roundabout laughed, but stopped abruptly upon hearing Milord's sober reaction: "How quickly Lord Ventblanc returns to matters of business." With alarm I realized that he had reverted to the lowest degree of familiarity in his address. The air chilled.

"I think only of the good of the Realm," Lord Pontieu replied.

"This conceit is the finest vapor of all," exclaimed Lord Roundabout. "Let us tax it and double our revenue in a twinkling!"

"Indeed, Lord Pontieu's haughty distillate jabs my nose like a barber's poultice," said Milord.

Glaring at both men, Lord Pontieu snapped, "I see that in certain quarters private commerce and pleasure are held in higher regard than matters of state."

"And in other quarters," Milord answered, his voice rising, "private ambition is cherished more than the warmth of fellowship. But these issues will be kneaded from several sides, in public, and by hands of different persuasions."

"Indeed they shall. Until we meet again in the Assembly this afternoon," said Lord Pontieu, standing up. "Good day, gentlemen."

He snapped the hems of his tunic into place like canvas in a brisk wind and strode to the entryway. Here he encountered Goighty, who hopped up and down excitedly in the mistaken belief that his master had at last emerged. This had the unfortunate effect of spattering the puddle of drool which had accumulated under his large paws, and his two agitated attendants jumped quickly to either side. Lord Pontieu waved exasperatedly at his manservant and stalked to his carriage, with Lizzault padding behind him.

Milord and Lord Roundabout waited until the doors were shut. "What of this devilish brew?" asked Lord Roundabout excitedly. "And how did he learn of it?"

Milord sighed heavily. "His knowledge is evidence of the dangerous breach in my security to which I alluded earlier." He lowered his voice. "For this reason I shall wait until later to explain the brew's origin and urgent purpose, Closelord."

Lord Roundabout nodded his understanding. "An extremely serious matter." He leaned back in his chair and rubbed his chin. "But regardless, I think it were wiser not to have broached the elixir to one of his ilk. He sees only its legalities and economics, and those through the dark lenses of political jealousy. In fact he could well force impoundment of the concoction!"

Milord sat reflectively for a moment, pursing his lips. Then he stood up, scanned the shelf of gilt-edged tomes behind him and withdrew a small volume. He opened it, applied a glass and read, " 'No excise or impoundment shall be levied upon any psychoactive decoction, essence, blend, or non-nutritive preparation of any kind, if its first social delectation shall have been in a company of fewer than four individuals.' " He closed the book and slipped it into his coat pocket.

"You sly bookwit!" said Lord Roundabout, looking sidelong at Milord. "A fancy bit of quick thinking, that. And I supposed you a clodhopper!"

"You didn't, Closelord Fontleroy," said Milord, modestly inspecting his nails. He glanced at his timepiece. "Come, we must be off," he concluded.

Lord Roundabout pushed heavily to his feet. "An astonishing development," he muttered, shaking his head.

We proceeded outside. The coaches glittered in the sunlight, their chassises adorned with magnificent arabesques of gold and amethyst. Lord Roundabout took his leave; his retainers assisted him into his caroche and they moved off.

Milord ascended into our carriage and sat fretting over events. The horses pulled away, their jingling traces accompanying the wheel-noise in a pleasant bourrèe. I was relieved to be alone with my master again.

From underneath our carriage came a sudden keen whine and then a *crraack*. We lurched violently to the right. Milord was thrown sharply against the wall of the cabin as we heaved to a stop. Confusion and commotion reigned. Finally Milord managed to extricate himself from the damaged vehicle, protecting me in his pocket with a cupped palm. The Mastermechanic came running out with Thindle Spinkite at his side.

"An explanation, if you please, Mastermechanic," said Milord, brushing himself off.

"At once, Sire." He and Thindle bent to examine the underpinnings of the carriage, where the trouble was immediately evident: the fore axletree was broken. In fact, it had been partially transected by a sharp instrument, and the stress of motion had completed the fracture. Thindle and the Mastermechanic looked at each other, afraid to put the obvious into words.

"Sabotage," Milord said quietly.

Lord Roundabout, seeing our trouble, had turned about and now joined us. He stared at the broken axle. "What sort of devilry is this, Closelord Cantilouve?" he exclaimed.

"A whole company of possible culprits has just departed," said Milord, referring to Lord Pontieu's entourage.

Lord Roundabout frowned. "They wouldn't stoop to such, such a …"

Milord looked meaningfully at him. "Perhaps not," he said. "But I suggest you instruct your men to inspect your equipage most carefully, Closelord Fontleroy."

"Of course." Lord Roundabout stood peering at the damage and shaking his head, a deliberation which floured his coat with wig powder. He looked up. "And then be so good as to allow me to convey you to the Assembly," he said. Presently we joined Lord Roundabout in his carriage. He banged a mahogany knocker at his side, a signal to his driver above to depart.

"Lord Pontieu's chicanery will not prevent us from debating his proposals," said Milord with determination.

"Caution, Closelord — what proof have we?" asked Lord Round-about, raising his brows. Milord cleaned his spectacles, shook his head and cleaned them again. Both men turned and gazed heavily out their windows.

The luxuriant countryside rolled past. To our right floated fields of balloonberries, swaying lightly on their tethers in a cool breeze. Amongst them stood several bolo trees full of chirping curlews and yellow-black willymuffies, endlessly discussing the best approaches to the tasty berries. From time to time one of their company would swoop down between the tethers, nimbly avoiding the sharp lines as the plump berries twisted and curtsied in an effort to garrotte the raider.

Finally the hungry bird would find a slower fruit and plunge his beak into its soft underside, sucking its sweet sap in a delicious, light-ning-quick sip. Then he would fly triumphantly back to his jabbering confreres, bragging of his exploit even before perching again in the tree. Behind him the berry would begin to shrink and sink slowly to the ground.

The road's margins were decorated with peonies and meadow-cusp in delightful scalloped patterns. Clouds of Albanderry's famous rainbow dust rose slowly from under our rear wheels, swirling and refracting the sunlight into fascinating patterns. We approached the Louvian Marsh, an area of dense willowbrush and other constantly steaming vegetation. Two underfootlings jumped from their stations on the accompanying supply wagons and applied varnish-cloth to the wheels, to prevent their being stained by the marsh's unpleasant waters. That stain is a sickly green which, once affecting wood or skin, does not fade for weeks. This circumstance alone should keep travel through the marsh to a minimum, but there is much worse.

One stormy night by a roaring fire, Milord told me of the many dangerous creatures that live there: sessile umbs, whose thin, fishy bones somehow support an immense quantity of blubbery flesh and whose only natural enemy is the mountainwitch herself; fit-sprites, no thicker than a hatpin and quicker than a dragonfly; and worst of all, the mallowjackal, a predatory creature with the speed of a wolf and the ferocity of a shrew. This menagerie should be enough to keep any traveler with half a wit away from the marsh; but unfortunately the swamp is strategically located between most of the forty-two manors and the commercial center of Albanderry, its port, and the Assembly. Consequently, impatience and circumstance conspire to send travelers through it almost daily. Though a well-harnessed wagon can traverse the marsh in less than two hours, one wagon in twenty never emerges on its far side, and occasionally one glimpses the half-sunken hulk of a broken carriage in the roadside gloom.

The steam rose thicker and darker around us as we proceeded and every sound acquired a strange, muffled quality. My two Lords suddenly scratched vigorously at the backs of their heads and looked at each other in puzzlement.

"I felt a strange tickling sensation at the back of my head," said Milord.

"As did I," said Lord Roundabout.

"An aerial blight?" asked Milord.

"You imply that my carriage is infested?" asked Lord Roundabout testily.

"Certainly not!" said Milord. "I only questioned whether some airborne contaminant, unknown to us both, might have penetrated the sanctity of Closelord Fontleroy's conveyance, and —"

The carriage slewed suddenly to the side of the road and skidded into the muck. It teetered for a long, dizzy moment and finally tipped over, throwing us in a jumble against the doors.

"Au secours! Help at once! Overdriver Axelman suffers an apoplexy!" shrilled a voice from above. The carriage now lay on its right side, thrust into a muddy hillock. With difficulty we crawled out the left door, which was now our ceiling, and stepped knee-deep into mud the color of rotting lima beans.

The Overdriver was contorted over his bench in a lavish display of falling sickness. Lord Roundabout put a handkerchief to his mouth and turned away, but Milord solicitously placed his arms under those of the unfortunate driver and, with an assistant's help, drew him to a relatively dry berth on the roadbank.

"He began shaking of a sudden, Milord," said the assistant driver, obviously terrified, "and before I could say Jack Spiddle we'd put roughly into port." He threw his arms around his chest and shivered.

"Never fear, Underdriver, the fault is not yours," said Milord, touching his arm. He bent over the young victim, carefully preventing him from self-harm as his convulsion subsided.

"Did you see anything pass by?" asked Milord.

"No Sire. But —"

"Yes?"

"It was nothing, Sire. Perhaps a speck of dust in my eye."

"Dust, in this foggy bath?" asked Milord with surprise.

"Perhaps the speck had a shape to it, but…" His face froze in fear and his voice trailed off. He stared at something above Milord's shoulder. We looked behind us in a start. A hundred yards distant there was a violent disturbance, surrounded by dull sheets of purple light, but because of the dense marsh gas no particulars were discernible. The stormy phenomenon soon subsided.

"Speak, Underdriver!" said Milord, shaking the man by the shoulders. But he closed up as tight as a periwinkle, and naught could induce him to amplify on his tantalizing comment.

Lord Roundabout returned, having refreshed himself by the application of moist hot towels, and ordered his servants to tend to the Overdriver. "We'll be mistaken for greenbeans for months," he complained in loud disgust, as his Firstvalet attempted futilely to clean his stained boots and leggings. Goighty had taken the opportunity to frolic in the marsh, narrowly avoiding the deadly claws of an umb, and had succeeded in converting his fresh carmine pullover to something resembling rotten cabbage-leaves.

"I fear the carriage is a total loss," said Milord, peering down the road into the cold fog. We could see no more than twenty feet ahead.

"Well then, it's the wagons next," said Lord Roundabout. He summoned his senior footling, who emptied his number three wagon for our benefit. I shuddered in fear for the safety of the attendants who would be forced for our convenience to walk through the marsh, though they armed themselves with short-swords.

But the rest of our journey was uneventful. We emerged into the vast brightness of the Peleplain, where we set to an earnest gallop and arrived at Albanderry Square in mid-afternoon.

Here stand the major institutions of the Realm: the central offices of the Protectioners' Guild, ensconced in an imposing structure of ruddy glowerstone; adjacent to it the Chancery and the Museum, and another building of less certain function. Various exclusive establishments lie along their flanks, such as the Pursuivants' Reserve, a spacious club to which only the most highly positioned thanes have access. And centered amongst them all is of course the Assembly, architecturally modest and yet conveying both security and prestige.

If the upper Square is reserved for the great engines of Lordly society, its lower portion is the center of Albanderry's ordinary commerce and daily life; and those familiar sights, sounds and smells are as much a delight to the senses as its great institutions are a tonic to the spirit. There at the Square's nether border, for example, is Fewtril's Haberdashery. From this shop's half-open windows waft pleasing odors of fresh linens and parchment. Carved on its low, massive front door is its famous trademark: a bootless urchin twirling a cane of polished ebony. Though clad mostly in grimy rags, he also sports an impeccable cravat of bright green silk.

A few doors further on is the Patulous Maw, a notorious eatery mobbed from sunup to midnight with sailors and itinerants of every stripe. From its rude apertures pour the rank smells of ale and mutton and the sweet, syrupy fragrance of what the seamen call 'flaps' — rolled-up flapdoodles dipped in molasses. It is by far the noisiest enterprise in Albanderry, roiling with the clatter of plates and the loud assertions of men unaccustomed to laws or walls.

Lining the Square's lower right edge is a string of squat, dingy agencies such as the Maritime Centrum and the Serfs' Permiture. Opposite them a popular hostelry swallows and disgorges its clients with the constancy of an anthill. Tucked away in a far corner of the quadrangle, largely below street level, is the Mascots' Society; its lack of activity and the dilapidated condition of its premises bring a pang to my heart.

Beyond all the offices and shops, the tangled headdresses of a hundred schooners and barkentines rise above their quays, vividly outlined against a sweeping blue sea. They sway gently to and fro, so that if one gazes steadily at them the whole Square becomes a gently rocking cradle. In its center sleeps a delightful green park, a gardener's jewel, resplendent with magnolias and hundreds of bright flowers.

We halted in front of the Assembly Building, a surprisingly demure structure of common ivorystone, rising only two stories; its architraves and cornices are just sufficiently ornate to deliver its style from utter plainness. Above the mahogany door is the Assembly's simple coat of arms: three lozenges voided with thistles proper on a field argent (three empty diamonds with naturally-colored thistles on a silver background). Along the gilt jamb is a frieze, in which carved scenes commemorate great speeches by ex officio members. To either side, balding caryatids look on in attitudes of surprise and consternation.

Owing to our unpleasant delay on the road, the meeting was already well in progress. A watery light suffused the room from two large skylights. More than forty Lords were present, and the air was choked with the competing scents of their colognes. Several white-wigged heads turned as we entered, and recoiled knowingly at sight of the verdant discolorations on our clothing. We took seats in the last row.

His Lordship Mountbank Trillphyte, the Assembly's treasurer, was holding forth at the podium. He is a gaunt and nervous man, with a shock of brilliant white hair bursting from veiny temples. He frequently massaged one shoulder with the other hand as he spoke. His thoughts were flitting bugs, upon which he hopped like a frog, one after the next, but a certain devious sense of purpose was nonetheless apparent.

"In conclusion, shall we continue to flob about," he demanded rhetorically, "in search of some…some amaranth, that imaginary, never-fading flower? Are we condemned to interminable equivocation? Or shall we take a more realistic posture, reined by firm guidelines approved in this Assembly?" He scanned the chamber intensely for a long moment and stepped down.

Milord leaned over to his neighbor and inquired in a whisper, "To what point does the Treasurer speak?"

"He proposes a modification of Bylaws Article XII, Provision 73, such that the minimum number of Lords present at a first social broaching of a decoction shall be reduced to 'fewer than three'." He looked significantly at Milord. "As you can well imagine, this would have the effect of levying a princely retroactive tax, ostensibly for the purpose of road repairs," said the Lord with a grimace. "And there are provisions for Impoundment of Decoction, under special circumstances."

Milord sat bolt upright and turned to Lord Roundabout. "Lord Pontieu moves quickly, Closelord Fontleroy."

"The speed of his compromises would be the envy of any harlot," he agreed, his face darkening. "He has succeeded in subverting our valiant Treasurer to his own ends. I wonder what trifle he promised in return?"

"Lord Pontieu's pockets are full of tricks and inducements. I would guess that he offered Lord Trillphyte a few marvelous specimens of the spotted horde-frogs which he so avidly collects," said Milord. He put his hand urgently on Lord Roundabout's arm. "It is imperative that he be prevented from seizing my decoction, Closelord. The very future of Albanderry may depend on it!"

But Lord Roundabout's attention was riveted angrily on the podium. His jowls turned a livid color. "Jealousy and greed govern the man like rival duchesses," he said through clenched teeth. "By the Vapors, I'll speak to that!" He stood up, straightened his jacket and puffed to the podium as Lord Trillphyte sat down.

"It is," he began abruptly, "unlike anything we have ever seen." He hooked his thumbs into his vest, frowned and pressed his wattles deeper into his collar. "It is, in fact, like nothing whatsoever upon which this body has ever deliberated," he shouted.

A ripple of laughter stirred the audience at this mention, for his own body was the most deliberate in sight. He shook his head up and down several times, mistaking the chuckles for affirmation, and pulled briefly at his ear.

"From our Lord Treasurer Trillphyte we receive only an endless concatenation of stipulations, disclaimers and double-negatives, worthy more of some discreditable barrister than of a Lord of the Realm." He steadied himself against the podium like a ship's captain at his helm and launched into a lengthy diatribe.

Presently Milord's neighbor remarked in a whisper, "Lord Roundabout has embarked upon one of his more extensive discourses."

"Its object becomes less apparent as he proceeds," replied the neighbor's neighbor. Both fidgeted and consulted the hourglass on the wall.

Lord Roundabout expatiated for several more minutes, by which time he had succeeded in convincing himself completely of his position, and sat down with a sighing of cushions underneath his ample buttocks. Lord Trillphyte resumed the podium.

Milord began again in an anxious whisper, "I must explain the extraordinary significance of the…inhuman essence you tasted this morning, Closelord."

"Yes, of course," said Lord Roundabout with an earnest frown.

We were startled by the loud, plangent sound of a huge gong. On a short pedestal in the corner stood a pear-shaped individual with spindly legs. Across his tunic he wore numerous horizontal bands of rose-colored material, tied in ceremonial knots at his left side. His pudgy face was reflected in highly polished toe-concealments. In his left hand he held a ceremonial bronzed tongue; with his right he braced the framework of the still-quivering brass gong. "A condition of bifid discourse prevails," he proclaimed.

This, so Milord later explained to me, was the Chamber Annunciator, a sort of sergeant at arms whose role was created at the Assembly's inception, when it had proved impossible to reach a consensus as to a chairman. The Annunciator's job is to clarify the current status of all Assembly Proceedings. This he does at carefully defined intervals, or when certain specific events occur, both of which are the subject of a detailed and voluminous section of the Bylaws.

In fact, vigorous debate concerning the Gong Protocol still erupts frequently, fomented by various factions who feel that it favors one or another of them. Motions to Reconsider, Points of Order and other Ancillary Questions have become so numerous as to have required a thick backlog of Scheduled Proceedings. This backlog is increasing so rapidly that prospects of reducing it become more remote each day and is itself a matter for hot debate, when time permits, which is seldom.

In any case, the Annunciator had apparently specified that two Lords might occupy the floor simultaneously. Lord Trillphyte spoke.

"Lord Roundabout castigates our efforts toward greater goals. Yet in Executive Committee, within the very forge of social policy, he hangs back in imitation of a blushing shyleaf. For proof I present this transcript of last week's meeting, which demonstrates conclusively the man's reticent and ineffective character." He waved a sheaf of papers in the air.

Lord Roundabout shot to his feet and shouted, "Not so! Scoundrel! Evil blot upon the common conscience! For justification he flaps a license purchased at some illicit chancery, and thereby becomes a sore upon the body politic!"

"I speak with the freedom of complete certainty," Lord Trillphyte intoned.

"Lord Trillphyte has the advantage of being insufficiently knowledgeable to be uncertain," Lord Roundabout shot back. Around us were many growing smiles and comfortably folded arms; the audience was enjoying the duel.

"I move that the Ablegate Lord Roundabout's remarks be stricken from the minutes in their entirety," said a new voice to our left. Lord Pontieu stood, silhouetted against a tall window now streaked with a dreary rain, his lean hand poised in a delicate gesture. A few "seconds" rumbled automatically from around the room.

Milord shot to his feet. "Objection!" he spluttered. "This repressive motion serves only to further the grotesque proposal put forward by Lord Trillphyte. I move that Lord Pontieu's motion be Rescinded With Censure."

"Second, with Particular Urgency," Lord Roundabout chimed.

"Point of order," said Lord Trillphyte smoothly. "Lord Benefice's objection actually pertains to the substance of the previous question, rather than to Lord Pontieu's motion which is now on the floor. Furthermore, Lord Roundabout's second is out of order, in that his own statements are the object of the motion before the Assembly."

"It does not and it is not!" shouted Lord Benefice in exasperation. "The lean intent of my proposal is being deliberately and scurrilously distorted!"

The Chamber Annunciator sounded his gong strenuously, which set the strips of rosecloth around his waist fluttering. "A condition of quadruple conjecture exists," he stated. I drew a deep breath and hugged my pouch around me.

Milord muttered something vile under his breath and strode angrily down the aisle to the lectern. At the same time Lord Pontieu also stepped to the platform. Under Milord's waistcoat I bumped against his warm ribs and clung tightly to my holster-straps.

"I perceive that the gracious Lord Pontieu would suck the marrow of his colleagues' private interests," Milord began acidly. "Perhaps he is jealous of that imported vapor to which he was recently introduced. I have prepared a few remarks in this connection." Milord reached into his pocket and brought forth a scroll.

Lord Pontieu turned his back on the Assembly and looked at us with unexpected concern. He whispered in Milord's ear, "The scum of a flea's arse clogs your teeth; you flog pubescent girls in private."

Milord stared at him in wide-eyed amazement. "Whatever is the meaning—?" he stammered.

Lord Pontieu put an arm around Milord's shoulders, then turned to the Assembly and shouted, "Lord Benefice complains of chest pains. Fetch help at once!" He held up his hand in the universal succor-sign.

Without warning six attendants rushed from the wings and grappled Milord to a canvas stretcher. He protested and struggled, but this only served to confirm the impression that he had been taken abruptly ill. From the corner of my eye I saw Lord Roundabout shouting and waving his arms frantically, to no avail. Lord Pontieu looked on with false solicitousness as we were carried out of the building.

The 'attendants', I realized at once, were accomplices of Lord Pontieu. They wasted no time in strapping Milord's arms roughly to the stretcher, and under the pretense of administering a tonic, clamped a leather socket over his mouth. We were rushed to a waiting aid-coach and roughly dumped in. The doors were shut and locked.

Before I could try to assist Milord, unfriendly hands tied me into a burlap sack and threw me under a seat. Milord's muffled cries pierced me to the heart as we rattled into the street. Soon the wooden wheels jarred against the rough cobbles of an unfamiliar and disreputable banlieue, and occasionally slewed through the refuse in its gutters.

V

A DESPERATE VOYAGE

A rocking motion jarred my sleep: the sturdy shuddering of a big ship's loins as she wallowed in heavy swells. I fought with loginess. My *gnozzt* had swollen uncomfortably to twice its normal size. I was dreadfully famished and thirsty.

Squirming from the bindings fastened around my holster, I found that I was confined on the hard shelf of a tiny cuddy. From a crack in the wood a draft of cold salt air stung my nostrils. At my side was a crust of bitter hardtack which I gobbled at once, and a carafe of insipid water at which I lapped uncertainly.

A sudden panic seized me. I scrabbled blindly for a way out of my cupboard, to no effect, and sank down in a lump, striving to organize my thoughts. I was aboard ship — but where? Under what captain? I had no idea. Where was Milord? Or — the question gripped me like a fist — was he still alive?

As I picked anxiously at my claws I turned my mind to recent events. Lord Pontieu's ruse was in one respect typical of the knave: he could wring almost any reaction from an opponent — fear, guilt, surprise — and manipulate it to his advantage. But abduction and shanghaiing — these were overtly criminal acts! That his minions had also sabotaged Milord's carriage now seemed certain; indeed, it was because that sabotage had failed to prevent Milord's arrival in the Assembly, where he would oppose his plan of taxation, that Pontieu had resorted to this greater violence. Perhaps, even as I sat pigeonholed in a barkentine miles at sea, his henchmen were plundering Benefice Manor! The thought was sickening.

But even more frightening was the realization that he might succeed in stealing the witches' brew. Did he know that even his own survival would be threatened by such greed? Would he squander the witches' brew to please and aggrandize himself?

Certainly good Lord Roundabout would somehow — but in the sweep of events, Milord had not managed to bring him into the picture before our kidnapping! In despair I threw myself down on the hard, rough wood and closed my eyes.

A night and a day passed, during which I paced back and forth for endless hours in the dark. Hunger made its bed in my tiny berth. Never in my short life had I spent so much time away from Milord's reassuring company. I slipped helplessly into an abyss of depression.

Finally one morning there were voices in the corridor and my hatch was unlocked. Two cruel-looking midmates with blunt noses threw me into a cage and swaggered aft, where a rude discovery awaited.

They knocked at a low mahogany door and were answered by a muffled grunt. Inside was an unshaven lout, hunched over a chart-littered table under a guttering hurricane lamp. He wore a seedy, one-piece suit of dark green shalloon, heavily stained with grease and rum. He scratched absentmindedly at a scab on his chin and leaned his palm on the rusty sword dangling at his side. He looked up and slowly focused his eyes on me; they were filled with hatred and implacable greed. It was Salvemaster Worrant.

But this was no longer Milord's trusted servant, with his airs of unctuous refinement and obsequious guile. This was an ugly, pragmatic oaf, a traitor who had discarded all pretense of civility.

"So, Milord's faithful companion sees fit to join us aboard the *Obnounce Dittaneer*," he said, leering. He leaned back in his chair and picked at his teeth with a splinter. Through the grimy windows behind him were emerald-black waters roiling astern. The horizon was bare.

For response I only stared at him with contempt. He laughed with genuine amusement. A squeak came from under his arm, where I was astonished to see another member of my species.

That the Salvemaster should keep a mascot was itself an act of great arrogance, for only the Lords were permitted to do so; but that it should be a race-mate of mine was doubly insulting. I wondered where he had maintained his pet before coming aboard, as I had never detected the scent of another Filxxx, other than my own family, in Benefice Manor.

The Salvemaster's smile faded. "He's no pantywaist like you, Flick. Bilch here would just as soon chew your nose as spit." Taking his cue, Bilch hissed and displayed a set of menacing, needly teeth.

"I'm the master of this ship," said the captain, serious now. "I imagine you'll disrelish being amongst us hoodlums and iconoclasts. But Lord Pontieu has instructed me to keep you here til we meet him at his enclave on Hibblebar River, and stay here you will, fox-whelp. Not that there's anywhere you could go, except to the sharks." This was the first I had heard of Lord Pontieu's enclave, many leagues removed from his Manor.

While he prattled harshly on, I gained what information I could from a quick survey of the captain's sanctum. Its shelves held a variety of baubles and sea-trophies, most of them layered with salty dust; and to my right was a streaked glass cabinet containing four green bottlettes. Worrant had looted the brew! Had he already sold the other two bottlettes, or used them for his own decadent pleasure?

And what had he done with Milord? Was he here, and in good health? I signaled my question to Bilch, using the ancient method of retinal semiosis which is unique to our order of bivertebrates. He in turn squeaked to the captain, who said, "Oh yes, your sniveling Lord is aboard. You may see him again. If he cooperates." That Worrant understood the Filxxx tongue disgusted me, for he had always pretended not to; for years he had eavesdropped on my confidences to Milord. My hatred of this scavenger deepened.

He looked suddenly irritated at having given over the initiative and poked his mascot. Bilch penetrated my eyes with a counter-question, the reason for my being brought here: how much more did Milord have of the coin he had paid for the witches' brew, and where was it? Apparently Lord Pontieu was not content with having acquired the brew, nor with simultaneously taxing it in absentia and enjoying the resulting political gains — his greed extended to the enchanted pellets as well. Worrant had not been entrusted with access to Milord's wall depositorium; and if Milord were aboard ship, it was clear that he still stubbornly refused to divulge its location. I prayed that they hadn't dealt too roughly with him and vowed that I too would not yield to their pressures. I twitched my eyes negatively at Bilch.

The captain jumped up from his desk and advanced on me with his cheap rapier drawn. Frustration burned in his eyes. "You crapping twiddlysnit! You think you can resist me too?" I wasted no time emptying my *gnozzt* in his direction, and he toppled over in a heap.

Here I must at last explain that this vestigial organ, which is for the most part merely a nuisance now, was at one remote time a highly developed means of defense, regularly used by Filxxxs in combat according to strict codes of conduct. It contained a variety of poisonous liquors, which could be expelled in clouds, needle-like sprays, or condensed balls. Most of those regulatory mechanisms have been lost through disuse, and the many subvarieties of *gnozzt* liquid have become genetically homogenized into one less noxious entity; but this latter substance still exerts a most stunning effect, which is on occasion quite useful. I once mused that this unusual feature of my makeup was perhaps what had unconsciously attracted my ancestors to that supreme concoctor of potent liquors, Lord Benefice, and for that matter, Bilch to the Salvemaster; for their art was in a sense the ultimate sublimation of this repugnatorial gland.

One of my two guards went to revive the captain. The other made as if to strike me, but thought better of it. Fortunately he did not realize that I could not discharge my organ again til it had regenerated, which requires some two days. But he seized me from behind, thrust me into the cage and returned me to my quarters.

I immediately set myself to finding a means of escape. There was little to explore in my tiny cell, but if I stood on my hind legs and stretched and pushed with all my strength, I could just wedge my muzzle into a narrow hatchway giving on the forecastle deck.

I gazed at the moving sea, more hypnotic than a winter fire. The ocean's sunset breath was more sweetly scented than the fairest white oak aflame, and I breathed it deeply. The ship rose and fell, wallowing steadily through the titan swells, thrusting her beak carelessly through layer after layer of creamy spilling surf. My dreamy thoughts were kidnapped by sudden fatigue. Wishing that I were still home again with Milord in his quiet study, I lay down and fell into a profound sleep.

I was soon awakened by a scratching from a narrow crack between my shelf and the wall. Through the boards came a subtle greeting-odor which was strangely familiar. Moreover, I realized with a start that its familiarity was more than recent — it stretched back in time, even before my birth, as inviting as a mother's smile, urging me gently hither.

I began to enlarge the hole with my teeth, but stopped, wary of what might lie beyond. I had ventured far beyond my comfortable purview and might easily meet with orcs or elf-ichneumons, or other strange and treacherous creatures skilled in imitative trickery. But this coddling scent reminded me urgently, lovingly of hearth and cousin, of burrow and family.

Family! — the ancestral print was imbedded in this odor, engraved unmistakably upon its very moleculae. I resumed my attack on the hole with a will now, splintering the aging planks with my teeth and claws, no longer expecting to find some enemy bilge-rat or miniature ogre. In the dim light I could barely make out a small, furry face, its onyx eyes intently reaching for mine: Bilch.

After the shortest moment of hesitation, we embraced in the age-old fashion of kith-Filxxxs, apposing our ears, eyelids and paws in sequence, at the same time uttering a low churring sound. Then we both began eye-speaking at once, with the delicious anticipation of discovering the connections that bound us to each other.

It transpired that the matron-aunt of Bilch's fourth cousin was teat-mate to my sire's own closebrother. This meant that we were obliged by ancient tradition not only to avoid all injurious relations with each other, but also to engage in a special intimacy: 'duothelytoky', a sort of mutual parthenogenesis, which would result in two or four female offspring each. But it had been generations since our species consummated such relationships, which had been all but replaced by a more conventional family structure during our long association with men. Embarrassed, we averted our eyes in the darkness.

"Broodcousin Bilch," I began, searching for diplomatic delicacy, "the kin-patterns between us are strong, yet we find ourselves in the midst of complex pressures…" I groped. But Bilch was greatly relieved that I had taken the initiative, with its implied demurrer, and our embarrassment faded.

"You allude to priorities," said Bilch. "Here then is the first." He spread out some sweetmeats pilfered from the captain's table. They had been heavily salted for preservation during the voyage and tasted of the stale firkins in which they had traveled, but I fell to eating ravenously while Bilch supplied me with further information.

The ship was manned by a motley crew of scalawags and roustabouts, he said, whom Firstmate Crowell bullied mercilessly. We had driven near halfway to Hibblebar Estuary and Lord Pontieu. Worrant also had a large store of other contraband from Benefice Manor, which he intended to deal away to his personal advantage in port.

The tasties dissolving in my stomach fueled my brain, which now flooded with yet more questions. "Yes, Milord is relatively safe," he assured me, "but he has lost considerable weight." No harm there, I thought to myself with a smile. But something in the way he averted his eyes at the phrase 'relatively safe' bothered me. Was anything else wrong?

Bilch started to answer, but his ears twitched in sudden alarm. He said, "I must go, or I'll be missed. Later I'll return and show you the secret passageways." He turned and disappeared.

I peered after him. He had come and gone through the pump-dale, a wooden tube which conducts bilge water from the chain pumps back to the sea. He must know their timing well; woe if they were activated during his passage, for they would flush him away like a bilge-rat!

It seemed forever before he came back. Once again he thoughtfully brought sustenance for me, a crumb of scrod and slices of pelican egg. I swallowed them almost whole, more in eagerness to finish and be shown to Milord's quarters than because of my hunger, wolfish though it was.

"The nightwatch crew take their sport on deck, and the captain occupies himself with his fortune-knuckles," he told me. "Come quickly now, Flick. I'll show you the galley and the holds."

"To Milord first," I said, anxiously touching his furry side.

Bilch hesitated. "Lord Benefice is in —" he began, and cut himself off.

"Tell me!" I said.

He held my eyes for a moment. "Come, you'll see," he said. "Follow me closely, and not a sound."

He turned and skittered into the hole, and I behind him. The sound of gurgling water came suddenly from below, together with the rhythmic creaking of a chain pump. We dashed out of the trough in the nick of time, as tons of seawater flooded past. We moved along a length of spirketing and crossed to a stanchion, and shinnied up to the gun deck.

There we headed forward on the lee side, dodging amongst the cannon straining and creaking on their trunnions. Many of the gun ports had been left open, admitting an unfriendly wind. The walls were painted a dark red, to conceal blood spilled during combat. We looked at each other and shuddered. Finally we came to a pantry just abaft the manger, where Bilch pushed gingerly at a loose strip of planking and we looked in.

On a bunk lay Milord, his eyes closed. An aura of palpable cold surrounded him in the darkness. His arms, still clothed in the gold-embroidered jacket he had worn to the Assembly, were folded symmetrically across his motionless chest. His wig had been lost, exposing his curls of flaxen hair.

I almost cried out in terror, but Bilch restrained me. "He only sleeps," he said. "You see his forehead?"

A dab of white salve had been smeared above his regal brows. "That is Captain Worrant's Salve of Aestivation, which will retain Lord Benefice in a suspended state until it dissolves — more or less until we put into port," he explained. I suppressed a whimper, and with it the urge to lick the noxious cream from Milord's skin.

Bilch anticipated my thoughts. "Do not consider removing the inunction prematurely," he cautioned. "Its contact would probably kill you, and sudden removal would be a severe hazard for His Lordship as well." He gently turned me back. "Come, you've had a shock. We'll raid the galley again and then get some rest." We entered a hatchway and crawled to the ship's kitchen.

The cook, a stolid bumpkin tattooed from shoulder to finger, was whistling and wiping his hands as he finished his chores. He hung up his greasy apron, sucked lustily at a pocket flask and stood for a moment smacking his lips. We waited until he left, then helped ourselves to breadfruit and lardoons from the locker.

A rhythmic thumping came from outside, and we jumped to an open porthole above the flour bin to reconnoitre. The weather had freshened under clear night skies, and whitecaps jumped on the water like confetti. Six crew members stood at each side of the foredeck, arrayed against the railings; those on the port side wore white pullovers with broad red stripes, those on the starboard side blue. Behind them flowed the silvery sea, stroked by a full moon; above, the riggings were tangled in the silvery black night.

The thumps emanated from the hand of Firstmate Crowell, who thwacked a belaying pin against a thick roll of leather at his side. The men squatted and stood again in cadence to his beat. "Lively now," he called, and the men hopped and sweated at double time. This exercise continued for a short while.

The men suddenly called out in unison, "All warm!", and stopped. They drew flat paddles from their pockets and laced them to their palms. Then they fell to a crouch, and Firstmate Crowell introduced a lopsided metallic ball, the size of a large codfruit, onto the deck. The men immediately began madly waving their hands about, at which the ball slewed crazily back and forth between them under the paddles' magnetic influence.

"Second phase," called the Firstmate, and again began beating his roll of hide. The players resumed their kneebends, but without stopping their magnetic manipulations. With their arm-waggling and leg-pumping they resembled two rows of giant, colorful sea anemones in a stiff current.

Bilch nudged me and pointed out a modified scupper set into the deck at each rail. "The object of the game," he said. "First team to drive the ball in twice wins. And if weak legs slow a man from the beat, he's ejected."

The drummer's cadence accelerated noticeably and the contest intensified. The deck clanked and whirred with the ball's wild peregrinations. One man's calisthenics slowed; the drummer called his name peremptorily and he withdrew, grumbling and shaking his head. A moment later two opposing men, whose red and white shirts bulged over their bellies like spinnakers in a squall, gave in to their lack of conditioning and were forced to sit down, puffing heavily. The two teams were soon reduced to two and three players, respectively.

Presently a large swell hove up the starboard side of the ship, giving additional advantage to the three-playered team, who thus scored a point and threw up a gleeful shout. The players stopped to massage their tired thighs, and tots of hot spiced rum were passed around. Its tangy, fragrant steam, blown by a bracing breeze, set my mouth to watering. Firstmate Crowell covertly collected bet-payment from a companion, whose dull manner suggested a singular lack of wit. What man of sharp mind would make wager against the referee?

"It's surprising the captain permits them to play deck-whizzle," Bilch explained with his eyes. "The game usually ends in violence and tears. But then I suppose they'd riot anyway if he tried to deprive them of their only entertainment."

Play resumed, with rowdiness made more lively by the rum possets. A blue player mishandled a reverse-spin dribble, such that the ball careened against his opponent's shin and bounced into the blues' own scupper.

"Larboard takes the point," shouted the red player.

"Illegal use of leg!" screamed the first one.

"No kick intended," rejoined the other.

"Intent not required, Rule 38," said the first.

" 'Opponent's forward motion precludes citation for illegal use', Rule 47," recited the red sailor smugly.

"Cheating mugwump," screamed blue.

"Crap-eating lubber!" came the reply.

"Snitflicker!"

"Shite-bird!"
"Killfeather!"
"Budmash!"
"Bagwattle!"
"Baggywrinkle-rot!"
"Toss-pot!"
"Nullibist!"
"Pederast!"
"Blatherskite!"
"Humoralist!"
"Cake urchin!"
"Milkwort!"
"Cocksnoot!"

Their name-calling match was interrupted by the Firstmate. "The point stands, contest tied," he said with an air of decision. A rumble of discord arose, which he quieted by holding the ball up to signal the start of the last inning. "Play!" he shouted, and rolled the spinning puck between the two lines of men.

The players worked in earnest now, moving closer and closer to the ball as they tried to coax it to the scuppers. Occasionally opposing paddles clashed and stuck together, and play was briefly suspended while they were slid apart. The two pot-bellied players combined in a strong flanking maneuver and the ball inched toward the blue goal, but their pudgy legs again betrayed them.

"Ongly and Peltmailer to the bulwarks," shouted the Firstmate. The two glowered at him. The blue team immediately drove through their position and scored.

"Cheating shite-breath!" screamed a wiry red player at the Firstmate. "You eject them to win your wager money with Noment Slagpile!" Without warning he seized the ball and lofted it at Crowell.

The Firstmate dodged the throw and shied his hardwood baluster accurately at his assailant, opening a gash along one temple. Chaos erupted and the fighting men surged fore and aft, carrying their brawling and bashing from forecastle to taffrail. A moment later we ducked shards of flying glass as the ball hurtled through the porthole next to us with a splintering crash.

A smoky gas spread across the decks from an opening in the hatch-coaming and dulled the bright moonlight with its shadowy mist. We ducked back inside to escape the fumes. " 'Oceaneer's Ordinary'," Bilch told me, "the captain's preferred somnolent vapor. He uses it whenever they can't be managed otherwise." It was the same cloying scent of currant preserves which I had smelled during our abduction in the aid carriage.

The men's caterwauling quieted with the suddenness of a wave when it crashes against a velvety beach. All around the deck, sailors lay in impromptu postures of enforced sloth, propped awkwardly against winches and rope-coils, or splayed limply on the deck. One man hugged the binnacle in a parody of love. The rush of seawater against the hull grew suddenly loud, and the night breeze rattled the halyards in the sheaves above.

We wondered where the captain was, to have tolerated such wild-ness in his crew. Our unspoken question was answered in a moment by a cough.

We turned to find Captain Worrant gravely watching us, slowly nod-ding his head from side to side in studied reproof. His smell of cheap kippers and rum was overpowering; globulets of weeks-old grease adorned his wiry beard like tiny ornaments. He casually filled a small seashell pipe with tobacco as coarse as the nesting-stuff of an albatross.

"You disappoint me, Bilcher Pebblepaw. Our little guest should be confined, away from this...unpleasantness." He gestured at the broken porthole.

Somehow I was not frightened, perhaps because I had already bested the ruffian once, or perhaps because I knew myself to be a prisoner in any case, in or out of my jail-cupboard. But for Bilch the moment was pregnant with crisis: his collusion had been discovered, his role sud-denly and perilously transformed. He trembled next to me, and my hackles rose in sympathy.

The captain moved forward with a threatening gesture, more at Bilch than at me, and I knew then intuitively that he had somehow neutralized Bilch's *gnozzt* before he was weaned, making him truly a harmless housepet. I squeaked desperately at Bilch to run, but he was riveted to the spot by fear, so I shoved him through the stove's heat vent and darted after him. An instant later Worrant's thrown knife clanged against the loose grill behind us.

Bilch found his legs and we raced blindly up the duct. Soon we emerged above the cookhouse and stopped to reconnoitre. Below us half the crew continued to doze. I looked questioningly at Bilch, but he seemed to be in a state of shock. The alarm bell sounded nearby. We could hardly return to my cell — Worrant's goons would undoubtedly search there first — and I tried frantically to think of a place we could hide; but a ship was an unfamiliar thing to me then, and my mind was a blank.

We dove down a companionway and dashed aft, moving below from deck to deck, carefully skirting bulkheads if they resounded with voices or footsteps. Soon we had descended into the ship's bowels, somewhere amidships.

We passed the cable room and entered the gloomy hold. After we had sloshed through the bilge for some time, I was astonished to see a small sapling growing on the limber board. Its lean branches were adorned by a few tiny green acorns and virtually no foliage. How could a stray seed survive hungry gulls and leagues of wet sea air to put down roots in this chilly brine?

There was another such shoot, and another, and soon I was wandering in a forest of young hedgerow oaks. But their skins glowed faintly in the darkness like no normal oak, creating a visibility equal to that of a gray-clouded day on deck. The trunks were connected above by cross-limbs, in the manner of banyan trees, and thus clasping one another arm-in-arm they gave an impression of a single organism.

The air resonated with a slow, quiet thrumming, so subtle that it had been unnoticeable at first. Trees shrank and swelled slowly, about once for each eight or ten beats of my quick heart, pulsing sluggishly downward like huge, bark-covered caterpillars. Where they penetrated the limber boards and first futtocks, their roots bent aft like arthritic fingers, and with each pulsation the ship surged briefly forward. A botanical engine! It was the strangest discovery of my short life, as bizarre as the hallucination induced by the witches' brew.

I realized suddenly that Bilch was nowhere to be seen. I dashed among the trees, sending my retinal flashes in all directions in a desperate effort to contact him, but there was no response. Soon I found to my horror that I was quite lost in the bosky throng. This nightmarish miniature forest was a hall of mirrors, sending me from one trackless false start to another like schoolboys cruelly shoving a young newcomer back and forth. Panic crimped its chilly fingers around my spines and my legs wobbled like table jelly.

"Well, Bilch," said a voice in the thicket. To my right stood an aging sailor. Deep wrinkles invested his leathery cheeks like the creek-scars in a ravine, yet his skin, no doubt from years below decks, was as pale as young ivory. His chest, under a shoddy felt shirt, was the size of a brewer's tun. He was armed with a heavy iron poker, secured by leather straps along one leg.

His gnarled hands cradled a bell book, which he consulted intently as he leaned against one of the trees. He pursed and unpursed his lips incessantly as he read, in unconscious tempo to the tumescing and shrinking of the saplings. His bare feet were extraordinarily lengthy, as though they too would soon turn into roots and plunge downward in blind, hopeless search of earth.

His glance flitted at me with a twinge of doubt; he had mistaken me for Bilch. Too frightened to run, I hastened to produce a few squeaks by way of reply. He seemed satisfied with this and returned to the perusal of his manual.

"She's bearing east by nor'east at twelve knots," he said finally. "Now as I was tellin' you yesterday, Bilch, the canvas o' the *Obnounce Dittaneer* accounts for only half her speed, and sap-propulsion the other half. If the beasts be in a cooperative frame o' mind." He looked over at me again and patted his poker meaningfully. "Aye, the Grandmage's treethrusters can save us from any doldrums."

The magical trees had come from Mentharch's hand! — from the same legendary workshop that had produced the Unending Fountain of Clamjamfry and the protective butterflies on our coasts. But how ironic that the trees had been indentured for larceny of the very brew that could save him. I wanted to ask the old sailor how they had come to such a situation but dared not, for fear of revealing myself.

He slipped the booklet into his pocket, hoisted a bucket of thick slops and poured it into the bilge-water. "Soup's on, lovelies," he called out with sardonic cheer. "An extra ration, captain's orders. But he'll be wantin' some extra power for it, mind you!" A wave of pleasure ran through the thicket and their pulsing quickened. "You've more belly-cheer than your own master," he said irritably.

He crooked his neck and peered into the gloom. Still talking, he fell to a crouch and crept quickly amongst the trees. Suddenly he whipped his poker from its sheath and spanked it hard against a trunk. The tree groaned with agony, and tears of thick orange sap welled up in the bruised stripe on her bark.

"You think to sprout leaves again, eighty-three? Hah? Plant-filth! Let your mother and father make leaves in the sunny meadows of Derbandell — your job is to sap and thrust, sap and thrust!" He slashed a bushel of leaves from the tree's thin branches, at which it cried piteously. I covered my ears, unable to bear the plant-creature's pain.

The treemaster shoved the point of his iron prod up against a thick cross-branch, a highwayman pressing his knife against a victim's throat, and announced to his congregation, "Remember well your purpose here, you trunk-scum. Or I'll chop you to logs and let you bloat in the Hot Seas of Bluddhmuste!"

A shudder rippled through the trees. He threw himself into a hammock and morosely uncorked a flask of purser's rum. The captive trees continued their relentless pulsing and humming and their roots clenched the floorboards as before, yet I swore they surrounded their master an inch or two more closely. But if their positions had changed at all, the engineer was oblivious to it.

Within the depths of the thicket I detected an eye-flash, and a few moments later was reunited with Bilch. "I should have warned you about the trees, Flick," he said apologetically. "I forgot myself."

"No matter," I said. "You were upset. It is hard to lose the love of one's master." He nodded unhappily. "But we must brace ourselves to think of where we can go next."

"Forward. Look to the boards." He cupped his paws and paddled aside the shallow brine, bringing the floorboards into view, and showed me how to follow the direction of their grain. Soon we emerged from the bizarre copse. We continued forward to the pump shafts and ascended to the orlop deck, where the shouts and footsteps of searching crewmen reached us again from fore and aft. We waited until they receded, then sprinted to a larboard locker just below the cookhouse.

"We're well hidden now, Flick," Bilch said, collapsing against a bale of spare leggings.

"You're sure they won't look for us here?"

"They've undoubtedly inspected these lockers thrice while we were below. It's near the change of watch; we'll be undisturbed." His soft ears relaxed against his head, the first time I had seen them anything but hyper-alert since our first meeting; and he felt safe enough to squeak quietly in Filxxxish instead of eye-speaking.

We used wool swatches to wipe the bilge from our fur, then licked ourselves clean in the manner of cats, helping each other on the hard-to-reach spots. We nibbled some mackerel snack-skins that Bilch had kept in his pouch and lapped its sweet oil from our paws. I felt strangely content, unconcerned for the moment with my predicament, or Milord's. Exhaustion was stealing over me, but I was too tired to sleep.

Our dunnage-cramped quarters were rife with fish smells and the sour odor of damp wool. "The air is stifling," I said.

He looked at me in agreement. "The *Dittaneer's* strake is well above the water line here," he said. "Let's have a fresh breath." He began gnawing the hull-plank where it had once been damaged by some pirate's cannon. When he had gone half an inch or so I took up the chore, and soon we had a porthole. We looked out on the fresh, wind-raked sea and drank its wet scent. I pitied the sullen engineer, mean fellow though he was, swilling stale rum in his floating dungeon below.

"We must think of a strategy to pursue when we arrive at Lord Pontieu's enclave," said Bilch.

"Perhaps we can enlist the aid of the Protectioner's Guild, although I fear we would have little standing in their eyes."

"I wouldn't have any, being an illicit mascot," said Bilch. "And now no one's mascot at all, come to that." He looked so sad that I wanted to squeeze him to me. "But you are the legitimate protégé of Lord Benefice, and would be properly received."

"Then we must escape to the Guild offices the moment we dock." We discussed the plan. I was reluctant to leave Milord in the captain's hands for even a moment, but Bilch was right: it was I who would have to approach the Guild.

A silence fell, and we sat gazing at the ocean's puttering surface for a long time. Then beneath it a shadow began gradually to take form, a great boulder of darkness without edges. It glided through the sea in tandem with us, creating the illusion that it was the ship's own moon-shadow. But the moon hung before us, not behind, and there was no object in sight that might have been silhouetted by its pewter rays. The black mass absorbed light as absolutely as a deep well. We looked at each other in bewilderment.

Then from this dark thing came a sound, or rather a rich, masterful vibration, a fremitus so deep-pitched that we did not hear it but rather felt it under our skins. The very outline of Bilch's body shimmered next to me amidst the rocky buzzing. Shivers ran slowly the breadth of the ship and back, and once more again, and her planks and joists rattled and knocked like corks in a barrel.

The huge scotoma radiated into the depths of the ocean, an angry black sun, and coursed through it to the horizon. Soon the whole sea was harnessed to this leviathan by quivering reins of sound, and a crop of wind-grown tentacles danced and frothed on the surface like a storm around its eye. These myriad tentacles grew taller and taller, writhing and shaking, and sucked like waterspouts at the water below them; they took on primitive lives of their own, fighting against the strings of some demon puppeteer. These watery phantoms with melting knees stared wildly upwards and grasped at the very sky, driven by the great black thing that hulked in their midst.

Then the macabre dance suddenly subsided. The waves quieted and died away, leaving only a ponderous warbling. A mountain of longing swelled in the night air.

For an instant a whale — was it truly only that common creature? — floated near the surface. Yearning for half-forgotten dreams, the spirit sang a delicate barcarole into the star-spattered sky, and tugged wist-fully at the limits of its very soul like a woman pulling at a too-tight slip. A lovesick gondolier drifted on the waters, lamenting a rendezvous with oblivion, and eternity.

I sensed that everyone aboard had silently left his duties to turn an ear. The ship herself seemed intent upon the enormous tune as she plunged rhythmically through the spume. We listened.

A few cat's paws budded around the phantom and it disintegrated. The wind freshened. "The Tumulus of the Sea," Bilch whispered. "It is a miracle to have witnessed it. Most never do, in a lifetime of seafaring."

Bilch was so close to me that I could feel his warmth, and his pulse tapped against me like a clock. His upper lip curved in a way that I had mistaken for a snarl at our first meeting, but which was actually quizzical, even whimsical. He wore a lime-green scarf rakishly around his collar, and his rufous fur glistened handsomely in the silvery light.

"I wish that Milord could have seen and heard it," I said.

"Perhaps he did, in his sleep," Bilch said in a way that made me wonder if we hadn't all been dreaming.

For some time he had been stroking the long, downy dimple between my spines, just above my rump, kneading it gently to butterdough. Now his other paw touched my neck. He locked my gaze in his and began gently milking the nerve-fluid in each of my spinal columns to its nether nexus. A wave of warmth rippled through me.

Our ritual of duothelytoky had begun. We set our *gnozzts* carefully to the sides and moaned the ancient syllables of consanguineous consummation.

I turned and nuzzled under his chin, nipped his warm neck. He complained, but not severely. He seized my ear playfully in his teeth and cupped his paw more closely around my spines. With my paws I began probing his belly for its delicate points of nerve-succulence and coaxed them downward, letting them expand like bubbles rising slowly from the ocean floor. We moved inexorably towards our final embrace.

Bilch clasped me tightly to him, and in that pressure was not only his passion, but also his anguish at the loss of his master's love, loathsome cur though he had proved to be. Some of Bilch's pain was my own as well, for the Salvemaster had once been a valued servant of my Lord, faithfully attending to the unique products of his art and buffering him against treacherous parties. Our tears flowed together, and with them were released the fears and tensions of recent days.

Passion overwhelmed us in a rising swell. At last we curled up together amongst the burlap bales and fell into a deep sleep.

The ship's clock sounded eight bells — four o'clock in the morning. I lay listening to the wet lapping of waves against the ship's hull. Bilch half awoke and hugged me to him, pulling me into the little cold puddle between us. He giggled, pulled me to one side, and we fell asleep again.

Just before dawn I had a terrible dream of a huge bat, large enough to dwarf Benefice Manor. A squinched dollop of wet pink flesh — its face — was set starkly into a vast, coal-black body; its huge, tattered wings were ribbed with sinewy struts and beat the air downward with the force of a giant rug-beater.

This beast swooped low over the whitecaps, closer and closer to *Dittaneer*. Just when it seemed sure to collide and send us to the bottom, it drew up short, flapping and cawing, and perched in the yards. It screeched some guttural syllables and shrank suddenly to one-tenth its former size, plummeted through the quarter deck and thumped into the hold below. The ship groaned and listed under its frightful new ballast. I fretted and tossed, wishing desperately that we had some means of contacting the Grandmage, and fell again into a dreamless sleep.

When we awoke a brilliant sun shone through our makeshift porthole. We stretched and touched noses.

"I had a strange dream, Bilch," I said.

"As did I," he replied, cocking his head in surprise. We knew at once that we had shared the same nightmare.

But our vague anxieties were dissipated by a marvelous, buoyant feeling the ship now had: she was alive, leaping over the waves like a frisky young ketch. Even our cramped locker, spilling over with with warm yellow sunlight, took on the proportions of a stateroom. Through our porthole the horizon lay razor-straight across an azure sea.

I was suddenly troubled by a discrepancy. "How far do you think we are from Albanderry's coast?"

"Five leagues, perhaps six," he said.

"And we're headed east, roughly, to Lord Pontieu's enclave?"

"So I understand."

"Then in fine weather, from the larboard we should be able to see Albanderry's landfall as we're easting?"

Bilch looked at me, then out the porthole. Everywhere sunlight glinted brightly against the hard blue sea, unbroken by a speck of dirt. Without another word we turned and listened at our cupboard door, and hearing nothing but the hissing of the waves against the hull, tip-clawed out to the jeer capstan. We scrambled topside on the waist and crossed to starboard. There, in a fine milky haze not six leagues distant, were the low bluffs of Albanderry's southern coast.

"She's turned about since yesterday," I said simply.

"Yes, we're headed back to Albanderry Port, or beyond," said Bilch. "And such speed I've never seen — she must be making thirty knots or more."

Dittaneer was dressed smartly in full suit, from spankers to jibs. Her canvas bellied ataunt in a stiff wind, sheets breasting and straining like foot-racers at the tape. Her topgallants and royals took the wind in great gulps, bending the masts til I thought they would crack, and everywhere the tackle hummed like a bevy of harps. I peered over the bulwarks: the ship's hull rode high in the water, showing her garboard strake if not her keel. She drove through the spray like a crazed bird, as though spirited by some supernatural force.

Around us the crewmen had discovered that their efforts were superfluous and half-heartedly shuffled through makework tasks. Men lounged under the yards, idly sheaving ropes or stitching spare sails, and looked about anxiously. It dawned on me that there was only one port to the west: Catsmouthport, which is controlled by the Mountainwitch Consortium; and this fact, together with our impossible speed, could have only one meaning. Our dream-in-tandem of a monstrous bat arriving on board had been reality: the ship had been commandeered by a witch!

"Bilch!" I cried, "We're —"

"I know," he said. "Listen."

From the captain's cabin came a horrible voice, like the clenching of a wrain bolt by a rusty tool. "Wretch! Wimp-sot! No potbellied Gasmaster to protect you now," she said. Her words grated painfully in my ears.

In a shrill, cracking voice Captain Worrant replied, "Petolzia will destroy you when she learns of this vile calumny. The Lords —" His elbows bumped against the bulkhead as he backed against it in terror.

"Impudent slime! No mortal dictates destiny to Sisters!" There came the abbreviated *shwith* of his sword half-drawn, then a stomach-turning groan, and silence. A moment later the captain appeared on deck. His face was drained of all color, his eyes as hollow as a conch shell. He moved in a dream, unmindful of the brisk, raw wind flapping at his open shirt. His hands hung like limp halyards at his sides. He shuffled past without noticing us. Over his shoulder was slung a coil of rope.

He walked steadily forward to the beak and lashed one end of his rope to the cathead. Before anyone realized what he was about, he had fashioned a noose and tightened it around his neck.

"To the glory of Vulgia," Captain Worrant shouted, and leaped from the ship.

VI

A TRAVELING COMPANION

ilch fainted, which was just as well, for the retrieval of Captain
Worrant's still-twitching corpse was a nasty sight. Shaking visibly,
Firstmate Crowell took command of the ship — what command
remained to him, under the circumstances — and conducted a cursory
burial ceremony. The shrouded remains of Salvemaster Worrant splashed
into the sea. Almost at the same time, we heard Vulgia's banging and
bumping as she paced impatiently in her dank quarters below.

"Well, that's that," Crowell whispered, and turned to face the assembled crew. They stood rocking slowly back and forth on the rolling
deck, their faces still frozen with shock. Crowell looked blankly at
them for a long while, retreating into himself. Then he turned back to
the sea and murmured:

> " 'Tired pirates plow the spume and rave
> At canvas patches flutt'ring overhead.

They scour the sea for thrills and swag
But in their hearts dream only of the grave.' "

The wind rippled her consoling fingers through the men's hair. "He resisted her," Crowell said hoarsely. "To the man's credit, he resisted her," he added in a firmer voice. He shook his head and drew himself up with an effort. "All hands to your quarters," he said. "Kitchenmate, double rum tots all around." The men waited for a moment, then slowly moved away. Crowell stood at the railing, staring emptily into the sea for a long while before retiring into the quarterdeck.

Bilch was distraught. He moped about the rest of the day, saying and eating nothing. Crowell ignored us, and so we had the run of the ship, but Bilch took to our makeshift cabin and wouldn't stir.

Through the afternoon our course turned steadily northward. At sunset we entered the broad North Channel, which divides Albanderry from Catscat Isle. The wind was striking cold and abrasive now, bringing raw pink to the cheeks and tears to the eyes of the few men who stayed on deck. Again and again the *Dittaneer* plunged into the timeless blue sea, a whinnying horse shrugging the live foam from her nape and giving birth to churning turquoise froth at her stern.

Around us floated occasional crags of brash ice, a sparkling pale blue under the setting sun. Some of these icy skiffs were skippered by harbor seals, barking and ducking their heads on their slippery decks. In their black flipper-gloves, slick suits and whiskers they resembled nothing so much as strutting comic actors, with waxed mustaches on their muzzles. I persuaded Bilch to come up for a look, and their burlesque brightened his spirits. We waved and squeaked at them from the forecastle deck. Below us several crewmen attached bowgrace, or bunches of old, frayed rope, to the ship's hull, as a fender against the lumps of swiftly floating ice.

A school of pale lungfish took up escort. They disported in long arcs alongside the ship, puffing up to remain airborne as long as possible. They grimaced at us with their thick, rubbery green lips, then slipped back into the icy sea as smoothly as champagne bubbles. To starboard we saw a shoal of bean clams twinkling only a few fathoms beneath the surface, and at once the lungfish darted off in their direction for supper.

In the distance the highest of the Catscat Peaks trailed a long banner cloud. Gradually the broad, alluvial maw of Catsmouthport came into view and we heard the thunderous sounds of its notorious brontide. This roaring signaled the tumultuous meeting of the Perspex River, as tepid as a baby's bath, with the surging, frigid waters of the North Channel.

As the *Dittaneer* stood down to port, we gained a better view of this natural marvel. The two bodies of water boiled and growled almost without stop, clashing belly-to-belly like enraged bucks at odds in spring. The newly wedded water rocked back and forth in its rivermouth cradle, gradually settling as it receded, until the arrival of new tides from the Channel produced yet another violent clash. Even at our distance, the air around us was flower-fresh with bouquets of spray — the echoes of that endless argument of crystal-fresh water with salt flood.

We made for the northeast, where the piers and quays of Catsmouthport squatted in the bay, protected by a breakwater from the brontides. As far as the eye could see, the bluffs above them were a stony fortress, carved from solid basalt: tier upon tier of battlements, bartizans, parapets and embrasures rose threateningly upwards, melding finally into the massive foothills of the Catscat Mountains. Behind their myriad openings lurked every kind of war-engine: basilisks rearing their muzzles seaward, catapults poised with mighty loads, giant crossbows pointing their deadly fingers. It was a stark and upsetting contrast to my pretty Albanderry.

Movement to starboard: what I had mistaken for part of the quay battlements was revealed as an enormous battleship, ponderously leaving her moorings to take up a position on our flank. A moment later another dreadnought to port detached itself from its share of the mountain and stood down, pincering us between her seventy-four cannon and those of her sister. Most of the quays were actually ships, masterfully camouflaged to resemble their surrounding berths. Their crenellated railings dovetailed, as nicely as upper teeth upon lower, with granite embrasures on the piers, instantly marrying them to the land in a single, continuous unit of defense. A docking ship could thus be defended from pursuing invaders as securely as a pup kangaroo in its mother's pouch.

"Do the Lords know of this mighty installation?" asked Bilch.

"I have never heard mention of it. The focus of the Protectioners' efforts has always been to neutralize or prevent the witches' deployment of magic, not military strength."

"Then we must get word of it back to the Assembly. It is even more important than helping Milord." Bilch looked at me with regret, but there was certainty in his eye, too.

"The order of our priorities is irrelevant," I said irritably. "What can we do, a hundred leagues from Albanderry Port?" He was right — even more so than he realized — but perhaps I was annoyed at the suggestion that anything should take precedence over Milord. Bilch only nodded understandingly and shrugged.

We hove to and berthed. The ship shuddered, and Vulgia appeared on the forecastle deck in all her hideous glory. Men scrambled in terror up the ratlines to the yards. Her brown robes, unlike the decaying black rags worn by Petolzia, grew continuously from her skin like the smoldering of a volcano and drained into an accompanying hole which hovered above the planking behind her. She swept to the bowsprit and withdrew a gnarled, luminescent baton from her bosom.

Suddenly Petolzia materialized on the dock and confronted her. "Sow-puke!" she screamed. "Your barratry violates the Covenant of the Sisters!"

Vulgia jumped back, holding her cudgel before her. "Nameless filth! You destroy my spell-locked amulets from spite, jealous that they survived the stick-men's fire."

"Your petty baubles are dwarf-turds," said Petolzia, and retreated as Vulgia swiped at her with the cudgel.

"Coward!" screamed Vulgia. "You surrender our sacred brew to the bargaining of a puny mortal. And you merely coddle the pelleted stick-men with abrupt death. Return to your knitting and let me punish them properly for their abominations!"

Petolzia fixed her grotesquely hypertrophied eye on Vulgia. "Their fate is fixed," she spat, and looked cannily at her. "Perhaps you wish the survival of the father among them? That he might raise your bastard child to —"

"How dare you!" Vulgia screamed. She threw back her head,

shaking a garniture of sparks from her hair. These became ferocious, red-hot hornets which bored holes into her opponent's ragged gown.

Petolzia feinted and replied with an expectoration which became, in midair, an engulfing web of vermin. But Vulgia's fingernails, rusty blades with needly tips, spurted gouts of flame that rent the web to shreds of combustion. With the assurance of a wealthy dowager Petolzia flourished the ruchings of her skirts, broadcasting a deadly smoke; but Vulgia pointed her knobby hand at the sea and formed a waterspout, which drew off the noxious fumes.

Now a stertorous muttering arose, as each of them chanted every spell she knew, and the atmosphere between them wracked and crashed like stormy waves on a rocky shingle. The vile syllables struggled visibly in the burning air, weaving their sinewy hates, sputtering and wrestling with one another. An acrid stench filled our nostrils. Even the witches' airborne pests vanished, driven to cover by those bilious battle-fumes.

Their combat drew down the very skies around us, creating the illusion of night illuminated by purple lightning. I recalled the lavender disturbance we had seen in the Louvian Marsh, and realized that this was not the first time the two witches had fought. One of them — probably Vulgia — had incapacitated our Overdriver with a seizure en route to the Assembly, and had been prevented only by their own feuding from kidnapping us sooner. We owed our survival to their jealousy!

Their struggle continued for the better part of an hour, til finally they had exhausted their store of spells and incantations and were left only with sibilant whispers of pure hate. Slowly they circled each another, panting heavily, their breath crackling marshfire in the air.

"The preliminaries are at an end," hissed Petolzia.

"As are you," replied Vulgia. They crouched on the dock, screamed and launched themselves suddenly at each other's throats, fighting at close quarters like cocks with razored spurs fastened to their heels, hopping and kicking in spasms of fury and rage.

A stroke from Petolzia's foot opened a wound through Vulgia's belly. A hideous brown liquor flowed through that dehiscence and seared a hole through the dock-planks. Soon the poison introduced by the spur caused her head to swell with angry red blains and bleeding cankers. Her already dreadful features caricatured themselves, then parodied

that twice-hateful design. A malignant oedema surrounded each shriv-
eling eye and swelled her tongue in her still-spitting mouth, until it
stuck like cooling lava to her palate. Her hair retracted into rotting
dimples on her swollen scalp, and her fingers fell clanking to the dock.
Her smoke-clothes ceased to billow from her flesh and blew away in a
dank wind. She rocked forward and back like a balloon-doll in a breeze,
and Petolzia pinked her thin, wrinkled belly with countless half-thrusts
and twists. Vulgia fluttered feebly to the pier, sifted between its rotten
planks and was gone.

Petolzia quickly gathered up her victim's amulets and shrieked her
victory-call. She raked her nails ecstatically against the purplish sky and
jumped a sordid jig on the lonely quay. Then she swirled her filthy skirt
around her like a ballerina and spoke an ugly word which unleashed
a horde of gnattering, half-sized witchlings made in her image. They
swarmed aboard the ship like a legion of madding ants and ransacked
her, knocking crewmen over like bugs. Soon they emerged bearing
bags filled with every iron fitting and bit of brass on board. The four
bottlettes of brew were swiftly off-loaded and handed over to Petolzia,
and another detail of witchlings carried a bier with the sleeping figure
of Milord. Bilch and I raced down the hawsers and hid behind a bollard.

"Begone!" screamed Petolzia. The crewmen stirred from their daze
and manned the sails, hardly believing their freedom. In no time the
Obnounce Dittaneer was veering towards the horizon, her stout sails
and pulsing tree-thrusters painting a gurgling zigzag wake abaft.

We stood gazing at our departing prison-ship. Despite the trouble
she had brought us, her exit wounded me with a feeling of emptiness.
She was a fine vessel, but doomed to evil captainry. Perhaps Firstmate
Crowell would prove a worthier master.

"He'll have a job to keep her bilge-trees in line," said Bilch, guessing
my thoughts.

"Yes, and without her fittings I fear she will prove a coffin ship."

We turned back to an empty dock. The harridan and her henchlings,
the bottles of brew, the sacks of metal and Milord: all had vanished.
The terrifying fortress loomed above; a blustery wind nearly swept
us into the sullen waters below. The two crewless battleships heaved
slowly back into their berths like octogenarian turtles into their shells.

The only other sign of life was the drab species of barrenwort stubbornly clinging to the dank barbicans above.

We looked at each other in despair. Milord and the brew were in Petolzia's toils, and we were lost. If only the Gasmaster were here, or some other members of the Protectioners' Guild! Or even the Masterfootling, with the loyal petrel which could fly swiftly to fetch Grandmage Mentharch.

My sole hope for Milord now lay, ironically, in the power and durability of Worrant's Salve of Aestivation, which, because of the unexpected rapidity of our voyage, would not be likely to dissolve until some time after our arrival in Catsmouthport. Would it prevent Petolzia from awakening him for interrogation? If not, would he survive the shock? I churned inside at thought of his peril.

But our first need was shelter, for the bleak climate threatened a dangerously cold night. We started up the causeway towards the first rank of battlements, keeping within the roadside gutter to avoid detection, if there were anyone to detect us. For though this place seemed lifeless and bleak, we had to assume that such complex ramparts would be heavily garrisoned.

We came to the first rank of siege walls, and scaled it by wedging our legs in its crevices and working like squirrels. Beyond it was a broad strip of rough ground, fortunately neither moated nor manned. We descended the wall and ran across. The next rampart was lower and constructed of a lighter stone. From beyond it we heard a puzzling, repetitive clicking, explained a moment later by the grunts of pleasure and disgust of men gaming at dice. We climbed up part way and peered through a chink in the wall.

A heavy withe net stretched from the top of our barrier to the next, enclosing a courtyard below. A band of squat, swarthy thugs lounged about, chatting casually as they followed the dice-game played by three of them in their midst. They wore heavy chasubles of finished gray leather; on the cobbles around them, lozenge-shaped helmets of the same material had been tossed aside. They were ugly men, with the coarse, experienced faces of mercenaries.

"Ow, ambsace. Drat!" complained one soldier in a loud, nasal voice.

"Another day's wages gone," grumbled a second.

"Never mind, Gimbernat, the old witch'll find more lucrative duty for you," said a man to our right, polishing his halberd. This brought a mutter of sarcastic agreement from the group.

"Pah! The stingiest termagant I've ever been liege to," said Gimbernat sullenly.

"Watch your tongue," said the halberdman. "You joined us too late to remember Habblemat — Petolzia turned his eyes to hot cross buns for less impudence than yours." The atmosphere among the men sobered at this reminder.

Another man chuckled harshly. "Or maybe her Sister's bastard will tug your tongue out for you," he said, motioning to his left.

In a corner sat a strange, lean creature, obviously of a different race from the soldiers who guarded him. He wore a full-length olive jerkin, from which four powerful legs protruded: the two lower ones terminated in large, serrated feet, while the upper ones were armlike, ending in prehensile pincers. His apathetic face, the color of tin, sprouted a drooping antenna on each side. He sipped at a stone cup which gave off the powerful odor of opium-vinegar.

At the halberdier's reference to him, his bleak expression contorted in a spasm of anguish. He launched himself abruptly against the crisscrossed lath above, a giant bug leaping from a hot griddle. But the stout lattice held firm; bleating and cursing, he fell painfully back on the cobblestones.

The mercenaries found this vastly entertaining and guffawed cruelly. "The crow's in his cage, the crow's in his cage," they goaded in unison, and flapped their elbows in imitation of trapped birds.

"Shut up!" the creature yelled in a deep voice.

"Aww, the blittersnipe wants his fustilugs mother, so he can hide behind her smoky brown skirts," said a soldier.

"My mother's Sisters will avenge me," the creature ranted.

"Petolzia, for example? Who do you think destroyed your mother?"

"I don't believe it!" shouted the creature defiantly. This only sparked another round of rough laughter from the men.

"The creature is Vulgia's son!" I whispered. "We've chanced on the stick-men's illegitimate offspring." I told Bilch of the sordid encounter described by Haggleman Wimley; and this creature truly did resemble a monstrous praying mantis, as Wimley had suggested.

"It's true he'll never hide behind her skirts again, if ever he did," said Bilch. "He's in a sad, hopeless fix now."

The creature turned morosely away and lay on his side. Another spasm of grief wrenched his face, and when it had passed he sipped again at his narcotic cup. Already a crapulous future was etching itself into his un-human visage.

"He seems to have little witch's blood in him," I said.

"Yes, to find a resemblance would tax the imagination." We fell to studying him.

"But he has no nose!" Bilch exclaimed.

"Nor eyebrows," I said. And it was true. But so striking was his profound lack of expression, and so contrasting the intense, heartbroken frenzy that afflicted him at intervals, that we had not noticed the conspicuous lack of those essential features.

The creature crawled into the shadows. The soldiers tired of taunting it and turned to building up a fire as night fell. They huddled around the blaze and swilled mugs of cloudy stump-liquor, first skimming the thick beeswing from its surface with their blunt fingers. Bilch and I squirmed into a nook in the wall, as close to the fire as we dared, cuddling together to escape the chill.

The men prepared their dinner, which proved surprisingly savory for such a rude outpost. First they served a bog-myrtle bisque in ceramic bowls, nibbling a garnish of spleenwort between gulps. They clashed their mugs boisterously in several toasts, and wolfed large helpings of steaming magpie soufflé nestled in unrecognizable vegetables.

"Begad, Petolzia's a filthy one, but she doesn't skimp for rations, I'll give her that," said one diner.

"Aye," said his neighbor, smacking his lips, "let's only hope she doesn't poison us into the bargain." They pushed their plates away, sleeve-wiped their mouths and plunged into the desserts: clove-currant buns and giant green pies slathered with horehound bitty-cream.

By now Bilch and I were dizzy with hunger, and fed up with the taste of thick saliva swallowed over and again. "When they're asleep or distracted we'll do some grazing," Bilch said, and I heartily agreed.

Now the men prepared to entertain themselves with after-dinner music. From out of nowhere they produced instruments of every shape and timbre: trump-flutes and plump viols, dudelsacks and brassy helicons, a laughably old fashioned slotted gambrel. One man strummed a huge bladder-and-string; another hesitantly coaxed his bassanello. The yard rapidly swelled with a ragged gaggle of hoots, strumming, plinking and *blaaats*.

The halberd-bearer turned over the empty cooking cauldron, ascended his makeshift podium and waved the detached head of his weapon as a baton. The cacophony dwindled to a fitful silence. "'Strikers on the March'," he ordered.

Moans of disappointment arose on all sides. "Strike me instead," wailed one man, to appreciative laughter.

"All right then, 'Tootbird Reveille'," said the halberdier.

"Not again," whined a man to our left.

The conductor lowered his baton with a frown and looked at the dissident. "So name another tune, Snafflerat."

"'Swamp-Clown Polka'," Snafflerat called out immediately, looking left and right for approval. A chorus of enthusiastic huzzahs arose.

The conductor banged the shaft of his halberd on the cauldron for order. "All right, all right," he said irritably, "but with *panache*. Last time you played it as though you were being dragged around by bat-mules."

The men jostled and fidgeted. One blew the spittle from his reed, another cinched the thong on his notch-stick, and already the dudelsack player improvised an obbligato. The leader brandished his blade, waved an exaggerated downbeat and a deafening din blared forth, rattling us in our wall-chink like mice in a drum.

One man flailed a pair of lacquered tambours with a stiff brush; the halberdman pointed wildly at him and screamed above the roar, "You there, more ruffle." An ecstatic smile illuminated Gimbernat's weathered face as he sawed obliviously on his bladder-and-string; the conductor yelled at him, "More vibrato," with no discernible effect. The men blew and sawed and wrestled with their instruments, and stamped their feet in approximate tempo, and soon dark sweat-stains grew under the arms of their leather tunics. They played with undeniable gusto, but the intonation was considerably less precise than what I am accustomed to hearing from Milord's Harmonious Consort.

After a few repeats, the halberdman put a finger to his lips and with surprising obedience they lowered their volume by half. The bassanello players reduced their play to a simple beat-keeping, stepped forward smartly and sang ensemble:

> "Come join us in a giddy place
> Where dwells a rare and waggish race.
> This gleeful troupe of muddy buffoons
> Will welcome us with smiles and spoons!
> Come strut and be a blackfaced fop,
> Or hop and jiggle in their slop.
> We'll shivaree — it's not too far —
> A soirée in their bog-boudoir!"

The whole group bawled the refrain:

> "A swamp-clown is a lively sort
> To dance or tarry or cavort."

The conductor took the next two stanzas, his resonant tenor voice filling the yard:

> "Tumble in the murky mire,
> Twiddle your feet to heart's desire.
> Through the marsh, swim round and down,
> Be a freewheeling swamp-clown!
> Taradiddle and bonnyclabber,
> Pipe and fiddle, scream or jabber.
> Kick your legs into a spasm,
> Be a skittish paraplasm!"

And again they all chorused,

> "A swamp-clown is a lovely sort
> To dance or tarry or cavort."

Now Gimbernat puffed himself up like a bullfrog and sang,

"Pick beebleberries or helmetpods,
Or merely lounge among the clods.
Laugh and romp, no fear of drowning,
Galluptious times for true swamp-clowning!"

The men raised minatory forefingers, and Gimbernat cautioned,

"Don't glump or be in frownish dudgeon
Or play the fud or drear curmudgeon.
No snollygosters haggle here —
In this quag you'll find only cheer!"

And *tutti* they roared,

"A swamp-clown is a lovely sort
To dance and revel and cavort."

Two piddle-pipers sheathed their instruments and danced from the group, stomping a jig and singing, "Taradiddle, o'er the wall, bonny-clabber or not at all!" They joined hands and took a turn, then resumed their piping as the aging gambrel player abandoned his instrument and tottered through a gavotte on his knock-knees.

They worked the tune a dozen times, with ever more zest and less discipline. Finally their efforts dissolved into coarse laughter and gossip, and they recessed to loll about and slurp more stump-liquor. Then they lurched back to their instruments and fumbled again with their repertoire. The merrymaking continued into the night, and at last deteriorated into perfunctory clownage.

The men took to their bedrolls and the fire was allowed to smolder. One old soldier remained on watch with his back to us, quietly sucking a plaintive tune from his reed-willager. We stole down to the mess and made a quick meal from their leavings.

Turning back to our hole, we found their strange captive staring at us. We hesitated, unable to read the intent in his blank face and afraid to try to slip past him.

"You have knowledge," he said bluntly. At close quarters his voice seemed to emanate from a hollow tree-trunk. Bilch and I looked at each other and silently agreed that we had no alternative but to tell him what we knew.

"Your witch-mother was destroyed by Petolzia," I squeaked.

He nodded; apparently he had no difficulty understanding Filxxxish. "Then it is true." Again his neutral face contorted violently and we backed away in fear. He regained himself, poured a dram of sweet-smelling syrup from his jug and nipped at it. "The blue-black one is the most evil of them all. She has kept me trapped here like a faddle-bird since my earliest days, as a shame to the tribe. She even persuaded their Council to prohibit my mother from visiting."

A rush of air issued from his mouth-parts, in what I took to be a sigh. "You are Filxxxs, yes?" he asked.

"Yes," I said. We introduced ourselves. "And what is your name?"

"I have no name," he said.

A thick sadness clogged my throat. "But you must have a name," I blurted, and immediately regretted my words. To be without nose, eyebrows or mothering was punishment enough; but to go through life without a name was unthinkable.

"We'll call you 'Stitch'," Bilch said quickly, for it seemed the simplest solution: a hybrid of 'witch' and 'stick-man'. And it somehow reflected the notion that to be without a name was worse than being without a stitch of clothing, as it were.

"Then you know something of my fatherhood, too," Stitch said. His quick analysis of our neonym revealed an astute mind behind that blank face, a mind still sharp despite his incessant sipping of the numb-ing opium-vinegar. Indeed, that intelligence, which contrasted sharply to the moronic disposition of his wanton sires, was apparently his mother's main contribution to his makeup.

Bilch looked uncertainly at me. Should we tell him of the enchanted pellets? It seemed quite enough that Milord had been shanghaied by Lord Pontieu, sedated by Captain Worrant and kidnapped by a witch — yet here was still another menacing creature with a strong interest in Milord's acquisitions. What troubles were attracted to those accursed grains!

We took a circuitous approach, telling him of our voyage and

Milord's predicament, but omitting Haggleman Wimley's sordid account of Stitch's conception. He listened patiently, slowly twirling the cup at his side.

"You have not been complete," he said in his somber, hollow voice.

I feared to evade his probing any further, and reluctantly recounted the violent episode by the Perspex River. Whatever emotion this news aroused in him, his face remained unchanged; he only shook the last drops from his jug and growled irritably to find it depleted. Bilch, thinking that we had offended him, protested in a frightened voice that we knew no more, but Stitch held up a foreleg.

"I know." He pensively stroked the cup with the toothed processes that served him as hands. "You have reduced the number of my father's possible identities to about twelve, and for this I am grateful. Now you must guide me to them, for he and I would know each other instantly if we met." For the first time I noticed the bulge of compact wings concealed on his back. Though their size suggested that they were no more potent than those of a chicken, he implied that he was capable of powerful flight, unlike his tribe. Another power acquired from his mother?

Bilch and I conferred quickly through our eyes: we couldn't allow ourselves to be taken further away from Milord. "But your father and his brothers are imprisoned by witch-spell," I said, trying to sort through the dilemma. "Do you have the power to undo it?"

Stitch was silent a moment and then said, "No. I was never entrusted with amulets. But I can lay a web-trap for one of the witches, if she can be induced to come again to your Lord-master's manor, and force her to free my kin."

Bilch reflected for a moment, obviously skeptical. "Even though their entire coven wove the spell?" he asked.

"I think it could be done," Stitch said, but doubt weakened his words.

"Lord Benefice might well have some means to help you," Bilch said. Stitch tilted his head in what I construed as an interested expression.

"Yes, if he were free," I put in, picking up Bilch's lead. "Perhaps he could make some arrangement through the Protectioners' Guild, or…"

"Then the matter is simple," Stitch interrupted with an attitude of sudden resolution. "We must rescue Milord from Petolzia, our mutual enemy. And return to your home, and my tribe."

Tears of relief welled up in my eyes. Bilch dabbed at them, but was quickly overcome by tears of his own, and hugged me. We could hardly believe our luck at having found an ally in such desperate circumstances.

Bilch recovered himself and wiped his eyes. "We'll try to gnaw through the wooden strips above," he said, already scrambling up the blocage wall.

I started after him. But a sudden thought troubled me and I restrained Bilch with a touch. "How do we know where Petolzia has taken him?" I asked Stitch.

"She makes no secret of her lair's location. She fears nothing." I turned again to our climbing, but the thought of deliberately pursuing such a vicious hag cramped my stomach.

The watchman's reedy tune had long since trailed off, and he sat snoozing on his haunches by the fire. Bilch and I hiked up and began chewing on the laths. They proved to be no more than thin, layered frapwood, decorated with an elaborate bead-and-reel design. I surmised that it was some magical quality of this design, more than the physical resistance of the wood, that had frustrated Stitch's powerful shoulderings. But fortunately the engraving held no secrets against our sharp teeth, and we had soon enlarged an opening between the wall and the edge of the net.

We were startled by an enraged shout from below. I lost my hold and tumbled halfway down the wall's face, braking my fall only by clutching at its licheny stones til my legs were scraped raw.

"Alarm, alarm!" bawled the watchman. All over the courtyard the ruffians roused themselves from their drunken stupor and clutched at the weapons by their sides: short-swords, bludgeons and halberds, useful only at close quarters, but also a number of crossbows and deadly bolt-slingers. In no time they were stumbling towards our corner, some still hitching up their leather trousers or clumsily thrusting arms into their hauberks.

Stitch plucked me like a cookie from a plate and thrust me onto his back. The watchman was upon us, cocking his brawny arm for a sword-stroke, but I felled him with a burst from my *gnozzt*. Stitch nearly tore from my grasp as he propelled himself upwards through a hail of missiles. Luckily most of them were ill-aimed, being served up by startled, groggy men, and clattered harmlessly against the wall or sailed through holes in the net.

At the top of the wall Bilch joined us. "Hold to my neck," Stitch barked, and we clamped onto the fold of gristle below the back of his hairless head. He pushed off sharply from the wall. The splintered lath-edges caught his jerkin and ripped most of it off, revealing his chitinous gray skin and vestigial wings. With a twinge of revulsion I saw that he truly did resemble a huge bug, like his anonymous father.

We cinched forward to protect ourselves from the powerful whir-ring of his wings and shivered as the frigid Catsmouth air rushed past, chilling us to our bones. The shouts of the men below quickly faded away. To our right we heard the booming cry of a nocturnal gyrfalcon, but when the predatory animal flew close enough to see the fearsome roc on which we rode, it quickly aborted its assault.

Above us hung an incandescent full moon; darkness was just begin-ning to erode its edge. Despite the numbing cold, a part of my mind marveled at the strange fate that had brought us here, spurting into the ether astride this strange centaur, a hybrid of insect and witch.

A hybrid. Suddenly I remembered the lines quoted by Grandmage Mentharch: he would wear the witch's collar…

> "Til it's plucked off by a hybrid
> Of a savage and a witch."

Was our supernatural friend to be the savior of both Milord and Grandmage Mentharch?

VII

AN UNPLEASANT RENDEZVOUS

W e soared through the black night, and the crenellated embrasures of the huge fortress below shrank to pebbles in a gray mosaic. Above us the three major peaks of the Catscat Mountain chain thrust so far upward that we could but dimly make out the giant helm clouds impaled on their summits.

"Where is Petolzia's lair?" asked Bilch, his teeth chattering as he pressed against Stitch's smooth skin.

"Far up to our right. She lives near the coven's central cauldrons, for she has insinuated herself into a position of importance in their Council. But my guess is that she will soon leave her sanctum behind and plunder my mother's quarters. Where my birth occurred." The intense thrumming of his compact wings missed a beat, as did my heart. Stitch's escape, in which we had aided him, also meant a return to his very cradle — which, in Vulgia's permanent absence, Petolzia would now defile like some monstrous jay.

We veered left towards a deep coulisse amongst the stonework and began our descent. "Bilcher," I said in alarm, "what are we going to do when we get there?" We clutched each other as tightly as we clung to Stitch's neck-hump.

Overhearing us, Stitch said in a self-important way, "Have you forgotten the skills which those of my father's race possess against witch-kind?" But his rhetorical question worried more than reassured me, for batfowling is a skill usually employed by the stick-men as a group, with exemplary teamwork, and furthermore we were in the witches' own bailiwick. And Stitch, though powerful and intelligent, was yet a callow and overconfident youth, a green shoot by comparison even with Bilch and me, though we were far smaller in size. We had yet to see his judgment and skills tested.

We neared a hole in a huge serac. "My earliest home," said Stitch, "though I was taken from it before I knew myself and remember little of it." I smelled the faint spoor left by his departed mother. He swooped in a broad circle, reconnoitering, and then descended rapidly towards the roof of the hive. Now my nostrils twitched at a second, stronger witch-odor, acrid and fresh, and fear gripped my spines. The horrible realization struck me that Petolzia was already nearby.

"Wait, it's a trap!" I shrieked, but too late. Stitch, having no nose, had not detected the vile stench. He alighted, but his legs speared the roof as a fork pierces meringue; the granite, transformed by a magical cantrip, was now a kind of viscid papier-mâché rather than solid rock.

He sank helplessly. His wild leg-flailing only submerged us more deeply in the blubbery stuff, and within moments even his stubby wings had sunk. Bilch and I were forced to abandon our tenuous perch on his neck-fold and scrabbled onto the top of his hairless head. We skated wildly on its slippery surface til we caught hold of his twitching antennae, which bobbed like spars in a stormy sea.

Beneath us Stitch continued to struggle and kick, in a mighty but futile effort to climb out. Just before the foul jelly engulfed his face he shut his eyes and drew in a huge breath. Bilch and I climbed his antennae like two water-bugs on quivering reeds. Finally their very tips also slipped into the mire, and we threw our legs desperately outward in imitation of flying squirrels, hoping somehow to stay afloat. But the slime sopped and sucked at us like a huge leech. The central Catscat peak glowered scornfully down at us with the contempt of a haughty dowager: we were merely three pitiful insects wriggling helplessly in a fluctuant spot on her shoulder.

The dungish jam penetrated our mouths and we gagged. Bilch and I reached out frantically to each other, and yet wrenched at ourselves to avoid one another's eyes; for only one glance remained to share, one last visual embrace: that look of terrible familiarity when death comes to tear away the veil. But at last our accelerating panic was replaced by a warm, sweet resignation, and we opened our souls as easily as sharing soup. Then we slipped entirely into the muck and utter darkness.

For an eternity we drifted downward, a pair of flies in soft, black amber. I could just feel Bilch's touch at the tips of my paws. Gradually the realization dawned that we were not dying; for though we were as blind as seeds in a lemon, though the thick paste plugged our mouths and nostrils, yet by some miraculous alchemy we felt no need of breath for that endless time. To this day I cannot guess how long we spent in our eerie descent, nor do I understand the magic that sustained us, though later Grandmage Mentharch made a cursory attempt to explain it.

Then without warning we broke into empty space and plummeted down, whirling giddily through cold space. A layer of real stone and gravel ended our flight in stunning pain.

The impact scattered us across the floor of the hive. I groaned and rubbed my head, and strove to regain my senses. My supple body had taken the shock fairly well and nothing was broken. Faint starlight twinkled through the hole our passage had made in the ceiling; but already that tunnel, like a layer of mud through which a pebble has been dropped, was healing shut. To my side were pale puffs of breath-steam, large and small, rising above the motionless forms of Stitch and Bilch. And just beyond them rose another pair of breath-plumes, larger clouds drifting languidly above a mountainous supine figure: Milord.

I raced to him, my miseries and bruises forgotten, and licked his hand. It was frighteningly cold on my tongue, colder even than the great berrystone ring he wore, and perfectly still. I cuddled against his side, feeling only the texture of his waistcoat instead of his reassuring caress, and winced. I tugged desperately at his sleeve, but then remembered the dangerous cataleptic salve that imprisoned his consciousness, and the hazards of violating its spell. Reluctantly I backed away and sat emptily watching him; and at last turned my attention to the others.

Bilch seemed no more badly injured than I, though still betwattled by trauma. His fur was clogged with the greasy mire through which we had slid, and gravel-dusted overall like a wad of fresh dough rolled in wheat flour. With disgust I realized that I was similarly decorated, but there was no time for cleaning up. Beside me Stitch stirred. I tweaked his flank til he grunted and groggily sat up.

While they collected themselves I surveyed the cave. A clumsily hacked ledge of stone jutted from what I reckoned to be the west wall. Bits of half-eaten food decayed there, consumed by vermin. A bowl of brackish liquid stood precariously at the shelf's edge — perfume? — and next to it a well of liquid smoke, no doubt the source of the fumous eruptions that had constituted Vulgia's clothes.

Corpses of winged lice lay scattered on the floor, affording my first opportunity to see this witches' nemesis at close range and unmoving. They resembled muddy yellow hornets, the size of my collarbone, with brunneous blotches and twisted, barbed legs. Even in death, their mouth-suckers were set in a surly scowl and their bulbous eyes bored piercingly into mine. I shuddered.

Impaled on a hook above the ledge was a rotting chunk of grumelog, dragged from the humus of some dank forest floor. Swarms of black, saprophytic insects writhed and squirmed over it, nickering like fur-fleas. I inferred from the position of a gazing-stool in front of it that this buzzing lump of corruption had given Vulgia many hours of enjoyment in her wretched lair. If Thindle Spinkite could see this! The sight and smell would send a shock through his thin frame.

In the far corner stood a basalt chamber pot, reeking of excrement, and above this was Vulgia's slovenly pallet: a bundle of faggots, suspended from an overhead soffit by a giant web with strands as thick as hawsers from the *Dittaneer*. Dangling by one leg from this twig-clutter was an enormous, piebald spider.

My breath snagged in my chest like yarn on a cockleburr and a cold sweat sprang up on my neck. I recoiled, hissing and baring my teeth,

and aimed my *gnozzt* at the horrid thing. But the seconds crawled by —
it was an agony of time — yet the huge arachnid did not move.

"Nömmely is dead," said a hollow voice behind me. I jumped in
fright; but it was only Stitch. "She was linked to her mistress by a bond
of supernatural empathy, and surely perished at the same moment as
she," he said somberly.

I looked cautiously again at this lethal confection of chitin and
venom, and marveled that such a hideous monster should have been
mortally wounded by its own sweet sentiment — its one, invisible flaw.
No natural enemies save love itself!

This reflection led to the realization that the fallen Nömmely was
also a mascot, and consequently (repulsive notion) my colleague. This
grudging rapport was quickly replaced by gratitude for her death, without which I would have been little more than her bedtime snack, and
Bilch her dessert.

The sight of Nömmely brought Stitch fully around, and his grief as
well. His face contorted spastically. He fumbled at his pouch, found it still
empty of opium-vinegar, and trembled. But he was distracted by something under the ledge and picked it up tenderly in his shaking forelegs.

It was a large baby-rattle, fashioned from the humped carapace of
a crablike animal and containing a few of its own dried bones. Stitch
gently cradled this artifact of his infancy against his glabrous cheeks
and coaxed sibilant rattling sounds from it, while softly crooning this
brief cradle song:

> "A flea, a fly
> Go bye, go bye.
> Sleepy days
> Before you die."

At the corner of his eye glistened a large yellow tear. I felt a helpless
urge to comfort him, but could not move; the alien gulf balked between
us. Instead a hard, passionate resolve took shape: to avenge him, for she
had kidnapped Stitch from his own mother and then killed her. When
next I met Petolzia, I would somehow overcome her evil powers and
inflict a well deserved punishment. Perhaps the Protectioners' Guild

would help me and — But the object of my hostile musing could not be far off, for was it not her rank odor I smelled throughout the cave? Was it not she, after all, who had trapped us here?

Bilch joined me and transmitted his alarm: he too sensed Petolzia's imminence. Fear-static tingled in our fur. Bilch turned and shook Stitch's wrist-equivalent with his paws. "Stitch, get hold of yourself," he said angrily. "Your hour of combat is at hand!" Stitch only nodded his head slowly and sobbed; Bilch spat in disgust. We conferred briefly, but escape was out of the question while Milord slept. There was nothing to do but await Petolzia's arrival.

I surveyed our prison again. Though our entry-hole above had sealed itself, blocking the starlight, yet a glow still suffused the cave, and now its source became apparent: a translucent pastel pane that formed the room's east wall. Some impulse drew me to a closer inspection of this partition, and then to touch it.

At once the panel brightened and cleared to a bright crystal sheet. A garish, pulsing light threw our shadows jumping and bobbing in the witch-den behind us; and a drumming, insistent clamor, a non-stop rumbling and buzzing, aroused our ears to confusion and protest.

The source of this cacophony was Vulgia's private garden, enclosed within the now transparent panel. But no garden, or even jungle, was ever like this tangled sea! For this was a blooming, seething mass of twisted tubers and fronds, of luminescent boles and burls, of stamens and stipules and thorns and tendrils, and hyphae and inflorescences in unmeasurable profusion — a bright and bushy welter to send the mind reeling in panic. Every growth in that garden moved incessantly in its own peculiar way, like a fish in an aquarium: here a spray of orange spikelets swayed athetotically back and forth; there a shrub's black bark pulsed in some mysterious physiologic duty. Glistening gray ferns jerked and danced, and behind them a viscous purple liquor throbbed in the ropy veins of a squat tree-trunk. Never had I dreamed of such a nightmarish hothouse.

Bilch clutched my shoulder and looked about for some means of returning the enclosing barrier to its dark and silent state, for he had seen quite enough of this parlous nursery. But I could not contain my fascination. "Look," I exclaimed, and pointed to the right.

From a thicket fluttered a striped tomb-bat, her suckling baby nestled cozily under one wing. She flapped lazily to the left, traversing a narrow aisle in the center of the garden. From a bank of shrubs a brown tentacle darted upwards. Caught by surprise, the bat flitted awkwardly to one side, but this evasive maneuver dislodged her baby. It dangled in the air for an instant, squeaking shrilly in terror, then lost its hold and tumbled onto a broad, veiny leaf, which clapped shut with a sickening sound like that of a dead fish coshed against a stone. The nursing mammal was now only a squirming, leaf-wrapped lump, an inconspicuous nubble on the otherwise smooth surface of its leafy trap. Its mother flapped and cried frantically above, kept at bay by the darting tentacle. The baby's muffled squeaks persisted for one horrifying moment and then abruptly ceased. I turned away in revulsion.

But now it was Bilch who, engrossed by the weird drama, coaxed my gaze back to the scene. The devouring bush quivered and flew into a convulsion, thrashing forward and back in a vain effort to reopen its flat maw and vomit up the invader. The bat-lump swelled to the size of a fist and burrowed relentlessly down within the plant towards its roots, rending a jagged, gangrenous swath in the surface of the stalk as it pummeled its descent. Soon the entire plant took on a sallow, moribund hue, slumped to the ground and dissolved in a puddle of slime. Above it the mother bat circled in triumph, cawing and chortling, before soaring slowly back to her ally plants on the right.

Bilch gazed at this botanical guignol with a feverish interest that shocked and scared me. For a moment the conniving puppet of Captain Worrant returned, the miniature traitor who had bared his teeth at me so long ago, it seemed. Where was the lover I had taken? Where my secret trespasser against misfortune, my co-conspirator against witch-forces? I drew back in alarm.

A garter snake slithered from the leftward flora. Its small head and round, innocent pupils announced it as a benign worm, likely prey for some flying predator. It had hardly crossed the garden's barren central channel when a clawed appendage swept from the base of a cactoid growth on the right and clasped it with the crushing grip of a hawk.

At once the ophidian visitor revealed itself to be no tender, vulnerable morsel at all, but the tough lower member of a squat, gnarled tree standing a few yards to our left. Instantly it swelled to ten times its former length and thickness, becoming a ferocious tentacle with a ringed, raspy hide. It slashed lethally back and forth, an ogre's scythe whipsawed amongst a platoon of raw recruits. A phalanx of topaz-vines rushed to the counterattack, fastening countless suckers to it, until at last the thing ceased its flailing and lay as still as a brutally punished dog. Soon it sank entirely into the soil.

The sight of all this war and struggle left me exhausted. Did the two warring camps continue their deceptive sorties and counter-thrusts without stop? Or only when a curious touch illuminated their prison wall?

I bristled at a sudden dank chill. My nostrils smarted unbearably with the acrid vapor of burning poison-weed, and an eerie black light, infinitely dark, radiated from the back of the garden. At the far end of the pathway Petolzia erupted, cackling wildly and brandishing a dozen clinking bracelets on her spindly arms. It was a terrifying display, though I cannot say to what extent it was intended to paralyze us with fear, and how much merely a vain effort to disperse the cloud of parasites around her head.

The foliage buzzed with loathing. She clashed her bracelets together on both sides of the gauntlet, sending bolts of purple static into the brush, and the menagerie recoiled and snarled like leashed cow-cats. She strode the length of the path and into the cave, heedlessly searing a gaping hole in the panel.

Bilch and I tumbled backwards, head over paws to escape her advance, and jumped to the rock ledge. Bilch stumbled, knocking the smoke pot to the floor, and clouds of the acrid, suffocating stuff billowed upwards in the cave. But instantly that weird material clung to the walls and ceiling, regenerating itself continuously in place, just as it had on Vulgia's rickety body.

Stitch began frantically to saw his forelegs together, forming a few strands of silvery material in front of him. But it was too late: he had been taken by surprise, and in any case was in no condition to wage a fight. Petolzia loomed over us, making a staccato motion with both clawed hands. The sinewy circlets around her arms flew rattling through the clammy atmosphere and manacled Stitch's upper extremities to his lower where he sat, binding all four together as snugly as a bundle of firewood.

"You merely exchange one prison for another, stick-bastard," she rasped. Finding himself hopelessly pinned in his own former home, Stitch began to blubber uncontrollably.

"You will now remove the quell-paste from your puny master's forehead," Petolzia ordered, looking at me.

I flinched, but went to Milord's side and gingerly began wiping away the salve with a scrap of Stitch's jerkin, until only a faint layer remained. This soon evaporated and Milord stirred.

"Manservant Mumphreed…Manservant, remove my nightcap please," he mumbled. I pulled at his arm, but he only snorted and rolled over, so I pummeled his shoulder brazenly. He must wake up now!

"Hmm? Unh…" Milord muttered and all at once sat up, and rubbed his knees. He coughed from the smoke and asked me, "Where are we, Flick?"

"In Vulgia's own hive, Milord," I told him. There was so much to tell, I hardly knew how to begin. But in any case, Milord's attention was riveted on the grotesque sight and smell of Petolzia, who stood over him pointing her deadly fingers at his nose.

"The exact location of my prisoners," she said. Her breath was the exhalation of a sewer, and her nose dripped a bilious yellow rheum.

"I beg your pardon?" said Milord.

"The filthy stick-men, in my spell-cysts!" she shrieked. "Instruct your wretched Gasmaster to give them to me, or you and your ridiculous pets will suffer horribly!" I wondered just how she expected Milord to comply with this order, so far from Benefice Manor. Did she intend to transport us? And 'ridiculous pets', indeed! Did she think her swarming pests so lovely? Or Nömmely? The harridan advanced still closer above him, and where the hem of her rag-skirt touched his trousers, they shriveled like a moth flown too close to its candle.

Milord stretched sleepily and cleared his throat. "I shouldn't think your Council will be pleased to learn you've treated me so rudely," he sniffed. Bilch and I cringed, fearing that she would destroy him on the spot.

"I am supreme here," she raged, but somewhere within the utter cacophony of her voice was an unexpected hint of uncertainty, a note of hysteria that indeed confessed the existence of a social order to which she might have to answer. As though to reinforce her threats, Petolzia made a sprinkling motion and finger-thick snakes wound around Milord's arms like cables. He tried tentatively to flex them, but the snakes jerked taut, straightening his arms as gardeners adapt green twigs to their whim.

Milord yawned and closed his eyes complacently. "Allow me to remind you, Madame, of the existence of certain hypothecations and commercial treaties, formally endorsed by you and your peers, which obligate you, your agents and their consignees, to —"

Here Petolzia roared a syllable so violent and full of fury that description fails. It was at once a blood-curdling, chesty roar and a pathetic sob, sufficient to make Atlas himself cringe and massage his muscles in fright. She raged about the chamber, smashing things and slashing more holes in the garden wall with her spurred feet. She threw Nömmely's corpse amongst the plants, where it was promptly devoured by a giant trumpwort; she launched the grume-stump at Vulgia's hammock, dashing its twigs to splinters; and devastated the perfume-crock with a shock wave from the amulet hanging at her throat. The cologne's vile odor choked me to the brink of a swoon.

Milord crawled hurriedly away from her to the north wall of the cave, next to Stitch, and Bilch and I leapt from the ledge into his pockets. I took advantage of her distraction to communicate a few important circumstances to Milord: the theft of the bottlettes of brew, by Worrant and then Petolzia, though we knew not what she had done with them; Stitch's sad pedigree and Vulgia's violent death; and so forth. Milord was greatly saddened to learn of his Salvemaster's perfidious treachery, and much alarmed to learn that the witches' brew was again in custody of its makers, while more than half the lunar month had passed.

At last she regained herself somewhat and stood in front of us, her chest heaving, her straggly hair strewn wildly in a dirty veil over her face. "I'll drown you in brain sand and bog lemmings! I'll boil you in bugbane and roast you in solicitor's belch! I'll —"

"Piffle," said Milord, inspecting his cuffs, which had become slightly frayed during his long nap. Pride surged in my breast at his wondrous display of aplomb, though I feared its effect on her.

"I can well understand your vexation on account of the 'prisoners', as you refer to the offending stick-men," he said calmly. "But I cannot overlook the fact that those I previously returned to you were subjected to considerable…jeopardy, to frame the matter in its mildest terms." He was deliberately testing her. He glanced at the old shrew and recognized that she was again rapidly reaching her limit.

"But naturally I would consider making some concessions," he added quickly. "For example, I offer an item of great utility: an insecticidal bezoar, whose sponge-like action will effectively neutralize the gall-sting of your unwelcome companions." Here he glanced delicately toward the loathsome parasites swirling around her head, and at the dead ones littering the floor around us. Despite herself, interest flickered in Petolzia's eyes, more so in the beadier of the two.

"They are specially mounted in portable containers, which need only be emptied at intervals," he added with a note of technical pride. Petolzia hesitated.

Milord pressed his advantage. "And my barber-surgeons possess exceptional skill in the cosmetic reduction of that condition known as 'buphthalmos'," he stated, inspecting her abnormally enlarged eye with an air of discreet but sympathetic interest. "Or alternatively, you might wish to augment the contralateral globe, thereby creating ocular twins of stunning appeal and excellent function." I recalled the squabbling ministrations of Milord's physicians during the Gasmaster's illness, and chuckled to imagine them at the bedside of this ugly, spiteful old gummer.

Petolzia's interest was unmistakably aroused. Her protuberant eye brightened and swelled til she resembled a lopsided Cyclops, intently gauging the assertions of a desperate Odysseus. But now her calculating scrutiny gave way to the lowered gaze of vanity. She coyly brushed a lock of dirty hair from her face and plumped her skirt, and a faint tinge of pink informed her corpse-colored cheeks.

Milord made a debonair motion with his wrist and pushed his position to the hilt. "And of course we might include other succulent perquisites, such as —"

Petolzia abruptly tired of Milord's chaffering. "My prisoners!" she screamed. I wondered what additional magical guards Milord had arranged to secure the spell-cysts in his wall depositorium, for without such protections it would quickly crumble under an earnest assault by Petolzia or her kin.

Milord pursed his lips in mild dismay. "I fear we approach an impasse," he said ruefully. He drummed his pudgy fingers on the floor. "Though of course, an objective analyst might well ask which holds more importance for you: the prisoners themselves, or the amulets which they still clutch in their little pincers?"

This was a daring maneuver. For what could be more delicate than touching deliberately on a woman's jealousy? Petolzia would forever suffer from the knowledge that while her magical weapons had been vaporized by the stick-men's fires, Vulgia's had proved strikingly immune. In consequence she had been forced to a bitter humiliation: the acceptance of charity, in the form of substitute amulets provided by the Council.

Competing emotions played on Petolzia's wizened features: lust for Vulgia's invulnerable implements; hatred and jealousy of their dead owner; and contempt for Milord, and all other Lords as well. But her hesitancy was also plain to see, induced by Milord's shrewd offers and probing questions. He had impaled her will on an unexpected choice: the amulets or the prisoners. It dawned on me that Milord, doubtless with the Gasmaster's assistance, had cleverly held back from barter those spell-cysts which contained Vulgia's amulets. Petolzia had immediately destroyed the few pellets she had already received in trade, for the simple reason that they contained only her natural enemies.

Milord broke in on her rumination. "Of course, I would require the return of my bottlettes," he said smoothly. He looked at her without blinking.

This provoked Petolzia to another rage. "Never! Never again will the Council authorize the release of our precious coction to mortals!" she shouted.

"By what right do you speak for the Council?" croaked a new voice from the far corner.

Petolzia took a surprised step back. "Your Fulsomeness," she said, and curtsied automatically.

In the shadows shimmered an apparition: a hulk, glowing red like my eyelids when I close them against the sun, with two little dolls at its sides. Slowly the mirage came into focus, as three witches materialized — the witches' Council itself! They stood and surveyed Petolzia with an air of important judgment.

The central figure of the bizarre triumvirate was astoundingly obese; her stupendous girth dwarfed the two cachectic witches at her flanks as a cathedral looms over gargoyles on its balconies. She was clad only in a brilliant red robe, adorned with chains of rimecrust which descended like miner's ropes into the crevasse between her bosoms. The sallow blush in her unwrinkled cheeks implied a surprising degree of youth — no more than sixteen winters, I guessed. It was the first time I had seen such a stripling of a witch. And yet, as a member of the Council, she appeared to occupy a position of great power.

But the peremptory challenge had not come from her. Its source was instead the runtish crone to her right, and now that one waited irritably for a response from Petolzia. She stamped her knobby knees impatiently against the stone floor (for her skinny legs had met with some unspeakable amputation) and fidgeted with the hem of her tattered shift. Meanwhile the huge, red-clad adolescent next to her wrestled intently with the impossible problem of inserting her sausagy fingers into her fat nostrils, which she flared wide for this purpose.

Petolzia's mouth worked in a struggle for self-control. "I merely cite the Council's policy," she said at last, with unwilling deference. Her loss of face brought a cruel smile to the fat one's vacuous features, though she continued to grapple with her nose. The third witch, a wizened, rubbery thing half-hidden in the shadows beyond, confined herself to rubbing her hands and cackling softly.

"This is feckless," pronounced the amputee. "The Council requires no additional citation. And you have erred gravely by not reporting to us at once." Petolzia forced herself to another curtsy of acknowledgment, though she rather conspicuously gnashed what few snaggleteeth remained in her mouth. "However," continued the matron, "these infractions are offset by your successful extirpation of the renegade Vulgia, and the recovery of our elixir. On balance, the Council would be pleased." The red behemoth's smile weakened, and she left off her nasal explorations in favor of nervously sucking her enormous thumb.

I glanced into the broken nursery. The plants had ceased their end-less stabbing and parrying, and had taken up a most alarming project: everywhere they were pulling up their own roots from the rotten soil and becoming mobile! Indeed, some of them had already formed squadrons in excited preparation for an exit from their stony jail.

Even as I watched, a shrub inched to a gash in the panel and extended long, blood-red polyps through it. These stretched their goose-like necks to within a few feet of us and shivered with ghoulish interest. Stitch looked on in wary agitation, turning his head slowly from side to side; the giantess sniggled and pointed at his plight. I tugged frantically at Milord's pocket, but could not attract his attention.

Her Fulsomeness shuffled forward on her knees and continued. " 'Would be pleased,' we say. But you commit a much greater offense: attempted extortion of a mortal-in-contract." Her voice was harsh as pumice. "This arrogation of our authority threatens the entire Coven." Slowly she raised her scrawny arm and pointed it like some cancerous musket at Petolzia, who looked as uneasy as it is possible for a witch to look. "You will cease and desist; a Council deputation will resolve this matter with the Protectioners' Guild, in accordance with established protocol. Further, you will return the recaptured elixir to this Council at once, and remand yourself for further discipline."

Petolzia clenched her fists til green sparks sputtered in them. Breathing heavily, she backed towards the wall. From between the thin black sills of her lips a hiss escaped, a sign of rebellion which widened her superior's eyes with amazement and then outrage.

"You dare to question my directive?" Her Fulsomeness screamed, shaking with fury.

"Kill her, Mumma, kill her!" interrupted the fat witch in a shrill voice.

There was a blinding crash and purple smoke belched from the spot where Petolzia had stood. A blast of heat, as though a furnace door had blown open, threw us violently against the wall. But this very heat also saved us from the red polyps, for they shriveled up and shrank back into their garden.

With a touch of her amulet the witch-chief dissipated the smoke: no trace of Petolzia remained. "Her freedom will be short-lived," she said under her breath, and cursed vilely. Her giant daughter, already losing interest in the matter, dabbed perfume from Vulgia's broken pot under her arms. The third witch, for reasons mysterious to me, burst into uncontrollable weeping and began chewing the long, complicated queue into which her black hair was tied.

Her Fulsomeness turned on her stubby knees in silent rage and pointed her finger at Milord. I thought surely we had met our end, and Bilch and I offered quick prayers to Filfalxxx.* Milord leaned on his manacled elbows in an awkward attempt to rise.

"Kill him, Mumma, before the plants do!" piped her daughter, throwing the perfume aside.

But Mumma hesitated, dropped her arm and turned away in irritation. "Pah," she spat, and made a careless gesture with her other hand, at which the snakes disappeared from Milord's arms.

The huge one stamped her foot petulantly, shaking the floor of the cave. "Oh Mumma," she whined, "you never do funny things any more. Auntie would —"

"Silence, Phiddla!" screamed her mother, administering a vicious slap to her huge daughter's crotch. In the corner Auntie's weeping was abruptly replaced by insane giggling, which she attempted unsuccessfully to stifle with both hands. Phiddla sniveled and wiped her eyes with a fold of her red dress.

Milord stood up unsteadily. Bilch reached from his pouch and brushed some of the gravel from his coattails, while I preened the singed hair from his temples. He performed an elegant though shaky bow. "Your Fulsomeness," he said with a forced smile, "my associates and I wish to express our gratitude for your timely intervention."

"Do you?" she asked sarcastically.

"Indeed. And in return," said Milord grandly, "at the very next session of the Assembly I shall speak most vigorously against certain tariffs with which the Consortium is now unjustly burdened."

Her Fulsomeness regarded Milord with an intensity that sent chills down my spines and into my *gnozzt*. "That is awfully good of you, Lord Benefice," she said with stomach-churning emphasis. Milord rubbed

---

* Untranslatable; roughly, a semi-theistic entity composed of countless Filxxx ancestors.

his chin uncertainly; the outcome of our unexpected meeting with this grotesque trio was still much in doubt.

At last Milord took note of the attacking vegetables. "And if I may ask a trivial favor," he added hastily, "perhaps Your Highness would consent to provide us some assistance with transportation. At once." Several stalks of fighting saxifrage slithered rapidly towards us, their needle-covered bursicles weaving back and forth, and a phalanx of poisonous squall-marrow pods crept steadily toward Stitch. Milord took a reluctant step closer to the Council, away from the plants.

Her Fulsomeness chuckled. "We shall take the matter under advisement," she said. The three of them abruptly executed a series of coordinated triple pirouettes, flouncing their skirts regrettably high above their waists, and resumed their original positions.

"We have conferred," she said, peering at Milord, "and this is our conclusion. You, Lord Benefice, are on Catscat Mountain by virtue of a criminal act: abduction by an outlaw Sister. That individual is no longer in evidence, and consequently this Council is not accountable for her actions. Furthermore, you are an accomplice to the illegal escape of the stick-bastard. And finally, all of you are intruders in the private domain of a Sister."

This analysis of our unfortunate situation seemed to me terribly unjust. Milord obviously shared this opinion, for he raised his hand to interrupt, but thought better of it.

"Such offenses arouse the Council to severe displeasure," she continued, "and would normally inspire an equally severe retribution. However, we graciously take note of your significant role in the affairs of the Assembly, and therefore have elected to adopt a more neutral posture. Specifically, this Council now withdraws without further action. This is our decision." Her look of finality forbade any further blandishments.

She turned to leave, stopped and turned back. Pointing contemptuously at Stitch, still bound and sprawled against the wall next to his rattle, she said, "The stick-bastard is entitled to a prophecy." She stepped smartly behind Auntie and yanked her queue, thereby choking off her vacuous giggling. Auntie lowered her voice to an unlikely baritone and pronounced,

"An utter lack will lead to wrack and then
A fray will bring a final sting
From kin and angry men."

"So," said Her Fulsomeness. "His fate is sealed. For this reason alone we spare his miserable life." With a flick of her wrist she dissolved Stitch's bindings.

Auntie spun her hair-queue high above her head with both hands. "Vulgia's plant-pets make good company," she said and fell again to hysterical laughter, which Phiddla terminated with a crushing box on the ear.

The giantess pouted and gave her mother a spiteful look. "I wanted you to burn him up!" she said.

Her Fulsomeness jabbed Phiddla in the ribs with an elbow, at which the huge witch-child cowered and again resorted to lavish sniveling. "Out, Phiddla!" said her mother in exasperation. Phiddla turned and waddled into the wall with a loud *thlump*. "No, idiot!" her mother shouted, impatiently repositioning an amulet on her daughter's massive bosom. "Like this." They vanished through the wall, leaving an odor of vaporized pewter and sweat.

Auntie's disquieting prophecy appeared to forecast Stitch's death; and yet the oracular poem cited by Grandmage Mentharch — a bit of doggerel which had probably also been authored by Auntie, the only witch I knew of who was given to such rhymed prattling — implied that Stitch would remove his noisome collar. Stitch's future was a paradox. And what had Petolzia done with Milord's bottlettes?

But there was no time for contemplation. The plants now filled the cave with their hostile growling, and advanced menacingly on all sides: thorny black and gold bulbs, violet panicles smelling of antimony, umbels bearing circlets of curved teeth. The vicious swipe of an amber cud-thistle opened an angry scratch on Stitch's ankle, and his thick gray blood oozed to the floor. In a moment the plants would swell into full riot.

A devil's-tongue vine surged forward on the floor like the prow of an ancient ship and wound around Milord's foot. In panic Bilch and I squeaked and banged our paws on his chest, but he seemed unconcerned and merely stood rummaging in the capacious pockets of his waistcoat, muttering to himself. "Feline Navigator, no…Ovid Suppressant XIV —" he chuckled, as though at some pleasant recollection "— Red Moronish? Hmmph; a bit late," he murmured through tightened lips and scowled. "Ah! Noxious Fellium VI." He shook his leg absentmindedly as the vine coiled higher and more tightly around it.

Milord drew a small flask from his pocket and applied several drops of its ruby-red contents to his palms, which he then rubbed thoroughly together. He waved his hands above him in a complex pattern and recited loudly,

> " 'Furting foliage, recoil in soil!
> Philodendrons, wilt in silt, or
> Feel the sting of hateful philtre!
> Lurking lilies, pale and fail!
> Lie within your vile nest, lest
> This liquid bludgeon be your test!' "

Milord's cheeks got quite ruddy and his eyes sparkled. At once there was a sense of retreat among the plants, and their angry susurration subsided to a fretful mutter. Many of them crept back through the holes in the light-panel, sliding over its jagged edges into the garden. The vine on Milord's leg relaxed and dropped to the floor like a piece of discarded lingerie.

As a playing-card king bears his axe, Milord cocked his notebook in his right arm. "Halt, or feel my wrath!" he called sharply. The plant-assembly obediently ceased their movements, and a hush came over them. Milord consulted his notes again and intoned,

> " 'Crinkum-crankum, dirt to sky,
> Heekee-peek, transmogrify!' "

The plants hesitated and their murmuring rose in pitch. Milord waited, then reproached himself and hurriedly flipped through several pages of his manual. "No no," he said to himself. "Shouldn't attempt the whole mountain…Ah! The Crack. Yes, much simpler." Already his delay had provoked an ominous air of mutiny. He looked up, made a sign towards the wall behind us and said,

> " 'From root and stalk and monstrous pistil,
> Extend between these rocky teeth
> A tongue of fiery, pulsing gristle
> And take us all from cave to heath!' "

The plants coalesced swiftly into an imploding mass. Ferns entwined with black fuchsias, taproots crushed against bracts and calyces. They tangled themselves together more and more tightly, grappling and grunting like oiled wrestlers. From this inextricable bolus a single, orange-hot stamen gradually emerged, a glowing prong extruded from a blacksmith's forge.

The fire-tongue advanced steadily to a corner of the cave, pushing and probing. It quickly found a tiny crack, delved into it and drove forward inexorably, widening it into a crevice. The mountain shook and rumbled in protest, and chunks of dusty rock fell all around us from the ceiling, til I feared the entire cave would collapse; but at last the walls parted with a leviathan groan, exposing a crude passageway. A short distance beyond it lay an open landscape, bathed in the weak light of dawn — a sweet sight!

I looked questioningly at Milord. "A simple Spell of Incontrofutable Effraction," he said with a shrug. "One of the Grandmage's donations." I recalled the implements he had given to Milord during his visit and made a mental note to thank him upon our return. If we returned; and if he were still capable of understanding ordinary communication. But such fatalistic broodings were useless, and I shook them from my mind.

The fire-tongue retreated and began to separate again into its component plants. Still weak with despair and grief, Stitch could hardly stand on his own, but Milord dragged much of his considerable weight onto his round shoulders and hustled him into the newly formed exit. Soon we emerged from the tunnel and began our trek up a steep escarpment, walled on both sides by great bluffs of rottenstone. The air was chilly and still. Directly above, a gibbous white-stone moon faded away in the dawn.

The slope was copiously littered with talus, forcing each of Milord's footsteps to the test of a different-sized rock or boulder. Somehow he managed to trundle Stitch through that stony detritus for perhaps an hour, but then stumbled as fatigue and long-denied hunger overtook him.

"Perhaps the downhill course would be preferable," he said uncertainly. Bilch reminded him of the armed mercenaries and formidable military installations we had discovered below. Inspired more by exhaustion than reason, Milord shook his head and argued the question weakly with himself, but pushed on.

At last we crested a wide ridge. Stitch slumped down in a heap. Puffing heavily, Milord leaned against a boulder and we gazed down the mountainside. Miles below, Catsmouthport lay covered by a bluish haze, braced on each side by the fortified foothills over which Bilch and I had flown on Stitch's back. A rayless morning sun hung isolated in the sky like an orange, having no more effect than the moon on the nippy air around us.

A rustling noise jarred the silence below. Less than a furlong away, a clot of plants jostled and clambered noisily over the rocks.

Milord clapped his hands in dismay. "The error is mine," he said. "Instead of specifying 'present company only', I said, '…take us all from cave to heath'." Bilch pressed Milord's chest by way of consolation, which I thought a very sweet gesture; but I was too anxious for condolence. Already the plants' remurmuring swelled to a crescendo.

The fresh peril roused Stitch from his torpor. He pointed up the mountain. "There, in the fog beyond those crumbling pinnacles: no plants will dare pass into that brumous region, for it is haunted by the dead souls of an ancient warrior-race." The forbidding stratum to which he gestured was dressed with shiny verglas, portending much colder temperatures and even riskier footing. But there could be no doubt of our direction, for to both sides of us the slope tailed off to impossible cliffs, and Vulgia's murderous garden approached steadily from below.

We resumed our ascent in earnest. Stitch now shambled with us independently on all fours, occasionally testing his wings in chickenish hops. The way steepened. At every step Milord was forced to use his hands to guide his substantial weight; his lambskin gloves were soon torn to shreds, and his hands raw and bruised. He became quite testy, alternately castigating Lord Pontieu or the Council for our troubles.

"Blackleggery! Pontieu will pay dearly for his nefarious transgressions," he threatened, and roughly shoveled a rock down the mountain behind him. "The rudeness of her," he exclaimed in disbelief a moment later, "leaving us to fend for ourselves in this desolate environment. The Consortium's supply of lap-toys will be cut off!" Milord illustrated this last remark by slashing the air with one arm and almost lost his balance. He lapsed into an unwontedly sullen silence, which I did not interrupt, and we continued our trudging.

Normally Milord takes great pleasure in the use of sweet colognes and corporeal sachets, but now, after days of enforced slumber in dirty circumstances and the exertion of our hike, his scent was unpleasantly rank. Bilch shared a look with me and twitched his nose: we were no less in need of a proper bath.

Presently Bilch wriggled his ear as though irritated by a fly, and poked his head above the hem of our pocket. "Do you hear it?" he whispered to me.

"The plants are falling far behind us, Bilcher, never fear. In a few minutes we'll be safely hidden in the fog," I said, stroking his nervous ear.

"No, not that," he said. "Listen."

I cocked my head. From the mists ahead came an eerie creaking sound, like the *krretcch* of a dried house-clam being levered open by hungry shore-peasants. In my puppyhood that sound meant succulent bits of valve-meat in my dish after the nursing hour. But this was a more complex and disturbing report, faintly metallic and bearing a sense of many strains or even voices combined in one. Bilch's eyes told me he was as mystified as I. We settled in our pouch in anxious anticipation and sniffed at the frigid breeze for some clue.

The slope was not as steep now, and Milord and Stitch hiked briskly along a winding cliff under great overhanging brows of granite. Whenever the rock's face opened to the north, we heard again the puzzling *krretcch* from somewhere ahead. Our path narrowed dangerously along an especially salient outcropping, forcing Milord and Stitch to mince their steps above a frightening precipice; but then, much to my relief, the way gave onto an expanse of open terrain. A jumble of boulders thinned to a gravely surface, scattered here and there with sparse vegetation, and then to a wide field, covered with a thick carpet of grayish-red furze.

A hundred yards to either side loomed grainy black crags, whose damp lichen filled the air with a strong musty smell. A weak gust of wind fluttered at our backs, bearing with it a last faint echo of the clamoring plants far below, and died; then all was stillness.

Milord's gold-buckled shoes sank into the grassy quadrangle, and he stopped to reconnoitre. At its far end was the forbidding bluff of icy rocks, shrouded in mist, toward which Stitch had directed us. The cloud of steam over those rocks flowed slowly back and forth as we watched, more like a rising and falling tide than a bank of fog. It massaged its captive stones as the surf caresses a sailor's beached corpse; and with each ebbing deposited another layer of frozen verglas that glistened like snail-slime.

The fog receded further than before, and we could just discern a broad, low archway in the rock. Above this, brutally carved into the ancient stone, were runes the size of carriage wheels. Milord stared at them for a long moment, the skin next to his eyes crinkling into crow's feet, but could make no sense of them.

The hush was broken again by the strange creaking sounds, and we understood that they emanated not from the fog itself, but from the archway below, or something beyond it. Each of us heard different things in those sounds: Bilch whispered that the grating noise reminded him of the *Obnounce Dittaneer's* rusty deadeyes rattling in heavy seas, while I recalled Ranktwo Sparseman's unfortunate experiment with the bass herd-fiddle (a venture which was, thankfully, short-lived). "Farberwile?" blurted Milord in surprise, for he had thought to hear the ratcheting of the good Masterfootling's arthritic knees when he hurries, and looked at me sheepishly when he realized his mistake.

Stitch regarded us with an unreadable expression. "Come," he said. Milord followed him hesitantly toward the archway, his scuffed shoes squelching in the marshy heath. Bilch and I thought again of the horrors we had discovered in Vulgia's hive, and wondered with anxious resignation where Stitch would lead us this time.

The archway yawned ahead like a black throat, closer and closer, and the *creaks* came louder. Stitch stepped in and was instantly engulfed by the darkness. Milord stiffened, and I smelled his fear; but after a quick, hopeless glance behind, he followed. Instantly the dark mist surrounded us too, cold and clammy, and palpated us like an octopus. Milord stumbled blindly forward. "What manner of—" he cried, but in an instant the fog retreated as quickly as the curtain on a stage and formed a misty ceiling an arm's length above our heads.

We emerged from the arch onto a broad terrace of hewn granite squares, each perhaps twenty yards on a side. At the center of each such flagstone an enormous iron ring was imbedded on its edge, so that an orchard of circular iron dolmens receded into the cold haze as far as the eye could see. Each was as tall as Stitch, who stood three or four hands taller than Milord, and wide enough that a bull pig could easily have been driven through the emptiness it encompassed.

"You see here the undeniable evidence of a departed warrior-race," said Stitch, startling me with his deep voice. "The fabled Thug-rings of Thaum, rusting unto eternity." The source of the grating sounds was now plain. We gazed at the monumental array, groaning and creaking like a herd of mechanical cattle in the fog.

"Long ago the demiurge Thaum, captain of his legendary race, anchored them here as mounts for his huge engines of war. He easily subdued the Realm with those terrible juggernauts: catapults charged with dreadful, telepathic ordnance; volcanic mortars, whose range was the fear of half the world; and even a great lens, designed to focus the sun's fire on ships in the North Channel." The monstrous toroids loudened their chirking, as though in eager hearing of their own tale. "But despite their fearsome engines, Thaum's Thugs were at last defeated by unknown enemies and all of them put to the sword. Knowing that such a loss was more agonizing to Thaum than even a difficult death, his foes spared him and departed.

"Thaum was determined that his loyal thanes should know the depth of his esteem for them. By impulse of a sacred onager, or catapult, he discharged their bodies into the sea; but their valiant souls he encased in these rings, that they might grasp their legendary weapons forever, even in death. Finally, consumed by sorrow and grief, and having conferred his last respects upon them, Thaum threw himself far into the bowels of the earth, never to return.

"For centuries afterward, particularly when coaxed by squalls or night-spirits, the soul-rings used to raise their voices in mighty, booming cries that rattled up and down the mountain, inspiring fear even in the witches' ancestors. But Thaum's enemies denied his troops their last intended honor: they left behind them the corrosive chill-fog, which as you see has long since destroyed their great weapons.

"Now the rings, heartbroken with longing for their beloved master, bereft of their awesome weapons and shot through with rust, can only mutter hoarsely to each other of their certain dissolution in salty air and time. Many of their cries are recollections of some unique fragment of history — that gaudy, bloody garment with which Time arrays herself; but most are tragic wish-songs, beseeching Thaum to return again."

This explanation lent their croaking a fresh poignancy, and subtle differences in their voices became apparent. From deep in the foggy shadows came an especially desperate *cree-eak*; perhaps its singer was recalling a friend's death in battle, or expressing some unbearable pang of grief for Thaum. Another, feebler creak conveyed the dutiful territoriality of an old mutt, barking through grizzled whiskers by his master's hut; and yet another bore an inexplicably quizzical twinge. The rhythmic chorus was as mesmerizing as a sea of gigantic crickets.

The fog descended again without warning and thickened, and choked off all but the hardiest of the creaks. It became a still, deliberate sleet, taking us in its grip with the certainty of a vise. Milord gasped for breath and pulled at his coat, but it had become as stiff as a cerement and gave no more warmth than shavings of ice. He stamped sluggishly back and forth, hugging his shoulders. "I fear we shall freeze," he said hoarsely. Bilch and I huddled further into our pouch, with little effect.

Throughout our climb I had vaguely assumed that we would make a fire when we stopped; but now the realization dawned that there was absolutely nothing here to burn. Stitch gathered some loose stones into a crude bulwark, but as there was no wind to shield against, it had little value, and even he began to shiver. I felt the first stirrings of despair.

How many hours passed I cannot say, for time itself was slowed by that terrible and malicious freeze. Now and then I looked up at Milord's grimacing face, hoping he would extract some marvelous spell or condensed nourishment from his wallet, but to no avail. We huddled together and occasionally glanced blindly into the mist, and listened. The creaking sounds drifted back and forth on all sides, reduced but stubbornly refusing to be suppressed altogether.

Soon it seemed we no longer paid any attention to the urgent signals of gnawing hunger within and cold wetness without. We wanted only to listen to this plaintive symphony, and awaited its every next note with indescribable yearning. Milord shifted our sitting-stone closer to the nearest ring, drawn to it as though by a magnet, and listened; then he wanted to be closer still, but found the moving of the stone too tedious a chore, and abandoned it to sit on the frigid ground directly in front of the ring. Through its great center-hole we could view the others, but it was to the song of this one round device that we now devoted our full and eager attention. Its occasional vibrations thrilled us with a special joy and satisfaction, as if it were an old friend just returned with marvelous tales of adventure; we told each other how smooth and plangent it sounded, and wondered at the countless numbers of soul-voices speaking from within its mysterious recesses.

Soon Stitch sat within the ring itself. He spread his forelegs in an attempt to straddle one of its two curved trunks where it entered the terrace, and pressed his ear close against its coarse, rusty metal. He began humming in a low, hollow voice, anticipating the ring's next emanation, and when it came he shuddered with pleasure. Bilch and I nodded our heads in mad, earnest agreement. Milord repositioned himself more closely with each syllable, and let his coat fall open to the freezing cold. We were entranced.

"I want nothing more," Bilch said with a fervent sigh, and crawled from our pouch to lie against the ring.

"Yes," I said at once; for no other thought or plan could match the irresistible appeal of those endless voices. Stitch curled up where he lay and closed his browless eyes, and abandoned himself to rapture. Milord pressed his chin deeper on his breastbone and sank against the cold metal. Already Bilch was unconscious, his paw pressed against the vibrating rust.

My last thought, before I too fell into oblivion, was of a legendary shipful of sailors on the black waters of ancient Greece, and of the Sirens who stirred their passion.

VIII

AN EVENTFUL FLIGHT

M y coma was interrupted by a vivid dream: a tall blur of brightly colored stripes, floating in gray mist. I giggled at its pretty hues — pumpkin orange, buttery yellow, a brilliant claret — and thought, "It wants to drift away!", which seemed a wonderful idea.

Below this puzzling apparition was an enormous, rectangular lemon cake. I squeaked brashly to be given a crumb of it, but this ill-mannered plea only aroused a crackling pain in my parched throat, and so I tried to escape again into dreamless blackness.

But the mirage persisted, and now Lord Roundabout drifted from the scumbled stripes into our forest of rings. Like a chubby windmill he tried futilely to wave aside the clouds of freezing fog. "Lord Benefice?" he called, "Friendlord Cantilouve... are you here?" His urgent, muffled shouts were like those of a traveler banging at the door of an inn on a dreary winter night.

He wandered to our pitted brown ring. "Aha! Here you are!" he exclaimed, and called excitedly over his shoulder to someone hidden in the mists. He bent down and peered at Milord from under his bushy, ice-caked brows and shook him, without response.

"And Flickamerry!" he said. His voice echoed as though in some distant, empty gallery. In my dreamy state I thought this very amusing and laughed out loud. He seemed so excessively concerned! "Hallo? That is Flick, isn't it?" he inquired again, a bit irritably.

A gust of frightfully cold air raked me and I came full awake, and discovered that my dream was reality. Lord Roundabout smiled wearily through the layers of ice on his pink cheeks. He turned aside Milord's frozen lapel and cupped his mittened hands to shield me from the wind. Seeing Bilch he asked in some surprise, "And who might your friend be?" But without waiting for an answer he scooped us both into his watch pocket. It was as warm as a fresh-baked muffin, and his generous waist made a wonderful pillow. To his credit, Lord Graham Fontleroy Roundabout did not wait for explanations or pressure to help a mascot, or even a mascot's friend!*

Two of Lord Roundabout's burly retainers appeared and lifted Milord to his feet. He was still obtunded, and thick flakes of rust were imbedded in his ears and neck where he had slept against the ring. Lord Roundabout drew off his heavy fearnought cape and threw it over Milord's shoulders, then rubbed his chest and lightly slapped his cheeks, until all at once he came to himself and exclaimed, "Closelord Fontleroy!"

"Closelord Cantilouve!" returned Lord Roundabout, beaming, and embraced him. Their joy was equaled only by my own. But Milord was at the edge of exhaustion. His cheeks were as hollow as a lightning-gutted tree, and bruised, frostbitten skin showed between the tattered remains of his gloves.

"Where are we?" asked Milord, stupefied. He swayed on watery legs, holding Lord Roundabout at arm's length, and sought his eyes.

Lord Roundabout smiled and nodded in the bland manner of one whose hearing is weak; for he had girded himself against the seductive

---

* That sympathy proved vital some years later, when events took an unexpectedly difficult turn for Albanderry's mascots.

power of Thaum's rings by stuffing his ears and those of his men with clots of beeswax.

"What place is this?" repeated Milord, but Lord Roundabout only put his arm through Milord's and coaxed him away from our ring, which protested the separation with a wild groan. This agitated Milord and he turned back, but the two footmen at once restrained him. Bilch and I were also powerfully drawn by the ring's plaintive creak and tried recklessly to enlarge the peephole in our pocket, but Lord Roundabout had doubled it over in such a way as to prevent our escape.

He produced another wad of beeswax from his cuff, divided it in half and deftly inserted the two plugs into Milord's ears, whereupon he ceased his struggling and smiled sheepishly. "What magnificent silence!" he said. Lord Roundabout shrugged helplessly and pointed to his own blocked ears. "I said, 'What magnif—'" Milord repeated at the top of his lungs, but stopped himself. Both men burst into laughter and threw arms over one another's shoulders, and turned to our waiting airship.

For that had been the basis of my bizarre dream: a towering, gaily decorated balloon, lovingly stitched from colorful taffeta and swollen with heated air. A narrow banderole snaked from a whip-pole at its top, emblazoned with Lord Roundabout's green-and-silver heraldry. The tall sac strained impatiently at its guys, puffing and crinkling like pastel curtains in a country kitchen window.

On the terrace below the balloon was its boxy yellow cab, or gondola—the giant pastry I had imagined. And this was a confection of sorts, for its floor and sides were luminous wafers of beveled saffron gemstone, supported by a lacy net of wicker. Its chest-high railings were decorated with ornate Vitruvian scrollwork, which alone must have required six months of diligent labor from a dozen woodscribes. The cab stood on legs of delicate jamwood, exquisitely carved in the eccentric cabriole style, which exuded a subtle raspberry fragrance—a welcome contrast to the fog's dank, meaty scent. Withal the artisans of Albanderry had crafted a marvel of aerostation.

"Stitch!" said Milord, stopping suddenly. Our unlucky guide still lay limply in the ring. Milord pointed to him and made urgent gestures to Lord Roundabout, who replied with a bewildered expression:

did Milord seriously suggest that a stick-man should accompany us? Milord nodded vigorously, gesticulating to the effect that explanations could be made later. Lord Roundabout probed him with a long, grave look, but at last reluctantly motioned to his footmen to assist.

The two pursuivants had been standing by, slapping themselves and blowing clouds of steam through raw, pursed lips. At Lord Roundabout's order they looked amazed. Servants and humble they might be, but the handling of a stick-man was obviously a task they regarded as vile and far beneath their station. I recalled that yeomen of their class traditionally come from Albanderry's coastal provinces, where savage bands of stick-men still marauded as recently as twenty years ago.

There was an uneasy moment of grumbling and backpedaling, which Lord Roundabout terminated with a stern glance. They bent to the chore, their movements eloquent with loathing and resentment, and soon the still-unconscious Stitch had been trundled into the cab. His gangling form took up more than half of its width.

In the gondola a third footman stood pumping a bellows at the mouth of a forge. A broad, round pipe conducted its heat upwards into the balloon. But the frigid atmosphere had nevertheless reduced the balloon's thermal mass to a critical point and threatened to shrink it irreversibly. "Halloa, Yeoman Threefoot!" shouted Lord Roundabout, spinning his arm over his head, and the forgeman responded by redoubling his efforts. Shrouded in a foggy orange glow, he gave the impression of a ghostly devil reveling at work in a fiery den. Soon the balloon regained its bosomy swell and tugged lustily at its tethers, buffeted by gusts of chilly fog. We bundled into the cab, and the three yeomen made preparations to take off.

Lord Roundabout fussed over a pelorus, sighting through its slotted vanes this way and that into the fog, and finally gave the signal to throw off the guy-ropes. The ship gave a sharp jerk and leaped sideways from the terrace. We yawed out of control, narrowly missing several rings, and Stitch was flung like a lump of coal into a corner of the gondola; but after an anxious moment we rose directly upward. The rings moaned and creaked feverishly below, and I swore they struggled at their stony moorings in vain hopes of escaping with us.

We broke abruptly through the fog's upper surface into a dazzling clear blue sky. Bilch and I hugged each other for joy.

"Oh la! Ahoy!" shouted Milord, for a jagged black crag lay dead ahead at the terrace's edge, on collision course. The forgeman plied his bellows furiously, his black coattails flapping up and down, and his mates threw what seemed half a cord of wood into the furnace, til with a buoyant pulse that pushed my stomach halfway into my mouth we lifted just over the top of the deadly rock, so close that I could see its crown of lightning-scars like streaks of melted brown butter.

Now only the spectacular Catscat Peaks loomed before us, wearing their cottony queen-shawls of pure snow. The sun shone with splendid candor, and shady rainbows shifted in the striated canopy over our heads. The dreary fog below quickly became an innocent blanket sliding slowly back and forth over its concealed rocks and rings, and beyond it the nasty slope we had climbed before our hibernation dwindled to a distant smudge. Far to the east we could just see a ridge of white haze marking the North Channel, reduced to a trickle.

The ship's gyrations gradually petered out, and we floated smoothly through the sky on a steady wind out of the west. Lord Roundabout doffed his greatcoat and loosened his pocket, allowing Bilch and me to scamper out. He removed his earplugs and pointed to the east. "That is how we bear," he said, "though much maneuvering and good luck will be necessary to reach Albanderry."

Milord was too distracted by his disheveled condition to interest himself in our course. His elegant frock suit was damp and rumpled, his gloves were in shreds, and grime smeared his neck. Lord Roundabout put down his pelorus. "Forgive me, Closelord. Please refresh yourself." He gestured to a privacy cabinet in one corner of the gondola. "The accommodations are less than we enjoy at home, but…"

"Thank you, Closelord Fontleroy," said Milord. He disappeared for a short while, during which Bilch and I also took the opportunity to preen ourselves, using a pan of hot water kindly provided by the forgeman. Milord emerged in a simple but well cut suit of ruffled gray twill. He had washed and applied a salve to his hands. His hair was brushed with a pleasant tincture and he appeared well renewed.

The temperature was now delightfully balmy. My Lords flumped down on the plush couches lining the gondola's walls; Stitch remained sound asleep in a corner. One of the footmen descended through a trapdoor into the storage locker below and emerged with baskets of food. Soon the forgeman served us possets of ale-milk mulled with the poker from his furnace, and thoughtfully included a separate pannikin for Bilch and me. The hot beverage was crusted over with a layer of tangy shepherd's cheese and laced with succulent morsels of brown frizzle-bread.

"Delicious!" said Milord.

"Brassbounder's Restorative," said the forgeman modestly. He added something extra to his cup from a small flagon and took another loud sip. "It makes a hearty tipple, doesn't it, Your Lordship?"

"Indeed," said Milord. More condiments and canapés were circulated, and the refection left us all feeling much more ourselves. We had entered a warm updraft, an incongruous phenomenon above those frigid mountains, and drifted aimlessly, high above the northeast corner of Catscat Isle. Fleecy clouds scudded all around like great white boulders, pierced occasionally by a soaring sea-duck or gull. From time to time Lord Roundabout's retainers fed the furnace another faggot of lignum capsicum, the extraordinary wood which burns with an intensity far out of proportion to its modest weight.

"How long had you been stranded there, pasted to those dreadful doughnuts?" inquired Lord Roundabout.

"No more than a brief snooze, I suppose," said Milord. "Why? What is the time?"

"Not the time, but the date, Closelord!" Lord Roundabout pursed his lips and counted off his gloved fingers. "Freeday's passed, and Mitreday, plus two...seven days since you disappeared, I reckon it."

Milord sat bolt upright. "Seven days!" he exclaimed. I had been counting on my claws: one day from the time of our abduction til my fateful meeting with Captain Worrant; a bittersweet day with Bilch, and Vulgia's nightmarish arrival that night; a day of swift sail to Catsmouthport, another night in Vulgia's hive — a total of only about three days, though it seemed an eternity. Yet seven days had passed! I communicated my calculations to Milord, who was shocked.

"We lay enthralled there for four days and nights!" he said in amazement, and immediately glanced around the sky. The moon was nowhere to be seen.

"It could be no more than half-full at most, Milord," I told him, and he answered with a look of deep worry.

"Four days amidst that ferocious cold? Never!" said Lord Roundabout. But there was no escaping the numbers. After some discussion it was concluded that only the soul-force of the rings could have accounted for our miraculous sustenance. We owed our lives to those imprisoned spirits, who had maintained us as surely as a mother nurses her whelps. And we had left them without so much as a word of gratitude or farewell.

"But what of your finding us?" asked Milord. "What clue —"

"Beginnings from the beginning," said Lord Roundabout. He applied a thin film of butter to a slice of bannock-loaf and chewed it thoughtfully.

"When the attendants carried you off, I ran at once into the road, but the aid-carriage had already disappeared. Lord Trillphyte appeared at my elbow and advised me that Lord Pontieu had made 'appropriate arrangements' for your care, a phrase which I found more disturbing than reassuring; and promised to keep me informed." He paused to drain his mug. "Why I listened to him at all is a question to which I have no answer, Closelord Cantilouve; it were better I had taken the advice of a bog-snake." He adjusted his wig, but finding that its powder had become disastrously soggy from melted fog-ice, he disappeared briefly into the privacy cabinet and emerged with a fresh coiffure in the pompadour style, which I thought rather daring.

Lord Roundabout drew a deep breath as though making a confession. "In answer to my anxious inquiry the following morning, Lord Pontieu told me peremptorily that you were in Saint Lester's Infirmary and were not to be disturbed. The cad even presented me with a missive, purportedly from you, which stated that you were on the mend and 'doing as well as one could expect,' and so forth. But its hand was foreign.

"I went immediately to my Protectioner in Residence and displayed the counterfeit note. He joined me in an urgent visit to Saint Lester's, where we presented ourselves at the offices of the Infirmary Director, Sir Montimus Applepill, and demanded to see you.

"His secretary coldly informed us that your convalescence had been complicated by catarrh and possibly dropsy, and that he was under strict orders to allow no visitors. But we were quite importunate and insisted on seeing the director himself.

"After some difficulties we succeeded in being shown into Sir Applepill's chambers. He appeared quite surprised. 'But isn't His Grace well enough attended in his manor?', he asked us.

"We looked at each other in shock. 'You mean he isn't here then?', I asked.

" 'Why no,' said the director, quite nonplussed. We departed in rather unseemly haste, I fear. I understand that his 'secretary' vanished shortly thereafter, and is even now being sought on charges of Extemporaneous Deceit.

"We next inquired at the Aid-carriers' Guild, where we were not surprised to learn that they had attended no one with chest pain in over a month. Indeed, their members hadn't been called to duty at all for some three days, during which, sustained by a crude imitation of your 'Vimplicate VII', they had pursued a nonstop game of 'prisoners' canasta'. The competition had culminated in violence, and they were quite surly." Lord Roundabout poised a pinch of snuff on his wrist, inhaled it briskly and expelled the contents of his nostrils expertly into a lace hanky.

Milord was visibly upset upon learning that one of his more famous essences had been counterfeited by the hoi polloi. "I will attend to that," he said heatedly. "Such illicit stillery must be vigorously stilled." I coughed. "Quashed," he corrected himself, and glanced aside at me to make a note of his intention. Milord had begun to rely on me as a sort of amanuensis, a role with which I was very pleased, and Bilch gave me a proud glance.

"Quite," said Lord Roundabout sympathetically. "Well, we found ourselves at a difficult juncture, and devoted considerable thought to our next thrust. My Protectioner proposed raising the matter at a Special Session of the Assembly, but here two difficulties presented themselves: first, the circumvention of customary procedure (not to mention the Agenda of Ancillary Questions) requires two weeks' advance notice, unless one declares a Situation of Consummate Emergence; and as we had no concrete evidence of foul play, we were loathe to pursue the latter option. And in either case, we would have had to overcome Lord Trillphyte's skilled parliamentary parries.

"The second difficulty was that Lord Pontieu had conveniently absented himself from the Assembly for an indefinite period, citing pressing business and the re-marriage of a third cousin. Consequently he would be unavailable to answer our public complaint. To confront Lord Pontieu in person we deemed most unwise, for he had retreated to his enclave on Hibblebar River, a secluded location in which he would doubtless resort to even more drastic measures than those he had visited on yourself, Closelord. Therefore my Protectioner and I concluded that the only thing left was to consult with your Gasmaster Bickle."

A look of extreme discomfort passed over Lord Roundabout's face. He abruptly stopped his narrative, produced a blunt pipe and devoted excessive attention to filling and lighting it. Unsolicited consultation with another Lord's Protectioner is an extraordinary step, without acknowledged precedent, and too delicate a matter to be addressed even indirectly in the Assembly's Bylaws.

Milord smiled and said quietly, "You had no choice, Closelord Fontleroy. I thank you." Lord Roundabout shifted in his seat and twiddled his pipe, and pulled his chin and harrumphed.

"At any rate, upon my arrival at Benefice Manor, the Gasmaster was pacing your study in a state of extreme distress. I believe he found your unexplained absence quite heartrending, Closelord Cantilouve. He nonetheless received me with great warmth, and even took the liberty of broaching a thimble or two of your Clarissimus XIV, in hopes that its clarifying influence might rectify our disorganized thoughts. We sat for some hours by the fire, turning our ideas over and over til they were thoroughly overcooked, and delving into the question from every angle until we were dizzy, but made no progress.

"It was an offhand remark by the Gasmaster which at last illuminated the abyss in which we floundered." Lord Roundabout sucked at his pipe and blew a cloud of tart smoke into the cavernous balloon above. For a long moment the only sounds were the rhythmic chuffing of the forge-bellows and the sough of balmy air along our wicker bulwarks. From his station the lanky forgeman gazed steadfastly at nothing in particular, while his two mates leaned dreamily at the railings on either side, jaws in hands. In their black suits and top hats they looked like chimney sweeps on a roof, silhouetted against the sky.

"And what was his remark?" asked Milord at last, when it appeared that Lord Roundabout had dropped the thread altogether.

He pocketed his pipe and peered curiously at Milord. "The Gasmaster's comment was, 'It's puzzling that Petolzia should have missed her appointment.' Evidently she had been due to deliver more of the extraordinary brew which you had so shrewdly broached with Lord Pontieu and myself. The Gasmaster indicated that she had previously been quite reliable in her appointments, much to the regret of your household. And he was quite put out that his careful placement of the day's vapor-barriers had been wasted effort.

"At that moment we looked at each other in simultaneous inspiration: her failure to keep such an important rendezvous implied that she knew you would not be there to oversee the transaction!" Lord Roundabout thumped his seat triumphantly. "And witches being witches, we considered it highly probable that your precise whereabouts were known to them as well."

Milord looked pleased. "How splendidly clever of you, Closelord Fontleroy," he said. In a tone of greater gravity he added, "In a moment I shall confide to you the terms and significance of those transactions in more detail." He stood up, folded his hands behind him and turned to look out over the spectacular panorama. "And what then?"

"The following morning we met with the Master—" he referred to the Protectioners' Master Guildsman "—and proposed a conference with the Consortium, a plan which he heartily supported. In fact he was quite prepared to stake his prestige on the matter, and even insisted that the Council itself attend."

"Good fellow," put in Milord.

"It was assertive of him, particularly as I understand the Council had not personally met with a Guild representative in almost a decade. And on such short notice! Their current identities were a matter for keen conjecture and even a wager or two. But they agreed to it, and we convened at the amphitheatre only two days later.

"The Council was most truculent and undisposed to candor. But curiously enough, the Master's arguments and persuasions proved entirely unnecessary, because of an unexpected actor in the play, so to speak, who revealed rather more information than her cohorts wished."

Milord laughed. "Perhaps an actress, actually? Rather large and clad in gaudy scarlet rags?" he asked innocently.

Lord Roundabout's mouth fell open like a gapeworm's. "You've met that bloated hoyden?"

"We had the pleasure of making Phiddla's acquaintance in a witch's own hive, no less."

"Pleasure indeed," said Lord Roundabout. "And what —"

"I'll explain by and by, Closelord; but forgive my interruption," Milord said.

"Well, she dominated the meeting from the start, clodhopping roughly on protocol and chattering blithely on, much to the annoyance of her superiors. It was rather delightful to see them so vexed, I confess. They were quite unable to inhibit her babbling, and wasted a number of moderately powerful spells in the attempt.

"She blurted the events with which I suspect you are already painfully familiar: your kidnapping by the loathsome Vulgia, and then by the equally repugnant Petolzia, who I understand is still at large. How despicable!"

Milord combed his fingers wearily through his hair. "The hearing of it is more exhausting than the reality," he said, "particularly as I slumbered through both crimes."

"I shall shorten the account," said Lord Roundabout apologetically. "*Enfin*, she indicated that you had been trapped in Vulgia's hive, and mentioned something about an unpleasant garden…"

"Such a motley collection of rude vegetables as you cannot imagine, Closelord!" said Milord.

"Ghastly. And you were abandoned in their midst?" Lord Roundabout was incredulous.

"By the Council itself!" said Milord. "Did she not say so?"

"No, for at that moment the vixen's mother interceded and pretended this was Petolzia's doing." Lord Roundabout's face turned a livid pink and he pounded his knee. "Scurrilous! By the Guild, the Council's treachery will not go unanswered." Milord motioned to

Yeoman Twofoot, who offered Lord Roundabout a platter of aromatic towelettes, and in a few moments he recouped himself.

"At any rate, we saw that there was no alternative but to attempt to locate you in Vulgia's hive, though we had only the vaguest notion of its location, which the Council of course refused to divulge. But by fortuitous coincidence, that very afternoon an itinerant magic-monger appeared at Roundabout Manor." He grimaced as though tasting an unripe lemon. "He offered for sale a torn map of the Catscats, showing the locations of the witches' hives, as well as the dwellings of various other imaginary creatures. He purported that this chart had been manufactured half a century ago by an anonymous thaumaturge, in connection with an unsuccessful campaign against the witches; I was subjected to a lengthy explanation of their feud, with which I shall not bore you. He was a most boorish and greedy lout, I must say, and would accept no fewer than fifteen bezants for the brummagem."

Milord smiled and had difficulty containing himself. "And no doubt you haggled with the fellow at some length," he suggested, laying heavy emphasis on the verb.

Lord Roundabout was taken aback. "I see the fisherman goes to more than one pond," he said drily.

Milord chuckled. "No fish were ever so troubled by such a simple worm. And I wager we've not seen the last of one Haggleman Wimley."

"Undoubtedly true, Closelord." The two Lords looked pensively at each other.

"But his chart was helpful?" asked Milord.

Lord Roundabout shrugged. "It was the only bit of intelligence available to us. And as I shall relate, it proved essential in one particular, though it galls me to confess it." He adjusted his vest irritably. "So there you have it: on that basis my footmen and I prepared our little expedition, while the Master Guildsman and Gasmaster Bickle remained at their posts."

Here it must be pointed out that Lord Roundabout's balloon-ship, though wondrously constructed, was virtually unnavigable. The use of balloon-and-cabs is largely confined to Freeday recreation, when they can be seen sailing gaily in the skies with prettily dressed ladies you-hooing from their railings. Lord Roundabout and his small retinue were thus particularly brave to have undertaken this hazardous mission, so far from any chance of help. And our voyage was far from over!

Indeed, I sensed that unnavigability was only one of the hazards we would have to face, for behind Lord Roundabout the three forgemen stood talking together in an undertone, while glancing hatefully at Stitch's sleeping form. It was inevitable that their resentment would seek further expression.

"And the journey itself?" Milord inquired.

"It was a harrowing excursion, to be frank. Capricious winds pummeled us at every turn, so that to avoid collision we often had to fend off the jagged peaks with long wooden booms." He waved at a bunch of tall spars stowed vertically in one corner.

"One morning the atmosphere became so treacherous that we were compelled to descend, collapse the balloon and portage into the next canyon." He closed his eyes in weary recollection of that grueling event. "At night we anchored by throwing our drag rope down amongst the boulders and hovering perilously in the updrafts, while keeping an anxious watch for witches.

"We scoured the southern face of the mountains for several days without success. The Haggleman's chart proved inaccurate in the extreme: naught but melt-riddled glaciers hulked where peaks were marked, and empty ravines yawned in place of witch-hives. But some intuition drew us further upward, and there the map saved the day. For scribbled in one of its ragged corners, almost as an afterthought, was the name, 'Thaum's Terrace'. The notation even included a caution against the seductive songs of its Thug-rings. Lacking any other reasonable destination, we elected to explore that gloomy loggia, and found you."

Lord Roundabout drew the scrap of parchment from his pocket and showed it to Milord, who scratched his chin thoughtfully. "It has the appearance of a palimpsest: notice the repeated erasures and overlying quill marks." He held it to the light. "Its mark suggests a cheap and recent vintage...Yes, see here: the sign of Fewtril's Haberdashery, in Albanderry Port. A bit of flummery, Closelord!"

Lord Roundabout was crestfallen. "It seems a comedy of errors led me to you, Closelord," he stammered, "each of them cancelling the other, resulting in gratuitous success." Milord began to object, but he said, "No, no use in putting it at the feet of our errant friend Wimley, or elsewhere; the fault is my own." He quoted a popular verse:

> " 'The man who goes to market for seeds,
> But comes home with a bushel of weeds,
> Should put the blame where it's been purchased:
> In the mirror, not the merchant'. "

Lord Roundabout sighed heavily. "But then I suppose there's no use brooding about it." He crumpled the map and tossed it to the winds.

Milord took his friend earnestly by the arms. "Serendipity is no cause for embarrassment, Closelord," he said. "Your bravery and devoted friendship are my dearest treasures."

Lord Roundabout returned the embrace with relief. "And mine," he said fervently. He smiled and produced a queerly shaped flask, and shared its delicate amber contents with Milord. Their mood soon waxed at once ebullient and pensive, and both sat consulting with themselves amidst frequent "hmmms" and other ejaculations which trailed off at once into silence.

At last Lord Roundabout said, "It seems we have descended from the trading of important news to a species of trivial periphrasis."

Milord looked mildly surprised. " 'Periphrasis', Closelord?" he asked. "I would say rather, 'persiflage'."

Lord Roundabout laughed. "No, no, Closelord Cantilouve," he said with a hint of pleasant scorn. " 'Persiflage' implies a sort of frivolous banter, a form of exchange which is quite beneath us, informal though we may be at the moment. 'Periphrasis', on the other hand, connotes innocent circumlocution, of which our conversation is certainly an excellent example."

"Not at all," said Milord, zestfully taking up the semantic gantlet. "True enough, 'persiflage' denotes light raillery or chat, whose value is perhaps open to question; but the meaning of 'periphrasis' is darkened by an implication of superfluity and stained by a sense of… of pointless verbal detour, as it were."

More scholastic subtleties and intellectual embroidery ensued, accompanied by much nose-pulling and, finally, enthusiastic nods of agreement. My Lords shared small witticisms, allowing them to dissolve slowly in their minds like sweet lozenges, and so passed another hour of warm chummery. But then Milord's mood sobered, in recollection of the urgent mission to which the Grandmage had compelled us. In stark terms he acquainted Lord Roundabout with the desperate circumstances into which the wizard was being squeezed by the passage of time itself.

"That explains the disturbing rumors in the Assembly — that the Grandmage has taken to his sickbed." Milord nodded. "And — but Petolzia has stolen the brew!" said Lord Roundabout in consternation.

"Yes, and even their Council could not induce her to return it. Though I suppose they have more elsewhere, or could make it on short notice. Conceivably I could trade more of my pellets for it upon our return, but it appears that Auntie herself was responsible for the curse." Milord banged his palm against his seat cushion in vexation.

"Auntie? Pellets?" said Lord Roundabout in bewilderment. Milord provided him with quick explanations, at which he lapsed into a brown study.

I tried to imagine the state of Mentharch's wits. Did he still dream and concoct? Or was he slave to a raving lunacy by now, discharging his vitality in gratuitous epithets and the purposeless flailing of limbs?

The afternoon neared its end. Bilch amused himself with a game of bumblepuppy, cleverly assembled from a few loose strands of wicker and a pilfered stick of wood. The forgeman was relieved by Yeoman Threefoot and snoozed on his bunk next to the cabinet. With dusk came that lull when the wind, having blown all day in one direction, prepares to blow the other way all night and pauses in the decision. The sun hesitated above a purple-streaked horizon, as though smitten by an unexpected thought, or reluctant to leave our company; but inevitably she slipped beneath her mountainous sheets, making them glow a rich yellow, then cinnabar and finally a dull vermilion.

Something had been gnawing at the back of my mind and now pushed suddenly into awareness: it was Stitch's continuing, utter inertia. We had not heard his hollow voice since the beginning of our flight many hours before, though it would have been very like him to interject a solemn pronouncement on the sustaining force of the ring-souls, or some highly questionable theory as to Petolzia's whereabouts. I am ashamed to admit we had quite forgotten him, but in that moment discovered the reason: it was, simply, the raw biological gulf which separated us, and which diluted our affection for him. For his alien hulk differed as sharply from both human and Filxxx anatomy as a cockatrice differs from a church mouse. And perhaps I wanted to suppress my growing consciousness of the footmen's angry resentment of his presence, a resentment which potentially threatened our entire expedition.

Stitch was sprawled in a corner like a discarded toy. Droplets of a thick milky substance had popped out on his rubbery skin, a sickly sweat which soaked the ragged remains of his doublet. Even as I looked he was suddenly overtaken by shaking chills and threw his extremities out like a sick starfish. He hurkled violently across the cab, scattering kindling and gashing the bench cushions with his hard, angular extremities. The yeomen cursed and jumped aside to avoid being cut down like saplings. Lord Roundabout climbed a corner stanchion and Milord backed uncertainly away.

Presently his jerkings slowed and he lay gasping on the floor. Milord knelt at his side. He examined Stitch's drooped antennae, draping them in his palm as a woman considers a bolt of cloth; he gently spread Stitch's mouthparts and prodded his grooved, fibrous tongue, and found it badly dried; and inquisitively pinched the thin webs between his serrated foot-parts. The plant-cut on Stitch's fetlock had festered, and bubbled with a morbid brown fluid which Milord carefully avoided.

"His leg wound has induced a septic condition, and in addition he suffers from a syndrome of withdrawal from opium-vinegar," Milord announced. I recalled the first part of Auntie's latest prophecy — 'An utter lack will lead to wrack' — and saw that it had come true, though his infection appeared far more dangerous than his pangs of withdrawal from narcotic.

"The need for treatment is urgent," Milord stated. He fished a vial of dark syrup from his wallet, decanted an aliquot into his palm and rolled it as a breadwright kneads dough, until it took the shape of a cheroot. He adeptly inserted this bolus at the back of Stitch's tongue and stroked his throat to induce swallowing. Lord Roundabout stood by in an attitude of queasy distaste, though despite himself he turned an interested glance now and then; the yeomen growled and muttered among themselves.

"No more than a simple compound of camphor, feverfew and a diluent," Milord said without looking up. He applied a gummy squill-plaster to the fresh bruises Stitch had acquired during his seizure; and with strips of clean balloon-linen from the repair locker he fashioned a poultice of opopanax (also known as Hercules' Allheal), which which he swathed the wound on Stitch's fetlock.

Lord Roundabout expressed amazement at these veterinary skills. Milord asked him, "Have you heard of Cornfumble's Vermifuge, Closelord?"

"A widely accepted treatment for the braxy," he answered with a puzzled expression.

"Correct. Its inventor was Scampil Cornfumble — Father Benefice's chief hostler and a most accomplished quacksalver. I was fortunate to learn a few of his simpler treatments before my Turning Year."*

"A most practical skill," Lord Roundabout said without conviction.

Soon Stitch's shaking subsided completely, his breathing deepened and he fell again into a profound sleep. Milord covered him with a blanket and gently secured him in a makeshift berth under the bench.

The yeomen meanwhile stood in a mutinous huddle, leaving the forge untended. Our great round sail began to luff and we lost altitude. Lord Roundabout turned to their corner and said sharply, "Yeomen, tend to your forge!" but they did not budge.

Yeoman Threefoot said insolently, "Stick-creatures belong underground, Your Lordship. Not coddled like babes!"

"Under sod and lye," Twofoot said vehemently, stepping forward next to his mate. "Did my mother's brother die at stick-men's claws for naught?" he demanded angrily.

"He is a rightful passenger on this vessel," said their master, but there was uncertainty in Lord Roundabout's voice.

---

* Milord referred to his fifteenth year, after which, being considered of age, he was expected to avoid such rude environs as the stables and to assume the demeanor and responsibilities of a Lord proper.

"Overboard!" snapped Twofoot.

Lord Roundabout glanced hesitantly at Stitch — did the thought of sacrificing him cross his mind? — and then at Milord, who said softly, "The choice is yours, Closelord."

As he vacillated, the yeomen exchanged terse remarks in their coarse provincial dialect; what little I grasped was not pleasant. They reached a quick consensus. Yeoman Onefoot hefted a thick piece of kindling and whacked it in his hammy palm, while his mates drew lengths of rope threateningly between their fists.

Decision wrote itself in Lord Roundabout's features. "There is no choice," he said under his breath. He fixed the footmen with a stare. "Your conduct is malicious and oppressive. As captain of this balloon-and-cab I hereby give final warning," he stated. The yeomen took another menacing step forward.

Lord Roundabout drew a blunt flintlock pistol from his vest and fired. A tiny swatch of black cloth jumped from Yeoman Twofoot's epaulet, rested for an instant on the railing and flew off into the darkling sky. The reek of burnt gunpowder filled the cab.

The three yeomen stood in shocked silence, transfixed like dolls; Milord still knelt on the floor at Stitch's side as though paralyzed. Lord Roundabout blew the ash from the pan of his pistol and coolly reloaded it, stuffing another ball into its muzzle with a short rod.

"Hold, Your Grace!" Yeoman Onefoot said desperately, dropping his lump of firewood into its bin. "We meant no harm!" Twofoot and Threefoot hastily threw down their ropes and crossed their arms in front of their chests to indicate surrender. Lord Roundabout lowered his weapon.

"Back to your stations," he commanded. "Think only of your duties, and pray for mercy from the Assembly upon our return." Yeoman Threefoot busily set about re-stacking the firewood and sweeping up its splinters, while Onefoot and Twofoot vied for the bellows. Milord pulled Stitch's sleeping form as far from them as possible.

Lord Roundabout mopped his brow and sat down. "We'll take watch by turns tonight, Closelord," he said in a shaking voice. "Careful watch. I'll take the first." He folded his arms, flintlock in hand, and elevated his feet. Milord nodded in somber agreement.

An uneasy truce prevailed. Milord kept his friend company for half an hour, puttering nervously with the odds and ends in his pockets for lack of anything else to do. Presently the footmen finished their chores; two of them fell into their bunks, leaving Yeoman Threefoot to his duty at the forge. Night fell, and the gemstone walls of the cab glowed a luminous yellow under a bright moon, now less than half full. A cloud of tiny sulphur-moths glittered like atomies around the car.

Under Milord's wary eye Yeoman Threefoot prepared his bedding, comfortable though hardly luxurious, and a little pallet next to it for Bilch and me. We fell at once into an exhausted sleep. It seemed only moments later when Lord Roundabout gently roused Milord to his watch.

"All's well, Closelord. We drift steadily on course," he whispered. They were reassuring words, but in his voice was the distress he felt on account of the mutiny, for such a rift between a Lord and his servants was utterly unprecedented.

Beside me Bilch slept peacefully. Catseye Peak and its cordillera receded several leagues behind us to the south, but even at this distance the sight of them raised my hackles. We floated over a series of toothy volcanic foothills, from which the moonlight chased long, tangled shadows into countless narrow cols and valleys. The chiaroscuro was beautiful but frightening, for an airship forced to land here would be chewed to shreds on those merciless crags. I glanced anxiously at the forge, where Yeoman Twofoot faithfully plied his bellows, and at the balloon, which showed no tears.

Milord rubbed his face and sat up. "Keep a sharp eye," said Lord Roundabout, and handed over his pistol. With a quick "good night" he padded to his bunk, rolled in and at once fell asleep.

"I shall," Milord said belatedly. But he frowned at the feel of the weapon's weight and threat, and set it aside. The bracing aroma of piping hot sweetsheaf tea rose from a butler's table; he poured out a cup and smiled at me. Being awakened in the middle of the night was not to his liking nor mine, his smile said, but we could still enjoy our good company!

I felt suddenly overwhelmed. Threatened by angry footmen so far from home, sucked away by uncertain winds, seeing Stitch struck down by a possibly fatal illness, the wizard's dilemma — all were more than I could bear. I'm afraid I quite lost my poise and indulged in tears of self-pity, though I plead extreme fatigue as an excuse.

Milord put a finger to his lips and took me gently in his hand. "St. Augustine remarked that the world is like an olive press," he said. "Men — and Filxxxs too, I should think, though he didn't say so — are constantly under pressure. Only the true oil remains in the vessel, while the dregs of the press run away to the sewer. But to be under pressure is inescapable, Flick! 'Observe the dregs, observe the oil and choose,' St. Augustine said, 'for pressure takes place through all the world: war, siege, famine, the worries of state.' We must welcome the pressure and the friction, for it will refine us and make us noble." I nodded dutifully, and from his bench Lord Roundabout snorted in his sleep as though in agreement.

I studied Milord's wise face. That I could be as true as he! Our tribulations had taken some of the flesh from his frame and fine wrinkles had started at the corners of his eyes; but the profile of his nose had lost none of that same noble straightness which one sees also in the most graceful marble columns, and already his cheeks had regained their pink bloom.

We floated silently over the desolate northeast corner of Catscat Isle, land as flat and uninteresting as a kitchen towel. Overhead the balloon was a shadowy carousel of moonlit colors. Its hem undulated like a jellyfish against the black velvet sky, rippling quietly in the tepid night air; and when it blew inward the bright, less-than-half-moon peeped in like a streetlamp at a passing carriage. Mesmerized, I fell asleep and dreamt of warm blankets and the familiar comforts of Albanderry.

The morning air was chilly, but the sweet aromas of frying piglet bacon and baby potatoes reassured me even before I opened my eyes that the rest of the night had passed uneventfully. Bilch yawned and squirmed awake at my side, and we jumped down to await our serving.

My Lords sat at table, linen napkins tucked up to their ears. A large pot of Tillyphrump tea steamed comfortably between them, and sweetcakes with slices of fresh tangerine further embellished the feast. The footmen had already taken their porridge and crullcakes and attended to their duties.

Lord Roundabout tapped his pudgy finger on an outspread chart. "The difficulty is to avoid being drawn into the devilish Winds of Conflation," he said. "They blow perpetually clockwise, and thus we took advantage of their southern sweep to reach you; but now we must somehow evade them so as to return to Albanderry."

"A pretty task," said Milord, dabbing his lips.

"Very pretty," said Lord Roundabout, "for if the attempt fails, we face a protracted voyage over the Northern Wastes. A possibly one-directional voyage." He looked grimly at Milord. "Only last week Bumbailiff Yannigan was drawn into their endless churning while on an innocent Freeday jaunt." He referred to the Assembly's former sergeant at arms, a universally liked gentleman whose position had been gradually overshadowed in recent years by that of the Chamber Annunciator; consequently his job had been eliminated altogether upon his retirement.

Milord was shocked. "Not our own Bumbailiff?" he asked, but Lord Roundabout already confirmed the fact with closed eyes and a sad nod. There was a heavy silence between them, in which I heard the unspoken conjecture that Bumbailiff Yannigan, melancholy at his loss of station, had actually sought his own demise.

With an effort Lord Roundabout continued. "Prior to my departure I consulted Albanderry's wittiest aeromancers, but they could say only that the Winds' centrifugal impulse is quite variable; none would attempt to predict its precise behavior in a given month." Bilch urgently notified me that he had no desire to be spun cock-a-whoop into the Northern Wastes, a feeling I heartily shared, and we communicated as much to Milord. He fondled our backs absentmindedly.

"But we must return before the new moon," Milord exclaimed. "Well before it, in fact, so as to have time —"

Lord Roundabout shrugged helplessly. "I know, Closelord," he said quietly.

Milord rotated the chart to read it. "Perhaps we could —" He was interrupted by a groan from Stitch and left the table to examine him.

He was delirious. Moreover, though Milord's poultice had reduced the suppuration in his wound, its margins had indurated and curled apart as though snarling, which left the injury dangerously exposed.

With a probe Milord cautiously lifted off the rancid bandage and threw it overboard.

Lord Roundabout put down his silverware and looked on squeamishly. Pointing out the relevant parts of Stitch's leg, Milord said worriedly, "The cannon bone is threatened, and consequently the aitchbone, whose loss would be a disaster. The wound must therefore be left open to the redeeming air, to heal secondarily; and I shall have to administer a carminative."

He directed a meaningful look at Lord Roundabout, but the significance of his remark was lost on him, as it was on me. Milord groped amongst the accoutrements in his wallet, withdrew a thumb-sized ball of waxy material having an odor of cardamom, and at length induced Stitch to swallow it between groans. He retreated promptly to the windward side of the car and motioned to Bilch and me to join him without delay. His reason was soon apparent: with an agonized grunt and prodigious force, Stitch expelled an astounding quantity of intestinal gas.

The stench of this flatulence was appalling. Lord Roundabout gasped, lunged to the railing and desperately gulped the breeze like a suffocating goldfish. Then he instilled into each nostril a dose of snuff sufficient for six Lords, sneezed til his temples turned an alarming red-purple and lay prostrate on the bench. The three yeomen blenched and swayed in their boots; then they pressed kerchiefs to their faces and likewise stumbled to the rail, methodically emptied their stomachs and collapsed in their bunks. But Milord, having carefully positioned himself upwind, reported only a mild and transient nausea. I felt only a brief malaise, but Bilch escaped even that by burrowing deep into our holster and swaddling his nose in pocket-lint.

Stitch meanwhile belched several times and, appearing much relieved, lapsed again into a deep sleep. In a short while the brisk wind freshened the cab and Lord Roundabout regained himself, though his color was rather ashen. But the yeomen remained in their bunks, and Milord was obliged to act as forgeman.

"By the morrow I anticipate much improvement in Stitch's condition," he said, looking pleased. He shoved a fresh log clumsily into the furnace. "Scampil Cornfumble was at a loss to explain the precise means by which this medicament heals such traumatic phlegmons, but its efficacy is not in doubt. I remember —"

With an annoyed gesture toward his incapacitated footmen, Lord Roundabout said tartly, "I suppose we should also be grateful that the animal's noxious eruption was not fatal." He drew a lace handkerchief from his shirt and blew his nose exhaustively. "One might say that the purgative greatly aided the patient, but nearly annihilated his household."

Milord poked absentmindedly at the embers and hmmm'd. "The preparation was a carminative, Closelord," he said primly, "not a purgative."

This bit of pedantry restored the color to Lord Roundabout's cheeks. "I conceive the need for treatments of finer anatomical focus," he said with great emphasis, "and less…effusiveness." He made an irritable lifting motion with his palms.

Milord nodded enthusiastically and folded his hands behind his back. "I fervently share your wish, Closelord Fontleroy. The requirements of medical science are truly limitless," he said, and gazed thoughtfully upwards into the balloon.

Lord Roundabout made a little plosive noise of disgust and abandoned the topic in favor of occupying himself grumpily with the repair of his pelorus, which had been slightly damaged during our ascent. Milord poked again at the logs and amateurishly adjusted the forge-valves.

Presently Lord Roundabout sighted through his navigational instrument and frowned, and anxiously consulted his compass. "The same winds which brought us so efficiently to your aid now hinder our return, Closelord Cantilouve," he said. He peered up into the sky, where the sun neared its zenith. "Confoundment!" he swore, and stamped his foot in exasperation. "If only there were some means of…of tacking, as any ordinary sailor can," he said.

The compass now pointed steadily north by northwest. We were being drawn helplessly into the swirling Winds of Conflation, just as he had feared, and faced a truly circuitous journey over the Northern Wastes. The only factors in our favor were the good supply of victuals in the storeroom below deck and the likelihood of continued mild temperatures.

The northern horizon gradually took on a dull sheen, and soon an endless expanse of flat gray brass covered half the world, as far as the eye could see. "We are above the Endless Ocean," said Lord Roundabout. "No one is known to have seen its far shores, much less return with their description." A look of hopeless resignation stole over his round face, though he tried to conceal it.

Bilch and I could find nothing to occupy ourselves, and moped about the cab in a state of ennui. For hours we floated in silence, prisoners above an enormous void. Our only evidence of motion was the slow procession of distant mountains in the south; but though those landmarks steadily receded, they did not disappear entirely, a fact which stoked a small fire of hope in our breasts.

The fleet winds whisked us through the skies faster than we realized. In mid-afternoon the terminus of the North Channel came into view, ahead and to our right. Its roiling blue waters, scarred with whitecaps, leaped forward proudly like a stag in spring; but that robust creature then plunged mindlessly into the dreary, mouse-gray sea, where it was lethally diluted.

To see such a ribbon of beauty being continuously snuffed out was, in an elusive and subtle way, horrifying. Bilch squeaked that it was like watching an endless column of smartly uniformed soldiers marching to a cliff, accompanied by the rat-a-tat of snare drums — and throwing themselves off, one after another. An unpleasant feeling, like hunger magnified, gnawed at my stomach.

Milord watched the spectacle with a sad, fascinated smile. "We are merely clots of dust and energy, Flick," he said, "though we persist in thinking of ourselves as far more."

"Mayflies," said Lord Roundabout with a soulful glance, and tapped his pipe empty.

The sun disappeared without notice behind a layer of high cloud, leaving a colorless dusk. We had described a broad arc across the southern expanse of the Endless Ocean, and approached the Northern Wastes. Countless leagues of cold, bleak tundra stretched into the distance on all sides, the color of dead trees. Under the sky's southern eaves a few runty thunderheads grumbled and sparred listlessly with one another amidst weak blinks of sheet lightning. A few sultry drops of rain spattered against the balloon. Yeoman Twofoot roused himself and passed out light ulsters, and with a sulky expression took over at the forge.

We flew swiftly over the savanna at a height of perhaps five furlongs. The wind took up a monotonous whistling and rocked the cab like a cradle. Lord Roundabout pulled his collar up around his nape and squinted into the distance. He had given up the trouble of maintaining his wig, so far from proper society, and took the sparse rain on his bare scalp.

"What life do you imagine thrives below?" inquired Milord.

"The sickly green thatch seen everywhere is muskeg. And there are many pernicious species of weeds, which are said to provide sustenance for umbs, though personally I doubt that those repulsive creatures venture so far north."

I recalled again Milord's vivid description of umbs: "They look as though they have been clumsily sculpted from a mass of translucent blubber," he put it, "set impossibly upon a rickety armature of thin fishbones. A large, cruel maw is concealed by thick folds of fat, whose color suggests uncooked oatmeal, and a pair of deadly claws completes their gruesome anatomy."

Milord looked regretfully down and pointed out a flock of ugly birds pecking at the desolate desert floor. "A troop of spotted bustards, unless I'm mistaken," he said.

"True enough," said Lord Roundabout in surprise. "The anatomists maintain that their gizzards are as tough as fossil-scabbards, which would suit them well to their thorny diet." The approach of our ship scattered them in all directions, hissing and squawking.

There was little else to see in the lingering dusk, and conversation languished. Yeomen Onefoot and Threefoot revived, morosely completed their evening routines and retired. Indifferently we ate a light supper. An anemic, waning crescent moon ascended, bathing the balloon in a glaucous light which made Bilch most anxious. He fretted nervously back and forth on pretext of checking that the lockers were secure; perhaps he already sensed the nearing of tragic events. But my Lords were greatly refreshed by their meal, and despite our desperate circumstances a paradoxical sense of well-being came over them. Milord leaned expansively back in his chair and invited his soul.

"We are no more than bare-hipped primitives, stumbling through mud and light, mysteries even to ourselves."

Lord Roundabout listened, pursing his lips and tamping his pipe. "Quite right, Closelord. Mere blinkards, wrapped up in our tense little imbroglios. We flit pointlessly here and there like butterflies, oblivious to the splendor of the universe…"

From the corner came a harsh voice. "Oblivious to many things." The source of the interruption was Yeoman Threefoot, who sat staring at the floor in the shadows. He raised his head and glared at us.

After a startled pause Milord mumbled, "Well, one always fails to see certain things…" but his voice trailed off.

Lord Roundabout's knuckles whitened around a fork. For the first time I sensed the depth of the strain between him and Milord, for in truth he had been no more eager than the yeomen to take Stitch aboard, and had done so only as a painful concession to his dear friend. Now the well-intended deed embarrassed him deeply, and the situation threatened to explode in his hands. "Oblivious, Yeoman?" he spluttered, pointing his fork at Stitch. "You think me blind to the implications of this creature's presence?" The question met with dead silence.

Milord interceded, directing his attention to a point halfway between Lord Roundabout and the footmen. "I feel certain that the Lord of Roundabout Manor would not knowingly have trod on the sensitivities of his thanes," he said, attempting a diplomatic assault on a very difficult peak. It was a gallant effort, which he followed hastily with others of equal character, but the footmen would say nothing more.

No words, that is, but a gesture more eloquent: with a brand from the forge Yeoman Twofoot lit a cheroot — a luxury not permitted servants aboard ship — and stood puffing it insolently, in explicit sympathy with his bunkmate. Defiance quickly poisoned the air. I cringed further into Milord's pocket, where Bilch, always the practical one, advised me to see that my *gnozzt* was in readiness.

Milord touched Lord Roundabout's clenched fist and said urgently, "The infringement is of no importance, Closelord; overlook it."

Lord Roundabout struggled visibly with himself. In a sudden burst of speechless anger he threw his fork overboard into the night.

A thin, victorious smile spread like a stunted plant on Yeoman Twofoot's face. The firelight danced on his narrow, harsh features and played through the gaps in his teeth like a jack-o'-lantern.

Milord stood up hastily from his seat. "Perhaps some rest would do us all good, Closelord," he said loudly and held out his hand.

Lord Roundabout hesitated, then reluctantly handed over his pistol. "Mind you stay awake, Closelord Cantilouve," he said hoarsely. He mopped his perspiring face with his napkin, cast a final deadly glance at Yeoman Twofoot and retired to his bed, where he spent some time vehemently arranging his bedclothes. Soon his labored breathing dwindled to quiet snores.

Milord looked consolingly at Yeoman Twofoot. "I can well understand your anger, Footman," he said.

Twofoot turned slowly towards him. "Can you, Sire?" he asked bitterly. "Can you know the horror of seeing your cattle snared and struggling in a batfowl net? Your barn burned in the night? The sight of pitiless pincers on your child's neck?" All at once the image of that terrible scuffle was starkly visible in his heartbroken eyes, the memory of a hideous night that had left him permanently scarred and embittered. And now he was forced to share close quarters with such a raider, to whom his own Lord gave aid and comfort!

"Easy, Tom," Twofoot's mate said gently from behind him. "Easy. You twist a knife in an old wound."

Twofoot whirled. "I, Onefoot? I twist it?" he demanded incredulously. "And I suppose Tim here sharpened it, eh?"

"That's not what I meant and you know it," said Onefoot defensively from his bunk. The argument quickly heated up, but they spoke in their rough dialect and I could not follow it.

With a loud "Bah!", Twofoot broke off and returned to the furnace.

Milord said, "Be assured that I bear you no ill, Yeoman Twofoot. I deeply regret your loss."

Twofoot scowled and slammed the forge door with a clang. "Bear ill or not, it's the same to me, but I'll not stoke a blaze for one of his kind." He jabbed a finger at Stitch, stalked to his pallet and threw himself on it, to murmurs of support from his mates.

Milord heaved a sigh and looked out over the vast tundra. Its utter blackness was relieved only by the occasional faint twinkle of a phosphorescent plant; the moon's weak, waxy light could not penetrate it any more than sunlight reaches into the ocean's depths. Our glowing orange cab was a conspicuous island, blazing uninvited in empty darkness. Milord looked back at the footmen: all three had turned their faces into their pillows and seemed to sleep.

He leaned against the rail again and ruminated. "It's time to consider our plans when we arrive again in Albanderry," he said with a sigh. I looked at him in some surprise, for the likelihood of our return seemed to have been flickering out. "Never doubt our survival, Flick," he said with a smile. "Have faith!" He dabbed my nose affectionately, and Bilch's too.

He talked quietly for some time. I hardly noticed him slumping in his seat, nor can I recall just when either of us fell asleep. A thumping and scraping awoke me, as of some large deadweight being cat-hauled over a wooden barrier.

I peeped drowsily from my pocket to see Yeomen Onefoot and Threefoot silhouetted in the yellow moonlight. They were struggling to lift Stitch to the railing. He moaned and tried stuporously to push them away with his forelegs, but in a moment they would succeed in pushing him overboard! I shrieked and scratched wildly at Milord's shirtfront. After what seemed an eternity he called out, still half asleep, and fumbled for the pistol.

Now the blackguards had the stick-man's rubbery body perched on the railing, ready to be jettisoned. Yeoman Onefoot stood on the bench, his back to the empty air, and tugged at Stitch's shoulders, while Threefoot cursed brutally under his breath and shoved upwards at Stitch's woody thighs like a longshoreman.

The scuffle awoke Lord Roundabout. "Satan's breath!" he swore and rolled from his bed. He lurched heavily into Yeoman Threefoot and both men toppled against the privacy cabinet in a tangled heap. With the sudden loss of Threefoot's support, Stitch's shoulders slipped from Yeoman Onefoot's grip, just as he was delivering a mighty tug; Onefoot fell backward against the rail, levered over it like a teeter-totter and disappeared. It happened so quickly that not even a syllable of protest escaped his lips. Stitch flopped back onto the bench.

Lord Roundabout tried to wriggle free of Yeoman Threefoot, an effort compromised by his simultaneous attempts to smooth the wrinkles from his nightshirt. Ironically this worked to Roundabout's benefit, for his unexpected movements, together with his substantial weight, frustrated Threefoot's efforts to thrust him aside and get up, and pinned the footman against the cabinet. But now Yeoman Twofoot advanced from the corner, nervously gripping a sharp dirk. Lord Roundabout blinked in disbelief.

"Stay!" shouted Milord, awake at last, and pointed his pistol. Startled, Twofoot turned towards us, and in that moment Lord Roundabout delivered a powerful kick to his shin. Twofoot yelled and hopped back and forth like a frog, clutching his leg. His knife clattered to the floor.

Threefoot at last extricated himself from Lord Roundabout and stood up, cursing him in dialect. He drew his own toad-stabber, but Lord Roundabout seized his ankles in a short-legged scissorlock from where he lay. Threefoot danced an awkward jig to escape the hold, dragging Lord Roundabout haltingly along the floor.

Milord had leveled his pistol and debated his aim, but with a sharp roll Lord Roundabout wrenched Threefoot's legs and toppled the footman headlong against the forge. He screamed as his outstretched palms pressed against the red-hot bulkhead, and he fell to the floor in agony. The awful odor of seared flesh filled the air as he sat isolating his crippled hands in the air like an injured fiddler crab.

I believe it was this terrible smell which pushed Yeoman Twofoot beyond some internal limit. His life had already been burdened by the brutal loss of home and family, and now he had seen one mate plummet to certain death, the other terribly maimed. And in addition he would have to answer for the unforgivable crime of assaulting his own Lord. He sat down heavily against the base of the bench and sobbed, still clutching his kicked leg with one hand and gesturing helplessly with the other.

Lord Roundabout heaved to his feet, breathing heavily, and surveyed the tragic scene. "Are you hurt, Closelord?" he asked between gasps.

"No," Milord said weakly.

"This is a sorry issue to our venture, Closelord."

With a shaking hand Milord put the pistol on the tea tray and pushed it away. "Sorry indeed, though the fault is mine for insisting that Stitch be brought along. Obviously a terrible example of oil and water." He shook his head. "A concocter of my experience should not have been so foolish as to attempt such an impossible mixture."

"Nevertheless, I must apologize for the churlish behavior of my footmen," said Lord Roundabout.

Milord looked sadly at him. "Three tragedies are apology enough, Closelord," he said. Collecting himself, he prepared a soporific powder for Yeoman Twofoot, who sat mumbling incoherently, and wrapped Threefoot's hands with medicated bandages. Stitch had fallen again into a state of sick sleep on the bench; we left him there and returned to bed. Lord Roundabout, deeply troubled, remained to stand watch and tend the fire.

Another day passed. We had consumed the better part of our stores, both food and firewood; and this reduction in mass, plus the absence of Yeoman Onefoot's weight, allowed the ship to soar giddily through the sky, though the forge did little more than smolder. Twofoot lay blithering in his bunk, interrupting his verbigeration from time to time only to raise his head and stare wildly at Stitch; Milord could hardly induce the yeoman to swallow even liquids, and feared for his survival. Threefoot meanwhile withdrew into a morose silence and responded to any attempt at communication only by propping his damaged hands accusingly before him. He took the spoon-feedings which Milord gave him, but never asked for more. Lord Roundabout fell into a brown study, greatly sombered by the mayhem which had befallen his once-faithful servants.

Stitch at last turned a critical corner in his convalescence and awoke. His leg appeared to be mending adequately, though he would have a conspicuous and deforming scar. He was still as weak as a newborn hummingbird, but ate so voraciously that our provender ran low and rationing was taken under serious consideration. Bilch and I spent much of our time perched on Stitch's shoulders as he half-reclined on his section of the bench, both for the better view and to help him with his food. He had little to say beyond somberly thanking us all for saving him. Lord Roundabout gruffly acknowledged his gratitude but otherwise avoided him, a behavior which Milord imitated in the interests of repairing their relationship.

My Lords were reduced to performing the menial tasks required on a balloon-and-cab, though Bilch and I did what little we could to assist. On the second morning after the brawl we sat together in a stagnant mood. The day seemed endless. Bilch and I had already diagrammed our family tree twice, and had defeated each other ad nauseam at a Filxxx version of noughts-and-crosses. We ate a tasteless luncheon — I cannot even remember what we served ourselves — when all at once the air again smelled of water and we heard a faint swashing sound.

Lord Roundabout jumped up and studied the eastern sky. "Lake Plinthimus!" he shouted. In great excitement he opened up his chart, now thoroughly crumpled from repeated consultations, and pointed to a bluish blotch in its upper right margin. "The Winds weaken and turn here; on this point the aeromancers were quite firm."

Milord leaped to the rail. No more than six leagues ahead lay a large lake. Its azure water exhaled a whitish vapor, and thin wisps of cloud drifted above it at approximately our altitude. Milord stared for a long moment, then pointed and exclaimed, "For a fact, the clouds move south!"

"South and west, Closelord, and back to the North Channel. And then we shall cool the forge and descend smoothly near Trillphyte Manor, or perhaps even my own!"

"This demands a celebration," said Milord with exuberant resolve.

"Indeed it does," agreed Lord Roundabout, and nimbly danced a little gigue. He retrieved a bottle of ancient port from a marquetried cabinet and poured it gurgling into two glasses.

"To Albanderry!" he shouted, clinking Milord's glass high in the air.

"To salvation!" said Milord, and they drained their glasses.

"To salvation," Stitch added gravely from his seat, and received for reply an uncomfortable look from Lord Roundabout, and a sheepish one from Milord.

"To salvation," echoed Yeoman Threefoot sarcastically from his bunk, and hoisted two nonexistent glasses in his bandaged hands. Yeoman Twofoot thrashed his head on his soiled pillow as though chained to it, and the air of celebration wilted as quickly as it had arisen. Lord Roundabout curtly re-corked his port and stowed it again in the cabinet, and withdrew into himself.

Soon we sailed over the Plinthimus. From a distance it appeared to be calm and peaceful, but from above we saw that it was a wild and grumly sea, whose pale blue waters churned and moiled without stop under their white vapors. I was grateful that we rode high above it, enveloped in our warm lobe of transport.

An hour passed and another, during which Bilch was nowhere to be seen. A brief search found him half-conscious in a corner amidst his scattered playthings. His breath was shallow and rapid and his eyes were misted over; and he had begun to enlarge at the flanks, like the face of a boy whose cheeks are pinched by an affectionate uncle. A quick inspection of his back confirmed that the dimple between his spines had deepened considerably — another sign of the corporeal fission that would rend him into two, or four, female descendants. In short, he was beginning to 'show' like a gestating woman — the result of our duothelytoky aboard the *Obnounce Dittaneer* — and would be unconscious until its culmination in a fortnight or so.

He turned his eyes feebly to me and tried to smile. "Goodbye, Flick," he whispered.

I hugged him and burst into tears. Bilcher Pebblepaw, lost! For though his personality, and even a few fragments of memory, would be incorporated into his offspring, yet he was dying. It was a birth and a death, together.

His eyes closed and he slipped away. "Goodbye, Bilch," I said.

Milord smiled down at me and gently tucked Bilch into his waistcoat pocket. "Never fear, Flick. Bilcher Pebblepaw — that is, the Bilches — will be welcome in Benefice Manor. And we'll find some means to persuade the Assembly to allow multiple mascotry in this instance; it's not unprecedented." Good Milord! His kindness overcame me, and I wept with gratitude.

But soon my emotions gave way to a more sober realization: if Bilch was showing, why wasn't I? It could only mean that our union had been but half successful — that I myself had failed to conceive. Such a quirk of nature occurs in only a small percentage of unions like ours, and aroused my very mixed feelings. On the one side, I had found a door to my future unexpectedly locked; I was an empty husk, where I had expected to be a full vessel. But on the other, longevity in my present form would consequently be greater, and who is not grateful for long life?

Bilch was now truly hibernating, his normal functions slowed almost to a stop, and yet he changed more radically than a baby in its womb. Each day would see his body further sculpted by a divine hand. I straightened his silk neckcloth and all at once felt terribly lonely. Milord cuddled me to his side.

"What unexpected turns this life brings, eh Flick?" he asked. I snuggled further into his vest and nibbled at the sweetmeats he had hidden there for me. Already I yearned for the company of Bilch's offspring.

My thoughts wandered, and presently it occurred to me to wonder why Goighty had not accompanied Lord Roundabout. I looked inquiringly at Milord. He was glad to have a point on which to draw out his friend, who had quite sunk into a mood. "And how is Goighty, Closelord Fontleroy?" he asked brightly.

Lord Roundabout appeared doubly pained. "He receives an unpleasant series of injections intended to reduce his copious production of saliva, Closelord," he said regretfully. "To now the treatments have succeeded only in souring his disposition. Perhaps you know of some easier remedy from Scampil Cornfumble's therapeutic armamentarium, and will be good enough to advise my quacksalvers upon our return."

"Of course," said Milord, but he was chagrined to have touched unwittingly on a painful subject, and conversation died.

The rest of the day passed uneventfully. After a spectacular sunset and a light meal we retired.

Dawn brought mad excitement. My Lords crowded the rail, pointing and shouting like schoolboys. "Yes, quite right," said Milord, shaking his head up and down.

"And Knucklebitt Point!" announced Lord Roundabout. He was buoyant.

We had reached the North Channel again, but much further south than before. Its broad ribbon flowed ebulliently no more than five hundred yards below. To be so close to home again and free of kidnappers, witches and contrary winds! Our circumforaneous voyage was almost at an end.

Lord Roundabout started forward and snatched a telescope to his eye. "Closelord!" he exclaimed in alarm. Milord already stared downward at his side. Their excited expressions became abruptly grim. I jumped to Milord's shoulder and peered down with him.

Along the shore a dozen giant gray centipedes flailed their scores of legs in the surf, pitching first to one side and then the other. Milord took the telescope from Lord Roundabout and studied them. Silently he held it for me to see.

The twelve 'centipedes' were in fact long skiffs, whose ungainly motion was due as much to their slovenly construction and warped planks as to the waves and crosscurrents in which they struggled. On several of them a clumsy attempt had been made to rig lateen sails, but the crude booms had snapped or listed uselessly. The centipedes' wiggling 'legs' were actually long oars, pulled by fierce, heavily armed stick-men.

IX

A BLOODY STRUGGLE

Stick-men, seizing a beachhead on Albanderry! All told there were some two hundred and fifty in the amphibious assault, not counting their skittish bathorses, nor the ferocious warrior-boars tugging impatiently at short tethers in the sterns of the boats. Never have I been so frightened, not even by Petolzia herself. But true to their station, my Lords kept their heads and calmly studied the invaders, chins in hands.

"They must have marched across the marshy wastes of southern Catscat Isle, a tour de force in itself," said Milord.

"Yes, and hacked their longboats from the oak groves near the coast; and then it was a simple matter to ride the strong North Channel current past Catsmouthport — but under the witches' very noses!"

"Doubtless they moved by night, or hid in the fjords," said Milord.

"Hmmm... For once I find myself wishing the Consortium had been more vigilant. Perhaps they were again carousing at one of their infamous convocations."

Milord nodded. They studied the enemy a moment longer through their telescopes, and Milord murmured, "Their armor is quite varied."

"It is a motley assortment," replied Lord Roundabout. Tunics of chain mail were the rule, but in addition a few stick-men bore stout ailette-plates on their shoulders, or protected their chests with sewn leather broignes. All had greaves on their sinewy legs. Some covered their hairless pates with ornamental casques, while others wore simple iron skullcaps from which makeshift antenna-sheaths sprouted; and a few lacked any sort of headgear.

"And the weapons!" exclaimed Lord Roundabout, for these, glittering in the morning sun, were just as diverse. Many stick-men carried such typical weapons as clink-clubs and web-poles; but others held sheathless brackmards — those razor-sharp broadswords well suited to cutting and thrusting at close quarters — or their smaller relative the scramasax, a gruesome weapon with a groove cut specially into its shaft to prevent wound-suction and thereby increase its victim's bleeding. Still other soldiers cradled crossbows or ratchet-slingers in their forelegs, and several platoon leaders fondled harquebuses or musketoons.

"They are well prepared…one would think they had been scavenging battlefields," said Milord.

"That's it!" said Lord Roundabout, slapping the rail. His face darkened. "The perfidious insects have plundered Grillefoate!" He referred to a hallowed battlefield on the southeast coast of Catscat Isle, where a valiant battalion of Lords withstood an invader's brutal attack some four centuries ago, saving all of Albanderry. The fallen heroes were ceremoniously buried with their armor and weapons, and no ancestors are more revered by the Lords than they. But now it appeared that the stick-men had desecrated the glorious plain for its battlegear.

Milord was shocked to his marrow. "Say not, Closelord," he whispered. Lord Roundabout was purple with rage and grief. He bit his fist and turned away, and bumped squarely into Stitch.

It was the first time our alien companion had stood up since the ascent, and he loomed over my Lords by half a yard, his head reaching nearly into the balloon. Lord Roundabout backed angrily away and reached into his jacket.

"I beg Your Grace's pardon," Stitch said in his flat monotone.

My heart skipped a beat as Lord Roundabout withdrew his hand, for I thought surely he had drawn his pistol. But he held only a handkerchief, with which he brushed his lapels. "Pardon granted," he said.

"I am grateful," said Stitch.

"Properly so." Lord Roundabout turned irritably away. His laconic response filled me with relief.

"Their degree of organization is surprising," Stitch volunteered.

"It is surprising," Milord replied. "How do you explain it?"

"My mother sometimes referred in vitriolic tones to one named Seerit," said Stitch. "He was believed to be much shrewder than his kin and knowledgeable in matters of war. I suspect he has incited them." Though he towered over us, Stitch stood partly stooped. In this limp pose I read his heartsickness at these ominous developments, which portended the destruction of his own species, of his adopted protectors, or both. I reflected that fear and uncertainty can do more harm to the posture than does disease or old age.

"But where would they obtain fresh powder for their firearms?" Milord asked.

"A simple matter of combining brimstone and charcoal with niter, which is abundant in the earth at Pelburn's Precipice," said Stitch. He peered at the boats. "But I cannot say what equipment is concealed in the sterns." He pointed to the bulky loads abaft each skiff, which threw their patched canvas coverings into pointed folds.

"The contours of some suggest bombards and catapults, though I am at a loss to identify others," said Lord Roundabout from the railing. "Powerful weapons in any case." Milord shuddered in response.

Squeezed between those blanketed engines were the stick-men's grunting warrior-boars, two to a ship. They stropped their deadly tusks incessantly on their short tethers, which provoked the nearby bathorses to nervous prancing. "The boars are said to be impervious to witchspells," said Stitch, "though readily wounded by conventional means."

Mention of the boars spurred Yeoman Twofoot to a sudden grasp of events. He frantically piled every available pillow and blanket around him as a barrier and cowered into the corner of his bunk. This in turn inflamed Threefoot, who seized a poker in his bandaged hands and prepared to thrust its red-hot tip at Stitch.

Now Lord Roundabout did produce his pistol and pointed it at Threefoot. "Sit down, Yeoman," he ordered. Threefoot faltered in mid-swing. Lord Roundabout directed the gun squarely at Stitch's featureless face. "Swear allegiance, stick-man, on the blood of your ancestors."

The gray fold of skin at the back of Stitch's neck quivered. "I swear it," he said.

Threefoot's face twisted into an expression of giddy disbelief. "You accept the word of this reptile?" he demanded shrilly.

Milord interceded. "Has it not struck you as strange that he has any word at all," he asked quietly, "rather than the mere jabber-clicks of a stick-man?" Threefoot blinked; Lord Roundabout pursed his lips thoughtfully.

"Richer blood than a mere stick-man's flows in his veins, Yeoman," said Milord. "He assisted in my rescue, and my mascot's. He is capable of allegiance and I vouch for him." Threefoot lowered his poker a few inches and looked doubtfully at Stitch; obviously these larger considerations had not entered his mind. I don't believe Lord Roundabout had fully perceived Stitch's hybrid nature either, much less guessed that it was a witch who had given him his intelligent speech; perhaps his suspicions would be aroused when he realized that Stitch could fly.

"The matter rests, Yeoman," Lord Roundabout said gruffly. "Return to your duties."

Threefoot struggled visibly with indecision — to give in or fight. For a moment I thought he would simply weep. "No!" he burst out at last and slashed wildly at Stitch.

Stitch's response was lightning-quick. He plucked the poker from Threefoot's grasp — its glowing end melted a painless groove in his pincer, emitting a puff of acrid yet sweet smoke — and shoved it harmlessly into the forge. Badly shaken, Threefoot retreated to his bunk and then descended below deck to the storage room, where he remained.

These events had distracted us from attention to the furnace, with the result that our altitude was now reduced by half. The stick-men, their boats secured on the shingle, spotted us and churred like evil crickets. One of their lieutenants jabbed his sword in the air, and his troops opened fire with ratchet-slingers. A barrage of sling-bolts whizzed upward and pinged against the cab, slicing through its layer of wicker and ricocheting off the underlying gemstone. Sunlight shone like pin-stars through perforations in the balloon and we fell another twenty yards.

Lord Roundabout jumped to the furnace, stoked it and pumped furiously at the bellows. Milord set about heaving unnecessary supplies overboard to decrease our weight. With help from Stitch he jettisoned the privacy cabinet, which crashed into the centerboard of a boat, scattering a dozen stick-men and neatly removing the leg of a tardy one. The cab tilted at a giddy angle and we surged upward, replenished with heat.

At Lake Plinthimus, Lord Roundabout had again donned his wig in anticipation of our arrival home, but that foppish appurtenance now departed briskly into the wind. This proved to be a stroke of luck, for the stick-men took it as some sort of weapon and diverted their fire to it. The toupee danced on a volley of grapeshot and rained white powder; this aroused them to further defensive frenzy, and with a mighty roar a harquebus blasted the wig to shreds.

We ascended rapidly out of range, and my Lords heaved sighs of relief. But one catastrophe followed another. Yeoman Twofoot, his worst fears realized by the invading horde, gave out a blood-curdling scream. In a frenzy he threw off his bedclothes, dashed to the far bench and hurtled into Albanderry's breezy air.

Milord rushed to the rail, but too late. For one endless heart-stopped moment we heard only the surf below and the flapping of the wind; and then a faint, sickening thud. In a moment Yeoman Twofoot's body was swarmed over by a dozen stick-men picking curiously at his clothes.

But we had no time for grieving. The strand receded quickly in a fresh westerly breeze and the white towers of Benefice Manor shone less than half a league ahead, surrounded by their beautiful paths and gardens like the whorls in a green and white lollipop. My Lords studied the geography through military eyes and discussed plans of battle. Milord pointed here and there, noting avenues by which the stick-men would be likely to approach; Lord Roundabout nodded sagely and used a counting device to estimate the number of his thanes. They fell readily into this martial role, for the Lords' past history is one of warring clans; indeed, those feuds still smolder, though thinly disguised in parliamentary dress. Both men looked repeatedly toward Dinthrup Downs, the jumble of heath-covered ridges and swales north of Benefice Manor.

"The Downs are critical," said Milord.

"Exactly," Lord Roundabout agreed even before Milord had completed his remark. For the Downs occupy a strategic position, being centrally situated amongst the forty-two Manors. They are a refuge from which an enemy can make uninhibited sorties, especially under cover of night, and prepare fatal ambuscades for any pursuers.

"Can we prevent the stick-men from attaining them?" asked Milord.

Lord Roundabout turned to Stitch. "What do you estimate their speed of march to be?"

"Perhaps three times that of men, but their boars and equipment will slow that by half."

"Roughly half a day, then, to the Downs," said Milord, sharing a glance with Lord Roundabout.

"But do you reckon that they have the wit to see the importance of that position?" asked Lord Roundabout. "Or will they be content with a simple frontal assault?"

It was a crucial question and Stitch considered it carefully. He stood up straighter now, having cast his lot irrevocably on the side of men. "I am uncertain, but I would not underestimate Seerit. He is capable of anything. He might even split his forces and attempt both strategies."

"Continued reconnaissance from balloons is essential," said Milord. "From them we can also throw down wads of powdered thatch, at which they will squander their munitions." Lord Roundabout blushed and stroked his scalp, but indicated his agreement.

Suddenly from above came a noxious whirring. Milord cocked his head this way and that, thinking it a hornet, but it was the sound of Petolzia's broom. From out of nowhere she drove at us, veering right and left with the intensity of a tornado and the relentlessness of a screw. Already she was so close that I could see the unraveling hem of her shift and the caruncles on her leering face.

Lord Roundabout leaped to the corner, untied a braided cord and yanked on it with all his might. A rip-flap opened at the top of the balloon and the ship dropped like a pear from a tree. I thought he had gone mad. Milord seized a strap in the nick of time to keep us from being thrown out of the cab, and the floor was jarred by Yeoman Threefoot in the storeroom below as the ship's fall slammed him against his ceiling.

Above us a powerful bolt of purple static singed the air harmlessly, and I understood that Lord Roundabout's maneuver had narrowly dodged a lethal charge. Petolzia zoomed past only yards above as he prepared to throw down our landing grapnel, while warning us to avoid its trailing coils of rope.

We flew a mere fifty yards or so above Milord's westernmost orchards, while Petolzia executed a broad half-circle turn to the north. Now she bore down on us again; I saw that we could not avoid her. My Lords prepared themselves for the shock.

She twirled her broom, twisting the air in front of her into a rotten spiral as easily as an absentminded schoolgirl fiddles with a lock of hair. The black, turbulent cone pierced the heart of our balloon. We whirled in a wild tizzy, out of control. The floor bucked, throwing the forge through the deflated balloon, and pans and linens flew back and forth like grains of rice at a wedding. There was a shattering, deafening crash and then quiet.

The sun filtered prettily through the blossoms of a jacaranda tree. Splotches of purple shadow played against the shattered yellow gemstone of the cab. We rested in a tangle of crumpled wicker and foliage, draped by reams of multicolored taffeta. I looked around in dread, but Petolzia was nowhere to be seen; evidently we had passed inside the protective influence of the Gasmaster's vapor barriers.

Lord Roundabout was wedged in the crotch of a large branch, his waistcoat snagged conveniently on either side of him like a sling. Milord's fall had likewise been gently broken by the oversized nest of an expectant osprey, which squawked angrily at us from a safe distance. Next to me Bilch still snoozed safely in his pouch.

Stitch had landed thorax-first on an angled branch, but his leathery hide and sturdy construction had absorbed the impact well. I reflected that it would have gone differently for him if we had crashed a few days earlier, when he was still so sick.

But the storage room below us was smashed to smithereens. Lord

Roundabout clambered along his branch a short distance and poked at the wreckage. He pulled aside a section of panel and peered into the compartment. "Yeoman Threefoot met his doom here, Closelord," he said quietly.

Milord nodded; somehow it seemed inevitable. "At least he was spared the sight of Yeoman Twofoot's death," he replied. There was little else to say. With Stitch's assistance we managed to climb out of the tree.

My Lords stood reconnoitering at the edge of Milord's favorite cherry orchard, its delicate whites and pinks dotted here and there with the blazing lavender and green of jacarandas. A broad, empty field lay between us and Benefice Manor. At its other side was an excited cluster of Milord's servants, with the unmistakable profiles of Masterfootling Farberwile and the Gasmaster in their midst.

The whole clot of them rushed to greet us: the Masterfootling, Gasmaster Bickle, Thindle Spinkite, Trumpmaster Rampbleu and Kitchenmaster Traysmith, Floorsteward Smithkline and virtually the entire household. Milord's fewterers wrestled with their yapping greyhounds and stumbled on leash-tangled legs; the blacksmiths and coopers flapped along in their leather aprons, and bakers clapped their floured hands with joy. All soon bowed or kneeled before Milord, shouting, "Your Grace!" and "Welcome, Sire!" I was happily greeted too, and even Mistress Breadwright gave me a pleasant wink. Lord Roundabout worriedly consulted his timepiece at Milord's side, while Stitch held himself back in the tree-shadows.

Masterfootling Farberwile stepped forward, overcome with emotion, and said, "Welcome home, Lord Benefice, a most gracious welcome from all your faithful servants!"

"My worthy and devoted family," said Milord with great feeling. "I am fortunate indeed." A grave look from Lord Roundabout reminded him of our situation. Milord drew a deep breath. "But I must inform you all of terrible circumstances. Even as we stand here, hundreds of stick-men invade the coast of Albanderry."

A shocked gasp went up. Thindle Spinkite detected Stitch amongst the trees and cried hoarsely, "One of them stands there! Attack!" Stitch leaped instantly to the top of a jacaranda and prepared to fly away.

"Hold!" shouted Milord, raising his arms. He explained hastily that

Stitch had saved us and had sworn obeisance to the Lords. "He is to be given safe conduct," he ordered. There was a long moment of jostling and uneasy discussion, subdued only by repeated assurances.

"Now then," he began. "The assignment of tasks is urgent. Fellscribe Thinklefine, immediately dispatch messenger loons to all the Manors, informing them of the invasion and urging their speediest mobilization; include Lord Pontieu's enclave as well. Floorsteward Smithkline, you will appoint division leaders for the transformation of our serfs to armorers, bowyers and the like, to be mustered in full before sunset. See to it that sentinels are posted in a quarter-circle to the north and west. Masterfootling, secure all defenses of the Manor itself, and direct Kitchenmaster Traysmith in the management of provisions and supplies." Milord motioned to the wrecked balloon and sadly lowered his gaze. "And arrange a detail for the burial of Yeoman Threefoot, who perished during our forced landing."

As swiftly as their collective joy had changed to alarm, the latter was replaced by firm purpose. In moments most of the group had dispersed on their critical errands, leaving the field littered with chef's hats and gardener's tools, awls and aprons and a dozen other sorts of peaceful paraphernalia, all suddenly rendered superfluous by *force majeure*.

Lord Roundabout took Milord by the arm. "I must conduct similar preparations at Roundabout Manor, Closelord." Thindle Spinkite ran off to summon a supply wagon for him. "I shall see to it that reconnaissance balloons are launched immediately, each furnished with signal mirrors and messenger loons to inform us of their findings," he added.

"Godspeed, Closelord," said Milord. They embraced. Without further ado Lord Roundabout climbed into the wagon and rattled off. He would have to circumvent the Downs to the east, and could not be expected to arrive home before nightfall.

Only the Gasmaster, Thindle Spinkite, Ranktwo Sparseman and several footmen remained to assist Milord. We returned to the Manor, with Stitch following at a discreet distance. Milord established a command post in a day room with a wide view to the north and west. Its French doors opened onto a terrace where Stitch could remain in earshot without actually entering the manor, which would have made the remaining household intolerably uneasy.

Over a hasty meal Milord briefed the Gasmaster on our journey and discussed operations. The armorer was called in and helped them to don hefty hauberks, greaves, helmets and shortswords. As afternoon waned, a dozen balloons ascended in the distance, their gay colors sadly out of place. The sun hid behind a large cumulus cloud, rendering signal mirrors useless, but soon Ranktwo Sparseman ran in breathlessly, clutching a wad of parchment.

"Your Lordship, a message by loon, from Lord Pinkleton's airship."

Milord plucked the scrap eagerly from his hand. "Two contingents, as we suspected," he reported. "Their main force to the Downs, and a lesser one advancing in our direction." In a softer voice he added, "And they have already reduced the village of Carfuffle."

After a moment of silence Stitch said, "Seerit knows the location of the pellets and will assault Benefice Manor."

Milord and the Gasmaster looked at him in grave agreement. How Stitch must feel now, I thought, knowing that he was powerless to help his unknown and ensorcelled father, trapped in a box of pellets only a few steps away! I wondered whether his sire heard him, or knew of his presence.

Milord rubbed his chin thoughtfully. "Ranktwo Sparseman," he ordered, "locate the Floorsteward with all speed and instruct him to assemble his troops on the west field."

"At once, Sire," said the Sparseman, and ran off.

Milord then beckoned to Stitch, who stood aside with him. "I give you my word that when the enemy has been defeated, I shall negotiate with the Consortium for the release of your father and his kin."

I thought Stitch's features would again sustain one of their emotional spasms, but he contained himself and said simply, "I thank you greatly, my Lord."

"In return I ask a crucial favor." Milord motioned again and Stitch lowered his earhole to his new master's lips. Milord spoke in a voice so low that even I could not hear, though I strained my ears from his vest pocket. Stitch nodded his knobby gray head in understanding and hopped off in the direction of Milord's armory.

Soon Floorsteward Smithkline appeared and bowed, and saluted. Beyond him marched four platoons in perfect formation. An amazing transformation of Albanderry's peasants had taken place: where cobblers had quietly stitched shoes only hours before, now determined soldiers shouldered musketoons; where common thanes had humdrummed their daily duties, doughty warriors now gripped the pommels of oiled broadswords and stared proudly from between armored cheek-plates, their gaze riveted to a single purpose.

"Well done, Floorsteward," said Milord.

"Thank you, Sire."

"They approach from the west. Deploy your men accordingly. Take advantage of the swale." By this Milord meant that since the stick-men would have to pass through the low marsh beyond his orchards, the Floorsteward should keep to the proximate high ground; this would offset the advantage of surprise which the swale's concealing marsh gas conferred on the enemy.

"Yes, Sire," said Floorsteward Smithkline. He turned smartly and set his troops marching at double time. As they retired, my eye was caught by a blur streaking to the north some twenty paces off the ground. It was Stitch, well armored in leather scapulars, mail and a visored helmet. He paused in mid-flight, silhouetted against the setting sun, and gazed back at us; and flew off again.

Milord retreated to a balcony on the third story, with the Gasmaster puffing behind him. They stood anxiously surveying the horizon through thick telescopes. Beyond the orchards, marsh vapor hugged the ground, obscuring our view, and thickened as twilight descended.

"A regrettable advantage for them, to attack by night and from a cloud," Milord said worriedly.

"The men have prepared calorescent flares, Sire, and an ambush," said Gasmaster Bickle. Milord looked at him with appreciation and relief.

Time passed with mountainous slowness. Milord twitched and put the spyglass to his eye again. "Activity in the swale," he whispered.

"It can be none but them," the Gasmaster stated.

"Commence firing!" Milord ordered.

The Gasmaster raised his arm and a booming *thrump* jarred us from a trench in the field below. There a squat mortar licked its thick lips with tongues of smoke and flame, illuminating the soldier next to it in an orange glare. With linstock in hand he looked like a devil just arrived from hell and brandishing his trident.

An instant later a hollow appeared in the marsh gas, followed by a plume of fog and dirt and a delayed thud. A score of stick-men erupted from the fog, and another twenty, their antennae twitching violently. From the nearby trees bright yellow flares sputtered to life and threw the savages' shadows in all directions, like moths fluttering around candles.

"What a scabrous lot!" exclaimed the Gasmaster. "They look like… like huge lutes, yet they bound like chickens!"

Another mortar-salvo detonated behind the stick-men, reducing their two platoons to a panicked mob of fewer than thirty troops. From the trees sounded the crack of musketoons and several more fell, pints of gray blood streaming from their wounds.

Now their lieutenant sought to regain control, barking orders in their harsh, clicking tongue. They dressed ranks and the center stick-man in each platoon unharnessed his warrior-boar. The deadly animals plunged into Milord's ranks, sending up cries of terror and pain. I could only imagine what grisly damage they wrought with those razored tusks, with which they rooted out men's lives as readily as ordinary hogs unearth truffles.

The stick-men leveled long, sharpened pikes and charged into the trees, but were thrown back by a devastating volley of musket fire. In an excess of bravado one soldier pursued them too closely, waving his broadsword with more threat than effect. A stick-man turned unexpectedly and with a twist of his pincers fatally scragged the man's neck. Five of Milord's troops slew that stick-man, then ganged up on a warrior-hog and impaled its blunt, snouty head on their halberds; its humped body thrashed and kicked, and lay still.

The stick-men were reduced to a dozen. They regrouped under cover of the marsh gas and emerged driving a giant bog-harrow before them. This juggernaut was nocked with a hundred barbed spikes and scythes, to mow down any living thing in its path.

Behind this invulnerable monster the stick-men appeared to have the upper hand. But Milord's forces wisely retreated into the dense orchard where it could not penetrate, and sniped with crossbows at its drivers. Their quarrels buzzed like angry bees amongst the stick-men, and one by one they fell. Their lieutenant sustained a mortal head-wound and lay dying on the ground; the remaining five warriors abandoned him and their bog-harrow and fled into the marsh.

Milord's troops cried out their victory. They threw down their weapons and exulted on the field of battle, dancing clumsily for joy. But when Handman Armright stumbled over the body of a fallen com-rade their mood abruptly sobered, and they grimly set about picking up their dead and wounded.

Milord turned away. "See that those who gave their lives receive Most Significant Honors of the Realm," he ordered.

"Yes, Sire." After a pause the Gasmaster added, "I fear we shall not be so lucky against their main force, where Seerit must be in command." He raised a forefinger. "I recommend utmost cooperation among the Lords — a pooling of resources and strategy, without reservation." He looked shrewdly at Milord, for both knew well that Lords Pontieu and Trillphyte would be unlikely to share this attitude.

Milord inspected his telescope. "Yes…Dispatch loons to con-vene the Assembly here at dawn, Gasmaster, in full battle regalia. Express the absolute necessity of attaining a quorum. And instruct the Floorsteward to post double watches through the night."

"At once, Your Lordship." Gasmaster Bickle retired.

Soon the Floorsteward arrived, confirmed that Milord's orders had been carried out and gave an accounting of casualties: six dead, none seriously wounded.

"They will be well and duly honored. Form a detail to retake our armor from the dead stick-men; let the men rest and eat. Prepare to march shortly after dawn." The Floorsteward saluted and withdrew.

Milord returned to his apartments and prepared a cradle for Bilch in a drawer of his armoire. I tucked him in and jumped to Milord's lap. "Come, Flick, we'll have a taste of my Somnolus XII. It will help us to sleep," he said. I was happy to join Milord in that libation and retire with him to bed, but we slept fitfully nonetheless.

It seemed only a few heartbeats before the roosters rudely summoned us again to unpleasant realities. There was a fluttering of wings at the window, and Stitch stood on the balcony. Milord threw a robe hastily over his shoulders and met him.

"What news?" he asked urgently.

"Their caravan is entrenched in the Downs. I approached on the ground and pretended to have fended off an ambush by one of your patrols, Sire." He pointed out several slashes he had deliberately administered to his tunic, inflicting only scratches on his body.

"And what is the shape of their forces?"

"They are encamped in four squadrons of sixty, with three platoons in each squadron. Their heavier weaponry includes ballistas and bombards. And bog-harrows."

"We have already met that giant's garden tool in our first engagement," said Milord. "There is no reply to it but retreat and an alliance with trees, but those maneuvers were effective. As to the other weapons, we shall have to rely on offensive surprise or speedy evasion. What else?"

"They intend to infiltrate the Manors by night: the first will likely be Lord Roundabout's."

"We shall prepare accordingly. And you were able to disseminate the false information as I instructed?" Milord asked.

"Yes, Sire. I was challenged by a platoon sergeant and ordered to remove my visor, but fortunately they were distracted at that moment by an escaped warrior-boar, and hurried my report. I stated that I had gotten the intelligence by torture of a captured soldier. They will expect a counterattack from the west."

"Excellent," said Milord. "Go on."

"Seerit leads them, as we suspected. He is carried everywhere in a luxurious enclosed litter and wields absolute power. I witnessed a meeting between him and three lieutenants." Stitch hesitated.

"Omit nothing, Stitch," Milord said firmly.

"He took his wine from…from a roofless skull, gruesomely embellished with skiddle-stones." Stitch's resonant voice wavered.

"Speak, Stitch," Milord implored, rubbing his forehead. "Time presses upon us like a vise!"

"The configuration of its broken teeth identified it as the skull of Yeoman Twofoot."

Milord swayed on his feet. He caught his balance by clinging to the drapery and looked away. "I thank you for your reconnaissance," he said hoarsely. "Take nourishment from the Kitchenmaster, and a short rest. You will join us in battle today." Stitch executed an awkward salute and left via the balcony. Milord lowered himself wearily into an armchair and sank into the rumination of grief.

The eastern sky paled to a delicate saffron-gray. The crickets' nightsong died out. A swiftly moving coach-and-four glinted on the brow of a distant low hill, followed by a cloud of glittering rainbow dust and a faint clattering. It descended gradually into the grounds of Benefice Manor. Another coach followed and another, their noise swelling like an ocean wave, and soon sixteen were reined in the courtyard. Their lathered thoroughbreds stood loudly blowing out their lips and tossing their long manes like women at the bath, while their postilions solicitously curried and watered them.

And what magnificent horses they were! They proudly modeled their crimson caparisons like ladies at a ball, displaying the mailed gorgets on their throatlatches as though they were diamond necklaces. Their carriages followed behind them like trains of velvet, emblazoned with heraldry; and platoons of smartly uniformed soldiers stood by as debonair escorts.

The Masterfootling welcomed the arriving Lords in the receiving chamber below. Milord waited until the sounds of anxious greetings and repositioned chairs had subsided, and descended the stair. Their buzzing abruptly ceased as he entered the room.

I studied the faces of Milord's colleagues: there was Lord Roundabout, showing his usual good faith and courage and holding his quick temper in check; here were Lords Pinkleton and Munchfirth and Hobday, and a dozen others; but Lords Pontieu and Trillphyte were absent. In the expressions of all was reflected that sense of unity which is brought about, sad to say, only by a great calamity. But a troubled perception was also apparent: that it was Milord who had brought this catastrophe upon them, however indirectly. No doubt Lord Pontieu had been busily spreading vicious rumors during our absence.

Milord strode briskly to a table in the center of the room and unfolded a gilt-edged map of Albanderry. A last few coughs and chair-shovings died out. Skipping all preliminaries, he announced, "My Lords, I declare a Situation of Consummate Emergence."

"Ayes" echoed on all sides.

"Carried by acclamation," said Milord. "The stick-men's lesser salient toward Benefice Manor has been repelled," he continued, to loud murmurs of approval. Milord glanced at the Gasmaster, who stood respectfully by the wall. "We believe they will now concentrate in Dinthrup Downs, thence to strike in any direction under cover of dark. Therefore we must surround them and attack by surprise, before nightfall."

This sparked a dozen animated conversations, which Milord quieted with a gesture. "But before proceeding to a discussion of strategy and tactics, I wish to dispel a misconception which, like a tenacious and repulsive weed, may have taken root amongst this august group. My sudden removal from the Assembly a fortnight ago was not the result of illness; it was a scurrilously staged abduction."

A shocked titter filled the room and rapidly grew to a brouhaha. "When circumstances permit," Milord said loudly above the noise, "I shall reveal its perpetrator, who, I hasten to add, is not with us at this moment. In the meanwhile, I caution my esteemed Favorlords to disregard any malicious allegations."

The many anxious conversations in the room became noticeably lighter in tone, and Lord Hobday blurted, "Welcome home, Favorlord Cantilouve!" to a chorus of "Here here!"s.

"I am grateful," Milord said. "Truly grateful for your warmth. But now to the pressing business at hand. Our counterattack requires a Commander of Forces, whose nomination is now open to the floor." All immediately named Milord himself, and he said, "I accept the duty as charged. Let us next proceed to the election of an Honorary Captain, whose privilege it will be to lead the first assault."

Lord Roundabout smiled conspiratorially and prepared to stand, but Lord Munchfirth was quicker. "Favorlords, I wish to nominate Lord Pinkleton, whose unique blend of bravery and élan are well known to all."

Lord Pinkleton rose. "I thank Lord Munchfirth for his gracious and accurate comments. The forces of Pinkleton Manor are justly famed for their ferocity, dazzling martial livery and unique battle-songs. But with infinite regret I must withhold them from consideration, in deference to your own warriors, Lordreserve Munchfirth; for their courage and panache are superior even to mine."

Lord Munchfirth had resumed his seat, thinking the matter settled, but now bounced up again. "The bravery of your stalwart thanes is exceeded only by your own too-fine modesty, Lordreserve Pinkleton; I must therefore insist on their nomination. Recognition is universal that they deserve this accolade in all respects."

"Tut tut," said Lord Pinkleton, "I could not consider this —"

Milord waved his arms as though pushing through cobwebs in an attic. "My Lords, my Lords, with due respect to the marvelous accomplishments of all here, I must point out that there is one other member of this Assembly, regrettably not present, on whom this honor would be most suitably bestowed. I shall entertain a superseding motion to designate Lord Maurice Ventblanc Pontieu as Honorary Captain of the Realm."

Lord Roundabout said loudly, "So moved, so moved," looking right and left. After some delay he succeeded in rousing general support and the motion carried. Lords Pinkleton and Munchfirth sat down heavily and waved handkerchiefs before their faces.

"Now then, to the plan of battle," said Milord. "We —"

"I rise to a point of order," interrupted Lord Sprightleigh.

"Proceed," Milord said impatiently.

"The pennons carried by the Honorary Captain must be specified. As Pursuivant Keeper of Heraldry, I recommend a fleur-de-lys sable in the dexter chief point; in the hoist, arms argent, or perhaps gules; and the device, a lion rampant —"

"Sable? Sable?" Lord Hobday jumped to his feet and clenched the back of a chair with whitened knuckles. "The tincture of the dexter chief point must obviously be murrey, and in the hoist a cross patonce! These considerations are apparent even to a tittlebat!"

"Poofff," said Lord Sprightleigh, hopelessly throwing up his hands. "Just as well fly the mascot's chevron and color it puce." I thought this a gratuitous insult to my class, but no doubt such remarks are commonplace in the Assembly, where mascots are in general not permitted.

Passionate groans arose on all sides, though whether they implied agreement or dispute with Lord Sprightleigh's rejoinder I cannot say.

Lord Hobday turned from his opponent to Milord. "I move the formation of an ad hoc Subcommittee on Martial Ribandry, to be chaired by myself and consisting of not fewer than seven —"

Milord banged the table. "The motion dies for lack of a second!" he shouted. There was a stunned silence. "I remind this Assembly that we are under attack. By savages." He paused and said in a quieter voice, "There is no time for brabbling. In a moment I shall delineate your substantial responsibilities in our campaign, Lordreserve Hobday; and your learned heraldic services, Lordreserve Sprightleigh, will again be much in demand at its conclusion. For now the agenda must be addressed." Somewhat mollified, the two sparring Lords sat down.

"We have reason to believe that the enemy expects a two-pronged counterattack from this Manor and Lord Trillphyte's to the northwest. Consequently we will instead surround their flanks and attack from the rear." There was an air of assent. "Lordreserve Hobday will coordinate our brigades by signal mirror from his balloon above the center of the Downs; do not answer his signals, lest you reveal your own positions.

"My Protectioner in Residence will now brief us as to the enemy's weaponry."

Gasmaster Bickle took the floor and quickly reviewed what we had learned about the stick-men's equipage. His answers to a few technical questions were interrupted by the brusque opening of the door. Lord Pontieu strode in, followed closely by Lord Trillphyte.

"I regret our unavoidable delay, my Lords," Lord Pontieu said without waiting to be recognized.

"To the contrary, your timing is exquisite, Lord Pontieu," said Milord. "You will be flattered to learn that you have just been unanimously elected Honorary Captain of the Realm."

"Delighted indeed, though I —"

"While I am now Commander of Forces," added Milord.

Lord Pontieu was taken aback. "And I thought you slept, Lord Benefice."

"Twice, and both times artificially," Milord replied drily. "But fortunately I received assistance from unexpected quarters, as well as from proven friends." Lord Pontieu sat down, momentarily nonplussed, while Lord Trillphyte stood nervously rubbing his left arm.

"As Commander of Forces I hereby order and direct you, Lords Pontieu and Trillphyte, to deploy your battalions at the western extreme of Dinthrup Downs, there to repel the anticipated thrust of the stick-men into that area. Lord Trillphyte, you will no doubt find this assignment pleasing, for it permits you the immediate defense of your own Manor."

"Lord Benefice is too magnanimous."

"Quite so," put in Lord Pontieu, affecting a haughty stance. "And too presumptuous. I rise to a point of privilege: with what authority are these designations made? Article IX, Provision 26 of the Bylaws states clearly that, in Situations of Consummate Emergence —"

His listeners became suddenly preoccupied with the examination of their timepieces. "Urgent motion to adjourn," called Lord Roundabout, seconded simultaneously by Lord Munchfirth.

"All in favor?" asked Milord, and was inundated with "ayes". There was a symphony of shoved-back chairs, which drowned out Lord Pontieu's exasperated shouts of "point of order", and in a twinkling the Lords had exited. Only Milord and Lord Pontieu remained, warily eyeing each other while Lord Trillphyte stood uncertainly at the door. Lord Roundabout remained comfortably ensconced in his armchair.

"Well done," said Lord Pontieu quietly. "I had no idea you aspired to such…eminence."

Milord ignored his barbed remark. In a businesslike way he said, "Keep me informed of your position and strength, Lordreserve, by mirror or loon." Lord Pontieu appeared to study Milord's nose for a moment; then he turned and stalked from the room, with Lord Trillphyte trailing behind.

Lord Roundabout heaved a sigh of relief. "A battle within a battle, Closelord."

"His energies will be put to good account."

"But do you not fear he will be entirely overrun, facing the stick-men without support?"

Milord brushed a non-existent thread from his vest, then peered at him above his lunettes. "We cannot afford to be too heavily burdened by scruples in matters of war, Closelord Fontleroy," he replied sternly. "And in any case he will be relieved in good time. With luck."

Lord Roundabout sighed and stood up. "I will take up my position on your right flank, Closelord. We shall drive the enemy into the sea!"

"And celebrate afterwards," agreed Milord. Lord Roundabout embraced him and left.

Milord rolled up his map. "It will be a long day, Flick." He stood gazing at the empty chairs for a long moment and walked outside to the courtyard. Soldiers and horses milled about under a light drizzle, anxious to be on the move. "Splendid!" said Milord, looking at the wet gray skies. "The rain will suppress the dust. No point in flaunting our position and course for enemy scouts." He conferred with Floorsteward Smithkline and Masterfootling Farberwile, while I hopped down and wandered among the troops.

Morale was high. The men fingered their weapons and exchanged the confident ribbings of well-prepared soldiers. A dozen additional battlewagons had been drawn up, loaded with ordnance and provisions of every kind. But one of them was conspicuously and puzzlingly different: a makeshift box, closed on all sides and hastily mounted on simple wooden wheels. From within came nervous grunts and bumping and the sounds of hooves. Through the small holes in its roof escaped a sour but enticingly feminine odor.

Final preparations were completed — lashings checked, ranks counted, orders confirmed. I raced back to Milord, realizing belatedly that I could not bear to be separated from my Bilcher Pebblepaw. He gravely advised me to leave Bilch safely in his chambers, but I insisted and with Thindle's help fetched him hurriedly from his drawer.

Milord entered our carriage, accompanied by Gasmaster Bickle. A blast from Trumpmaster Rampbleu's cornet set everyone in motion and we lumbered onto the road. Only Thindle Spinkite and a skeleton force of footmen were left behind to maintain and defend Benefice Manor.

The air was soon swollen with the ominous tramping of soldiers, the jingling of horse-traces, the clatter of equipment. A few remaining rain clouds evaporated under a warm sun. An hour passed, and we rested briefly as the water-bearers passed their bougets around to animals and men. Then we marched and rolled again over low, barren hills for two more monotonous hours.

The Gasmaster peered through his periscope. "We approach the Downs, Sire."

Milord looked through the device. "Position the men as planned." We reined up on a rise of clear ground. Milord and the Gasmaster climbed to the armored housing on our carriage roof and studied the landscape through their glasses.

A labyrinth of hillocks and ravines extended half a league to the north, and twice that distance to east and west: Dinthrup Downs. Here swales dipped into impenetrable shade; there a cluster of low hills blocked our view as the shoulders of adults frustrate a boy in a crowd. The thick, scrubby foliage provided perfect cover for an enemy, and stick-men might have been concealed as close as a furlong for all we could see.

Lord Hobday's balloon soon floated high above. His mirror-flashes confirmed that the other Lords had taken up their circumvallate positions. The brigades of Lords Pontieu and Trillphyte were already engaged in the west, his message added, and were rapidly depleting their supply of munitions in pitched battle; fortunately the accuracy and power of the stick-men's bombards appeared to be poor.

Milord signaled to the Floorsteward. He drew up the odd, boxy wagon so that its left side faced the Downs and lifted its hinged siding. Within stood three plump female shoats, blinking in the sudden sunlight. After a moment of confusion they bolted out, flushing a covey of quail, and disappeared into the brambles.

The Gasmaster scratched his head in bewilderment. "Three pig-mares from Hostler Pimfix's stables," explained Milord. "Their naturally attractive fragrance has been rendered even more irresistible to the male of the species by the instillation of Corporeal Magnifier III into the appropriate glands."

Gasmaster Bickle chuckled. "If the great Scampil Cornfumble had possessed such an essence, his stables would quickly have overflowed with piglets!"

The hogs revealed their zigzag course by a wake of rustling brush in the ravine below. They had gone perhaps five furlongs when we heard the roar of warrior-boars and the pigs' answering squeals. "There!" said Milord, pointing as he looked through his telescope. The foliage shook with commotion as the warrior-boars wrenched free of their leash-poles and charged in a frenzy to mate with Milord's swine. His ruse thus simultaneously revealed the stick-men's positions and subverted a major element of their arsenal.

"Well done, Sire!" congratulated the Gasmaster.

Milord smiled and gave the signal to attack, and with a deafening crash our mortars vomited their loads. Lord Hobday's mirrors relayed the order, and all along the horizon our allies contributed with noisy puffs of smoke. Clumps of trees and chaparral exploded in the brae, followed by the clicking groans of injured and dying stick-men, and more stertorous hog-squeals.

The enemy answered with hidden ballistas. Leg-sized quarrels whined in all directions from those fearsome giant crossbows. One pierced the shields of our carriage as easily as Stitch's legs had punctured the puddinged roof of Vulgia's hive, and I gave thanks to Filfalxxx that we were no longer sitting there. Another volley buried itself harmlessly in the ground nearby, but one found its mark, removing a large plug from the neck of Milord's lead mare, like an apple core. For an instant she looked bewildered, then flopped over dead, dragging her whinnying harness-mates down in a terrified, bloody tangle. Hostler Pimfix and two assistants rushed to quiet the panicked team and cut the unfortunate mare's corpse from her traces — a gruesome chore.

The birr of battle filled the air. Platoons of soldiers from a dozen brigades charged into the Downs from three sides, flushing stick-men from their hiding places and clashing brutally in hand-to-hand combat. A lieutenant stick-man (his rank declared by the chevron crudely affixed to his helmet) took three arrows from Lord Pinkleton's cross-bowmen. He toppled to earth and more arrows turned his byrnie to a pin cushion. Two of Lord Roundabout's men fell, a single sling-bolt piercing them both. Their mates answered with a raft of spears that turned a stick-man's shield to a collander; then they threw a rope net over him so that he struggled like a fly in a spider's web, and quartered him with their swords.

Slashing his huge broadsword right and left, a stick-man waded into a column of troops from Lord Sprightleigh's manor. But one of that Lord's men wielded a sword-breaker knife, an unusual tool having a series of square, toothed notches cut into its edge. He ducked the stick-man's strokes and deftly exserted his weapon. Thus gripping the sword as a glazier grips his pane, he snapped it to shivereens, and his comrades rushed in and delivered fatal thrusts with their halberds.

To the north, Lord Munchfirth's men threw barreled pitch on the bocage, set fire to it and blew the flames before them by means of large bellows mounted on caissons. The stick-men retreated downhill before a wall of flames — all but three, who attempted to vault the fire. With swipes of their rapiers Lord Munchfirth's thanes severed the major thews of the threesome's hind legs, and they met a hamstrung and fiery death.

From his balloon Lord Hobday's men threw out pads of thatch saturated with white powder. A few stick-men potshotted at them, but by and large the distraction was ignored. Clearly Seerit and his savage troops learned from experience.

A gust of wind from our right carried wild strains of drumming and piping. Lord Pinkleton's ferocious host crashed brazenly through the brake under gaudy banners. They smote huge kettles and pierced the air with raw blasts from their crooked flat-pipes. Saint Gladden himself would have screamed in exasperation to hear their nerve-rasping dissonance.

But it served a dual purpose. First, it frightened and confused the enemy. Many stick-men cringed and picked irritably at their ears, and with rearward glances betrayed thoughts of retreat. And the dissonant concert secretly coordinated the soldiers' own advance through its specifics of pitch and tempo. Their complex maneuvers were executed with remarkable precision, like a dance rehearsed a hundred times. In the time it takes to drink a small pot of tea, Lord Pinkleton's brigade deployed themselves in superior positions and soon enfiladed a platoon of stick-men with accurate musket fire.

A mirror flashed frantically in the west. "Lord Pontieu, in trouble," said Milord. "His caravan has been ambushed by the stick-men's vanguard."

"The Honorary Captain requires our assistance," said Gasmaster Bickle. "And no doubt Lord Trillphyte needs it as well."

"Send a loon to Lord Munchfirth, dispatching him and two

additional brigades to Lord Trillphyte's aid," Milord ordered. We learned later that they succeeded in rescuing him in the nick of time from a vicious siege, though Trillphyte Manor was badly damaged.

"To Lord Pontieu, respond that we come to his aid at flank speed," said Milord. But instead of wheeling the balance of his forces to the west, he gave the signal to commit them to our front lines. They galloped into the heath, their long maroon-and-gold gonfalons fluttering above; and now Stitch followed close at their side.

A phalanx of stick-men rushed at Milord's men. Stitch waded valiantly into the fray, quickly dispatching two enemies with the same number of swings of his blade. His appearance at first confused them, and they refrained from attacking him; but after twirling their antennae madly to each other, half a dozen sprang from cover to surround him. He took several light wounds before Milord's troops drove the attackers back with a musket fusillade. But just when he was able to disengage, an officer in Lord Sprightleigh's militia, believing him to be a stick-man, shot Stitch from behind with a musketoon. He fell with wounds in both haunches.

The Floorsteward sent a detachment to his rescue, and they carried him quickly from the field to the hostler's aid station. With dread I recalled Auntie's mad prophecy: "A fray will bring a final sting, from kin and angry men," and rushed to see him.

Stitch was quick to reassure me. "Not critical wounds, Flick. I shall mend in a week or two." His optimistic prediction was confirmed by a smile from Hostler Pimfix. With relief I scrambled onto Stitch's litter, threw myself onto his neck and kissed it for good measure.

The fighting raged into the afternoon and gradually lulled. My Lords' forces retired again to the north and south boundaries of the Downs, occasionally sniping into the brush with crossbows or muskets, or making quick sorties when they saw an advantage, but all the while advancing slowly in parallel to the west. In this manner we squeezed the stick-men's flanks, forcing them towards the twin peaks at the Downs' western extreme.

Milord consulted again with his generals. "The outcome is no longer in doubt. We shall have them bottled between the peaks," said the Masterfootling with enthusiasm.

"A natural bottleneck, true enough," replied Gasmaster Bickle, "but in such a narrow defile a single house cat could block the entry of a thousand cellar rats."

"Correct," said Milord. The Masterfootling's smile vanished. "I have no intention of trying to pry them from that crevice, in which two stick-men could hold a battalion at bay. Instead, the southern half of our forces will circumvent the peaks on this flank, to the relief of our Honorary Captain; leave only a token force to occupy the enemy's attentions from the peaks' eastern side. Instruct all forces remaining on the northern boundary to proceed to the far western end of the peaks, where the terrain is clear, and attack if conditions favor it." The Gasmaster and the Masterfootling saluted and retired.

With that we began marching in earnest, riding first into a dale choked with puckerbush, then over a series of reedy hummocks. The sky turned again to cold slate and oozed a fine rain. After three hours of slogging we crested a low hill and met a terrible sight: on both sides of the coastal road most of Lord Pontieu's men lay dead or dying. He and his Protectioner were surrounded by stick-men, commanded by Seerit in his litter. The savages were about to tear their prey to pieces.

We were detected, and Milord angrily reproached himself for not having sent pickets ahead to scout. Seerit pulled aside the goatskin drapery on his litter and showed his blotchy gray face. His eyes swiveled independently in their turrets, alternately sucking information from his surroundings like leeches, or conspiring with each other like assassins in an alley.

He motioned and two stick-men took his prisoners' necks in their pincers. The Gasmaster gasped and held his chest. Seerit uttered a few gutteral syllables whose meaning, even without translation, was all too clear: stand clear or see his hostages beheaded.

Milord had to make an instant decision. If he opened fire, the two prisoners would certainly lose their lives; and while there would be little remorse at the death of that abrasive schemer, Lord Pontieu, the loss of a Protectioner was a far graver matter, for the Guild's importance in the diplomatic and commercial life of Albanderry is beyond estimation.

Milord gave the order to stand down, and our soldiers reluctantly lowered their weapons. The Floorsteward sent runners to the brigades reining up behind us, to inform them of the situation.

Lord Ponticu faced death in silence; no pleading or wheedling escaped his lips. I reflected that cynicism strengthens the stomach — or perhaps he was simply paralyzed with fear. But his Protectioner spoke up. "Have courage," he called out, which struck me as an astonishing remark from one in such a desperate position, for certainly it was he who was most in need of that precious commodity.

Deeply moved by his colleague's expression of faith, Gasmaster Bickle climbed to the roof of our wagon and formed his blunt arms into the Protectioners' 'Sign Ordinary of Infeudative Resistance.' That signal, he told me later, can be adequately explained only in the Guild's secret tongue, but the terms 'deep respect' and 'love of universal order' approximate its meaning.

With a gesture of his antennae Seerit ordered his minions to proceed to the south. Now our two contingents began a tense ballet, sidling like two opposing magnets along the road. As long as Seerit's cohorts kept their scissor-like pincers around their hostages' necks, we were helpless; yet because our forces outnumbered them ten to one, they dared not force the fight. I retreated into my pocket, numb with dread, and shared my fears with Bilch, though he could not hear me.

The stick-men backstepped warily along the far side of the route, while Milord's wagons and men trundled along this one. The other Lords' brigades followed slowly a furlong behind us.

At this delicate juncture we had an unexpected visitor. "Saint Gladden's fire!" Milord swore. I peeped from my pocket to see none other than that blowsy swagman, Haggleman Wimley. He sauntered down the middle of the road from the north, seemingly oblivious to our desperate straits.

"Retreat or be fired upon," the Floorsteward shouted. Wimley only smiled angelically. "I say stand down!" repeated Milord's lieutenant.

The Haggleman nodded and waved a loop of brass chain over his head. From out of nowhere a hundred colorful shapes materialized like a mirage, accompanied by the shuffling of boots and hooves.

It was an entourage of phantoms and freebooters the like of which I hope never to see again. Here were overgrown cacodemons, twitching their puffed noses like hares; a troupe of sour-faced bogeymen shambled there, dredged up in foul weather from the Louvian Marsh. Then came a band of Calisthenian bullyhuffs, alternately punching their hairy, clenched fists in the air or hiking up their kilts and racing in an arm-locked circle til they were no more than a blur. A gnattering of bump-dwarfs pranced in purple kilts; bog-matrons twitched leather crops under the tails of their apathetic giraffes.

"A menagerie suitable for display at a witches' convention," the Gasmaster whispered in disbelief.

Milord laughed humorlessly. "Lord Roundabout will be amused and irritated all at once." He scanned the columns of troops stretching into the distance behind us. "For the sake of his spleen I pray his attentions are elsewhere."

The Haggleman halted his followers and presented himself with a flourish to Milord. "I came as quickly as circumstances permitted, Your Lordship." He wore fingerless gloves and a badly frayed surcoat; his squalid hob-boots were splashed with mud. A ridiculously large sapphire, obviously paste, was slung around his neck on a length of twine. "I trust that the forces under my command will suit your requirements." With a sly smile he added, "And meet with your generous approval."

Milord winced. "Requirements, Haggleman? For a ragtag assortment of hobgoblins and dunce-ghosts?"

"Don't let their variety fool you, Sire!" he blustered. "They are a ferocious lot, quite capable of dealing death and disaster in all directions! Notice, for example, their deadly swords." He pointed out the weapons strapped to their legs: thin bodkins of lacquered marsh-reed. As he spoke, a poltfooted catawampus stumbled into its neighbor and turned to dust like a meadow puffball.

Milord sighed. "I shall take the matter under advisement, Haggleman. In the meantime —"

Haggleman Wimley stepped rudely forward and poked his face uncomfortably close to mine. His scraggly beard reeked of kippers and sour ale. "Ah, the little fox, and glad to see you again," he said. I took the liberty of snapping at him, at which he bulged his eyes in mock fear. He saw Bilch snuggled next to me and chuckled insolently. "Well, so now it's Calipash and Calipee, too! And the little fellow is about to drop a foal or two, if I'm not mistaken. You'll soon have a dozen of them, Sire, and a dozen dozen, if you're not careful."

The cheeky lout! Thinking he would not understand my Filxxx dialect, I informed him that his behavior inspired me with bottomless contempt, and I wished him a lifetime of lumbago and personal failure. "Tsk tsk, such impudence," he said, making a face. As an itinerant magic-monger he had evidently been forced to acquire a smattering of foreign tongues, for which I give him some credit.

Milord ignored his gaucherie and mine. "Doubtless by contributing this ludicrous collection of footpads and conjurer's blunders you hope to obtain some pleasant sinecure, Haggleman."

The Haggleman attempted a blush. "Sire, I would not presume —"

"Of course not," said Milord, cutting him off. "Very well. I allow you and your mangy cavalcade to accompany us at a distance of two hundred paces, with this condition: on no account attack the stickmen without my explicit order, for as you see they hold two important hostages. Is this clear?"

"Naturally, Your Lordship." He grinned and puffed himself out and stuffed his hands conceitedly into his pockets. Milord waved him away.

Milord turned to Gasmaster Bickle and confided, "When the moment of battle arrives, as it must inevitably, his magical poltroons will be trounced like mites and he will abandon any thought of compensation."

"Without a doubt, Sire," the Gasmaster murmured thoughtfully. "The churl's lack of moral fiber betrays him. But he is resourceful. With proper guidance he could be of some use."

Milord laughed. "You give him too much credit, Gasmaster. Even Grandmage Mentharch's alchemy could not place Haggleman Wimley on a narrow path."

We turned our attention again to the hateful Seerit and the dilemma he forced. Under a lowering gray sky behind him lay the desolate shore, where a weak tide lapped at the stick-men's abandoned barques. Seerit hesitated, apparently debating whether to attempt an escape into the North Channel. But with a surly shake of his head he ordered his tribe to continue south and east, towards Benefice Manor.

Without warning a lizard-like creature bolted from the Haggleman's entourage and gnashed its teeth at a stick-warrior, who instantly opened its piebald underside from collar to tail with a thrust of his scramasax. Its caul was a shimmering, slimy green and bubbled away to nothing on the ground; the rest of its carcass shriveled to a husk and blew away like a tumbleweed.

The brief combat aroused Haggleman Wimley to passion. "Charge!" he cried. The Gasmaster waved his arms frantically to our rear to indicate that Milord had not given the order to attack, and narrowly succeeded in preventing a general assault.

Screeching and howling, Wimley's battalion of paraplasms trampled off the road. Some lobbed grenades of cheap black powder wrapped in green starch, which either fizzled in midair or disappeared altogether; others spun their bodkins overhead in what they undoubtedly considered a dazzling display of martial art. The stick-men coolly awaited this motley onslaught, their brackmards and clink-clubs at the ready. In a trice they clubbed, bisected, deflated, disemboweled, pulverized or otherwise eradicated Haggleman Wimley's entire gang of buffoons. That courageous leader had meanwhile kept himself well to the rear of his forces, and already spurred his broken-backed mare in the opposite direction.

Fortunately this debacle failed to rouse the stick-men to counter-attack. They resumed their wary advance, forcing their two prisoners ahead of them. With horror I soon saw that we were less than a furlong from the main courtyard of Benefice Manor. Milord cast about desperately for some means of creating a distraction, in hopes of allowing the stick-men's two hostages to escape; then our forces would have a relatively easy victory.

But no such diversion was forthcoming. Milord called for the Floorsteward. "Bring Stitch forward," he ordered. In a moment our now battle-proven friend lay on his litter next to Milord.

"Yes, Sire?"

"I require translation. State that I am willing to parley with Seerit."

Stitch twirled his antennae and boomed several long clicks across the road. At first there was no response; then Seerit's adjutant indicated that Milord's proposals would be considered, but surrender was out of the question.

"Advise him that I am willing to discuss a trade," said Milord.

"Seerit's freedom, with stipulations, in return for the release of his two prisoners." Stitch barked and clicked again.

Seerit's adjutant gestured harshly with his forelegs: all the pellets must be turned over; he and his troops must be given unconditional freedom. In addition they required transport for their injured, the keeping of their plundered armor, and six of Milord's finest silk chemises for Seerit himself.

The Gasmaster lost his temper and spluttered incoherently. Milord frowned. "At least some of the pellets must be retained at all costs. We must temporize. State that we are taking his demands under consideration."

As Stitch relayed this message, Lord Pontieu's patience suddenly wore thin. "Get on with it, Lord Cantilouve," he shouted in annoyance, and was rudely cuffed about by his captors for interrupting.

"No fear, Lord Ventblanc; matters are proceeding," Milord shouted calmly back. Seerit consulted with his adjutant and two lieutenants.

The invaders were now only a stone's throw away from Benefice Manor and heedlessly crushed Milord's favorite hedges as they advanced. At the main entrance two footmen stood at attention, staring motionless before them though the stick-men inched closer and closer. The Gasmaster flinched. "Milord —" he began in alarm, for he had noticed it too: their rigid stance and glassy eyes were more than the hallmarks of duty — the two retainers were under a spell.

In the plaster behind them a crack appeared, and another. The wall bulged and the two footmen toppled over like dolls. With a deafening crash the entire wall collapsed in a cloud of rubble-dust, exposing Milord's den.

Furniture and *objets d'art* lay scattered everywhere in the dust. Milord's books had been ripped apart, their sheets of vellum strewn about like autumn leaves. The neck of his favorite brass candelabra was bent in two against the splintered remains of a cherished mahogany credenza.

In the midst of this chaos stood Petolzia.

Her attention was focused on Milord's depositorium. It lay at her feet, still encrusted with chunks of marble and plaster from its surrounding wall, which she had shattered with a spell. She stooped to clutch the cubical vault in her hands, but its protective essence bristled red sparks, at which she yowled like a drenched cat.

Her glance found the stick-men. With a startled shriek she flew backwards, her straggly hair stiffening like bear's hackles. She shook her amulets in a dazzling pattern and a putrid, quivering mass of colorless plasm descended from nowhere, entrapping half of the stick-men like flies in a blancmange pudding. Some of the remaining savages fled in terror, only to be blown up by explosive petards which the Floorsteward had planted on the Manor grounds as a barrier to invasion; others began frantically setting up their long poles and magic webs.

Lord Pontieu and his Guildsman, seeing their captors' attention diverted, darted to the safety of Lord Pinkleton's ranks. "They are secure," Masterfootling Farberwile reported. "Open fire at once, Sire!"

"No," Milord said thoughtfully. "Against stick-men we have effective weapons, but not against Petolzia; with luck they will destroy each other. Hold your fire." Looking rather chastened, the Masterfootling restrained his troops. But one of Lord Pinkleton's platoons, apparently not hearing the order or in an excess of zeal, unleashed a fusillade of crossbow arrows which felled many of the surviving stick-men.

Seerit himself now jumped from his litter and seized a web-pole in his claws. Flanked by his adjutant and two guards, growling and clicking, he charged at Petolzia. She shrieked and released another noxious spell; but this was neutralized by a wave of the adjutant's web, and she turned and flew into the Manor. The four stick-men stormed after her.

"My own Manor will be ransacked before my eyes," Milord said brokenly.

Lord Roundabout had joined us, and put a consoling hand on his arm. "I'm afraid we have little choice but to restrain ourselves, Closelord. To intervene in that deadly exchange would be suicidal." Milord tightened his lips in agreement.

Drawn by some dangerous impulse of curiosity, I leapt from Milord's pocket and dashed into the foyer, where I watched from the shoulder of a statue as the chase raged from antechamber to mezzanine. Petolzia's tattered black form streaked back and forth, leaving a trail of broken tables and statuary. The stick-men crashed up and down stairs in wild pursuit, shattering gilt-framed mirrors and portraits in their wake.

They cornered her at last in the dining hall and joined in hideous combat. Seerit jabbed his magical pole before him like a shortsword and whipped at her with its lethal web-strands; Petolzia responded with a Spell of Ructious Cataclasm, which destroyed Milord's buffet and chandelier but left the assaulting stick-men unscathed.

Seeing that her spells were ineffective, Petolzia withdrew a conventional weapon from her skirts: a deadly mace, studded with countless cleats and razored vanes. With dreadful and messy swiftness she lopped off the heads of Seerit's three henchmen, spattering gray blood over the dining room walls.

Seerit backed warily into the foyer. Petolzia waltzed close to him, flinging her mace viciously back and forth. Seerit answered with swipes of his broadsword. He held his batfowl pole before him like a cudgel and flicked its magical web-strands, at which she ducked and bobbed her head like a boxer. She discharged fiery spells from her fingernails, but Seerit dissipated them with his pole as a rod takes the lightning.

Seerit turned suddenly and bolted into Milord's den. I followed and scrambled up to a shelf. He thrust the abandoned depositorium under one foreleg and prepared to flee through the gap in the room's wall, but Petolzia circled outside with the speed of a crow and blocked his exit. She pointed to the box and imitated the clicking language of the stick-men. Though I understand little of that tongue, her gist was obvious: "Give the box to me and have your freedom."

Seerit responded with ugly syllables and a blunt gesture. Petolzia cursed and threw down her mace. By sheer force of her volcanic will she now pressed him slowly backwards towards me, wearing him down relentlessly like an arm wrestler. He threw a broken chair at her but she dodged it; he parried her advance with pincers and sword, but she feinted and raked huge gashes in his neck with her fingers. He crumpled to the floor. With her fists she knocked the pole and box from his grasp and gored him in the upper abdomen with an elbow.

I discharged my *gnozzt* at Petolzia's face, and its liquor splashed in her lopsided eyes. She shrieked, momentarily blinded, and in that instant Seerit retrieved his pole and thrust it at her with his last strength. With a sound like 'poink' it pierced her scrawny chest.

She moaned in surprise and slumped to her knees, panting heavily.

Bubbles of dirty pink froth welled up at the corners of her mouth. She wrenched the pole from her chest. It made a horrible sucking sound as it emerged, and left a green-black hole that led into a bottomless, evil vortex from which I had to wrench my eyes away. Seeing that her death was inevitable, Seerit smiled in satisfaction and died.

The combat outside had ceased, every stick-man in the area dead or taken. Our troops stood by, gazing in dread and fascination at the awful scene in the Manor. Milord and his two generals stepped through the gaping hole in the wall and into the remains of the den.

Petolzia slid onto her back, the breath ruckling in her lungs like stones in a mill. She looked up at Milord with a wistful expression. "I regret I did not avail myself of the perquisites you described," she gasped. "Particularly the bezoar, to rid me of these rotten wasps…" Even as she spoke, the parasites buzzing above her began to drop like flies on a sill, dying as her life-force faded.

"You'll soon be rid of them," said Milord.

The death-mask came over her face, a foul and final thing even in a witch. With a fleeting, ugly smile she said, "An evil mind is a comfort," and perished. Her body dissolved in a wisp of bitter smoke.

Cheers went up outside. With a huge sigh of relief Milord perched me on his shoulder and offered a sweetmeat from his pocket. "You tipped the balance, Flick. Clever fellow!"

"A lesson for us all," said Gasmaster Bickle.

"A fine day for mascots!" put in the Masterfootling.

Milord stooped over Seerit's corpse and picked up the depositorium. He placed it on a righted table and began to turn its release levers, but jerked his hand away. "Your protective essence tingles even a Lord's fingers, Gasmaster."

"My apologies, Sire." Gasmaster Bickle briefly blocked our sight with his broad form as he performed a series of secret ritual gestures and rhythmic gargling noises. "There we are, Sire."

Milord lifted the vault's lid, removed the gold-and-ivory box and raised the lid.

It was empty.

X

A BOTANICAL AVENGER

Milord looked blankly at his Protectioner. "Perhaps you removed the pellet-box for safekeeping...?"

The Gasmaster was shaken. "No, Sire, certainly not."

Milord pointed to the smudge on the floor where Petolzia's form had evaporated. "Then she must have removed them."

"I think not, Sire, as we saw her struggling with Seerit for your depositorium." He was mortified, for it was his own oversight which had allowed her to penetrate the Manor at all: in the flurry of preparations for battle, he had neglected to establish the day's fresh vapor barrier. The mistake was too painful for mention.

"True enough," said Milord, deeply troubled. "Well, form a triple detail to search for them at once; they must be located." The Gasmaster saluted and dutifully set off.

I recalled that Salvemaster Worrant, Lord Pontieu's only known spy in our household, had been unaware of the location of the pellets, for he had tried without success to learn it from me aboard ship; therefore he could not have taken them. Had another of Pontieu's henchmen raided the depositorium in our absence? This too seemed unlikely, for the Manor had been well guarded by Milord's pursuivants during that time. And still later, only two days ago in fact, though it seemed an age, all of Pontieu's belligerents had been unavailable for burgling, swept up as they were in the whirlwinds of war. The pellets' disappearance was a mystery.

We returned outside. Dirty clouds fussed and scudded in a cold afternoon sky. Under the Masterfootling's direction, work gangs began clearing the Manor and grounds of their gruesome debris. The stick-men's corpses were unceremoniously piled in an empty battle wagon, which trundled off, escorted by a dozen yapping coach dogs, to be burned or dumped into the sea. Milord delivered a brief speech of praise and gratitude to his victorious brigades and dismissed them; he promised medals to the fallen and generous stipends to their widows.

Milord retired to his terrace room to confer with Lord Roundabout, and I ran to check on Bilch. My mate continued to snooze and swell in his drawer as peacefully as a strawberry in a patch. I kissed him and said a prayer to Filfalxxx, and tucked him in again.

The battle had taken only two days, but the exhaustion of a fort-night swept over me. Anticipating a snooze before supper, I returned to Milord's chambers. He had exchanged his uncomfortable greaves and mail hauberk for a comfortable satin robe, and reclined on a couch with a decanter of his famous Pale Restoratus IX. I jumped gratefully into his holster.

"Our highest priority now is to inform the Assembly of the grave circumstances prevailing," he said thoughtfully. "Perhaps collectively, by means of some exceptional diplomatic or economic pressure, we can induce the Council to rescind Auntie's curse."

Lord Roundabout had also removed most of his armor. He stood across the room clad only in his rouge battle-pantaloons and quilted under-tunic. With the Masterfootling's assistance he was attempting to shrug free of the crude ailettes protecting his shoulders. "A reasonable proposal," he said, tugging at his upper sleeve. His shoulder popped suddenly free of its armored covering, and he toppled to the floor. With a flurry of apologies Milord's servant helped him to his feet and hastily fetched an extra robe for him from Milord's closet.

"Or perhaps we should simply offer to return all of their confounded pellets when they are found, if the witches will recant," Milord continued.

Lord Roundabout snorted in disgust. Savagely tightening the sash of his robe, he said, "Whatever initiative we take, my intuition suggests that Lord Pontieu will find some excuse to oppose it, though our efforts redound to the benefit of all Albanderry."

"Even he would not be so vile," Milord said, but his tone was dubious.

"Time will reveal just how badly Lord Pontieu's colors have been stained."

Their colloquium continued for some time longer. I fell into a doze, which was penetrated now and then by snatches of conversation. At last Milord took a deep breath and stood up. "For now, food and rest, Closelord." He invited Lord Roundabout to sup and stay the night, an invitation which his faithful friend gratefully accepted. We shared a light repast, graced with conversation no more profound than Lord Roundabout's terse praises of the lamb pie and my concurring squeaks. Early in the morning we would leave together for the Assembly's first plenary session since the impromptu council of war; we would ask the help of all the Lords to rescue Grandmage Mentharch from the insanity so maliciously imposed on him.

Evening fell. My energies revived, and taking some tidbits from the table, I paid a visit to Stitch and brought him up to date. I was gratified to see that Hostler Pimfix had taken a fascinated interest in his care, thus assuring a swift recuperation from his wounds. With his natural stoicism Stitch accepted his isolation in the stables, for he understood that it was necessary while anti-stick-man passions cooled. He happily thanked and congratulated me for my revenge on Petolzia, and asked kindly after Bilch. I left him with a tiny volume of Filxxx lore to amuse him during his convalescence.

It occurred to me that Thindle Spinkite had not reported to Milord since the battle. This was perplexing, as he had been nominally in charge of the Manor during that time. I slipped through the fragrance-ducts to his nook.

He stood in an odd posture, his gangling form sagged against the wall, and absently caressed something in his hands. At the sound of my claws on the wooden floor he gazed forlornly down at me for a long moment. Without further greeting he said, "Stranded here alone, that's what I was. Alone and faced with temptation in a great household. Can you blame me, Flick?"

"Blame for what?" I squeaked. He held out the box of pellets. Thindle, a thief! I stared at him in shock.

"I know, it's hard to believe. Too much frustration, and for too long." I backed uncertainly away, fearful of the change that had come over him. "Oh pish, Flickamerry, I haven't become an ogre, ready to swallow you, ears and all." He chuckled emptily.

But how had he even known of the pellets, I asked?

"The household knows more of His Grace's affairs than he realizes." He sank down on his bunk and closed his eyes. "Filching them was the simple part. His Lordship protects a vault well from evil magic, but neglects to guard against simple burglary. But now what in the name of the Realm can I do with these devilish pips?" He combed his fingers wearily through his thinning hair. "Petolzia's dead, and in any case I wouldn't have the stomach to deal with her... And I've no connections to bargain with the Witches' Council." He gazed up at his tiny, yellowed windowpane. "Not a well thought-out crime, was it, Flick?"

"You have no conception of their importance. You must return the pellets at once," I told him firmly. "No matter what; and throw yourself on Milord's mercy."

"It will be the end for me, Flick." He fondled the box as a man tests the edge of a knife: with satisfaction and desire, but also with fear of the pain and death in it. He lifted the filigreed ivory lid. The glistening grains pulsed and squirmed like worm-beans. The sound of an ocean wafted softly from them — the emanations of the stick-men's souls? Or the aura of their binding spell?

He slammed the box shut and took several hard swallows from a flask under his pillow. "All right then. A man can't live forever under a cloud. Come to that, he can't live forever, cloud or no." He stood up. On his door hung a carved *kalakxx*, or soul-freshener, which I had given him one Salvers' Eve. He stroked it with both hands and pushed out of his tiny chamber. From the Kitchenmaster he requested an audience with his master.

I ran upstairs ahead of him and found Milord at his desk. Masterfootling Farberwile stood at his shoulder, presenting the final reports of battle for his review. I slipped into his holster.

"A few stick-men appear to have escaped our siege at the peaks, Your Grace. And some thirty of them remain penned under heavy guard near Trillphyte Manor, awaiting disposition."

Milord was pensive. "We must —" There was a faint knock at the door, which the Masterfootling attended. "Ah, Underfootling Spinkite. Yes?"

Thindle entered and bowed, licking his lips nervously. "I have neglected to make my report, Your Lordship." He shifted his weight uneasily from one foot to the other.

"There were no difficulties during our absence, I trust?"

"None, Sire." He half-turned away and cleared his throat. "Ah, there is one small matter, Your Grace…" Milord leaned back in his chair, sensing something amiss.

"I thought it might be wise to secure certain of Your Lordship's valuables, in case events turned for the worse." With a tremulous hand he took the box from his pocket and placed it on a table.

Milord sat looking at him in silence for a long time. A drop of sweat moved slowly down the side of Thindle's face. "And why have you waited til now to inform me of this?"

"Well, Your Grace," he stammered, "I thought — well, that is, it seemed that with circumstances being as they were, and…" His voice trailed off.

Milord stood up, moved to the window and stood gazing out, hands folded behind him. "The punishment for theft from a Lord is quite severe."

"Yes, Your Lordship," Thindle whispered.

Milord studied the image of black fields and darkened serf-huts in his bay window. "You've held the rank of Underfootling a long time, haven't you?"

"Seventeen years." The words rustled like dried grass.

"Seventeen years… quite a drought. Perhaps you've already had the punishment, and only now commit the crime." Milord turned and positioned himself in an armchair. He opened a velvet presentation case on its arm and reverently lifted out a cloisonné medallion.

"This is an honorary badge, given me years ago by the Protectioners' Guild. Tell me, what does it mean to you?"

"A rare and special honor, Your Grace," Thindle said with hushed fervor.

"An honor, yes; but what else?" Thindle was silent.

Milord put great emphasis on his next words, clipping them like an overgrown hedge. "It is also a symbol, Underfootling. A reminder of the enormous responsibility exercised by the Protectioners' Guild: a duty than which there is none greater in Albanderry. Particularly now that we face —" Milord caught himself "— especially now."

"Yes, Your Grace."

Milord's voice rose. "Those who are initiated into the Guild swear an oath which is as binding as any witch's spell. There is no recorded instance of violation of that pledge, whose syllables are unknown even to Lords." The Masterfootling looked on solemnly. Thindle's knees trembled, and he steadied himself with three fingers on the back of a chair.

"Now. I am faced with two problems. The first is the security of Benefice Manor, which has already been compromised on several sides. Indeed, faithful men gave their lives to preserve it, while you threatened it perniciously from within.

"The second problem is closely related. The Gasmaster, on whom our security may soon depend more than you realize, no longer has a chief assistant, for Salvemaster Worrant is dead." Shock registered in Thindle's face, though he said nothing. Speculation had been rampant in the household concerning Worrant's disappearance, but Milord had cautioned me to absolute discretion, and word of his tragic fate had not yet escaped Milord's closest advisers.

With some uneasiness he continued. "And so a novel possibility comes to mind. Do you see it?" Thindle only tilted forward slightly. "I mean apprenticeship to the Guild."

Thindle was dumbfounded. The lines in his face, previously frozen in shock, now relaxed like an idiot's. "Guild?" he said without hearing himself.

"Exactly. It is an arduous and demanding road, Spinkite! But if you succeed, perhaps even the position of Assistant Protectioner is not inconceivable."

"Your Grace, I —"

Milord waved him to silence. "I thus present you with a choice: this program, or…the alternative."

Thindle was as pale as chalk. "Your Lordship is too merciful."

Milord rubbed his chin. "Possibly so. But you accept?" His servant nodded, though it is hard to say how much of that motion was merely a consequence of the involuntary swaying which overcame his lanky body. "Then the matter is settled. Arrangements will be made on the morrow." Milord glanced at the Masterfootling, who acknowledged the order with an imperceptible movement.

Thindle regained himself somewhat and bowed repeatedly, saying "Thank you, Your Grace!" each time, and hastily took his leave.

Milord sighed and looked tiredly at his senior servant. "Speaking as my general, do you approve of this paradoxical strategy?"

The Masterfootling massaged his hands in thought and studied the ceiling. "I recall Spinkite's conflict with Ranktwo Sparseman's cousin years ago, Your Grace. It soured the underfootling's disposition like bitter verjuice in a well. But if sweet water still flows at that well's source, a traditional punishment would certainly not bring it forth."

Milord closed the medallion case and set it aside. "Responsibility of great magnitude is itself a form of punishment," he said to himself, and shook his head. "The man must be carefully watched, lest I have made a terrible misjudgment."

"So he shall be, Your Grace."

Milord took the box of pellets in his hands and frowned. "Again these monstrous grains…" He made a little noise of disgust and wrinkled his forehead. "In the morning we shall analyze what might be their best disposition."

"As you direct, Sire."

Milord dismissed the Masterfootling and with immense relief retired to bed. I cuddled next to him under my comforter. A waning crescent moon, hardly a sliver, shone with dwindling brilliance through the mullioned windows. It was a warm, humid night and

Milord's darkened bedchamber was rife with mysterious scents from the gardens. I lay awake trying to sort them out, while Milord slipped immediately into deep slumber.

I wondered at the state of the Grandmage's wits: was he still capable of casting a spell, or even of deciphering the runes in his own workshop? Did he rage wildly about his castle? Or had he taken feebly to his bed in despair and confusion?

The midnight hour passed. All creatures know instinctively, without hearing the strike of the clock, when that precious moment arrives, for we sense then that the darkness will no longer continue its inexorable deepening. The fading hope of dawn swells quickly to a certainty, giving easy birth to prayers.

There was a sharp knock at the door. The Masterfootling requested an urgent audience. "Your Lordship, Kitchenmaster Traysmith has made a startling discovery."

Milord sat up and threw a robe over his shoulders. Still rubbing the sleep from his eyes, he propped himself in an armchair. I jumped to its arm. "Yes? What is the time, please?" he mumbled.

Traysmith stepped forward. "Forgive me, Your Lordship; the hour stands only at two." Milord grunted and gestured for another candle to be lit. "Handman Armright and the Cellaress were searching section twelve of the potherb cellar," Traysmith continued, "and encountered the missing Footling Stonebrew."

Milord fumbled grumpily with his robe. "And?"

With a note of surprise the Masterfootling put in, "We had assumed that Stonebrew accompanied Salvemaster Worrant when he defected, Your Grace, and therefore that he met some unpleasant fate, perhaps known to yourself."

Milord was now fully awake. "To my knowledge Footling Stonebrew was not among the Salvemaster's accomplices." He stroked my head, and I confirmed with an upward glance that I had not seen Stonebrew aboard the *Obnounce Dittaneer*. "Continue your account, Kitchenmaster."

Traysmith hesitated. "His condition is…unhealthy, Your Grace. He lies on a bed of straw in a disheveled state, quarreling animatedly with himself in a fragment of mirror. He asks again and again why its reflection fails to reverse his image up for down, as well as right for left, and slyly offers various theories in reply. Then he parades about his cell, mumbling child's rhymes. In effect, he has gone quite balmy."

"How strange!" said Milord. "And how very sad. Is any cause apparent for this unusual illness?"

The Kitchenmaster averted his pale blue eyes. He thrust one hand into an apron pocket and withdrew two green bottlettes, one empty and one unopened. "These containers were next to him, Your Grace."

"Ho la!" Milord shouted. He jumped up, nearly knocking me to the floor, and seized the full one from his servant.

Traysmith recoiled in alarm. "Your Grace, I had no —"

"No fear, no fear, Kitchenmaster!" said Milord, hoisting the bottlette jubilantly like castanets over his head and doing a little jig. "Stout fellow! You have saved the Grandmage, and Albanderry!" He threw his arms around his astounded servant and hugged him, then abruptly stepped back and gave himself over to an intent examination of the bottlette. He rubbed its metal netting, tested its bung with a fingernail and found it intact, and peered at its hazy contents against the light of a candle. "Thank you and well done," he said in a satisfied voice, and sat down again. "A double-standard bonus for Handman Armright and the Cellaress, and twice that for yourself; and see that Footling Stonebrew is attended by the physicians."

"At once, Your Lordship." The puzzled but happy Kitchenmaster turned and left.

Milord slipped the bottlette into a pocket of his nightshirt. "His pilferage exacted a high price," he murmured.

"Fortunately the potion's very potency prevented him from consuming it all, Sire," said the Masterfootling.

"Yes…" Milord drummed his fingers momentarily on the arm of his chair and jumped up. "Summon Hostler Pimfix at once, and instruct him to release Grandmage Mentharch's signal bird." The Masterfootling bowed and set off in haste.

Milord dressed quickly. He awakened Lord Roundabout and excitedly briefed him of the discovery. We tumbled downstairs and gathered over a pot of tea to await Mentharch's arrival.

But more than three hours passed with no sign of the wizard, and our excitement sank into consternation. The eastern sky turned a pale gray — I recalled the elegant color of Lord Pontieu's suit — then oxblood, and the fresh yellow of ripe bananas. My Lords sat anxiously in the receiving chamber, sipping much more tea than they wanted and chewing their crumpets without interest. The Gasmaster and the Masterfootling stood silently against the wall as another hour slipped by.

"Seven o'clock and he has not arrived," Milord said quietly.

"Perhaps the calamity is already upon us," answered Lord Roundabout.

"And there is no other means of communicating with him —?" Milord said desperately, glancing at his servants.

The Masterfootling replied with a series of scholarly frowns, culminating in a helpless shrug. The Gasmaster only looked more dolefully at his shoes and murmured, "The location of the wizard's castle is known only to himself and his small assistant."

"But did Hostler Pimfix not note the direction taken by his messenger petrel?" Milord persisted.

"He stated that it flew straight upward, Sire, as though diving from the clouds, but in reverse, and was quickly lost in the night skies."

Lord Roundabout grunted and stood up. "Just as well leave for the Assembly then, Closelord; we can be notified by signal mirror if he arrives during our absence. And perhaps one of our peers will know of another means by which to contact him."

Milord reluctantly agreed. "Through the Marsh?"

With a grimace of distaste Lord Roundabout replied, "The gong is silent until noon, Closelord Cantilouve, which allows ample time for travel; impatience would only stain the clothing." He referred to the insipid green discoloration by which his suit had been soiled during our previous trip through the Louvian Marsh.

"The Coast Road, then?" said Milord, concealing a smile.

"The sea air will freshen our wits," agreed Lord Roundabout, snugging his waistcoat over his hips.

Milord wrapped the last bottlette carefully in a doubled linen napkin and showed it to Lord Roundabout. "I dare not let the potion out of my hands again, Closelord; we will take an armed escort." Lord Roundabout nodded soberly as Milord secured the potion in an inside pocket next to my holster. It gave off an icy, feverish tingling like that of

Vulgia's monstrous garden, and made me shiver. In the opposite pocket he placed the box of pellets, whose aura was almost as disturbing. It would be an uncomfortable journey.

We adjourned. The morning air was wonderfully crisp, the horizon sharp against a perfectly cloudless sky. The fields of Benefice Manor had been scrubbed by windy hands, and showed their roan skins to a cool white sun. We packed into our carriage and snuggled under our trotcozies, while a dozen armed retainers took to their nervous mounts alongside.

Milord skimmed through the morning's parchment dispatch as we rattled off. "Pfff," he said, throwing down the journal, "Lord Pontieu has already filed a Petition for Summary Recompense for his losses in battle. The knave would have us lace his boots as well!"

"Lord Pontieu is an arrant clinchpoop," Lord Roundabout said vehemently, jabbing his pink hands in the cold air. "And this Petition is a new height of impertinence!"

Milord touched the thin frost on his window. " 'Impertinent behavior is the sally of an ulterior man,' my father once said. He meant that it is a villain's way of testing those around him. A prompt and forceful response is the best rebuttal."

Lord Roundabout's lips tightened. "Force in the form of…?"

"Proof. Proof of his treachery, Closelord." Milord energetically rubbed a large disc in the window's condensate, replaced his hands under our lap blanket and peered out at the passing fields. "We must have witnesses."

"But the entire Assembly witnessed his dissimulation when you were abducted."

"And the entire Assembly was deceived by it, Closelord," said Milord. "No, we must locate at least one of his accomplices, and bring that man's testimony before our peers." He stroked my neck affectionately. "If only a mascot's word carried more weight, we would have our witness, and a fine one at that." If Filxxxs could purr, I would have done so then.

"A simpering malcontent," Lord Roundabout muttered. He added something about bile and an intolerance for breakfast, and lapsed into a morose silence for the rest of the journey.

Soon we turned south and jounced into the Coast Road, where we were joined by other carriages en route to the Square, and their drivers exchanged formal waves with ours. Across the broad, glittering reach of the North Channel, the volcanic foothills of Catscat Isle yawned upward to their forbidding peaks. In the sunlight along the shore fluttered a few braided butterflies — the magical creatures deployed by the Grandmage to offset a witches' curse of geological magnitude — but many of them faltered in flight and only narrowly escaped being engulfed by the crashing surf. Alarming evidence of the wizard's waning powers!

I fell asleep. It seemed only a moment before we arrived in Albanderry Square, where the mood was ebullient. Carriages disgorged their occupants in front of the Assembly and moved off, leaving clusters of Lords happily greeting one another in the warmest degrees of address. They loudly shared their tales of battle, and embroidered them further with each re-telling. In the Square's central plaza, another group pointed up into the branches of an ancient magnolia tree, chuckling and nudging each other in recollection of some boyhood episode. Elsewhere Lords strolled in pairs and threesomes, engaging in bright badinage.

At sight of Milord a cry of welcome went up from the nearest clique and quickly spread to the others. Soon dozens of admiring Lords and pursuivants were jostling around us, to shouts of "Well done!" and much hand-pumping and affectionate touches. I was proud of my master, but the pressing crowd made me acutely claustrophobic, particularly as I was already squeezed between the disquieting auras of the bottlette and the box of pellets. Hopping out of Milord's holster, I darted between the forest of legs to the plaza.

I stopped by a wooden bench to catch my breath. An old man sat there, sadly contemplating the dappled shade between his thin knees. Something about the way he hunched forward in his worn clothes was oddly familiar. I jumped to the end of the bench and studied his face. The wrinkles around his eyes had been precociously incised by something more than time and wind — some unspeakable sight perhaps, or grave responsibility thrust too soon on young shoulders. He had presided somewhere, at a contest, or game — that was it! — a game of deck-whizzle, disputed by stripe-shirted men on a sultry night at sea, while he hammered a solid leather drum with a wooden pin.

It was Firstmate Crowell. But now the tattered breeches hung from his lean frame like storm-ripped sails from their yards, and his usual air of insolent vigor had been replaced by one of bottomless fatigue. He looked at me for a long time. At last he said in a flat and melancholy way, "Well, here's a familiar rascal." Then, as though the matter were concluded, he leaned back and returned his tired gaze to the crowd of furled masts in the harbor below. He withdrew a splinter of wood from his pocket and applied it absentmindedly to his few remaining teeth.

(I have often observed this phenomenon in people grown weary of the world: a thought flits across their minds; we catch a glimpse of it in their eyes just before it disappears, like a bird into a dark wood. Then, after a long delay, they reluctantly give voice to the vanished idea. In the silence that follows we are disturbed by a vague uneasiness.)

Milord's colleagues were dispersing to enter the Assembly building, and he beckoned. I ran to him and squeaked my discovery of the *Obnounce Dittaneer's* sole survivor. "So our witness arrives, and with marvelous timing." He pressed Lord Roundabout's arm, and both strode purposefully to where Crowell sat.

Milord stepped firmly in front of the seaman. "Firstmate Crowell, I believe."

Crowell continued gazing with an impenetrable expression at the forest of masts. Slowly he pocketed his toothpick, shuffled to his feet and executed a clumsy bow. "Good morning, Your Lordship."

"The morning is rapidly improving, at any rate. Though for a sailor in port, never quite satisfactory, isn't that so?"

"A sailor always wants a ship, Sire." Crowell's eyes widened as he recognized Milord and realized the sudden import of his situation. "I had no choice, Sire, on pain of death," he blurted, his voice suddenly loud and querulous. "I beg Your Lordship's forgiveness."

Milord stiffened. "No choice, Firstmate? On whose order?"

"Why, Captain Worrant's, Sire. But —"

"Of course, but who commanded him?"

Fear dilated the sailor's eyes. He took an agitated, involuntary step backward. "Your Lordship, I was commanded to say nothing."

"And I command you to speak."

Crowell struggled visibly with himself. "Sire, I knew nothing of what the Captain did. I only —"

"Firstmate, you see correctly that you lie between two great ships, and fear your tiny boat will be swamped. But there is no help for it. Pick one ship and leap."

Crowell looked desperately right and left, but encountered only the stern face of Lord Roundabout and a few idle strollers. A gust flew up from the piers with the tart smells of fish cuttings and tarred ropes. In the distance a gull was outraced by her competitor to a bit of orange peel and cried bitterly.

"Support me and enjoy my protection; resist, or labor in indecision, and more sorrow will surely be yours," added Milord.

Crowell lowered his eyes. "It was … it was Lord Pontieu," he whispered.

Milord nodded without surprise. "Be assured that you are under my protection from this moment, Firstmate. For now, remain here until summoned." He turned to consult with Lord Roundabout. The Firstmate slumped like a rag doll onto his bench.

I jumped down, drawn by sympathy to the broken man's side. From my Lords' huddled conference came snatches of urgent conversation: "…implications of this…conspiracy to engage in barratry…breach of Lordly duty," and so forth. Crowell took on the haggard look of a condemned man.

But I was eager to learn the fate of the vessel that had carried us to Catsmouthport, and tactless enough to indulge that curiosity. I touched his trousers questioningly. A heavy sob wracked his body, and he buried his face in his arm.

"All right," he said at last, exhaling deeply. "I suppose the telling of it might bring me some ease."

He waited until I thought he had changed his mind; but it was only that same habit of delay, of weary reticence, to which I have already alluded. "We made way well enough for two days, though the lack of brass and iron was a trial. The winds were favorable and the men fought less than usual. But then without warning the thrust-trees took Pinleaf prisoner and mutinied. The only wonder is that they didn't do it sooner, considering how cruel he was to them.

"They made up for his stinginess by swilling their food-slops like common pigs. Without his brutal pruning they grew like fireweeds and choked the rudderstock, and we blew aimlessly out to sea. In two days we reached the Dallydrums, where not a breath of wind stirs the year round. With neither thrust nor sail, we were stuck like a fly in pone-pudding."

I shivered in the morning sun. My Lords concluded their tête-a-tête, shook their heads decisively and strode towards the Assembly. It was the only time Milord has ever forgotten me; but I could not resent him, burdened as he was with matters of extreme gravity. And in any case I wanted despite myself to hear the rest of Crowell's terrible narrative.

"Until then they had confined themselves to the hold. But as the rebellion blossomed, they began wrenching their way inexorably up through the decks, one after another, pushing forward til we were confined to a few bulkheads in the bow." Crowell lifted his head bleakly from his sleeve.

"Picture us trapped there, hearing nothing the day long but their devilish thrumming, and the slow cracking and splintering of wood! And at night they tortured us by humming evil dirges. It was dreadful, I tell you.

"Then, to make matters worse, our water and rations began to run out. One night Ongly and Peltmailer couldn't take any more. They sneaked down the sternpost, armed only with shortswords." He sagged against the bench. "There was a scuffle, and then…" Crowell looked at me through a mask of horror. "The screams, Flick…The *screams!*"

With a shaking hand he fumbled in his shirt pocket for a well-chewed pipe. "It was a dullard who saved us finally, though the salvage was only temporary. We lay in our bunks the next night, forced to listen to the awful sounds of creaking planks and tree-chants. Suddenly Noment Slagpile exclaimed, 'Vapor!'. Of course, he meant the gas that Captain Worrant, rest his soul, used to spray on the men when they got too rowdy.

"At first light we hung tackle and ratlines on the hull. Slagpile pulled himself to the Captain's cabin and pinched a few bottles of Oceaneer's Ordinary. We knocked together a crude system of tubes from scraps of wood, forced them into the hold and caulked over the hatches. It was a tricky business, snuffing out those blasted trees without getting tangled in their murderous branches, or putting ourselves to sleep as well, but we managed it." He put down his pipe unlit.

"We set to carving a new rudder and oars, but starvation and thirst struck before we could use them. One by one the men died. I am the only survivor, unless you count the Treemaster, such as he is." He sighted down the narrow street which connects the bottom of the Square to the quays. It was through that grimy backwater neighborhood that our captors had whirled us so long ago, it seemed. "He's there, Flick. It's what he deserves, I suppose, though it seems a harsh end."

I was bursting with questions, but held my tongue. "I remember little after that, but somehow the *Dittaneer* found her way back home. There's not much left of the old girl now; she'll be lucky to get barge duty, if you want to call that luck." He spat bitterly. "They'll use her for a rubbish-scow." With bitter sarcasm he added, "You'd think a great magician like Grandmage Mentharch would have taught his wretched plants better manners."

"But how was it that such a work of magic came into private hands at all?" I asked.

He seemed to understand me, though I squeaked in Filxxxish; but his expression again became vacant, losing even the spark of sarcasm which had briefly enlivened it. He turned away, and I feared he would retreat irrevocably into himself while I was still anxious to learn more; but in a moment he faced me again, his mouth twisted into a sardonic smile. "You and your Lord must be the only ones in Albanderry who don't know."

"Lord Pontieu stole it," I guessed.

"Hardly," he said with a hollow chuckle. "The damned thing was rented."

"Rented? To whom?"

He shrugged again, irritably. "To Captain Worrant's agent, I suppose. To anyone. At the Maritime Centrum they're as easy as your purchase of a penny-pudding." He shook his head. "A sorry day it is when a great wizard leads his miracles to the common marketplace for lease."

Sorry indeed! Had Mentharch been forced to such a reckless venture by ordinary economic pressures?

Crowell initiated a sigh of resignation, but it ended in a cynical grunt. "Well, there's no help for it now. Let's only pray the cobble-rot strikes his filthy trees, and we'll take our chances with the doldrums." He banged his pipe out against the edge of the bench.

We were interrupted by the boom of the Assembly gong, readily audible even from the Square. With a quick apology and farewell to my sad informant, I dashed across the cobblestones to the door of the Assembly. In the mascots' holding area I glimpsed Lizzault, Lord Pontieu's repulsive mascot; he was luffing next to his new companion, a charming frilled lizard, and other creatures waiting impatiently for their masters. A steward tried to divert me to that chamber, but I slipped between his boots and found Milord, and popped into his warm pocket.

Lord Trillphyte stood at the podium. "Hear all present, hear this: by authority of Albanderry Assembly, I announce the presence of a Quorum Sufficient." Three peals of the gong convincingly punctuated his sentence, and he stepped down.

The chuffy-cheeked Gong Annunciator swept his eyes severely around the chamber. "Item the first: Lord Munchfirth has petitioned to speak concerning Article XVI, Provision Thirty-seven of the Bylaws. This Provision details constraints on fish-serfs having an annual income of fewer than fifty bezants." How quickly the toils and grief of war were forgotten! Would no one speak with gratitude of Milord's brilliant leadership?

Lord Munchfirth separated his corpulent cruppers from his seat-cushions and assumed an expository posture at the podium. "It is my sad duty to address this august sodality on an untoward subject; I shall confine myself to a brief exordium. I refer to those anemic fish-workers who labor under the indefensible limitations imposed by this august Assembly —" he bit off the word with trenchant sarcasm "— to achieve their meager subsistence."

Milord and Lord Roundabout whispered urgently back and forth, debating whether to break in with a Point of Order to reveal the Grandmage's dilemma. They decided to wait until Lord Munchfirth had concluded his remarks.

The speaker adjusted his pince-nez and quickly warmed to his subject. "Condemned to truckle and scrape for long gray days amidst the parings and scales, never questioning their lack of those sweet entitlements which others take for granted, they press their rusting work-hooks into dead and dying fish…Cowering and exhausted by daily struggle, their aching backs bend under officially sanctioned bullying." He put a hand to his back in a gesture of rheumatic sympathy. It was well known that Lord Munchfirth hoped his Ciceronian eloquence would gain him the coveted position of Most Harmonious Speaker.

"But meanwhile there also flourish those unscrupulous scofflaws who, oblivious to the regulations oppressing their less fortunate neighbors, succeed in filling their purses with ill-gotten coin." He raked the congregation with a withering look. "…while this Assembly basks in pretense and delicately turns its eyes and ears away to pleasant diversions!" He banged the lectern, his wattles shaking like jelly, and thundered, "Nullibists! Marplots! Mugwumpery and obfuscation prevail at every side, nurtured by a dastardly coalition in our very midst, who daily fill this once-dignified hall with their bursts of garbled hoo-ha!"

Enthusiastic shouts of "Hear hear!" surged like swollen waters on all sides, but were interrupted by a vigorous blow of the gong. "Lord Gracewright Cantilouve Benefice rises," intoned the Annunciator.

Milord rose, and all hailed their victorious Commander of Forces. Milord spoke without taking the podium. "My Lords of the Realm," he began in a voice heavy with concern, "I thank you for your recognition. But I regret that my comments must address a matter graver even than that so ably expounded by Lord Munchfirth; graver by far." Milord planted his feet more firmly under him and held out his arms. I sensed that he was greatly relieved to be sharing his burden at last with his peers.

"Less than two fortnights ago, an extraordinary meeting took place at Benefice Manor. It was initiated —" Milord steered his glance methodically around the room "— by Grandmage Mentharch himself." An astonished murmur rippled through the audience.

"Today, even as we nudge our bloated agenda from its berth, that vital wizard's wits weaken and dwindle, stung by a witch's curse!" This dreadful report precipitated a brouhaha, above which Milord shouted, "And unless he receives the anodyne in my possession within two days, he will become an imbecile, drooling and gibbering in some dark corner of his castle!"

Lord Pontieu stood up at the other side of the gallery, and with his customary air of conceit signaled a desire to be heard. The Annunciator banged his gong again and again, agitatedly proclaiming a State of Bifid Discourse, and at length brought about a decrescendo in the commotion.

"Lord Benefice asserts a marvelous need, to be sure," Lord Pontieu began smoothly. "Protected by such urgent requirements, any Lord's concoction would be immune to Article XII, Provision Seventy-three, whose revised principles of taxation Lord Benefice has already disputed in this very chamber." Discordant rumblings arose here and there. "Accordingly, a logical man inquires, what proof is there of this awesome crisis?" He cocked his head innocently. "And why has Lord Benefice waited until now to inform us of it?"

Milord reddened. "I aver that the safety of Albanderry is at stake, and you impugn my integrity?"

Pontieu ignored the question. Abruptly replacing his air of contrived innocence with one of scornful ridicule, he demanded, "Perhaps it is you, Lord Benefice, whose wits, strained by the pressures of wartime command, now shrink from the acceptance of ordinary and legitimate law, and fabricate this fanciful story solely —"

"This is foul slander!" Milord thundered, and all at once I saw Pontieu's strategy: to arouse him to such anger that he lost sight of his purpose. For a fact, Milord's heart already raced and pounded uncomfortably next to my holster. "And just where is this essential 'anodyne'?" Lord Pontieu asked contemptuously.

Milord grabbed the linen-swaddled bottlette from his pocket and thrust it high overhead. "Here!" he shouted. "It is the Mountainwitches' own brew! The curative must reach the Grandmage's lips before the morrow's morrow, or even the Guild itself will be helpless against their evil whims!"

Lord Pontieu grinned wolfishly. With the deadly calm of a storm's eye he stepped to the podium. "Under the previously cited Provision of Article XII of the Bylaws, I demand impoundment of this decoction, to be surrendered at once for disposition by the Executive Committee."

Nervously massaging his left arm, Lord Trillphyte joined him from the wings. "The Office of the Exchequeur concurs."

Milord looked around him, stunned; a dead silence filled the hall. No event could take precedence over implementation of the Bylaws; and already a marshal of the Assembly strode down the aisle to take possession of the bottlette.

"Clangorous twaddle!" bellowed Lord Roundabout, jumping into the fray. He stood and glared balefully all around. "Lord Pontieu is dissolute and flagitious, and not to be trusted!"

"This is malicious defamation!" returned Lord Pontieu, angrily pointing a lean finger at Roundabout.

"No defamation exists where the accusation is accurate," Lord Roundabout retorted. "This much is incontrofutable." He crooked his finger at a runner, who went quickly to the exit and said something to Milord's retainers.

"In a moment I shall present a witness, who will testify that Lord Maurice Ventblanc Pontieu conspired in malversation of the most evil variety; specifically, that he contrived and implemented the abduction and imprisonment of Lord Gracewright Cantilouve Benefice on the high seas, and committed other acts of larceny upon his person..." Lord Roundabout's last words were drowned in a wild uproar.

The marshal now stood uncertainly before Milord, who had replaced the bottlette in his coat. "Marshal, do your duty," shouted Lord Pontieu.

"Stay!" responded Lord Roundabout. "I move that the concoction in question be placed in a State of Imminent Escrow, pending the outcome of the matter before this Assembly."

"Second," Lord Hobday said immediately.

"The motion is out of order," said Lord Trillphyte. "An Act of Impoundment is in progress."

"The instigator of the impoundment is himself the object of criminal investigation!" returned Lord Roundabout.

During this exchange the runner returned, his eyes wide with fright. He mumbled something to Milord, who shot a grim look at Lord Roundabout and strode violently from the chamber. I hunkered in my pocket to keep from being thrown out. Behind us mad squabbling and confusion erupted as Lord Roundabout continued the jousting on

Milord's behalf, while Lords Trillphyte and Pontieu vainly exhorted the confused marshal to place Milord in irons.

Floorsteward Smithkline waited outside. In a shaking voice he said, "Please come at once, Sire." We walked back to the middle of the Square and into the chilly pools of shade under its huge magnolias.

On the bench Firstmate Crowell sat slumped on his left side, in what I mistook for a posture of simple dejection; but Milord's keen eyes immediately detected a tiny bead of fresh blood on the bony protuberance behind his right ear. "Nape's Bodkin," he said under his breath. "Poisoned. Its merest pink is death." A few yards away were the two retainers under whose guard Milord had left the Firstmate; they guiltily pocketed their playing cards and slunk into the shadows.

Milord leaned against a kiosk, thinking furiously. Never have I seen him so agitated. I had no idea how the Assembly would deal with such extraordinary and unprecedented circumstances. And how would Milord, having made such a deadly accusation, face them without his witness? At any moment I expected to see the marshal emerge with fresh resolve from the Assembly building.

I looked again at the vacant face of Firstmate Crowell, hoping to find there some silent proof of Lord Pontieu's complicity, or at least some indication that the sailor's terrible weariness and suffering had at last been relieved by death. But his lifeless features were as absent of meaning or explanation as a desert gulch.

I ransacked my mind for some solution to Milord's dilemma. The rest of the crew had died aboard ship, according to Crowell. Or had they? On a sudden hunch I jumped from Milord's pocket and began running toward the wharf.

Hardly knowing what I looked for, or where it was to be found, I darted across the park, past the shops and into the collection of squalid shanties and buckling boardwalks beyond. In every doorway slouched some sleazy tout or petty thief, his cosh or dirk conspicuously displayed in a back pocket. Mascots were plainly not welcome here. Two mangy dogs ambushed me from their filthy niches, but I dashed to safety just in time.

What I sought was under a pier. Its dense tangle of branches filled the space between two pilings and clung to them with the ferocity of a spinster-clam; its roots clutched the wet black sand as though in rigor mortis. But where an entire grove had flourished aboard the *Dittaneer,* only a few transplanted trees survived here, governed by their thick central trunk.

Bits of moldering plaid cloth were invaginated into the thick bark, and a twisted iron poker protruded from the crotch of two branches. But the most chilling details came more slowly into focus (for perhaps my mind, seized with fear and revulsion, resisted them): two spatulate human hands, nestled in a whorl of leaves above; and in the center of the gnarled branches, clenched like a coin in a greedy fist, the Treemaster's head. His wrinkled, ivory-white skin was now the color of wood, and a knot gradually replaced his narrow nose.

His mouth twisted slowly, the way a snail turns its head. "Bilch," he croaked.

"I am Flick," I replied reflexly. My words echoed distantly in my head, as though spoken by someone else.

Suddenly the branches labored in a mighty contraction, squeezing his head til I thought it would pop like a roasted nut. Agony distorted his face. From the branches came a mocking whisper: "Sap and thrust! Sap and thrust!" it said and the branches writhed again, compressing his features like rubber.

"Can I help you?" I squeaked desperately.

The tree relaxed its grip. He was silent a long time, struggling to the surface of his sea of pain. "Yes, you can help," he said at last. "Kill me."

In horror I backed away and dashed toward the Square, slipping in the rotting refuse which filled every crack of that broken street. An old termagant launched a meat-ax at me from her window; with a shower of sparks it clattered on the stones only inches away. In the next block a surly tomcat sprang into my path, convinced he had found a delicious mouse for supper, but instead tasted bitter *gnozzt* fluid.

After an exhausting upward slalom I found Milord, still pondering his situation next to the benched corpse of the unfortunate Firstmate. Meanwhile the clamor from within the Assembly grew and grew, til I thought its old copper roof would burst into the air. With infinite relief I threw myself into Milord's pocket.

"Where have you been?" he asked anxiously.

In urgent tones I outlined the essentials of my discovery. "But then … then he's our witness!" he exclaimed, and rushed back inside.

"Particular Urgence! Particular Urgence!" Milord called as he pounded through the doors, but his exclamations were lost in the thunderous, swirling din that filled the hall. The Annunciator thumped his gong continuously, and the countless comings and goings to and from the podium were far beyond the aged Annotator's ability to record.

A dozen speeches and arguments flourished at once. At their center reigned Lord Pontieu, making eloquent but noncommittal gestures with his delicate wrists in response to queries from all sides. A man of his powerful nature could say nothing, yet all those around him would believe they knew precisely what he meant; but later they would find themselves quite unable to agree as to what he had said or promised.

Milord shouted to be heard, with no effect. He withdrew a tiny tablet from his coat and threw it into the air: an iridescent red and silver globe floated slowly to the ceiling. A stunned silence spread over the meeting.

"My accusation stands," he said. "The witness awaits the arrival of a deputation from this Assembly at the Twelfth Pier." I anticipated another endless parliamentary harangue over the appointment of such a subcommittee, but instead there was a general scramble for the exit that left several Lords bruised and groping for their snuff. In a few moments the entire Assembly had quitted the hall and stood milling about outside, loudly demanding their carriages.

My Lords wisely chose a side exit instead and walked briskly via a succession of small streets downhill. "What witness is this?" asked Lord Roundabout, gasping to keep up with Milord.

"Flick tells me of enchanted trees aboard the *Dittaneer* —" he looked sharply at me in sudden doubt "— empowered by the Grandmage himself, but commanded by one Treemaster Pinleaf, who now finds himself their victim; this wretched fellow was planted in port by the ship's salvagers, in the grip of his tree-captors, to live out what few sorry days remain to him. Presumably he can attest to Lord Pontieu's wrongdoing." A worried look spread across Milord's face, for it was hardly certain that the Treemaster had actually seen Lord Pontieu, or witnessed any of his crimes; and in any case the word of a man in his hideous straits would not be hard to impeach. Yet on his testimony Milord had staked his word to the entire Assembly — and on that, in turn, rested Mentharch's salvation.

The wharves were already in a wild tumult. Lords arrived by the score, their horse-carriages and retinues skittering in the muddy streets and maneuvering precariously along the piers like acrobats on wheels. Lord Sprightleigh's hansom tipped over and sank in the muck, precipitating a heated dispute amongst his retainers. Lord Hobday slipped on a patch of pier-slime and splashed into deeper water; vigorous rescue efforts were mounted at once, hampered by mischievous urchins who wiggled pier-planks under his rescuers' feet at crucial moments.

Hundreds of local denizens gathered, gawking and milling about. Rumors and wagers spawned like minnows. Young ragamuffins ran amongst the crowd, innocently offering to run errands or fetch snacks, while confederates picked their customers' pockets from behind. Strumpets materialized like frogs after a rain and brazenly winnowed a few males from the edges of the herd. To one side the Annunciator tried to establish himself on a discarded barrel, but repeatedly tripped on his ceremonial sash and plunged into the dirty sand, to the loud guffaws of a bystanding gang of wharf-bums.

A degree of order at last imposed itself, and Milord pushed his way through the throng. Gingerly stepping on boards laid over the mud by an underfootling, he approached the weird growth imprisoning the Treemaster. A hush fell.

"Identify yourself for the Assembly, please," he said.

The bushy organism shivered, and Pinleaf winced. "I am Treemaster Pinleaf, of the *Obnounce Dittaneer*," he said hoarsely.

"And who am I?"

"Lord Benefice," he said at once. His eyes bulged in pain as the tree compressed him again; but this wave of peristalsis was a bit of gentle physiology compared with the grinding, vindictive grip to which he had been subjected before.

Milord cleared his throat deliberately. "Now tell these good men exactly how you came to know me, and *on whose order*."

"Yes, Sire. It was Captain Worrant. He promised a fine bonus once the passage was done. Then he confined me to the hold, and the management of these damned bitch-trees." He knew perfectly well that this insult would bring on another vengeful squeeze, which it did; and he groaned as the powerful sphincters compressed him again, while all looked on in horrified silence. Even the riffraff behind us were quieted by the sight of his frightful suffering.

At last the relentless pressure eased. "But who was the Captain's captain, Treemaster?" Milord asked, his sympathy overcome by impatience.

"That was common knowledge, Sire, even to the cabin boy," he said weakly. "The man came aboard —"

With the agility of a fencer Lord Pontieu leaped forward and plunged his half-rapier into the Treemaster's eye. A shocked gasp erupted from the crowd. Blood and sap gushed from the wound; the branches thrashed about like the tentacles of a gigged octopus, scattering leaves and twigs everywhere, and Lord Pontieu jumped nimbly back.

He turned around, fastidiously wiping his bloodied hands and dagger with a silk kerchief. "It was the only thing to do," he said nervously. "His case was hopeless; I did him a service." This arrogant assertion met with restless murmurs; but conviction was lacking from that dissent, because for a fact it had been a kindness to relieve Pinleaf of his awful fate. Already Lord Pontieu took a deep breath and prepared to reassume his accustomed position of dominance. Behind him the tree's writhing eased, and Pinleaf's gory head sank slowly into its main trunk.

But Lord Roundabout would have none of it. "He named you!" he shouted from our right.

"No name but Captain Worrant's escaped his lips," retorted Pontieu, "who was in the employ of Lord Benefice. And in any case he was hardly more than a vegetable."

"He was no vegetable when he received your felonious orders, but a man as cruel and calculating as yourself!"

Pontieu replied to this accusation only with a complacent smile, which he dropped at once. "Now we must attend to the unfinished business at hand," he said sharply, and turned to Milord. Holding his silvery weapon half-upturned at his side, he said with menace, "Impoundment is now definitely effected." He extended his other hand, palm up.

Milord took a step back and glanced at the many Lords around us.

Some looked away in embarrassment or uncertainty; others found something of unexpected interest at their feet. A few strove to maintain expressions of sympathetic defiance, but silence stamped that bravado as counterfeit, a starched collar put on temporarily and only for display. Milord's face was as warm as a stove.

Only Lord Roundabout — true friend! — made to defend Milord with the poignard concealed in his gold-headed cane. "Stay," Milord said softly, restraining his arm with a firm touch. "We have had enough bloodshed for one day." Milord reached into his coat; the motion of his arm was definite, but it shook as he withdrew the bottlette.

In one gesture Pontieu snatched it from him and thrust it into the outside pocket of his jacket. With a bark of laughter he said, "Now we see that Lord Benefice's franticism was no more than a thin disguise for his own selfish interests."

Lord Roundabout purpled and would have lunged but for what happened next. Lord Pontieu turned and took a step. A root from the tree-thing arched its back like a frightened cat in front of his shoes. He stumbled, clownishly flailing his arms for balance, and plunged head-long against the trunk. Around him slithered a sinewy appendage, and another, and in an instant he was lashed as tightly as by a deck-winch to that mighty column.

"Summon the wizard! Release me!" he screamed.

Not a soul stirred. A hundred tendrils of plant-flesh spiraled rapidly around his perfectly tailored suit and locked him in their clasp. He tugged futilely at his bonds and screamed again. "Help! I confess! By the Fire, help me!"

Lizzault darted to the aid of his master. Lord Pontieu's mascot resembled a bundle of swiftly moving shadows, for even the bright afternoon sun could not penetrate the deep clefts in his thick hide. With the power of a catapult he launched himself at the tree-monster. In mid-flight his ferocious jaws flew open — the sturdy muzzle under his snout parted like a cutting of lemon rind — exposing six rows of glistening teeth.

A spray of branches realigned themselves into a noose. They yanked Lizzault's voracious jaws backward as though peeling a large banana, while another and straighter branch, sharp and deadly, plunged deep into his wide-open maw. He disgorged a volume of dark brown blood and thrashed from side to side; then he lay still, and was sucked inexorably into the tree.

Meanwhile another branch-coil snaked around Lord Pontieu's neck and squeezed, tighter and tighter. His narrow face bulged and turned dark red. The engorged lips worked, but no further sound issued from them. In moments his eyes took on the congestion which the most incorrigible sot requires a lifetime to cultivate. They rolled slowly upward into a fixed and permanent stare, as blind as baked apples. Lord Pontieu's limp, slender frame began sinking into the welter of branches.

"The brew!" blurted Milord, and leaped toward the monster.

"Closelord!" Lord Roundabout shouted. He and Lord Munchfirth bolted forward and restrained him, unintentionally cuffing me roughly in my pocket as they grappled him to a halt. We narrowly escaped the wildly whipping branches.

"But it must be retrieved!" Milord insisted, trying desperately to shoulder his friends aside.

"It is no use," Lord Munchfirth said with calm finality. "The Guildmaster himself could not save it now." The precious bottlette in Lord Pontieu's pocket disappeared under churning folds of twilled cloth and living wood; soon it would be buried deep within the tree's phloem.

The tree-monster thrummed with malignant satisfaction. The only other sound was the *sloppet, sloppet* of wavelets against a ship moored nearby.

With an effort Lord Sprightleigh said hoarsely, "Move adjournment til the morrow." The gathering slowly dispersed.

XI

DARK ENDS
AND BRIGHT FUTURES

We rolled along the Coast Road in silence. The loss of the witches' brew, after so much struggle and horror, was too painful for discussion. I calculated that the morrow would be the twenty-eighth day since Auntie's curse; its evening would bring the wizard's mental demise. My stomach was empty, but it felt as though I had eaten a lump of uncooked dough.

The mighty sun's health failed once again, and soon a black, pin-poked dome covered the earth. Above the horizon floated the moon's remains: a luminous eyelash. The carriage chilled, and Milord fastened the top button of his greatcoat. "How ironic," he said at last, to break the silence. "No Lord received more than a bruise from two hundred stick-men, yet a lowly vine inflicts our first traumatic death in living memory."

"A goblin vine," Lord Roundabout replied absently. He studied the low, black hills rolling past and heaved an uneasy sigh. "Well, ironic or not, it's no more than he deserved, after all."

"You sound unconvinced," replied Milord.

"I should have preferred an easier solution."

"As would I. But circumstances raced past us like greyhounds, Closelord. And Lord Pontieu's own greed led him to his destruction."

"They did, and it did. If only the Firstmate had lived to testify!"

"Yes, 'if only'," said Milord. "And his murder remains to be solved, a matter which I shall place high on the Assembly's agenda, when that is possible; though whomever Lord Pontieu hired for the scurrilous task has undoubtedly fled and gone by now."

"I fear you are right." Lord Roundabout rubbed his forehead tiredly. "It has been a harrowing day, to which my digestion will respond in familiar terms." His prediction was immediately confirmed by the escape of several uncomfortable grumbles from beneath his waistcoat.

"You must answer its complaint firmly, Closelord Fontleroy! With a slurry of capsicum and lime, taken at bedtime, or perhaps a mash of potatoes boiled with cilantro." This advice precipitated an earnest discussion of stomachics and other remedies, but the exchange was curtailed by a shout from the driver.

"Your Lordships, mirror-flashes from Benefice Manor!"

Orange bolts of light emanated from the glass-and-flame apparatus in the signal turret atop the Manor, and my Lords pressed against the icy window to interpret them. Simultaneously they shouted, "He has returned!" But their excitement was immediately assassinated by the realization that they would arrive with empty hands. They shared a glance which said, more loudly than words, "To face Albanderry's premier magician as failures is the bitterest regret."

The driver coaxed his horses to their best gallop. We passed three farms, and three more. Lord Roundabout heaved a sigh of resignation and asked, "A military assault on the tree?"

Milord shook his head. "Too great a risk of damage to the bottlette."

"But there is no time left for the economic and diplomatic actions we considered earlier," said Lord Roundabout, spurred by impatience.

"True." Milord bit his lips and rubbed his gloved hands together.

I wished that I had Bilch to consult with again; he seemed always to have some insight into such difficult enigmas. "If only the good Lady Benefice were still here, she would hand me one of her clever suggestions, like a freshly starched suit of clothes!" Milord said, as though echoing my thoughts. Lord Roundabout added a similar rumination concerning his own Lady, though her lack of practicality is exceeded only by the unwavering sweetness of her temperament.

My Lords continued to pick at the knotty problem, and soon concluded that their only course would be to transport the wizard back to Albanderry Port, in hopes that even a degree of proximity to the tree-swallowed brew would somehow be of value. Perhaps, having come from the wizard's own manufactory, the nautical trees would respond favorably to his presence.

Milord lapsed into a nervous silence. Lord Roundabout drowsed fitfully in his chair, and punctuated his nap with an occasional soft grunt. Some intuition prompted me to tell Milord of the additional revelation from Firstmate Crowell — that Worrant had leased the tree-engine from Mentharch for use aboard the *Dittaneer*. He drew back in astonishment.

"Leased?" he ejaculated.

"At the Maritime Centrum," I squeaked.

Milord stood up so abruptly that he bumped his head on the ceiling of the carriage, and I nearly fell out of his pocket. He rubbed his head and paced to and fro. "Did the Firstmate aver that these transactions had been taking place for some time?"

"He implied that a previous captain had enjoyed the tree-engine's power," I replied.

"Then Mentharch's resorting to such unorthodox dealings was not an effect of the curse, but a reflection of an impecunious condition, which I had not suspected." My head swam with all these combinations of economics and sorcery: taxation of the witches' brew, the leasing of enchanted trees…No doubt Vulgia's vicious garden was also no more than a collection of rented props, subject to complicated contracts, liens and rights of estoppel!

"Leased," he muttered again. "That changes everything! We must be prepared. I have in mind a strategy in which the pellets will figure prominently, provided we are able to rescue the Grandmage." Milord anxiously patted his jacket to confirm that the box of pellets was still there. He withdrew into himself, a consultation which I knew better than to interrupt. The last two hours of our journey passed with agonizing slowness.

At last we drew into the courtyard of Benefice Manor. Mentharch's coach kneeled brokenly against the curb. Its once-dazzling colors were pathetically faded, like the hull of an abandoned boat when it has baked for months in the sun. The Masterfootling hurried down the front steps.

"The Grandmage arrived only a short time ago, Sire," he said, wringing his hands. "I have taken the liberty of summoning the physicians to his care."

"Of course," said Milord, bolting the steps two at a time. Lord Roundabout puffed behind us.

The atmosphere in the house was desolate. The servants had withdrawn to their quarters, sensing the arrival of death and hiding from it. Even the crickets were silent, as though listening for some fateful event within.

With foreboding I imagined the sight, the sound, even the smells of a great sorcerous power reduced to — to what? To the staring and babbling of a pap-nursed crotchet, obsessed with his posset and his bowels? Or, yet more hideous, was he an out-and-out idiot, exerting no more influence upon the world than a turnip?

And if the moon renewed itself before we found some solution to his dilemma, what would be the disposition of Mentharch's magical paraphernalia? Would Gwarph, an unknown, be entrusted with those precious tools? Or had the Grandmage perfected some agreement with a lesser thaumaturge, whose agenda might be dangerously at odds with the needs and goals of Albanderry's society?

The Gasmaster met us in the foyer and in hushed tones transmitted more disturbing news. "Sire, there have been reports of witches in restricted areas, and even overt harassments at Hobday and Munchfirth Manors."

My Lords accepted this intelligence grimly but without surprise. "They are well aware that his powers fail," said Milord.

"The cobnosed hags will next invade the Assembly itself," said Lord Roundabout.

They looked at each other in the sudden horrified recognition that this was indeed a possibility. "Hurry," said Milord. The Masterfootling led us to the south wing, where we entered a guest chamber.

A few dying embers glowed in the fireplace. Before it on a narrow couch lay Grandmage Mentharch's frail body, clad only in a coarse gray shift and his burdensome horse-collar. A crumpled nightcap rested precariously on the bed's edge. His dazzling white hair, once a fluffy bush, was condensed by sweat to damp lumps on his pink scalp.

In a whisper Lord Roundabout blurted, "He is no more than a scrawny shrub."

"Clinging to a cliff in a storm," added Milord.

Across the room was a small chaise, with a large candle burning at each end. Milord's three physicians were crowded onto it, and I was alarmed to see that they had withdrawn into the Posture of Penultimate Condolence: each clamped his left knee to his chest and splayed the fingers of his other hand like a frightened octopus before tightly closed eyes — a configuration reserved for incurable cases. Their silhouettes flickered grotesquely in the gloomy candlelight.

The wizard had been facing the hearth, but now slowly twisted his neck towards us. Lord Roundabout gasped and palmed his cheeks in dismay. Milord's legs jerked.

Grandmage Mentharch's shrewd, lively face was no more. It was instead a clayish, apathetic mask, fashioned by some merciless ghoul; his gleaming yellow eyes had been replaced by dark, feverish eye-holes which opened into a black cavern — the 'empty sack' threatened by Auntie's evil stanza. Gwarph emerged from a dark corner and searched my Lords' faces. Seeing at once that we had failed to bring his master's antidote, he returned to the head of the bed, where he set about one-handedly plumping the Grandmage's pillow and mopping his forehead with a moistened cloth.

Milord bowed to the wizard, something I had never known him to do towards other than a Lord. He sat down at the bedside, leaned forward and asked softly, "Can you talk?"

In Milord's vest pocket I was as close as he to that terribly harmed magician, no more than the distance between the ends of a loaf of bread. To gaze into the dilated chasms between Mentharch's temples was to be sucked into a deadly black vertigo, and I clutched at the hem of my pocket in panic. But somewhere deep within his eyes I thought to catch a glimpse, a flicker of some tiny light like that of a shooting star on a dark and moonless night — a last fragment of his powerful mentality; and in wild, illogical hopes of somehow contacting it, of reaching out to it across that near-infinite void, I activated my retinal semiosis, which I had not used since before Bilch retreated into his hibernative gestation. My small flashes of pale green eye-light disappeared into his cranium.

Whether his words were in response to Milord's query or mine, I cannot say, though it is of no importance in either case. "Cockalorum," came his faint warble. His lips hardly moved again: "Clackdish." Then he was silent. His dementia was all but complete.

I recall the day that my own father died, and the mountainous weight that settled upon my heart and back. No laborer, though he may struggle under four hundredweights, knows that oppression; and I believe it was with that same sense of utter weariness that Milord now pushed to his feet.

"You may dismiss the physicians, Masterfootling. Prepare a carriage suitable for our return to Albanderry Port."

Gwarph glanced in surprise from Milord's face to that of the Masterfootling, and Lord Roundabout's. Farberwile apprised him in a quick undertone of our plan to relocate the wizard to the site of the remaining brew, enveloped though it was in the renegade trees. All at once Gwarph threw down his cloth and dashed from the room. My Lords exchanged expressions of astonishment.

"What can he be about?" asked Lord Roundabout.

"A shocking case of abandonment," the Masterfootling suggested with contempt.

Milord looked down at me for some insight; but as Gwarph was an assistant rather than a mascot — and a wizard's assistant, at that — he was governed by a code of conduct of which I knew nothing, and I could formulate no theory.

The Kitchenmaster and two handmen were summoned. On Milord's order they obtained a litter, and with infinite care the Grandmage, now bundled in blankets and comforter, was carried from the chamber and down the front steps. "Direct the Hostler to bring Stitch from his lair," Milord added, and Handman Armright trotted at once towards the stables.

The wizard's coach was nowhere to be seen. One of Milord's larger battle-carriages loomed in the courtyard, pressed into service again. Its spacious troop-chamber easily accommodated a comfortable chaise for the Grandmage, with room to spare for my Lords, the Masterfootling, Ranktwo Sparseman and the two handmen. Gasmaster Bickle was left in charge of the Manor, in case the witches' increasingly brazen assaults moved in that direction.

Stitch fluttered to the door of the carriage and saluted smartly. Our veteran friend was sturdily outfitted in brown tunic and double sash, and appeared greatly strengthened. He carried a small valise. "Good evening, Sire," he said in his woody voice.

Milord motioned him to a seat, and Ranktwo Sparsemen drew the doors closed. "It appears you have made a fine recovery, Stitch. I am delighted."

"The result of Master Pimfix's craft, Your Grace, for which I am grateful."

"And welcome."

We composed ourselves for travel and again began the trip from Manor to Port. It seemed we had spent the last week rattling back and forth between those two stations, but this was by far the most trying of the excursions, both physically and emotionally. The ride was rough, unlike that in Milord's luxurious standard carriage; my Lords later complained of backache and boneshave, and even I, though cushioned in Milord's holster, was uncomfortably buffeted about. And constantly before us was the tragic figure of Grandmage Mentharch, staring emptily at the ceiling. At his side the two handmen had the sickened expression of green recruits in battle.

Milord tore his gaze from the wizard to Stitch's tall, angular form. "We must discuss your future."

"I am prepared for a life of service, Your Grace," Stitch replied instantly.

Milord shook his head. "And I would gladly have it; but you would forever be a fish out of water. The household would obediently say consenting words, but in their hearts rankle and make plots. Inflammation and grief would be the inevitable result." Stitch lowered his gaze. "Yet clearly you cannot return to live among your father's brothers, because your valiant combat on my behalf — for which I shall always hold you in grateful remembrance — has set you irrevocably apart from them." Stitch's shoulders trembled as he waited silently for Milord's conclusions.

"Thus we have a contradiction. And from contradiction comes growth, whose ultimate effect, though it may hurt more sharply than the wounds of battle, is to make us noble." Stitch forced a nod of agreement.

"Now: I have in mind an excellent situation for one of your unique abilities. I hope to confirm it soon."

Hope relieved Stitch's sad expression. "I shall adjust myself for a new beginning, Sire."

"Excellent. And remember this: our friendship is made of sterling, and cannot be weakened by distance or the ill will of others."

"I am indebted, my Lord."

Milord stood up and opened a porthole. Beyond the Downs, the sky was intermittently illuminated by dull purple flashes, in which I could just see the tiny, distant silhouettes of witches whizzing back and forth without restraint. Later we learned that noisome fig wasps had infested Lord Sprightleigh's cattle, and that Lord Munchfirth's barley fields had been overgrown with a noxious species of milkwort; and for months afterward Lord Hobday's every sixteenth word, though he struggled to avoid it, was 'grugle', or something similar. The effort of counting his words drove him nearly to distraction.

Milord returned to his seat and puttered through the few magical charms remaining in his pockets, and petted me betweentimes. I slipped into an anxious doze, from which an especially sharp jounce or sway of the carriage startled me now and then into an awareness of the darkened cabin and its occupants. Lord Roundabout half-reclined on his chaise, exhausted; Ranktwo Sparseman idly stroked a braided signal-cord in the corner. Stitch sat dutifully upright, clenching his pincers together in a manner that suggested either prayer or a method of sharpening their edges.

Our wooden wheels bumped and banged loudly in the road's ruts. Raising his voice above the noise, Milord asked Masterfootling Farberwile, "Have you any further advice?"

The senior servant frowned and thumbed quickly through his Compendium of Exceptional Circumstances. "Sire, in his most famous tract, *Lustrations*, Furibund alludes to a conflict between 'a troupe of significant individuals' and 'a grasping entity'. Unfortunately a lost portion of the passage has been replaced by the dubious conjectures of a lesser commentator; but its last few lines are intact from the master's hand. They predict intervention, to salutary effect, by 'an asymmetric personage of diminutive stature', as he puts it."

Milord raised his eyebrows. "The passage is obscure, to say the least." He reached to the Masterfootling's lap and turned the chapbook around. "You find this reference useful, in general?"

"Oh yes, Milord," he said enthusiastically. "Its author is often somewhat babblative —" he wiggled his fingers in demonstration "— and at times indulges in unvarnished frippery, to be candid. But it has been quite helpful, especially in the management of Your Lordship's third-level servants." He blushed and hastily re-pocketed the tome. Milord leaned back again in his chair and pursued the subject no further.

We arrived at last in the center of Albanderry and circumvented the Square. Milord stood up and opened the hatch cover; I jumped to its hinges to reconnoiter. The dawn air was unpleasantly damp. Layers of red clouds were matted in the eastern sky like bloody fur. To the north, flashes of purple witch-light continued unabated. In their shanties the locals were deep in the hard, oblivious sleep of the indigent.

Milord poked his head through the opening. A little tatterdemalion was picking at trash in the mouth of an alley. "To the right here," Milord said to the driver. The waif jumped aside as we turned into the narrow passage.

A few moments later we emerged at the Twelfth Pier. All was quiet. On the deck of a ship a lookout huddled in his peacoat, motionless; on the yards above him, sails were furled like young leaves around their stems. Even the gulls seemed to have been detained elsewhere on unknown business.

Beneath the wharf was the tree-thing, the *Dittaneer's* former engine, glowing a faint gray in the early light and humming in a soft, deep register. Mounds of dirty sand were banked up around its muscular roots,which continued their slow pulsing and thrusting as though they would push the entire earth into the underworld. Since yesterday the monster had almost doubled in size and now held three pier-pilings, not two, in its woody grasp. I shuddered to think of the food — two mean men — which stimulated its growth.

With a look of discouragement Milord lowered himself again into the cab. "What do you make of it?" Lord Roundabout asked him, turning from a porthole.

"It waits," Milord said simply. I had half expected to find Gwarph wrestling with it in a heroic effort to recover the brew, but he was nowhere to be seen.

With a rough gesture the Masterfootling secured a ring of keys and other implements on his belt. "It wants a good tree-barber," he said sourly.

Milord only grimaced in reply. He ordered his pursuivants to take up the Grandmage and we piled out the rear doors. Stitch was appointed to stand guard over the wagon. Cautiously our entourage stepped from the boardwalk onto the sand and approached the tree-creature. Its clenching and humming quickened, and its gray glow intensified. The handmen reluctantly carried Mentharch's litter as close to it as they dared, perhaps fifteen yards, and set him gently on the sand.

We stood about uncertainly for a time in the lonely, stagnant air. No whispered words came from the tree; no further sign of reaction to the presence of its creator. At last Milord called out in a tentative voice, "Your maker requires your obedient cooperation, Tree-engine." The creature's branches shivered like the arms of an exotic dancer. Seeing that it responded, Milord added more eagerly, "Present the glass container within you."

It quivered and shook, and made a sound like the belch of a green moose. Drops of noxious orange sap flowed down the side of a secondary trunk; an aperture appeared in its bark and enlarged to the size of an apple. From this orifice it disgorged a small white object, whose lean, oblong shape suggested one of Lord Pontieu's handbones.

Milord recoiled. "No, no — a bottle," he said in dismay. The tree's emetic efforts continued with greater energy, as though its trunk were one large esophagus, and at length it spewed out other items: the treemaster's leather poker-holster; Lord Pontieu's largest gold ring, rumored to contain a deadly poison; and a bolus of owl-scat. Its vomiting ceased. The newly formed hole sealed itself into a smooth commissure, and the organism resumed its steady, rhythmic pulsing.

"A bottle," Milord shouted once more. The tree was oblivious.

"And what now?" Lord Roundabout asked in despair.

Milord shook his head. He threw a vexed look at the Grandmage, who lay staring emptily at the lightening sky from his cold, sandy bed. Milord's legs weakened and he groped for support; Ranktwo Sparseman hurriedly brought up a portable stool. Lord Roundabout threw himself down in a lump at our side.

My Lords sat and contemplated their leggings. A fragrant breeze rustled the muggy air with fruity hints of a faraway island.

"I recall Lady Benefice's last remark," said Milord. Absently he stirred the sand at his heels. "I was... I was heartbroken, for on that day I realized that the bed in which she suffered was her last. She said to me, speaking of death, 'It's terribly simple, Gracewright: try not to waste too much time thinking of it'."

Lord Roundabout pursed his lips and also explored the sand with his fingertips. "A wise bit of counsel, Closelord," he said softly.

Ranktwo Sparseman set up a table and silently spread out a tray of meats and sauces, but no one moved to eat. The wind freshened and the Handmen, squatting next to the Grandmage's litter, pointed their heads into it like dalmatians. Standing above them, the Masterfootling dug a grain of sand from his eye with a blunt forefinger.

Along the docks a few arriving longshoremen cast curious eyes at the odd group encamped below them: displaced barristers, abducting a sick grandfather? Overdressed gypsies, on some bizarre pilgrimage to a pagan tree-god? Each laborer in turn startled more to see Stitch behind us and put a hand quickly to his dirk; then, realizing that the stick-creature was somehow allied to our company, shook his head and with obvious misgiving resumed his steps.

The silence was almost complete, eroded only by the stirrings of those few early seamen and the rippling of a flag or two. The moon, cruelly pale and innocent in the growing daylight, floated like a scoop of cake above the horizon. Soon it would shed its flat white fullness and a thin, glowing scimitar would appear at the edge opposite that of a month ago. Nudged by a swell, a nearby schooner bumped against its dock.

Silence. It hit me all at once: the trees were silent! I scratched excitedly at Milord's shirt.

He looked up from the beach and his eyes opened in wonder. "Closelord!" he shouted. Both Lords bounced up and advanced toward the tree-thing.

To say that it had wilted would not be correct, for it kept its shape. But it was perfectly still, and no longer hummed or pulsed or glowed, as though some intrinsic, activating force had suddenly ceased. Its cloud-colored luminosity was gone, leaving a dull, lifeless ochre; and its texture, rubbery and vibrant before, was now that of a spider's corpse forgotten in a cupboard.

Milord clambered up a bank of root-humped sand. "It has failed entirely," he said. With cautious amazement he touched its bark and found it dry as bone meal. "Handman Berryplain, a sword!" he shouted. "At once!"

"Yes, Sire." The weapon was fetched from the carriage's armory and placed in Milord's good hand. He pierced the organism's trunk, hesitantly at first, then repeatedly, and accelerated his foins and remises til he would have made of it a dry sieve, had he not struck something harder than its starchy matrix.

In growing excitement he glanced at Lord Roundabout — his friend exhorted him, "Yes, Closelord, yes!" — and deftly opened its trunk with three quick swipes, exposing its pulpy system of circulatory tubes. He probed the spot which had resisted his piercing and artfully dissected out its surrounding material, then threw his épée aside and delicately seized the carved-out chunk of xylem.

"Now we shall set Lord Mentharch free!" His excited slip of the tongue — calling a wizard Lord — seemed somehow appropriate, a well-deserved token of special sympathy and respect for the mad magician.

He chipped away the concealing deadwood. But I knew, by the absence of the potion's characteristic tingling, that the shard he was about to extract was not the bottlette. He delivered the Treemaster's bell book, its brass clasp dented by Milord's probing rapier. With a word too coarse for Lords of the Realm, Milord pitched the offending book angrily into the low tide and attacked the tree-cadaver anew. Lord Roundabout obtained a sword from the wagon and also hacked away. With the alacrity of adolescents at a fencing lesson they lopped off limbs, which dropped like dried cucumbers onto the wet sand. In their reckless enthusiasm I feared that my Lords would shatter the bottlette if they struck it and lose the therapeutic brew forever to the coastal winds!

"Milord," I squeaked at the top of my lungs, but he did not hear me over his labored breathing. A sweat, the rising sap of long frustration, dampened his suit. I tugged at a stud in his shirtfront and repeated my interjection twice, and at last, more because of need of a moment's rest than to attend to me, he left off his hypnotized swinging and stabbing. Lord Roundabout also paused, which was just as well, for he was consumed by a fit of wheezing.

Milord groped for a kerchief. I withdrew it for him from his pocket and said, "Milord, may I suggest another approach?" He looked at me in some surprise as he wiped his brow — his mascot, proposing a plan?

"Why risk damage to the bottlette?" I asked. "I am quite sensitive to its presence; allow me first to search the tree, Sire."

He looked blankly at me and lowered his sword. Uncertainly he said, "Yes, Flick, of course. A fine suggestion."

I jumped from Milord's shoulder to the wounded trunk and scrambled up. I dashed across its lower branches, to right and then left, leaping over the gaps and stumps left by my Lords' sword-strokes, and then explored the tree's tangled upper stories. My paws stumbled over a pale, smooth-skinned knot; much later, recalling our adventure by a fire, I realized with horror that it must have been one of Lord Pontieu's knuckles, slowly turning to wood.

But the tingling sensation was not to be detected. I looked down at the anxious faces of my Lords and squeaked, "Nothing yet." Then I crisscrossed the same territory again, like a hound ransacking a field for a misplaced bone, with the same negative result. In disappointment and alarm I descended the trunk; but at its base a faint signal touched me from somewhere deep beneath the center of the mighty bole. I chirped like a bird over a buried worm.

Now my Lords set to their work with a will and quickly hewed a yard-high segment from the trunk. The handmen heaved the carved-out cylinder to the side, leaving the remaining base almost flush with the ground. The upper portion of the trunk and its branches, deprived of support, dipped and swayed. "Caution, my Lords!" shouted the Masterfootling, pointing upwards; but the tree's bushy superstructure remained safely attached to the pier and its pilings.

In its base the openings of the tree's severed vascular tubes were laid out like the pipe-holes of a mighty organ, and it was from one of these that the tingling emanated. Contracting my *gnozzt* as much as possible, I plunged in like any gopher, before black fear could paralyze me. (Later that fear afflicted me retroactively, so that Milord felt compelled to dose me with a draught of his Vimplicate II, which he dissolved, to my regret, in oil of castor.)

The walls of the passage were slippery, like well-rubbed leather. Slowing my descent with extended claws, I slithered downward and to the left in the tube. In this manner I slid for several yards, though it seemed a league. Behind me the last faint glow of daylight vanished. By the grace of Filfalxxx, I possess the most sensitive retinas in all of Albanderry, but the darkness was so complete that I could see nothing. I was a mole.

The shaft suddenly steepened and enlarged, so that I lost my grip and fell through space. Something slammed into my side, emptying my lungs and nearly popping my *gnozzt*. I fought for breath, scrabbling with the smooth barrier.

I was sprawled across a wedge which divided the passage in two. My whiskers twitched and something prickled the skin under my fur: the unmistakable tingling of the witches' elixir was strong in the passage before me. I climbed into it and squirmed against its walls to slow my descent. But after slithering a distance equal to a man's height, a sudden claustrophobic terror stopped me: what if the bottlette broke as I approached, or when I tried to drag it to the surface? I would be overwhelmed, lethally engulfed by its fumes in that confined space.

Go back! I thought. Why risk death by asphyxiation? Surely Milord's retainers could excavate the area. But such an excavation would probably take more time than the Grandmage had left, for I was now many yards below ground. And to make matters worse, the tide was rising — I might drown in water from above before I suffocated in witches' brew below. No doubt Milord was already trying frantically to stave off the advancing salt water with impromptu dikes, and —

There was no time to lose. I slid blindly downward with less caution and more speed. The air was stifling, due as much to the dank surrounding earth as to the brew, whose presence was now overpowering. The passageway branched twice more; its caliber decreased so that I barely squeezed through. Its spiraling course approached the tree's central taproot and finally emptied into a hollow, vertical shaft, where the emanations from the brew were almost unbearable. My legs brushed against a hard object in a mesh — the bottlette in its flexible metal net.

Its base was wedged at the junction of the two shafts, but it wobbled in place if pushed. Fortunately it was upright, so that I could gain a fair grasp of its neck, particularly if I also threaded my upper extremities through its netting. But when I hugged it thus, the tingling coursed through me intolerably. I backed away and rested for a moment, gathering my will.

I took a deep breath and gathered a bunch of the netting like a puppy's scruff in both paws. I backed upwards and pulled. It resisted, and for one frightful moment I thought the tree had again come to life, dragging the container down in response. I tugged again til I thought the net would tear, and at last the bottle came free. By pushing against the sides of the tube with my lower legs, I could crawl slowly up the passage like an inchworm in reverse.

The bottle bumped and scraped against the walls — I feared it would shatter each time — and every turn was a struggle of maneuvers. Where the two channels coalesced into one larger tube, I sank my claws into the walls' tissue; thus engaged, I pulled the bottle up alongside and ahead of me, squeezing it against the wall and then shouldering its bottom laboriously from underneath. Its unending tingling sent thousands of painful darts into my numb neck and back.

At last daylight peeped from above. "There he is!" Milord shouted ecstatically, and with a last desperate shove I pushed the bottlette to within his reach. He plucked it from the hole so sharply that my claws were nearly pulled out by the netting. He extended two fingers down into the hole; I clung to them and was pulled out, and saw the rising tide already lapping at the tree's decapitated base.

Panting with exhaustion, I collapsed in Milord's triumphant palm. "Well done!" he exclaimed, and kissed my neck, and beamed.

"Sound the bugles!" shouted Lord Roundabout. He mimed a bugler and hopped a two-step, splashing through the shallow water around the stump. Milord laughed, pocketed me next to his lapel and whirled behind him in the sunshine. The Masterfootling and Ranktwo Sparseman grinned, linked arms and followed, pulling the two blushing handmen with them.

From the wagon Stitch boomed congratulatory clicks and waved his pincers in time to the reel. On the pier three longshoremen dropped their bale-hooks and stared in utter bewilderment.

Milord burst into an impromptu song:

> "For the gizzard of a wizard we've a merry potion-O,
> A merry, burbling potion that will perk his spirits up!
> For the gizzard of a wizard we've a merry potion-O."

Lord Roundabout sang the stanza with him a second time and a third, and the party straggled to a halt. Milord wiped his eyes and heaved a happy sigh.

"No more delays," he said, abruptly serious. He walked deliberately across the sand to Mentharch and kneeled by his litter. The others formed a circle around us. Already a smile animated the Grandmage's lips like the shadow of a shadow.

Milord raised the bottlette in his hand and gravely spoke these lines:

> "No dearth of mind, nor witches' trouble,
> No preparation for a hearse;
> This wizard's wits I now redouble,
> And by this remedy botch their curse."

He extracted the bottle's bung with the knowing precision of a midwife. Lifting Mentharch's head from the sand, he pushed the ugly itch-collar aside and held the container's opening next to his nose. Though the wizard's respirations were slow and shallow, the potent fumes flowed into his nostrils like smoke drawn into a drafty flue, and in no time he had quaffed the entire contents of the bottlette.

Anxious moments passed. The bangles in Mentharch's matted hair sparkled. His sallow, wrinkled eyelids smoothed and took on a fine luster. Slowly his face filled with the delight of a child given a jelly candy. His eyes popped open: their vast store of coal ignited, flashing from black to yellow. His coma exploded into fierce cognition.

The magician cleared his throat and stood up, and Milord with him. Silently Mentharch assimilated his surroundings. His eyes probed the docks and the beach, taking his bearings — he had been absent a long time! With a shocked look downwards he discovered his drab shift, and by snapping the fourth and fifth fingers of one hand transformed it into a flowing white robe with a pattern of blue stars.

"Welcome," Milord said huskily, and was echoed at once by Lord Roundabout and the Masterfootling.

Mentharch scratched with both hands under his ungainly collar. "A fine welcome," he said testily.

"I am pleased that we were able to…" Milord's voice trailed off, for he saw that the wizard was not listening — his attention was distracted by the approach of a small, disheveled individual on the boardwalk.

The new arrival limped noticeably. His suit of violet chenille was badly ripped, and with each stride his better leg pushed through the garment's lower shreds to reveal a shoeless foot. Another rent in the fabric exposed the stump of his missing left arm. He slogged through the sand and stopped hesitantly in front of the Grandmage.

It was Gwarph.

The wizard frowned. "Where have you been?"

"Master, I —"

"Well? Where is the carriage?" Mentharch demanded.

The hapless dwarf cringed and stuttered his excuse so miserably that I could hardly understand his words. "Ma-master, the rear axletree was overcome by a tu-turbulence. I was forced to abandon the vehicle in a ditch near Carfuffle —"

"Never mind," Mentharch interrupted in a loud voice, doubly

irritated, for Gwarph's groveling explanation hinted at the location of their castle. "And have you tended to the vats?"

"Yes, Master." He threw himself abjectly on the beach and said in a small voice, "But I was compelled to deactivate Tree Number Two."

The wizard drew back in shock. "Deactivate? I gave no such order!" I feared a most unpleasant afternoon for the small assistant.

Milord uttered a little noise of surprise and understanding. "Gwarph has saved you," he protested, and pointed to the tree. "It ingested the witches' brew, and would not have given it up without Gwarph's intervention."

Only now did the Grandmage notice the sliced and lifeless hulk suspended from the pier behind him. "It is destroyed!" he shouted, looking with angry suspicion from Gwarph to Milord.

"Circumstances required that we —" Milord began.

Mentharch turned his back and floated to the remains of the tree. He passed his hand before it in a circular motion and recoiled. "A witch has tampered with it!" he exclaimed.

Intuitively Milord and I looked at each other and said together, "Vulgia!" She had perverted it during her stay aboard the hijacked *Dittaneer*. No wonder it had tried to devour the crew; no wonder it had refused Milord's demand for the swallowed bottlette.

"The perpetrator met her demise at the hands of a rival, Grandmage," said Milord. "At a more convenient time I shall be happy to supply details. For now, suffice it to say that your assistant's help was instrumental in resolving the dilemma."

Gwarph drew the wizard's lost riding crop from his armless sleeve and presented it with an imploring look. "I found your whip, too, Master," he pleaded.

Mentharch's craggy features softened. He patted his dwarf on the head, and with a twitch of his thumbs repaired his tattered clothes. Gwarph closed his beady red eyes, smiled and rubbed his master's leg like an affectionate kitten.

Milord coughed. "Now then. I believe we have other matters to discuss, Grandmage."

"Specifically?"

"Amulets," Milord said at once.

"Ah, well." Mentharch half-closed his eyes, folded his arms behind his head and reclined two yards above the ground. "Amulets, eh?"

"Of Consortium quality. Premium grade."

"I see. Number?"

"Unknown."

The Grandmage swiveled his head suspiciously. "But you can state with certainty that the number is positive and exceeds zero?"

"This much is certain."

"Display them," Mentharch said with a peremptory sprinkling motion of his fingers. Milord withdrew the pellet-box and opened it for inspection.

Startled, Mentharch jumped back and waved his arms and legs in midair as though he would fall from his invisible perch. "They are wrapped in a Spell of Cataplastic Condensation," he said reproachfully. "You said nothing of this!"

"A detail with which I thought it unnecessary to burden a thaumaturge of your stature."

"Detail!? Its undoing will tax my energy vats dangerously!" He scratched furiously under his leather collar.

Milord drew a regretful breath and closed the box. "That would never do. The limited resources of Grandmage Mentharch must be preserved."

"Limited?" he bellowed. "What vituperative jabberjowl makes such an allegation?"

"Certainly not I," Milord said innocently.

Somewhat mollified, the Grandmage produced a thick lens. "Let me see them again." He reopened the box and examined the pellets again, first with one eye, then the other. "A further difficulty is evident: they are guarded by ferocious stick-men!"

"This is no difficulty, but a bonus, for which I shall ask no additional benefits," said Milord.

"Bonus? Benefits?"

"Of course! They might profitably be put to work in the repair of roads, for example, or —"

"Who tells you I have roads to mend?" Mentharch asked with a sharp look.

"I merely speculate. Perhaps you would prefer simply to banish the noxious creatures to the Northern Wastes."

"Hmmph. A possibility."

"Now then. As to the modest benefits to which I alluded —"

"Very well, I accept." The wizard stood up. With a flick of his wrist he produced a capsule. It grew instantly to a series of nested boxes, ranging in size from that of a thumbnail to that of his narrow chest. Selecting one of intermediate dimension, he popped the pellet-box into it, collapsed the lot of them again and slipped the capsule into a waist pocket.

"A trifle, a trump, and twiddled for a show!" he sang, and clicked his heels high in the air.

"But we —"

"Tut, no compliments, please," he said modestly. "My feeble gymnastics are no cause for elaborate flattery."

Milord cleared his throat and pointedly folded his arms.

"All right, very well," Mentharch said irascibly. "Benefits. Have I not already given you sumptuous gifts, in the form of potent spells?" He walked briskly from the strand with Gwarph straggling behind him, and began to vanish into the morning air.

"But this is not at all what I had in mind!" Milord objected. Seeing that in another instant Mentharch would disappear altogether, he blurted, "Your collar!"

Mentharch did a sharp about-face. "How did you notice it?"

"No prying intended. But I seem to recall a bit of witch's doggerel in which a 'hybrid' was mentioned. By chance I may know the creature's location; it is even conceivable that an introduction could be effected."

Mentharch half-reclined in midair, but more cautiously than before. He remained translucent, so that the shanties beyond him wavered eerily through his gown. "Say more, please."

"I ask a modest concession or two," Milord began.

Mentharch waved his hand disingenuously. "A simple matter."

"I am pleased to hear it. I ask only your continued good will towards Albanderry's Lords and citizens."

"Given," he said impatiently.

"And I would have you consider Albanderry's fine institution of mascotry."

Mentharch's eyes bulged and he dropped his scratcher. "What impertinent notion is this? Privacy is a wizard's most precious possession!" He looked sternly at Gwarph, who had alertly cocked an ear at mention of mascots; the dwarf reddened and tried unsuccessfully to slink behind him.

"Doubtless this is true," argued Milord. "But consider the advantages of an intelligent mascot, capable of speech and flight, yet stout enough to serve also as bodyguard. The perfect complement to an able assistant," he added with a diplomatic glance at Gwarph.

Mentharch pulled thoughtfully at his narrow chin. "I shall take the matter under advisement."

"Excellent." Milord positioned his hands in the sign of Departure Under Moot Circumstances and turned towards our carriage.

"Wait! What of my collar?"

Milord put his finger to his cheek as though in sudden appreciation of a coincidence. "As chance would have it, there is a close relationship between the removal of your collar and the question of mascotry."

"In what sense? How so?" Mentharch said wildly.

Milord signaled to the carriage; in the blink of an eye Stitch hopped over the sand and bowed. He was clad in a flamboyant suit of gray and gold livery, modestly gusseted at the throat and shoulder. His presence induced violent vibrations in Mentharch's collar.

Masterfootling Farberwile stepped forward. "Will you accept this fine specimen, a chimaera of Mountainwitch and stick-man, as your lawful mascot, subject to the rights and duties thereto appertaining?"

"Rights?" bleated the Grandmage, flabbergasted. Gwarph looked on grimly.

The Masterfootling handed the wizard a thick scroll. "The covenant is briefly summarized herein, Sir. Its lengthier version, comprising some ninety-six volumes, is available from the Archives upon request, with a fortnight's advance notice."

Mentharch silently studied the unopened scroll. In a persuasive tone Milord added, "I would also point out that Stitch contributed substantially to the acquisition of the witches' brew."

"Very well," said Mentharch. "The relationship is in force." He waggled his finger sternly at Stitch. "But do not touch my energy vats, on pain of transmogrification! Or nibble at my trellises of fleecevine, whose flavor would cause you untold sorrow!"

Stitch bowed and touched his forehead three times. "He agrees to enter into your service as mascot," said Milord. "But I ask one additional favor on his behalf: that before you ostracize the stick-men ensorcelled within your pellets, you allow Stitch to meet his father, who is among them." Stitch glanced at Milord with an expression as grateful and soulful as his lack of facial features permitted. "Perhaps you could even find a suitable position for him on your premises," Milord added.

Mentharch ran his fingers through his hair as though harassed with impossible demands. "A delicate feat," he said, and blew out his lips like a horse.

"Your gracious generosity is a source of widespread admiration," said Milord.

Stitch stepped to the wizard's side and held up his opened pincer, at which he recoiled in alarm. "Already the perils of mascotry declare themselves!" he shouted.

Milord concealed a smile. "He merely offers to remove your noisome collar."

"Ah, well," Mentharch said with tentative relief. Stitch approached again. The wizard held himself with rigid uneasiness, like an emperor who fears his barber's razor.

Milord restrained Stitch with his palm. "One last detail, Grandmage, though it is a delicate matter of business which I hesitate to broach."

"Broach and divulge!" shouted the Grandmage in exasperation, pulling futilely at his collar.

"Very well. It is apparent from the course of events that the leasing of magical artifices to Lords and/or commoners poses significant hazards. I would therefore ask you to cease and desist from this dangerous practice."

"But this is unbridled wheedling! The leases are most lucrative!"

Milord shrugged. "Surely a magician of your resourcefulness can conceive some means of translating precious witch-amulets into bezants. And failing that, I stand ready to offer my extensive commercial contacts for your advantage."

Mentharch turned his head in disgust. A strangled syllable escaped his throat.

"I construe this mumbled interjection as a token of wholehearted assent," Milord said, and motioned to Stitch. Mentharch strove to confine his neck in the opposite curve of the collar as Stitch scissored the offending device neatly in half. It dissolved at once into a squadron of parasitic witch-wasps, which buzzed off a short distance and collapsed to the ground, dead.

Mentharch looked beamishly from Stitch to Milord. "Splendid! Did I not swear to the many advantages of maintaining a mascot?" He plucked a tablet and a square of silk from his pocket. "In gratitude I present my new associate with these gifts."

Stitch took the tablet delicately in his claw. It burst at once into a magnificent rapier, twinkling in the sun. He tested its balance with obvious satisfaction, and commented approvingly on its fine hornblende pommel and sturdy hilt. With quickening pleasure he took the swatch of silk, which altered at once into a slim sheath and belt of fine leather.

"I thank you, Grandmage," he said enthusiastically. His joy caused me some misgiving, for I could not recall an instance of a mascot's bearing arms in Albanderry, much less expressly acting as bodyguard, and the precedent was somehow disturbing.

Mentharch smiled modestly. "A trifle. So. I believe our business is concluded, Lord Benefice? You propose no further indemnifications, indentures or imposts?"

"None. I am quite pleased."

"Then our satisfaction is mutual. The amulets will permit me to reply in an especially well tailored manner to one Mountainwitch in particular," Mentharch said with a sly look. " 'Wear this necklace with an itch,' eh?" he quoted, imitating Auntie's smarmy voice with repulsive accuracy, and chuckled.

Milord shivered slightly. "I am relieved to leave these too-potent charms in your capable hands, and return to my simple concocting."

With sudden impatience the Grandmage said, "What a sluggish pace this discussion takes!" He hitched up his stockings and toed a bourrée, and sang in a quavering tenor voice,

> "Slug a bed and a sluggard be.
> Dull a knife and a dullard be.

Tom Kidd

Blink too much and a blinkard be!
All hale fellows, we!"

Gwarph waddled forward and took up the next verse in a rasping voice that seemed to come from a hole in the ground:

"Never be of divided mind, or a half-wit you will be.
Don't block my path, or a blockhead you'll soon be.
Ignore me and I'll make an ignoramus of thee!
All hale fellows, we!"

Mentharch stopped his dancing and frowned at his dwarf. "Clodpate! The key is F sharp!"

"Yes, Master," said Gwarph, shrinking away. The Grandmage abruptly whirled his arms overhead, and a circular carpet woven of bright yellow cornsilk and spindrift floated to the strand. Stitch quickly took his leave of Milord, and to me expressed regret that our dissimilar anatomies precluded a warm embrace; with a delicate but loving touch he bade me farewell. He snapped to attention by the wizard, sword braced neatly on his lean hip. Grandmage Mentharch stepped briskly onto the carpet, with Stitch and Gwarph at his sides. His brows jerked; the carpet floated straight upwards, rotating faster and faster til it became a blur and disappeared.

We stood watching the empty, sunny skies for some time. "Is his castle in the sky?" I asked Milord.

"What energy could sustain it among the clouds?" he wondered in reply.

"And where would it be on cloudless days?" asked the Masterfootling.

"I could not say," Milord said softly. He sighed and stroked my back.

"Well, that's done," said Lord Roundabout. "Taken all in all, I suppose we should be content."

Milord agreed. The handmen packed up our things, and with a last glance behind us at the broken tree-skeleton, we left Albanderry Port.

"I shall miss Stitch greatly," I said when we were home again.

The weather was fine, and Milord had elected to take a late-morning stroll about the grounds. "He proved a fine friend and ally, Flick," he said, nodding vigorously. "Perhaps the wizard will allow him to visit us from time to time. And remember: he is now entitled to seek membership in the Mascots' Society." This realization greatly brightened my spirits.

Milord sauntered back to the Manor, hands behind his back. Already the revived magician's benign influence was felt everywhere, and no sign of witchy intrusion was visible or reported. Milord paused to study a row of eucalypti. Tossing their bushy heads prettily in a quiet midday wind, the trees filled the air with their pungent scent.

"We have sense organs — our eyes, our ears, our noses," Milord said reflectively. "Stimulated by the world, they quiver and reverberate, communicating their excitements and sensations to us. And our minds in turn make one great assumption, perhaps the greatest of all: that the location of all that quivering and reverberation is out there, in the world. Out there, Flick! Yet in truth, trapped as we are in our envelopes of self, the commotion takes place within us, does it not? Within the eyes and ears and minds themselves — for where aught could it occur?"

Milord's philosophical mood grew quickly to one of bright agitation. His nostrils flared, perhaps stimulated as much by the sweet fragrance of the eucalyptus as by his epistemological thoughts.

"Now take this step, Flick," he said pedagogically. "Ask yourself, what, on the other hand, is a hallucination? And answer, it is merely an imaginary entity within ourselves, whose existence and venue we incorrectly assign to the world — an event within our senses and minds, believed to be external. Does that not sound suspiciously like our description of 'true' sensations?"

I looked up at him and shrugged. His wide, bright eyes, framed by their slender auburn eyebrows, reminded me of the windows of a curious old house. "Perhaps all our experience is, in actuality, hallucinatory!" he concluded excitedly. "A grand figment and nothing more."

The eucalypti swayed and twitched, as though agitated by Milord's remarks. "Those trees, for example. Look at them! Are they not merely a creation of our minds?"

I wish always to oblige Milord, and so I squinted til my eyelids cramped and my vision swam in red and black. The trees transformed themselves into fearsome, giant bloodybones, crashing their leafy ruchings together in the wind. In a moment they would wrench their enormous roots from the ground, march inexorably toward us and... My *gnozzt* quickly became swollen and tense, and a hiss escaped my lips.

There was motion to our right. Startled, I dove into my holster, but it was only the Kitchenmaster. "Luncheon is prepared, Sire," he said, bowing. With a white-gloved hand he directed us delicately to a sparkling buffet on the terrace.

Milord laughed. "Then let us respond to the hallucination of hunger," he said, and stepped delightedly to the groaning table. It was an excellent repast — joints of grouse simmered in plentiful pots of farmer's beans, and six desserts — and the visions of monster trees were soon forgotten. We lingered there for most of the afternoon.

EPILOGUE

A quiet week passed. Relations between Albanderry and the Mountainwitch Consortium returned to their former state of uneasy equilibrium. Through the Protectioners' Guild we learned that Auntie had been ostracized to the Northern Wastes, and it was rumored that the Grandmage had succeeded in confining her in Funk's Globular Suit, a hideous contrivance packed with sharp fibrils of marsh-scum.

Milord was elected by acclamation Burgess Preeminent of Albanderry Assembly. In consequence he was permitted to augment his coat of arms with the sumptuous devices of that office: a fimbriated bordure and roses azure in the dexter chief point. He departed in triumph from a special session of the Assembly as Albanderry's undisputed leader.

On Freeday morning Milord awoke in high good spirits. He exuberantly threw open the drapery (a chore normally reserved for Manservant Mumphreed) and basked in a torrent of warm sun.

"Saint Gladden's berries!" he shouted, hitting his palm with his fist, and paced about the room in his nightshirt, humming to himself. It was the day of the great celebratory banquet at Benefice Manor, to which every Lord and Compeer of the Realm was invited. "The evening will bring a splendid convocation of beglerbegs and panjandrums, all turned out with marvelous *panache* and *éclat!*"

But an even more exciting event took place beforehand. For it was that afternoon, amidst the pandemonium of preparations for the grand gala, that Bilch's birthgiving occurred. The Kitchenmaster summoned me in an excited whisper. "His Lordship wants you at once, Flick!" I raced upstairs and found, of all people, Mistress Breadwright kneeling by the drawer of Milord's armoire and tenderly offering sugar-tits to four squirming sucklings. Masterfootling Farberwile puttered about behind her, happily accepting her imperious orders for towelettes and other niceties.

The four babies' eyes were still closed, but they systematically palpated each other with their soft, still-moist paws. In this way young Filxxxs introduce each other to the sensations of the world, stimulating the growth of our nervous systems from the earliest moments of life. And each one nursed the others, a marvelous feat of developmental independence unparalleled, to my knowledge, by any other species. In a few days they would be scampering through the deep pile of Milord's carpets like children in a field of corn.

I was overjoyed, but at the same time their arrival brought a deep sense of loss. For their crib was also a catafalque, or bier, in which Bilch as I knew him had died, leaving only remnants of his unique soul to his tiny heirs. Of all the sexual strategies in which Filxxxs engage, duothelytoky is undoubtedly the most painful.

Milord hovered over the crib with an approving smile. "A state of quadruple parturition prevails," he commented, wryly imitating the Gong Annunciator. Then he dandled the infants one by one on his fingers and gaily proposed cute names for them while giving me sly looks, for he knew perfectly well that strict Filxxx traditions govern such nomenclature.

Mistress Breadwright served an impromptu collation of blithemeat tidbits in frumenty pudding. Milord broached a decanter of his most effervescent Ebullientia XVI, and we toasted the new arrivals. Members of the household looked in to pay their delighted respects, and soon everyone had met my new protégés. Milord's Keeper of Heraldry even presented them with a tiny pennon, showing simple tinctures and a fracted escutcheon. (Though I thought this no more than a harmless and touching gesture, the Masterfootling gave him to understand by a frown that a coat of arms for individual mascotlings was not appropriate. The incident served as a stinging reminder that the issue of multiple mascotry and their rights had yet to be dealt with in the Assembly; but that is another and complicated story.)

Fireworks exploded outside the windows, showering pink and yellow powder-puffs into the sunset sky, and Milord hastened off to complete his toilet and dress. Soon the Lords' most elegant broughams, decorated with fluttering gonfalons, began to arrive. In the courtyard, trumpets and vamphorns burst into ecstatic tantaras and majestic voluntaries, echoing like mountain voices in the twilight.

Lords and Ladies streamed into Benefice House, appointed with a degree of magnificence I had never before seen. The Ladies wore shimmering gowns of silk with lengthy trains of pleated brocade; their elaborate, scalloped headdresses were dotted with pretty tassels of pastel twill. The Lords favored sniptious six-piece complets of royal purple, jet black and silver, and carried tall ceremonial canes with handles of pure gold. Milord circulated energetically among his guests, creating an atmosphere that was at once electric and cordial.

Even mascots were attired with particular finesse for the occasion. Lord Hobday's nape-mouse modeled a fetching indigo jumpsuit, and Lord Sprightleigh's Filxxx, Harla, enchanted me in her pink shift. I jumped from Milord's pocket to boast of Bilch's offspring, and we gossiped for some time. What would become of Lizzault's mate-widow, now that he and Lord Pontieu were no more? Did Harla have relatives in her Manor? What did the mascot of —? Milord beckoned, making a face to show that he missed my company. I hastily made plans to visit both of them again soon and took my leave.

The plump Lady Roundabout made her entrance in a fuzzy gown of ochre and blurred pink. This garment, together with her soft, delicate skin and considerable rotundity, gave her the appearance of an oversized, ambulatory peach. Behind her Lord Roundabout fussed with his cane, which despite its extreme simplicity of design had somehow become entangled in his coattails. Goighty was mercifully absent; it transpired that he had mistaken a wad of upholstery paste for goose-liver paté, his favorite delicacy, and was indisposed.

The Trumpmaster announced Lord Trillphyte, who entered the foyer accompanied by his gorgeous daughter, Togala. He nervously adjusted his ornamental kneepieces as he walked — garish devices which perfectly exemplify his outmoded sartorial philosophy. At his feet rolled his 'mascot', Phrugge. This entity is actually a troupe of spotted horde-frogs riding in a series of fitted harnesses and slings within a rickety, wheeled apparatus, which they propel by pumping a horizontal crankshaft; but the eccentric gears of this device are quite inefficient, so that the frogs are always near the edge of exhaustion, and their master is obliged to feed them grubs almost continuously to keep up their strength.

Lord Trillphyte located us, contrived an ingratiating smile and approached. Obviously he saw Milord's political star rising and sought to take its coattails, so to speak, in his grasp; and the means by which he hoped to effect this ascent was now revealed.

"Good evening, Favorlord Benefice," he said, bowing deeply. "Allow me to introduce my lovely daughter, Togala. Togala dear, say hello to His Grace, Lord Benefice."

Blushing profusely, Togala minced forward in her plum-and-silver leotard. Blond frisettes adorned her forehead, and her slender waist was circumscribed by a sheer half-skirt, open at the front. Her nose, perfect when seen *en face*, was marred in profile by an unfortunate hump on its shaft; but Milord's fulminating smile suggested that he found this imperfection quite endearing. Her perfume was a reverie of morning meadows and white roses. With a shock I realized that this voluptuous girl was the same awkward hoyden who had galloped through Milord's hedges many years ago on a formal visit with her father.

"A very good evening, Favorlord Benefice," she gushed. How brashly too familiar of her to employ the third degree of address! But Milord was far too absorbed in the appreciation of her buxom qualities to notice her ungainly etiquette; and despite her obvious naïveté, I was forced to acknowledge that she was ravishing.

Milord took her hand and gallantly delivered a kiss. Lord Trillphyte stood close by, intently manipulating his fingers in a manner that suggested he already counted the increase in his political fortunes. Lords Hobday and Munchfirth approached to greet Milord, but were diverted and held at bay by Trillphyte to foster the tête-a-tête; but he in turn was distracted by a crescendo of croakings from Phrugge, and while he impatiently rummaged in his wallet for a few grubs to toss them, the Masterfootling deftly intervened and steered Milord back to his hostly duties.

The socializing swelled to a pleasant pitch as everyone chatted of old and mutual things. A warm tidal wave of Lords and Ladies flowed into the grand banquet hall to be seated at white-linened tables stretching from one marble wall to the other. I had a commanding view of the proceedings, for Milord had installed me on his shoulder in a Surveillant's Perch, fashioned for the occasion by his velvetsmith.

Milord opened the festivities by conducting several vibrant toasts with his superlative Clarissimus XVIII, far and away the finest *liqueur ordinaire* ever enjoyed in Albanderry. The first of eighteen fabulous courses was served: poached tulips in candied shells, dramatically carried in by the chefs on trays of polished ebony. This was followed by the Kitchenmaster's celebrated dairy topiary: cheeses whimsically molded into the shapes of mythical animals and garnished with cloudberries and shredded pancakes.

The entertainment began with a troupe of light-buskers, who pranced around the perimeter of the hall to the accompaniment of zithers and lightly stoppered trombones. A course of viands and fruit pastries in comfiture was quickly polished off, followed by a selection of wines. With each round Milord was the object of increasingly ardent urgings to speak. Each such entreaty was itself a lengthy oration, or took the form of a prolonged disclaimer to the effect that it was not itself a speech.

At last Milord rose. He wetted his lips with a dram of liqueur and delicately cleared his throat. "Your companionship is a joy to my heart," he said, and sat down.

This stunning display of breviloquence induced a moment of inert silence, followed by wild, deafening applause. Gasmaster Bickle now took the dais and delivered a message from Grandmage Mentharch: the wizard greatly regretted that circumstances prohibited his attendance, but he was pleased to send a token of his high esteem for Lord

Gracewright Cantilouve Benefice: an exquisite decanter, of crystal as thin as a ray of sunshine, and so light that it floated just above the table-top. The gift came to Milord's hand at his glance. The accompanying note said simply, 'In gratitude'. Milord was overcome with joy.

The guttling and bubblement grew yet more enthusiastic. The last of the servings was soon dispatched, and the guests withdrew to the main hall to begin the party in earnest. There they happily executed minuets, galliards and bransles through the night, to the accompaniment of pan-pipes, dulcimers and lilting sweet-songs.

It was sunrise before the last of Milord's friends departed. He reclined in his favorite channel-back chair, reveling in the hush of dawn and its sweet fragrances of honeysuckle and white-and-yellow checkerbloom. The gentle strains of 'Olights Cantapata' wafted down from the cantoria, softly sung by Benefice Choir to the accompaniment of a harmonium.

The singers retired, leaving only the gentle sounds of a fountain pip-pling in the patio. Milord was smitten suddenly by weariness. I pressed his knee anxiously.

"Yes, I shall confess to being a bit ramfeezled," he said with a noisy yawn.

I too began to nod off, but was awakened by a disquieting thought. "You won't barter for more of their unpleasant brew, will you?" I asked, looking directly up at him.

He hesitated and then laughed, as though at himself. "No, Flick," he reassured me. "No, henceforth I shall content myself with the prepa-ration of my own concoctions only. Though when dealing with the Consortium I may pretend to demand more of their nasty soup, and adamantly, in order to drop the claim with a great show of regret and thereby gain some other concession." His promise filled me with relief.

He sipped at his tot of mulled brandywine. "But I do not regret our little adventure, Flick. For the ancient Greeks espoused moderation in all things; and it follows that moderation should itself be moderated — by an occasional excess."

He smiled and dabbed my nose.

Colophon

This book was printed using 11,5 pt Adobe Arno Pro as the primary text font, with NeutraFace used for titles.

Special thanks to Steve Sherman.

Book composition & Typesetting: Joel Anderson
Typographic design: Howard Kistler
Map: Andrew Kim
Management: John Vance, Koen Vyverman